W9-BIH-607

RAVES FOR TIM SEBASTIAN'S
SPY SHADOW

"TIM SEBASTIAN HAS THE CREDENTIALS.
. . . You know this is a man who writes from deep
wells of experience. . . . Sebastian is excellent at
pace, crisp and taut in narration."
—*The Times* (London)

"WELL-PLOTTED INTRIGUE."
—*Library Journal*

"TIM SEBASTIAN LOOKS SET TO RIVAL
JOHN le CARRÉ. . . . Since Poland's problems are
always in the news, this is a political thriller with real
immediacy; meaty and gripping, a frightening book,
full of atmosphere." —*Good Housekeeping*

"A RIVETING READ . . . THE PACE IS FAST,
THE TENSION HELD ALL THE WAY."
—*Women & Home*

"WRITTEN BY A PERSON WHO KNOWS THE
SOVIET UNION EXTREMELY WELL, AND
WHO KNOWS THE SECRET SIDE OF THE
CONSTANT INTELLIGENCE WAR."
—Pierre Salinger, chief foreign correspondent,
    ABC News

TIM SEBASTIAN

SPY

SHADOW

A DELL BOOK

Published by
Dell Publishing
a division of
Bantam Doubleday Dell Publishing Group, Inc.
666 Fifth Avenue
New York, New York 10103

Copyright © 1990 by Tim Sebastian

All rights reserved. No part of this book may be reproduced or transmitted in any form or by any means, electronic or mechanical, including photocopying, recording, or by any information storage and retrieval system, without the written permission of the Publisher, except where permitted by law. For information address: Delacorte Press, New York, New York.

The trademark Dell® is registered in the U.S. Patent and Trademark Office.

ISBN 0-440-20846-7

Reprinted by arrangement with Delacorte Press, New York, New York

Printed in the United States of America

Published simultaneously in Canada

April 1991

10 9 8 7 6 5 4 3 2 1

OPM

FOREWORD

December 1970

Prague in winter. Like an old lady once beautiful, now bitter and sad. Across the Charles Bridge, with its figureheads and statues, Tristram could see it all— the splendor of Eastern Europe from centuries gone by, and the utter despondency and gloom that lay thick over the city like the snow.

Two years since the Soviet invasion. Two years from Prague spring to Prague winter. From daylight to darkness.

Get in there, they had said to Tristram. Get in there and see what moves. Who's left, who's active. Is there a dream among all the nightmares?

James Tristram, age thirty-eight and a salesman, he had written. Going bald, going soft, going nervous. But he hadn't written that. And then he had waited, a month, two months. And finally they had opened the door.

He had booked into the loveliest, the oldest, and the smallest of the hotels—U Tri Pstrosu, at the

Three Ostriches—and word must have gotten out quickly, for the contact hadn't been long in coming.

Hours after the sleek official Skoda had brought him back from the Foreign Trade Ministry, with the pile of boring leaflets about steel production and all the words of peace and friendship still ringing in his ears, there had been a knock at the door. Soft, then more insistent. Just as the defector in London had told him. The man standing there was somehow older than he'd expected, his face more lined. Or was it simply the shadows and the fear?

Tristram had gone out into the corridor and taken the note he was handed and the man had slipped away down the staircase. Outside the snow had gone on falling, covering his tracks as he crept home along the soft-cobbled streets.

The next night Tristram had shrugged off his peace-loving hosts, drunk the toasts to better cooperation, and headed for the restaurant where he'd been told to go.

It had been little more than an underground wine bar, but it offered Hungarian goulash on red-checked tablecloths. And he had taken it as much to warm a hole in his stomach as to enjoy a meal.

Later he had almost failed to notice them—the wafer-thin sheets of paper folded underneath the table napkin. Not what he'd wanted or even expected. But he took them all the same.

He had tramped home on foot. He felt depressed, hadn't come all this way for the kind of dissident claptrap even the tourists got handed. And yet that was always the danger with volunteers. You didn't get what you wanted—you got what they gave. The walk was hard going. The city was clogged with snow, the traffic at a virtual standstill. And he hadn't read the pages until much later. But as he settled down in bed they began to catch his attention.

It was a tale that began in Warsaw in August of 1944, a city without God, where murder was commonplace and executions the norm. As the Nazis prepared to dynamite the city, bodies appeared on street corners and excited no comment or interest. The living were the exceptions. The dead were the rule.

For a moment Tristram stopped reading, put the papers under the bed, and went to the door. Dressed only in his pajamas, he stood there for a while, feeling the draft sweep in along the floorboards, listening.

In this dismal city it wasn't hard to think of Warsaw, and the battle, and the treachery. Tristram withdrew the papers and turned the page.

They talk much of the noise of war, the terrible din of gunfire, of bombs and artillery, but on that night in August three men heard only silence.

From where they crouched in the sewers, deep under the capital, the fighting seemed almost remote. Death lay above ground, where the SS Kommandos wrought their own kind of carnage.

In a peaceful world the men would have just been starting life, beginning their careers and their training. Instead they had already trained to kill and kill quickly. In the months of urban warfare they had mastered guerrilla tactics, sniping, the manufacture of bombs. The short, sharp strike—the only weapons for a weak force pitted against a strong one.

The talk that night was of the uprising. A radio message had come in from the Red Army, now encamped on the east-

ern bank of the Vistula. The message had been simple. Begin an all-out struggle and we will cross the river and drive out the enemy.

For many hours the three men argued. Could the Red Army be trusted, would the Russians deliver, was it a trap that would seal Poland's tomb forever?

As they sat in the darkness, like an unholy trinity, they heard footsteps swishing through the low waters of the sewer and they reached for their machine guns, only to see the signal of recognition from a flashlight way down the tunnel. Three short flashes, one long one. Repeated three times.

The figure had emerged from the shadows and crouched with them. Another young face but not Polish. For a while they spoke English as he pleaded with them to accept the Russians' offer. He had information, he said. This time they were genuine. He could vouch for them.

They embraced the man because they knew him and loved him and then he was gone.

Next morning the wounded, broken city of Warsaw rose up and fought again.

Tristram looked around the room and shook his head. Where had the story come from? It read like a book, but none that he had ever heard of. Was it a diary?

The failure of the uprising and the failure of the Russians to assist had indeed sealed Poland's tomb. By the time the Red Army came in, eighty-five percent of Warsaw had been destroyed. The talk had been of liberation. But they had liberated a cemetery.

From the papers it seemed that only one of the three men in the sewer had survived. The man who had written them, with his mind shattered and dazed, but still with the clearest recollection of the young Englishman who had tricked the underground, tricked their city, hastened its annihilation.

And then the message for him alone:

There is more. Much more. The Englishman was recruited by a Soviet agent. Maybe after all these years they still work together. "Russki"—the Russian. Necessary to find them both. You'll be contacted again.

Tristram rubbed his eyes. How do you judge it all? he wondered. Some facts, some interpretations, and a story of betrayal almost three decades old. Maybe true, maybe half remembered.

And yet this was the only contact he had. And he owed the man a hearing, owed him his presence. Even if the truth were somewhere else, buried by time and torment.

For two days he remained in the garret room, feigning illness to the ministry, not even daring to go out for food lest he miss a call or a visit.

On the second day of his vigil he fell asleep at about midnight, hungry and wretched. And he didn't know why he hadn't heard them, for suddenly he was being forced awake with the terrible din and clatter of strangers all around him, shouting, swearing, smashing the door back against the wooden dresser. It seemed the cruelest of endings as they dragged him out into the street, banging him against the side of the armored personnel carrier, closing the door on a puzzle he had only just discovered.

In the years that followed Tristram could never look at a snowstorm without remembering that night in Prague when he was bound and tethered like an animal, then taken to market.

1

1992

Like sons with their father, the two figures helped the Russian onto the frozen river as the wind came in sharp and sudden from the steppes and the ice glistened in the midday light.

Beautiful. So beautiful. And it was still his country. For they still came out to visit him and listen to him, still looked to him for guidance.

He stopped for a moment, coughed, and blew his streaming nose. The younger men gripped his arm.

Maybe it was that which brought back the memory. For in those distant, endless days of Stalin, there had always been two of them gripping their victim, leading him toward the blank, scarred brickwork in the prison courtyard, tying his hands behind him to the iron ring. And then if the guards were busy, one of the security men would come out, quiet, almost nonchalant, and blow the victim's head away with a gun held behind his back right up until the last moment. The final deceit.

The Russian felt again the sense of foreboding.

And then the ice cracked beneath their feet and they stood still, watching the fissure arrow out across the surface of the river. Nature disturbed by man. An act of sudden violence.

They turned and strode northward. Memories were no good to the Russian. For when you live by treachery and terror there are no quiet places where the conscience can hide, no respite or repose.

The younger men looked at him anxiously, aware that his mind had taken a different journey. They walked on, three dark shapes crossing on the ice, the wind at their backs.

They got him to the dacha, the old wooden house at the edge of the forest, although he didn't need their help. The hands gripping his arm were respectful— almost comradely. The black limousine was still waiting for them, twin exhausts belching out smoke, the driver alert and anxious, for these were important men, men to be feared.

Inside they were served tea in china cups on a lace tablecloth, everything just so. For when you claw your way out of a dung heap of a village in southern Russia and make it to the top, these things matter.

It was then that they spoke of the plan. And in Russia you have only to say it once in the right ear. There's no need to belabor it. And the two young KGB officers left just before dusk, their feet crunching on the ice, their host's guidance and approval requested and given.

Later, when darkness had surrounded the house and the shutters creaked in the wind, the Russian's housekeeper brought supper—a tray of salmon from Finland. But he couldn't eat, couldn't sit still. The afternoon talk had excited him, the feeling once again of being at the center, in control.

He got up. Around the paneled study were the books that had traveled alongside him. Fellow survivors in the jungle of political intrigue that went back for decades. Not books—bibles. Thick dark tomes of Lenin and Stalin. Speeches they'd never written themselves, thoughts they'd never possessed. And yet they contained the life-force for Soviet society. He fingered them tenderly, blowing dust from the spines, patting them into place on the shelves.

What a Russia it had been! A country under orders, gripped by steel. No place for the limp, sweaty handshakes that were offered these days in Moscow. Whiners and weaklings droning on about reform and democracy. What had happened to the cruel strong men who had carried their passion into battles across a whole continent and promised it to all the others?

It was 3 A.M. before he fell asleep, nervous, restive, tormented by visions only half remembered. And the wind beat against the door, beggaring everything in its path across a thousand miles.

At midday they drove the Russian to Moscow's Sheremyetyevo airport. His cold was worse, the handkerchief, constantly at his raw and angry nose. In the flurry of cars and buses, the gaggle of tourists and guides, no one saw him step from a yellow Zhiguli and head for the departure terminal.

At customs he handed over a Canadian passport

and shouted with anger when the officer snatched his clothes from the small suitcase, then flung them back inside, leaving him to repack.

At immigration it was no better. The first guard called in a second, who whispered darkly into a telephone and then asked him to say his name out loud.

The Russian laughed scornfully and spoke in fluent English. "Such shit," he announced to the others in the queue. "I wonder that we ever visit this fucked-up country."

The outburst brought him much sympathy from the foreigners in the departure lounge and a scowl from the Aeroflot ground personnel.

And then he was inside the Swissair DC-9, with a cup of coffee in his hand, reveling in his disguise and deception. As they took off, skirting Moscow to the southwest, he looked out of the window and shook his fist at the frozen countryside, the little people, the clumsy, stubby trucks that wound their way into the Soviet heartland.

The red train was nearly empty as it pulled onto the foothills of the mountains and swung out above Lake Geneva. The Russian had taken a window seat, a scarf well up over his chin. His hands shook slightly as he turned the pages of a newspaper, or maybe it was the juddering of the train.

He got out at Blonay-sur-Vevey, a farming hamlet where the snow lay clear and unmarked in the fields around him. And he watched the train clanking up the steep track toward Les Pleiades and the Bernese Alps. The air was cold and pure, caught between the mountains. No wind, no sign at all of the world beyond the peaks.

The road tilted down to the hotel. An old family hotel where the nth son of the clan welcomes guests the Swiss way—half a smile, a clipped sentence, nothing intrusive, nothing to suggest that he's met you before if you want to pretend that he hasn't.

They relied on the hotel.

The Russian set down his briefcase in number 8 and opened the double doors to the balcony. And immediately he was clutching at the wooden frame as the dizziness hit him. There's nothing quite like a new fear. Old fears, like old friends, become comfortable, predictable. They might visit a little too often, but you can always usher them out. New fears jab at your chest, come and go without warning, take away your breath, like the cold air from the Baltic.

He sat on the bed and wondered about the man on the floor below. The fellow would have left London that morning in a hurry. What had he gone through to make the journey? What would he say when he went back?

He picked up the briefcase and stepped into the corridor. A young chambermaid curtsied and moved aside to let him pass. "And what's your name?" he asked in good German, for he had to know. Later, much later, he would need the names of all the people who had seen him. As he made his way downstairs he took in the scrubbed parquet floors, the finely embroidered curtains, the cuckoo clock, the details of a Swiss evening that he wouldn't forget.

Without hesitating he opened the door and moved quickly inside.

* * *

"A long time, my friend, a long time."

The Russian stared hard at the Englishman, trying to trace the damage of four decades. The hair, now gray and wispy, the extra chins, the blotches and veins that nature no longer hides. And what was left? The same authority, the same straight back and military bearing. No movements out of place or excessive. Self-contained, dangerous, the way he had been in the old days.

"I had not expected to see you again." The Englishman was sitting on the bed.

"That was our understanding, I agree. But this time a message was not sufficient." The Russian coughed and shook his head. "Let us not be embarrassed, my friend, you and I worked together many years ago when the world was in chaos. It was a war. We took risks. Drastic measures were necessary, drastic solutions."

He looked hard at the Englishman, but the words evoked no echo, no understanding. The man sat calm and expressionless, like a priest hearing confession. The Russian seemed unnerved.

"You look at me and you say nothing. . . ."

"I'm listening. I have no wish to discuss what is past."

"Nor I, my friend. But what we achieved then has been justified by history. You alone had vision. You saw the need for us to enter Europe, to liberate Europe, to prevent the Nazis from ever regaining power. You saw all that."

There was a flash of anger in the Englishman's

eyes. "Let's not get poetic. We did what we thought was best. Leave it there."

"Of course, of course. And I have kept to our agreement. . . ."

"Until now."

The Russian looked thoughtful. "It has not been easy. We covered our tracks. Sometimes I covered your tracks. There were people in Poland who did not forget you, people who sought you out. You have had a price on your head for a long time, my friend. Remember Prague. You had a man there. He came close to finding out certain things."

"Quite."

The Russian raised an eyebrow. "My friend, the kind of world that we helped to organize is in danger. Not from you, but from us. In Moscow these days they talk of reform, of democracy—and yet there is chaos. Our new General Secretary is a man out of his depth, floundering in water like a child unable to swim. He wishes for change, but he produces only confusion, doubt, and instability."

"He's your problem. You have solved such problems in the past."

"But it's your problem too. If the Soviet Union should disintegrate, then it will drag the world with it. There will be power battles in Moscow, blood on the streets, and our weapons will no longer be under firm control. Think about it, my friend. A nuclear power station in Chernobyl explodes and half of Europe suffers contamination. What about a nuclear missile? What then?"

"Then get rid of him."

The Russian smiled. "Don't you see, it is not just

the man. Anyone can kill a man. It is his ideas that are dangerous. It is his ideas that have to be killed. If he can be discredited, humiliated, that would be much more effective."

The Englishman got up from the bed and walked over to the window. He drew back the blinds, gazed out at the mountains, and listened intently. A quarter of an hour later he had made his decision. He didn't say anything, gave no signal, but the beginnings of a deal hung there unspoken in the small Swiss bedroom.

The Russian could sense the lighter atmosphere. Watch the eyes and the breathing, he told himself. It's all there.

He went over to the door to open it. "In two weeks the General Secretary goes to Poland. Think about it, my friend."

The Englishman moved back to the window. As with all the major decisions of his life, he felt quite calm, quite at peace with the world around him. But as he stood there the storm broke over the mountains with no warning. The wind began hurling hailstones at the shutters and thunder smacked down on the little hamlet.

"Good night, Mr. Tristram."

"Good night, Albert."

Tristram hurried toward the door.

"Off somewhere nice tonight, sir?"

He turned back toward the service commissionaire. He knew the man was a gossip. Radio Free Albert, they called him. And he bloody well wasn't going to tell him where he was going.

" 'Fraid not. See you next time."

Albert touched his cap.

As he hurried down the steps Tristram grimaced. How typical of the Service, with all its secrets and intrigues, to have a nosy doorman. And what if he'd told him? Yes, Albert, of course, old friend. I'm off to my ballroom dance class. Adult education, you know the sort of thing. Twist and grope. Just your cup of tea. Why don't you come along next time?

He cringed inside. That'd be wonderful. Albert would tell everyone. The cryptographers would get hold of it first, then signals, and pretty soon there wouldn't be a foreign station that hadn't heard of it. Know what our European analyst does in his spare time? Yeah, Tristram—that old bugger. He goes dancing. Ha bloody ha. He could just hear it.

Thank God he didn't go near the main building too often. Thank God they'd started farming them all out across the city. Thank God he was too low on the ladder to matter.

His house was a box at the end of a long, narrow cul-de-sac. "Nouveau Poor" a colleague had once called it. But that didn't matter. He could have afforded a better road, more space. But then there'd have been envy whenever anyone saw it, where now there was just pity. Poor old Tristram. What a hovel he lives in! That was much easier to cope with.

He turned his key in the lock and went straight through to the kitchen. Coke into the fridge, apples, loaf of white bread. And then upstairs for a bath, change.

And now he could smile at the thought of the dancing. He could do what he wanted in his own home.

That had been the great thing after getting out of Prague. Because in prison there'd never been any privacy. He'd expected solitary. But there'd always been two or three others in the cell, Czechs or foreigners, and he'd hated that more than anything else. The smell, the narrow confinement, the sharing of a predicament, when it would have been easier to manage on his own. And maybe they'd known that all along.

He ran the bath and lay back in it. Funny how things had gone full circle. Now that he wanted to share, there was no one in sight.

Of course that was where the dancing came in. You could reach out to people and that was accepted and natural. You could hold hands and sometimes dance close, although they didn't encourage too much of that. But you could pretend and imagine. And one day, maybe, there'd be a woman with warmth to give instead of take. And he'd be ready for that when it came. He got out of the bath and looked in the mirror. Yes, he told himself, more than ready.

A few minutes later Tristram telephoned the duty room and told them he was going out. It was quiet, they said. Not a sign of trouble anywhere in the East.

2

For a long time the four of them had sat in the car watching the old town square. They had come in from across Poland, rendezvoused ahead of time, smoked a cigarette together just to get the feel of being a team again. Talk of the families, talk of the weather, talk of the food that there was and there wasn't.

Outside they could see the carriages with the old cart horses coated up against the cold, snorting, stamping their hooves on the cobbles. Beneath the gaslights the drivers were wheeling and dealing, exchanging dollars, a joint or two, swapping stories. Tourist trade, street crooks. The end of a long winter's night in an Eastern Bloc capital.

Around two o'clock the Krokodil nightclub threw out its patrons, more tourists, a few of the local rich kids, the magician, resplendent in black cloak, his parrot on his shoulder, striding up the alley past the entrance to the cathedral. Minutes later came the click of high heels on the stone, the swish of an evening dress, a blonde in a long gown hurrying across the square toward the river. The stripper. And they knew where she was going.

In the end they got out of the car, stretched their legs, walked a little, kicked at the snow. The senior man looked at his watch and told them it was time to go.

And as the sun rose over the Ukraine and crossed into Poland, they dragged the old man from the apartment block dressed only in his pajamas and overcoat. The streets of Warsaw were wet from the thaw. The car weaved and skidded because they liked to play it that way. And the old man saw little except the dark statue of King Zygmunt, sword in hand, stooping low over the Castle Square.

His shins were bruised and bleeding where they'd kicked him but he barely noticed the pain.

I'm not afraid. Mary Mother of Christ, hear me . . . guard me the way you always have . . . deliver me from danger.

They never talk when they take you in . . . four thugs . . . always in fours . . . must be official policy.

Why after all this time? . . . It's years since we even had a march. . . . In the old days I always knew . . . all those years and I always knew why they were doing it . . . maybe someone had talked or some papers had been seized but . . .

Always I would prepare myself . . . work out a strategy . . . but I can't think anymore . . . please . . . give me time.

The car, which smelled of burned-out brakes and cheap fuel, had turned into the driveway of the Interior Ministry, and as they pulled him out into the courtyard he caught a glimpse of the blue winter sky, not a cloud anywhere in sight.

"Wake the bastard up." Passent lit a cigarette. Slumped on the metal chair, illuminated by the spotlight, the old man had fallen unconscious.

"What's the point?" It was one of the interrogators.

Passent took a step forward. The man's face was a stubble field. Too thin for his age. Passent could make out the curve of the rib cage beneath the nightshirt. No stomach, no waist, the baggy pajama bottoms suspended by faith alone.

You could tell he was nearing the tunnel. That's what they called it—the point at which torturers begin to lose their victims, the point where they start to sink inexorably. And then you can stop and give them water and all the injections in the world but you can't bring them back, can't put them together again. Once they're in the tunnel, they're lost for good.

Knowing he didn't have long, Passent moved in close, just the way he'd been told, speaking right into the man's ear.

"Remember the uprising, old fellow?"

"What of it?"

"Remember your British friend?"

The voice slurred. "I remember no Briton."

"Why did you agree to rise up?"

No answer.

"Why?"

"I . . . I don't know."

"Speak, old man, speak."

"It's gone . . . I don't know what you want."

Passent knew he would have to release the man. The rules were clear enough. The new rules. He had been wrong to open a file. Files required numbers and homes to go to. They set their own bureaucratic momentum.

In the old days he would have used the safe house. No files there. The baby unit would have been enough. So well named, for they could have reduced the man to infancy, owned him. Given time they would have coaxed the words—any words—from his mouth like a child learning to read.

"I said—wake him up," Passent barked again. Lipinski emptied a jug of water over the prisoner's head, the gray crew cut, the pale leather skin. The eyes flickered, opened. A hand rubbed them. The violent coughing echoed throughout the stone room.

An hour ago—it seemed like a day ago—the old fellow had asked Passent, "What happens if people are brought here and they're not guilty?"

Without thinking, the officer from the Interior Ministry had answered, "We make them guilty."

And what had the prisoner done? He had smiled.

Lipinski kicked the chair from under him. It was a favorite gesture, perfected over the years. He enjoyed it.

The old man felt a stab of pain as his back hit the floor and his breathing seized momentarily in shock. But because he was Polish and proud of it, he didn't make a sound. None of them ever did.

Passent pulled him to his feet, guiding the thin, shambling figure toward the door, framed in concrete. The room was airtight, clinical. The old man had sensed it. A place where human beings probed and betrayed each other, where no free spirit could breathe.

They had reached the door when the elderly figure moved. And suddenly Passent was crying out in pain as the prisoner seized his right hand with unbelievable force and twisted it behind his back, pushing it up hard against the nape of the neck, turning him, using him as a shield, as the interrogators rushed forward.

"Stop them." Such a soft growl from the old man. And Passent raised his free hand, as if to keep them at bay.

"Just one thing to say," the prisoner was panting, his breath rasping from the throat they had battered. "Today you win, maybe tomorrow as well." He gulped down more air. "But don't count on it in the future. Don't be too comfortable, don't sleep too deeply, don't walk in the darkness when you're alone."

He let go the hand and Passent turned, his face twisted with rage, his hand already clenching into a fist.

And then he stopped. Something in the man's face held him back. He couldn't be sure what it was—the defiance, maybe, the strength, an image of the tireless, irrepressible Poland, challenged and fought over through the ages. The land of his father. Your land, too, a voice told him, but he couldn't remember whose.

Passent shook his head clear. "For this I could hang your balls from the castle turret," he told the prisoner.

The old man laughed for the second time that

morning. "Your own would hang beside them the next day," he replied.

When they threw him out the prisoner walked half the length of Rakowiecka before noticing where he was. And yet he knew this street, knew it as if he had built it himself—the Interior Ministry, the barracks, the prison where they'd spent so many Christmases, wolfing their rations, still believing they lived in a wonderful country.

A bus took him to Stegny—the southern strip of the city, the dormitory for the children of the sixties and their thirties parents. Rows and rows of little streets, too numerous to count—all with their faraway names like Barcelonska and Paryska—dream names. Dug in along them were the squat, modern rectangles that housed the overspill from the inner city. They shouted out equality, prefabricated, pre-ordained.

The man got off the bus and limped across the muddy shoulder to a sidewalk. Of course they were lucky to have the new buildings. The Germans had blown up most of Warsaw and the Russians had put little enough back. Unless you counted the meat lines and the pictures of Lenin.

He could still remember the blasted city—just a pile of rubble, a few walls, a few pillars left standing like gravestones to mark where a city and a generation had once lived. That had been 1945, when the war and his world had ended together, when he had come back, not with hope or ambition, but simply to forget.

The old man entered block five, pressed the elevator button, and took what remained of his memories to the ninth floor. As the elevator slid to a halt a child held her face flat against the glass door. A tiny, wispy, blond thing in her pink skirt and English cardigan. He bent down to lift her, but the pain stopped him and she took his hand, pulling him into the apartment, sensing his unease.

She didn't notice the bloodshot eyes or the bruises beneath them. She couldn't discern what lay behind the soft, halting voice. She didn't know why he kept his back so straight as he sat down on the chintz-patterned sofa, and she missed the blood that he coughed into his handkerchief.

But when he fell asleep she covered him with a blanket and stayed close to him, just as if he had been her father.

Passent removed his jacket, securing it on the back of the door. It was light tan, the trousers flared and looked Italian. He looked Italian, they said. A short figure, the black hair thinning out into a vee on the forehead—the widow's peak.

He pulled the file toward him. The name on it was Zbig Lermontov and Zbig had given nothing. Not that people were supposed to give, Passent reflected. You extracted. They didn't give.

With Zbig though it had been pointless. The man had fought his way through the Nazi occupation and the riots of the fifties. He'd been beaten up by the Zomo squads in Gdansk in 1970 and 1980. In fact, Passent recalled, he'd been beaten up by some of the best and most experienced police agents in postwar Poland. So he wasn't going to break until he was ready. And when that happened he'd die with his mouth shut.

Passent felt no animosity toward Zbig. If it hadn't been for the message, he wouldn't have pulled him in at all. But then he had learned to follow instructions.

They had taught him the basics in 1968 at the Interior Ministry college in Lodz, then the KGB had offered a little more expertise in Minsk, and when Warsaw had finally got him back, short-haired and cocky in early '71, he had it down pat.

Of course, the colonel had reminded him, we do things our way over here. And don't forget it. The Russians may have been pleased with you, but Russians are Russians and Poles are Poles, and there's only so much fucking about *our* people will take.

Passent had heard the man out and kept silent. The colonel wouldn't be around forever. And it wasn't the colonel who had ordered Zbig pulled in. It wasn't the colonel who had met him in that coffee bar near the monastery, where the university students sported their jeans and leather jackets, played worn records on the jukebox, and pretended to be somewhere else.

He had recognized the Soviet diplomat without much difficulty. The black shapka hat was made in Moscow, so were the shoes. He wasn't the only one who saw it.

"What now?" he had asked.

"Just a few suggestions." The diplomat looked carefully around the room.

"Why so many suggestions these days?"

"We think it's time. Solidarity has had its fun. They've all had their little games, playing at politics, cuddling the capitalists. Now it's time to sort them out. Nurture the good, destroy the bad. Like collective farming." The fat face beamed.

"I see."

What Passent saw was a list of names that the diplomat slid across the table toward him—names from the trade union, the big names that had possessed such big mouths and opened them so loud. Such idiots, thought Passent. They hadn't seen where it was going. They'd all crawled out of the woodwork, said their piece, and believed a Solidarity government would protect them. They hadn't looked at the map.

Passent had gazed out of the café window and stared hard at his countrymen. The Interior Ministry had written down all the names and kept them till needed. The probables, the possibles, the diehards, the ones who were finished and would have to go. Warsaw had written them down and handed the list to Moscow. Now Moscow was handing it back.

Right at the top stood Zbig Lermontov.

The apartment had only two rooms, neither large. One was a real bedroom; the other became one when the need arose. Both were cluttered. Books burst out from the shelves, papers were piled on them, suitcases in the corners, jars of food, a stack of toys, a mound of clothes on an ironing board just inside the front door. A lived-in apartment, but lived in in a hurry. No one dawdled there. They sat a little, slept a little, and then departed.

In the early hours of the morning the child had left the old man. He had eaten little and spoken less. And now he slept heavily, his legs drawn up to his stomach, arms across his chest, head inclined against the armrest of the settee. She made her way into the bedroom, tucked in the blanket, and climbed beneath it. A tiny figure, yet oddly neat and fastidious. A little home builder, a little homekeeper. She was old beyond her years, the neighbors said. But then a child alone grows quickly.

Maya Angelica fell asleep to the ticking of the alarm clock that dominated the two rooms. Six hours later she awoke to the daily routine. She tidied away the dirty clothes from the day before, brushed her teeth in the bathroom, stroked the rough man's hairbrush through her curls, making them stand. She held one tight against her nose, peered into the mirror, and laughed at her reflection.

Then, as she always did, she tiptoed into the main room and ran her fingers over her grandfather's shoulders. Quietly she stepped back. And the child who had never known death, never seen it, never heard of it, began to scream so loudly that the neighbors came running from their apartments many floors above, pulling on their clothes as they went, slamming the doors, sprinting down bare passages with gray walls, fearful of the child's distress.

Zbig Lermontov, wartime and peacetime leader of the underground, had departed Poland during the night. And the screams from his granddaughter continued for almost an hour, because she didn't know why.

The tie line between Warsaw and Moscow crackled into life.

The Russian's nasal voice sounded tense, anxious. "You asked the old man the question?"

"Just as you instructed. He remembers nothing."

"You're sure. He could have been pretending."

"With the methods we used there was no room for pretending. Besides, he has never remembered anything. You know that. If he had, we would have acted years ago. The war destroyed his memory—like so many of them."

"Ha!" The Russian seemed to relax.

"Why do you worry about an old man who has lost his memory?"

"I, too, am an old man—I wanted to be sure."

The Russian replaced the receiver. For nearly an hour he went over the conversation in his mind, just to be certain he had missed nothing.

3

The mother of Maya Angelica caught sight of the police cars as she rounded the corner and her heart seemed to jolt. But habit made her walk on, slowly, precisely, head down. It was the conditioned reflex to the state militia, the training of a decade spent in People's Poland. It came with the milk.

Keep going, she told herself. They're not for you. Not this time. Not anymore.

A hundred yards on she could pick out the vehicles more clearly—the Polski Fiats, the blue-gray van with the shaded windows. An ambulance. Christ!

But by then she knew they were outside her entrance and the hard-learned discipline left her. She began to run toward them, holding the little suitcase in her left hand, the high boots tripping, slithering on the rough driveway, the yellow scarf fluttering in the breeze, her thoughts only for the daughter she had left behind.

Ahead of her two men got out of the van and took up position in the doorway, their legs wide apart.

Their hands were in their raincoat pockets, clutching the guns she knew they carried.

They made no move to block her and she pushed past them, leaning hard against the stiff glass door, taking the stairs because the elevator was out of order. Why did they let me in? But she knew that too. They wanted her out of sight, well away from the thousand windows and witnesses. And yet she had glimpsed one face high above her and the shimmer of a curtain. How many others were there? Who would watch and record? Who would agonize, turn away, and say nothing? It needed only one person to take a walk in the darkness and tell the movement. There had to be one, even out there in the urban dormitories, windblown and godless.

And then she remembered her father's words . . . in Poland you're never alone.

"Grazyna Garten?"

To Passent it seemed she was younger, fairer than the file had suggested, with the long blond hair in studied disorder.

She stopped in the doorway, mouth open. She could see the furniture had been moved around. A chair lay on its side.

"My daughter," she breathed. "Where's my daughter?"

"Please don't worry. She's next door with the neighbors. Fine but a little upset." Passent took a step toward her.

"Upset, why upset?"

"Sit down, Mrs. Garten."

"Who are you? What's happened?"

"Sit down!"

Grazyna felt the nausea rising but she couldn't move.

"I have to tell you that your husband's father died during the night." Passent cleared his throat. "The neighbors called us. I'm very sorry. Heart attack."

He touched her arm and somehow she was certain the tears would come. But they didn't. Instead a feeling of profound loneliness sank upon her in the little room, pushing her to the floor.

Zbig had died, Zbig, her father-in-law, her companion. Zbig, who had comforted her when Jozef had walked out. Zbig, who had led the underground in war and in peace. Dead here and found by her child. She shook her head, trying to clear the jumbled thoughts.

And then she could see it all so clearly—the van outside, the security men from the SB—the Sluzba Bespiecestwa. And now the smooth talker without a name.

They weren't there by chance. Zbig hadn't died by chance. Not he. Not after he'd spat for so many years in the faces of these clowns. They weren't sorry for Zbig or her. They wanted to know what would happen next.

Slowly she got to her feet and leaned against the sofa. The voice was a whisper. "I know, you bastard. I know." And she looked up at Passent and the hatred traveled between them. Grazyna never saw the man who hit her.

The stretchers were light and made easy work for the security men. And as they carried them toward the ambulance the breath from the two inert figures wound upward into the light gray sky.

From Stegny the convoy drove northwest to the domestic airport and was waved through the outer perimeter fence onto the tarmac. They halted beside a green transport plane, its tanks fueled, propellers turning, and inside the cockpit the blanket security clearance for an unregistered flight anywhere in Poland or outside. The gold card, they called it. Given only to the trusted. Rare and priceless.

Passent got out of the car and stood still for a moment, deafened by the noise. Low clouds had gathered over the airport. All other traffic had been delayed or diverted. In a few moments, he realized, they'd be lost from sight, their radio silent, quite alone in the skies over Poland.

The flight was bumpy and the turboprop had to fight hard in the thin atmosphere, droning its way south toward the mountains. At Krakow the two figures, mother and child, were transferred to a Sikorsky helicopter, painted blue and white, the colors of the national airline. And as they rose into the afternoon clouds the first tinges of red appeared in the west.

Twenty minutes later they flew across the foothills of the Tatras. Passent could make out the forests, half buried in snow all the way to Czechoslovakia. Smoke came from a few wooden chalets and then the helicopter was banking sharply, lowering itself into a clearing in the woods.

Grazyna woke for a few seconds and felt the cold, dry air. She was being carried through the pine trees, but her eyes wouldn't open and she passed out again as they bumped uncomfortably in the back of the four-wheel-drive Niva.

Passent called a halt in a small settlement overlooking the town of Zakopane. The engine was switched off and he was struck by the wall of silence around them, the hush of the forest, the chill that pointed to imminent nightfall. In the shadow of a cottage not thirty yards from them, he could see the couple standing stiff and motionless. Passent beckoned to them and they began trudging slowly toward him across the unmarked snow.

"Everything all right?" he asked.

"Of course it is. What did you expect?" It was the man who replied. Gruff old shit, thought Passent, with his army greatcoat and sheepskin hat. But who wouldn't be in his position? Former police captain from Gdansk, stoned by the crowds back in 1970 and now paralyzed down one side of his face. And look at his wife. Nothing to smile about there. She'd been in charge of the detention camp at Bialo-Leka during martial law. No softy that one. A great, triangular creature with arms and legs as thick as tree trunks. There wouldn't be any nonsense in her house. That was why he used it.

Between them all they carried the stretchers to the house. Once it had been a barn, and the windows, tiny and filthy, had come much later. Inside, in the semidarkness, Passent smelled cheap soap. They left the stretchers on the floor.

"You call every morning at ten. Understood?" Passent spoke to the woman. She nodded sullenly.

"We know the rules. Don't think we're stupid just because we live out here." Her lip curled at him.

"If you were stupid, I wouldn't be here," he replied, and turned back toward the clearing.

"Who are they?" The woman was calling after him, her voice echoing far away into the trees. Suddenly he felt cold and realized the sun had passed behind the mountains.

"It doesn't matter who they are," he yelled back. "Look after them well."

"If you'd wanted them looked after, you should have gone somewhere else."

As Passent stared at the woman her voice turned into a shriek of laughter. He could hear the cackling across the valley as he drove away.

A military helicopter returned Passent to Warsaw. The pilot had frowned at the Interior Ministry identity card and leaned across to open the door, gesturing to Passent to put on the headset and strap himself in.

As they flew he listened to the traffic controllers handing them through the military sectors. Much talk of "our boys." Brothers in arms, thought Passent, but the pilot didn't talk to him. The hatred between military and police was alive and well.

Halfway through the flight he caught a query from Soviet Air Defense as they passed within three miles of the border. The pilot answered curtly, then turned to Passent, raised the middle finger of his right hand, and thrust it upward in a gesture that left nothing to the imagination.

It was after eleven when they landed back at the military end of Okecie airport. There was no staff car, no escort. He had seen to that. Instead Passent hurried to the parking lot, unlocked the little Fiat, and headed fast into the city.

He parked as near to the Old Town as he could and continued on foot to the cathedral. The narrow street was packed and already he could hear singing from inside. The people didn't like it, but he pushed past them as gently as he could, making for the left side of the church, near the back.

He tried not to look at the faces. But the tapestry of students, old women, even soldiers in uniform, captivated him. At times he almost stepped on them, kneeling as they did on the bare flagstones.

Near the wall was a gap and Passent slipped into it. And when the time came to sing the carols, he sang his heart out, just he had as a child, when his family had thought it best to smuggle him into church lest it affect his future among the new atheist elite.

Again the congregation knelt, and Passent wondered if anyone else had brought such a heavy load into the church. The beating and killing of an underground leader, the kidnapping of his family in broad daylight, and the implicit offer of direct confrontation with the resistance—the ones who had never come into the open. All on orders from Moscow and they hadn't said why.

At the altar the intoning ceased and Passent got to his feet. It was midnight, and as the bells jangled high above him, he crossed himself and welcomed Christ into the People's Republic.

* * *

By then, to anyone who cared, it was eleven at night in the London suburb of Wimbledon and James Tristram was on his way home from the dance class at Walworth Junior School. He felt light, which he wasn't, and happy.

The waltzes had been especially good. True, the fox-trots had been less satisfying, but then the fox-trot always required a little more panache. And the tiny physics teacher who'd been chosen to partner him—any fool could see she was too small—had not been blessed with panache.

Tristram could still hear the tinkling piano, the strains of Gershwin in the third-floor classroom, with the desks and chairs piled up in the corner and the get-together afterward for coffee in the Cottage Pie. Nice, simple—a bit bitchy at times—but a perfect antidote to the academic and thankless tasks he performed these days for the Service.

As he opened his garden gate that night his mind was wholly on the mystical harmony of body and music and it was a long time since he'd thought of anything east of Dover or Berlin, east of Dresden or Warsaw.

Not that you could ever forget. He knew that. He put his key in the door. Simple things like that which you took for granted. But the years can soften the sting. Like a frightened dog, a frightened mind will one day come out of the corner and take from the hand that offers it kindness.

They'd been good to James Tristram, he reckoned. The Service had taken him back, a little hesitantly at first because they weren't at all sure where he'd been. But they'd taken him all the same.

Of course he could no longer go in the field. They'd put a leash on him now. Tristram had been grounded in research duties and left to go flabby and awkward. More often than not his plump frame was housed in a green sport jacket, worn full and tight like a sack. He had parted company with most of his hair—two gray patches nestled close to the ears. But his appearance evoked little comment.

In any case, the Director liked him, the old-school Director and Cornish too. Cornish the deputy.

And it was, he reasoned, a home of sorts, a kind of foster family. Not the first choice but the best there was under the circumstances. It never crossed his mind that the family might throw him to the dogs to be mauled alive.

4

The figure in the light blue parka and dirty sneakers had given no thought for his safety. It didn't occur to him that he might be in danger. At ten minutes to seven in the morning the outside temperature in London stood at zero. Only inside on the underground platform was it warm and seductive.

He could read the advertisements for stockings and typing schools, but it still took him time. He found English a strange language. For three years he had lived with it, bathed in it, but it would always be foreign. Such a frivolous tongue, without rules or principles, full of masks and disguises. Even if you knew the words, the meanings could so easily escape.

Deep under the city he could hear the hum on the rails, the faint rumbling far away in the tunnel. So he turned toward the opening to be ready to see the beast emerge, because that was dramatic, exciting. And he missed the footsteps behind him.

But then they were trained and he wasn't. They had speed and motive. They were fit and the adrenaline was well on its way around their bodies. And so he didn't stand a chance. Not he. Tired, a little drunk, such a long way from home.

In the airless room high above the Edgware Road, James Tristram got down on his knees and switched on the radiator, wheezing with the effort. It seemed to him that middle age had arrived overnight, a bit like a registered letter. You couldn't give it back. No one would take it.

The news of Zbig Lermontov's death had reached him an hour earlier. A courier had brought the mailbag over from Curzon Street. And it had seemed appropriate to say a small prayer for the old man. Not a sign of any deep religious faith, but a habit he had come to cherish after the Czechs had arrested him. Something to hang on to, something to do. An act he couldn't expect Cornish to understand.

"Don't you have any idea what's going on in Poland?" Cornish sighed and tapped the desk impatiently with a pencil. He looked out of place in the room. The dark blue suit fit too well, the tie was too perfectly matched with the yellow shirt, shoes unscathed and unscuffed.

Tristram grimaced. "I don't know why they pulled in Lermontov. He hadn't done anything for well over a year—who had? Anyway they beat the shit out of him, by all accounts."

"Whose accounts?"

"The usual. We still have one or two people left."

Cornish took off his glasses and rubbed his eyes. And in that moment, thought Tristram, he looked old —far too old to be in the Service, and yet they never really retired. "Of course Lermontov was one of those resistance leaders in Poland, wasn't he? All that running around in the sewers of Warsaw." Cornish sniffed for a moment as if he could smell them. "But that was a long time ago, wasn't it? Muddy waters, I seem to remember, like so much of that postwar stuff." He had drawn back the net curtain and was looking down into the street. Now he turned back to face Tristram. "You never did tie any of that down after Prague, did you?"

Muttering oaths and incantations, Ezekiel Morris, an ancient West Indian station guard, found the little figure sprawled on the platform beside a vending machine. He was unconscious and Ezekiel wasted valuable moments crossing himself and whimpering before calling an ambulance.

They took the man to St. Thomas's hospital on the South Bank, where the hospital chart listed him as a suspected mugging victim, the second that night. It confirmed serious abrasions to the chest and lower abdomen. The intern looked carefully at the face and felt for bruises under the hair but could find nothing.

With the hospital record completed, they summoned the police. A sergeant found the man's driver's license and radioed the number to New Scotland Yard on Victoria Street. Less than a minute later they knew who they had.

The noise startled James Tristram to his feet. The door opened, revealing a plump middle-aged woman in brown coat and hat, looking like a nanny.

He sank back into the chair.

"Ah, Martha." Cornish raised his bottom a half

inch from the chair, acknowledging Tristram's colleague.

"I've been to the doctor." Her voice carried no expression. Clipped and German. A statement, not a plea for sympathy.

"Oh dear, I hope everything's all right." Cornish seemed suddenly embarrassed, as if an intimate discussion of medical symptoms was about to follow.

Martha cut him off. "Of course."

"Good, good. Now that we're all here." He looked over to Tristram and back to Martha. "You up to speed on all this, my dear? Brain in gear?"

She folded her coat and placed it like a trophy on the desk beside Cornish. His kind, she reflected, didn't know any better. At school he would have been a bully, now he was a bore, putting women down, yet preening his long gray hair, strutting around in pin-striped finery. But when all the affectations were stripped away, she knew he was a hard man.

Cornish let his head track between them.

"I want to do something about Poland."

Tristram snorted contemptuously. "What did you have in mind—buying it?"

Cornish ignored him. "The committee has made a decision. That in itself may surprise you, but we want to use Lermontov's death to see what they can do—the underground. Have they all gone soft? Are they lying on their backs waiting for the Russians to tickle their fannies? Could Poland let the communists back into power?"

They looked blankly at him.

"In some ways they still have power," Tristram

sniffed. "They control the police, the army, the security services—that was their price for joining the coalition. Look at the rest of Eastern Europe—same there. First the revolutions—then the communists gradually took back all the top jobs, calling themselves democrats. And now all the underground movements are back in business."

Cornish looked bored. "Anyway, the new Soviet General Secretary is going there. Let's see if we can't stir things up for him. James? Martha?"

"Indeed." She hung her head.

Within an hour the injured man was moved from the general medical ward at St. Thomas's to a private room. Amid much shouting and recrimination, the previous occupant was wheeled away down the fourth-floor corridor out of earshot . . . an African diplomat who wished the hospital and its staff much bad luck and hoped their futures would be short.

A little way down the corridor a man in a beige raincoat sat on an armchair reading the newspaper. He told the sister he was a cousin of the injured victim and would wait until his relative woke up and he could be certain that the poor fellow was all right.

Such a nice man, thought the ward sister, such an educated manner of speech. It was of course quite unlike the speech of the new patient. But since he was unconscious and hadn't opened his mouth, no one could spot the discrepancy.

Left by themselves, they sat for a while not speaking. James Tristram and Martha Cedar. Two names never listed in a phone book, never to be noted on their way in or their way out.

From the distance came the rattle of a train heading for Paddington Station, the occasional ambulance siren. Tristram hated the noise, deafening by day, intolerable at night. There was simply no peace to be had. Typical of the Service to billet them in a slum. "Security, old man," they'd said. "Best if you're out of the building, but not too far away when we need you."

Every day a messenger would come to remove the sensitive documents, but sometimes for weeks on end there weren't any. And the two of them would huddle, each against a radiator, reading the statements of the political opposition parties in East Germany, Russia, most from Poland.

Normally they tried to be out when Cornish called. But this time he had artfully rung the newsdealers downstairs—the smiling Patel family—to make sure they were there.

"You want me to find someone for this little trip?" Martha looked down at the floor.

"It can wait till tomorrow."

Tristram left the office and the underground train bumped him slowly and with apparent bad grace southward across the river. So slowly in fact that the dance class in the Walworth Road had begun without him.

There were reproving glances and a price had been exacted. The only female left unpartnered was the tiny physics teacher he had suffered the last time and

Tristram gave an inward groan as she skipped toward him.

"I'm June," she said. And he thought, You're more like January, dark with a strong tendency toward gloominess. Short days, long nights, plenty of introspection. Wrinkles around the eyes that weren't from laughter.

And yet as the evening progressed so did the relationship. They even began to dance cheek to chest as the teacher grew bolder, pressing her tight black curls against Tristram's jacket, a shy grin between dances and a bony little hand that wedged itself in his as they circled the floor. One or two of the couples noticed and mouthed "sweet" at each other over the music.

By mutual agreement they bowed out of coffee at the Cottage Pie and took the underground train to Waterloo.

"What d'you do?" she asked him.

Without thinking, he looked over his shoulder—an odd reflex, and yet no one had asked for a long time.

"Not very much. Actually I work in an office in the city. Nothing exciting I'm afraid."

"Best thing." She smiled. "Then you can plan exciting things the rest of the time. I'm going to Russia next year."

"Good Lord. Whatever for?"

"I've never been there. I've got an aunt who went. It's awfully cheap. And she said everyone should see it. I mean it's important to know what it's like, isn't it?"

"I s'pose so. What's wrong with Spain?"

She pulled his arm. "Don't be boring. Everyone goes there. It's nice to be different."

No it's not, he thought. I wish I'd gone to Spain, wish I'd never set foot in Russia. And I wish I did something normal, like build houses or clean windows. Difficult to have any relationship if you have to begin with a lie. *I work in an office in the city.* What sort of nonsense was that? You can't start out with lies. They often come later. But you have to build on something a little better. Don't you?

They got out and walked over Hungerford Bridge toward Charing Cross. And it seemed natural to take June's arm, her plastic raincoat billowing over the long blue dress, to walk past the courting couples, the kissers and would-be kissers, unable to summon the courage.

As he knew he would, Tristram misjudged the good-bye on the platform. In a hurried, jerky movement his mouth connected with her chin.

"Couldn't we do that next time?" June put out a hand. "It's nicer to wait."

He hadn't known what to say, watching the little figure hurry away to her train. Better not to have waited, he thought. A kiss would have staked a claim—like putting down a deposit. Waiting might lose the opportunity altogether. Waiting was dangerous.

At St. Thomas's the man in the beige coat felt a tug at his arm. He shouldn't have dozed off, but really it wasn't much of a job, baby-sitting some third-grade East European.

"Your bloke's going to come round soon." The nurse was leaning over him. "He's a bit more stable now, better color, you know—vital signs and all that."

He thanked her, left the hospital, and walked to the nearest pay phone. He'd been told to dial just one number, say his piece, and that would be that. No need to make a meal of it.

The phone call had wakened Tristram just as dawn was seeping in over the Thames Valley and he had stood for a moment in the freezing bedroom, uncertain who had spoken.

Pulling back the curtains, he had seen the pool car waiting at the end of the road, just the parking lights on, just a shadow at the wheel.

There hadn't been time to dress properly and in his haste he had put on too many clothes—a jacket, sweater, even an overcoat—and that had made him hot and uncomfortable. And yet he wouldn't have missed the trip. Not this one.

As they drove in he could see that the short hospital night was abruptly terminated. The day shift was taking over and inside patients in dressing gowns filled the corridors. It struck him that the living were obliged to rise early. Only the dead slept in.

Entering the room, Tristram peered down over the inert figure, battered and now sedated. it wasn't quite the Jozef Garten he'd seen before. But the cleft jaw and the long thin nose jutted up from the pillow looked much as he remembered them.

He thought of the collection of abject casualties filling the hospital and marveled that of all the people in London, Garten should have surfaced among them. It was the kind of sudden and extraordinary coincidence in which he had never believed.

5

In Tristram's eyes Garten had not been like the other defectors. And he had known it from the start, from the initial debriefings, from the walks, the dinners, and all the small talk they had shared so many years ago.

Garten hadn't demanded fast cars and champagne the moment he'd arrived, hadn't been a nuisance. Instead he'd recounted graphic stories about a police chase through Warsaw, a gun battle in Lublin, a secret border crossing into Russia to meet the KGB—tales that the West had never heard.

And then he had disappeared from view, drifted from hamburger bars to cinemas; he'd waited at table, even driven a minicab. But he'd gotten on with life. He hadn't looked for trouble and it hadn't found him. Until now.

And yet even in the early days Tristram had noticed something the other debriefers had overlooked. Garten was an angry man, a hurt man who had made the wrong decision and would one day seek to right it.

For years he had been one of the mainstays of the Warsaw underground. He'd built new networks, serviced the old, led the state militia a five-year dance across Poland. And then something had snapped. Without any warning at all, he'd had enough, jumped ship, literally, in Sweden and the Swedes had passed him on to London. Later he had confessed he didn't know why he'd done it. He'd left a family, left a cause, left a country. And eventually, Tristram had felt certain, he would go back to reclaim them all.

The young Pole stirred, opened his eyes, saw Tristram, and closed them again. A nurse took his hand, feeling for the pulse.

Tristram didn't know for certain who had arranged the beating, but he could imagine well enough. It carried the hallmarks of standard KGB harassment. Nothing too drastic or gentle, but a point to be made on several points of the body. Always the face left clean. Maybe a couple of drivers from the Czech or Bulgarian embassies. They always looked on beatings as a treat.

Of course they wouldn't have been told the reason, that this was in the nature of a little reminder. A sign for Garten that they knew where he was, hadn't forgotten him, and that he'd never really be safe.

To Tristram it was more than that—an act of cynical cruelty. So cruel, he thought, to attack this man, barely twenty-four hours after the beating in Warsaw. And not just the beating of a fellow Pole, but of Zbig Lermontov, who happened, by anything other than chance, to be Jozef Garten's father, buried that morning in Poland.

* * *

Four hours later Garten was discharged into Tristram's care. His record of admission was destroyed, as was the chart listing his vital signs. As he limped out into the gray London lunch hour it was as if he had never been to St. Thomas's. He belonged now to Tristram.

A gift. And time and experience had taught Tristram that every gift has a donor.

The rain had stopped and Cornish moved unhurriedly toward the river. He could make out the blue light of a police launch as it puttered softly toward Westminster. The city was damp and quiet.

"You'll have to tell them to speed it up. The Russians are going to be in Warsaw a week early." The Director turned to his subordinate and scrutinized him under the streetlamp.

"I still don't see why—"

"I thought I'd made that perfectly clear." The Director stopped by the edge of the Embankment and leaned against the low wall. Classic Whitehall, thought Cornish. Gray hair, gray mustache, the suit and the brogues. The same fancy dress, same packaging, same train in from Kent or East Sussex, same pork pie at lunch, same half hour in the lavatory fighting constipation—same as everyone else. Only the papers on the desk would tell him apart—the papers and the special phones and the access to the Prime Minister and the intelligence staff, and the twenty or thirty thousand secrets swirling around in his head as he did the crossword puzzle.

It seemed, almost, as if he were speaking to the

river. "There may not be much time left. Everything in the bloc is becoming too nice and cozy. The Poles are signing pledges about democracy as if they've been doing it all their lives. And the opposition is swallowing it all. They've even started turning up for talks wearing coats and ties. By the time they find out what a con it all is, it'll be too late. We need an uprising, we need general strikes, we need a takeover of the party headquarters—if they don't assert themselves now, they may never get the chance again."

"Why don't the Americans do something? They're just as worried about the Kremlin leadership as we are." The wind gusted along the street, catching Cornish's collar.

"The Americans? Don't make me laugh," the Director said. "You think they could handle a covert operation? Look how they fucked up Iran/Contra. Bunch of dewy-eyed Marines handing out Bibles in Teheran. Forget it. It's us or no one."

"And if we fuck it up?"

"We'll have tried." The Director shrugged. He looked back to the road, watching the headlights waving like sparklers along the Embankment. Then without speaking, he turned abruptly to the left, moving out along the wet pavement, head down, feet shuffling.

Cornish watched him till he disappeared past the silver griffin—the tiny statue that stands as the only permanent guardian to the city of London.

"Did you have to kill the Pole?"

The Englishman rubbed a hand over his forehead. He felt sick, ill at ease. The overnight journey to

Switzerland had been awful. Now he'd have to go straight back.

"No of course we didn't. We could have just kicked his arse and hoped the underground would start a revolt in protest. Of course we had to kill him." The Russian snorted in contempt. "And even that was nearly bungled."

You're primitive, thought the Englishman. You used to be rough and have ideals. Now you're just rough and cruel. You're the worst of the old breed.

"I will compliment you, though, my friend." The Russian seemed to read his thoughts. "A good move to pick the son. Good to beat him up, make him nervous, disoriented. And so soon after his father's . . . ah, departure."

"We didn't know at the time that his father was departing, as you put it."

"Scruples, my friend? Scruples, after so many years?"

"Standards."

The Russian laughed.

"Let me offer you some. Keep this man in the Kremlin and you will see some standards you didn't expect. Want to know about all the money you're investing these days, all those joint projects, the grand new schemes? I'll tell you. It's going down the fucking drain, and it'll take you with it."

"I'm surprised you're telling me this."

"My friend, I'm surprised you don't see it. The longer this man is in power, the harder it'll be to clean up the mess. And then how do we restore order? Tanks? Riot police? Of course we do. Only we'll see who does the squealing and wailing after that.

You in the West and all the sniveling cowards you've produced."

The Russian was warming to his subject, his fists clenched, his eyes blazing, the sweat forming on his brow.

"My friend"—he leaned over and slapped the Englishman on the knee—"this is just the beginning."

6

Night came rapidly to the town of Zakopane. Grazyna could no longer see the mountains, but she could feel their presence in the darkness. The hostile, jagged edge of southern Poland.

She hadn't ever known captivity. Her friends had been interned, some had been jailed on criminal charges. She'd visited prisons and cried at the gates. But she, herself, had never been caught, never interrogated. In the underground they'd called her "little innocent" for she hadn't seen Poland through bars. And that meant she hadn't seen it.

Now she had.

Grazyna turned from the window. Maya was asleep on a trundle bed. The two of them had been herded up the narrow stairs to an attic room, with only a single window on the world. It had been the woman who took control. Grazyna could see it in her eyes. Hatred and indifference. "Stay still, stay quiet, and maybe you'll make it," the bitch had said. A simple key to life that Grazyna could keep or throw away.

Despite the cold outside, the room was warm and musty. Grazyna sat on her bed and felt the low wooden beams. She knew all about the code of survival. Her parents had talked of it when she was a child, her friends had talked of it when she grew up, and Jozef had talked about it for all those years that he had planned and plotted and helped to push Poland into chaos.

My husband, she whispered, and tried to picture the small determined face of Jozef Garten, who had walked out of the apartment building on a beautiful June day, bright blue cap on his head, holdall in hand, waving at the two faces pressed hard against the window.

Jozef, my teacher, Jozef, my friend, father of Maya. See you soon. Come back safe. She could remember shouting the words, then mouthing them through the glass nine stories up. And he hadn't come back at all. Hadn't ever written or telephoned, never bothered, never cared.

There were no tears left for Jozef Garten, she decided. They'd all been cried a long time ago. To fill the gap after he'd gone there'd been Zbig and the underground and that had been plenty.

Together they'd come up with the rule book for life in occupied Poland. The techniques for a life of danger and deceit. The only one she and her friends had known.

Of course there was another way and another type of Poland. Grazyna recalled talking to the mother of one of Maya's friends.

"I don't hold with this underground nonsense," the woman had said as they'd waited for a Warsaw tram. "Surely the time for hiding in sewers and typing those silly news sheets is over. I mean, after all we live next to Russia. And who's to say they're so bad? All right"—the woman had shrugged—"they lie and cheat. But what do you think happens in the West? Uh?"

She lay on her bed, trying to return to the present. Someone in the apartments would have seen her carried out, someone would have sent word. The movement would have been told. The movement would find her and get her out.

After all, she was family, Zbig's family. And they never forgot that. It was the rule and the promise: "We will not desert you." She thought of all the young faces, the farmhands, the shop assistants, the priests who burdened themselves with this sacred vow, often before they were twenty. Barely away from home, they were required to fight for a new family. It wasn't fair. Grazyna turned to the wall. None of it was fair. She laughed to herself. In the West they thought democracy had arrived.

She caught the noise as she turned—a footstep, halfway between stealth and openness. *My God*, she thought, *I was meant to hear it.* She turned on the lamp beside her bed, because no one should fight in the darkness and she wanted to see the enemy.

The man stood in the doorway. The ex-policeman, still standing the way they all did. Legs apart, weight evenly distributed, weapon in right hand. Only this time he carried a flashlight. He didn't say anything but she recognized the look. Men showed that look at any age. The young hopefuls, the past-it brigade. The

want and the certainty that it would be satisfied. In
the light from the small lamp she could see a scar on
his right temple. *Did we put that there?* The gray face,
hair neatly combed. *My God, he's even made an effort.* In
another place, at another time, she might have
laughed.

But she didn't follow the rules. It was she who
broke the silence. "Get out of here, I'm tired," she
told him, voice steady, nerve holding. For a moment
the face smiled and he seemed to know he had won
that round.

As he shut the door Grazyna was certain she would
have to kill him.

From his office in the Interior Ministry, Passent
could see across Rakowiecka to the prison. Along the
high wall the morning visitors were waiting to be
filtered in through the gate, searched, identified, sub-
jected to petty harassment.

It seemed like an unending stream of humanity,
and yet you couldn't feel sorry for them. There
would always be sacrifices for the greater good. So-
cialism was like that. Clear the dead wood from the
common path. Remove all obstacles. Only then could
the masses march forward in unison.

Odd how the words had stuck in his head, odd how
easily they came to mind. That was the training.
That was why the Russians were so effective.

Suddenly Passent's eyes narrowed. In the distance
he caught sight of an old, familiar shape, coated in
black, half hidden by the crowd. For a second the face
turned toward him and the hatless white head left no

room for doubt. He smiled. It was Dyadek, the priest. Dyadek the confessor and informer, the coward and the comforter. God's own gift to the state of Poland. Dyadek was visiting his flock. By midday, Passent decided, he'd be worth a visit himself.

Passent left the ministry on foot. An official Fiat parked outside Dyadek's block, a friendly wave from the driver, and Dyadek's cover would be blown. In any case, Passent knew it could take a lot less than that.

Warsaw was a city of suspicions, of rustling curtains, of whispers and winks. Trust had died in the onset of martial law. In the years after the prisoners and internees had been released, the underground had kicked in a ruthless campaign to discover its traitors. There had been many. They were sure of it. But they had never identified Dyadek.

As he left the building Passent looked again at the long line of people snaking into the prison. Each carried a bag and even from a distance he knew the contents—underwear, a bar of soap, chocolate, razor blades, and a few cigarettes. Some of it would reach the intended recipient. Much wouldn't. A lot depended on the generosity of the duty guards and it wasn't a quality they were known for.

Passent looked for Dyadek, but the man must have passed inside. Rapidly he walked to the end of the street and crossed in front of the Moskwa cinema. Behind it the road descended sharply. On all sides were the apartment blocks of the fifties. Occasionally an older building with bullet holes still pitted in the concrete. The battle scars from the German invasion, left intentionally unrepaired. It was a point of honor.

Some people recall the locations where they have loved or suffered or proposed marriage. But to Passent each street carried a different kind of memory.

As he walked scores of startled, sleepy faces came to mind, dogs that barked in the dawn light, wives who wept, and through it all the sound of police boots running on stone corridors. The old days. Now they had to be so careful, so precise.

Dyadek never locked his door. Thieves can always get in, he would explain. Passent had smiled. It was true enough. In the early days he had searched the flat himself and he was sure the underground had done the same. Everyone took out insurance, but in the end they all made their deals. Party member dealt with dissident, student with teacher—even policeman and priest. Dyadek and he making their pact across the great divide. Dyadek won leniency for his people, Passent won information. No format—but little drips, little accommodations over the years, as and when. No reports written, no records kept.

Passent stepped quietly into the dark hall and held his breath. The flat was on the eighth floor. The top. Below him he could hear a door open. It creaked a little on its hinges. Someone was listening. Passent remained still. Thirty seconds later the door closed.

So Dyadek had his lookouts and one of them had heard him. He removed his shoes and walked soundlessly across the wood-block floor. The embers from a fire glowed on the grate and Passent lowered himself into a chair beside it to wait. It must have been an hour before the door slid open.

The priest looked around the room accusingly and rubbed his hands. "D'you know its warmer in that fucking prison of yours than in my flat?" He flung his coat over a table and sat down opposite Passent.

"That's no way for a man of God to talk."

"How would you know?"

Passent could sense the raw nerve. And yet the man was good. He hadn't heard him coming.

"I'm sorry to come like this. . . ."

"Sorry? Whatever for?" Dyadek rested his feet precariously on the fender in front of the fire. "It does me no end of good when you visit. Think of it—a clumsy 'Ubek,' no offense you understand, blunders his way into my flat, thinking he hasn't been noticed, and spends an hour riffling through my things. It's wonderful." He laughed out loud. "After all, you do it to everyone else. Why leave me out?"

He pulled a bottle of vodka from under his chair, drew out the cork, and upended the bottle against his mouth. "Forgive the early hour," he muttered, "but prison depresses me."

"Who did you see then?" Passent's eyes wandered around the cluttered room.

On a bookshelf stood a handful of knickknacks—a silvery Eiffel Tower, a bronze Lenin with a paper hat, a House of Parliament. Stuck to the wall behind them, some cigarette cards, a small shell casing. Inside every Pole, Passent reflected, was a magpie.

"I saw a friend of Zbig's."

"Ah." Passent paused for a moment. "I've got a problem there." He chose a moment when the bottle was the right way up. Dyadek held his gaze.

"You're right, my friend," he told him, "you have a big problem." And he kicked the embers from the fire till the sparks flew up the chimney and out into the winter city.

7

Jozef Garten had lost all sense of direction. For three days he had lived among the semidetached houses and the privet hedges, the car washers and dogwalkers, with only Tristram to guide him.

Such a strange creature, that one, thought Garten. He had aged since they'd last met. Tristram was slower in his movements, but Garten could still sense the sleeping giant within him. An intellect, unstretched, unchallenged, its reserves untapped. God had granted no favors to his body, Garten realized, but had invested them instead in the mind. It walked its own paths, fed on its own impulses, triggered its own fulfillment.

They talked of operations both real and imagined and it was Tristram who led, dragging the younger man behind him. Tristram who would see the risks and the potential and Garten would often wonder how it could be. In Poland the underground had looked to *him* to plot and devise, but in the hands of the older man he was once again a student.

The little kitchen with its greasy walls became the

classroom, looking out as it did over a patch of soggy turf and a plane tree. In odd moments of sunshine a cat would stretch out on the fence and scratch itself.

The talking was reserved for mornings and evenings. In the afternoons Garten would set up the sofa bed in the sitting room and sleep, tired out by the remorseless questioning, the learning by rote, the sharpening of a mind that had lost its edge.

"You lived on a high in Poland," Tristram would remind him, "you all did. You were bugged, followed, harassed. You played cat and mouse, chased around, hid in your dugouts. You've forgotten what it was like. Very exciting. Now you'll have to speed up a bit. Remember, they've all been doing it the whole time you've been away. If you don't get back in the swing, you'll stick out the first time you hit the streets. And then they'll have you."

It was all right till the fourth day, but then the voice got on Garten's nerves. The petty lecturing, the know-all epithets about life in Poland, the condescending follow-me-and-you'll-be-fine assurances. And he lost his temper, just as Tristram had hoped he would.

They were halfway through lunch.

"Why did you never go to the Solidarity people here? You know, keep in contact." Tristram didn't look directly at the Pole.

"What Solidarity?" There was a sharpness to the question. Garten put down his sandwich. "You mean the distant cousins of West London? Don't be ridiculous. You call that Solidarity? A phone call to Warsaw at Christmas to the relations who're so old they can't hear you? You call that staying in contact, for God's sake?" He pushed the plate away. Tristram sat back.

"I'll tell you about these Poles here, shall I, with their holy Madonna badges and T-shirts, their key rings and posters from the good old days. But would they do anything to help? A few food packages, some cans of beans, and they all think they've saved Poland. They make me sick."

"I thought they had some influence." Tristram's eyes narrowed.

"We're not Jews, you know! There's no lobby for us. No homeland . . ." Garten tried to check himself but the words were out and Tristram was waiting for them. The latent anti-Semitism that so many of them carried, the automatic assumption that Jews are to blame, first, foremost, and every time.

"You know," said Tristram carefully, "I used to feel sorry for Poland—screwed by the Russians, blown up by Nazis, sold down the river at Yalta—but I don't anymore. We've paid the debt. We look after all you people who come over here expecting the bloody world. You're lucky we take you."

Garten rose angrily, his face flushed. The chair fell over behind him.

"You think this is such a paradise?" He waved his arm around the kitchen. "Wonderful Britain? What's so wonderful about all this?"

"Better than queuing three hours for a milk bottle in Warsaw, I'd have thought. Or can't you cope with freedom?"

"Freedom!" Garten made a face. "For four months I had no work at all—nothing. Then a pizza house takes me for a week. They throw me out. You know what I did then? Cashier at a cinema. Porno. Another week. You call that freedom?"

He was shaking all over now and Tristram's heart was singing. This was a real Pole, an angry Pole with all the passion and prejudice intact. Garten's temper would carry him through. Tristram was certain of it.

Only then did he tell him of his father's death, watching his eyes close, the color leaving his face.

The doubts came at daybreak. Tristram hadn't slept, hadn't even bothered to undress. Once he heard a child scream in a house nearby. In the shadows of the landing he stood, fearful suddenly, without knowing why. He went back to his room. And now in his mind he trod the streets of Warsaw, Garten's mentor, Garten's guide. Would the underground accept him back? Would they be ready to take action? In all the villages, and in all the factories and power stations, would the word get through and would Poland get up off its knees and stand? How many times can you beat a man before he stays down for good?

Tristram knew the risks. An uprising in front of the Soviet General Secretary, right before his eyes, street battles, flying stones, tear gas. It would certainly be the most powerful political signal in decades. Could Garten start such a thing?

Tristram looked out over the damp, gray garden, a London of Christmas leftovers and trash cans. If Garten could start it, where in hell would it end?

8

Martha Cedar wouldn't go to work next day. Wouldn't sit down in the little office with James Tristram, wouldn't chip away at the Eastern Bloc for the honor and glory of the Service. It would be the third doctor's appointment in as many weeks. The third time she had made the excuse. There wouldn't be many more times before they checked. She knew that.

It was something you learned about the British. They were dangerously unpredictable. They followed no patterns, acknowledged no rules. They would slide and shift and circle. But they'd get you in the end. And you never knew when.

It was late, well after eleven, and she had been early. That was one of the problems about being German, she decided. Slavish adherence to petty principles, followed by a massive departure from the ones that really mattered. An ideal recipe for guilt and depression.

The night was crisp. The wind scratched at her face, but she liked that. Nothing should be too comfortable. Don't ever let your mind settle, they had told her. The day you do you should grow a tail, fetch your master's slippers, and lie on your back with your legs in the air. You'll have lost it for good.

Two men came out of the building and gave her a sideways glance. Peter was always late. He didn't know how to hurry. She was surprised he could ever make the deadlines, working as he did for the BBC's German service. Peter wrote the political commentaries that were punched nightly into the Eastern Bloc from the studios in the Strand and the transmitters in West Berlin. He supplied the "gloss." In the BBC they liked to say he had "depth," but he wouldn't have it much longer. Peter would soon be giving up the work, staying in bed all day, unshaven and undressed, drinking himself into oblivion, eating nothing. She could visualize the scene so clearly in all its sad ugliness. For she knew him so well and knew he would never manage without her.

She took his hand as he emerged, books and papers under his arm, his long gray hair streaming in the wind like a pennant. But she knew that hand. The limp grip, the moisture. The hand that told her, "I've already had a tray of whiskeys and not much soda . . . and would you lead me home, take my shoes off, and don't talk too loudly. Better still, don't talk at all!" She could read all that, standing out there in the Strand as the wind flapped around her.

They stumbled onto the bus, but there was nowhere to sit. The theater audiences were out and on their way home—all with evenings to remember. Martha caught sight of a young couple staring at her. The girl pointed and then turned away laughing.

What right have you to judge me? she thought. And then, *How can you look into my life and find so much to laugh about?*

The bus was over the river, past the War Museum, almost at the Elephant and Castle. She pushed Peter off the platform, breaking his fall as best she could, controlling the crash onto the pavement.

He looked at her and grinned. Even in the darkness his nose looked red. "Sorry, my dear, so sorry."

She blessed their foresight in buying an apartment on the ground floor. And she removed his shoes—why bother with anything else?—and she sat in front of the gas fire wondering if there was any whiskey left for her. Or had he drunk that too?

Odd how drink had controlled so much of her life. She got up and fetched a rug from the bedroom, wrapping it over her feet, staring into the fire. It was drink that had given her young father the courage that night in 1961 when he'd left the two rooms they'd had in the Eastern zone and gone to the Berlin Wall. Except that it wasn't quite a wall. Not yet. Just a barbed-wire fence. And Father had used all his bravado to crawl halfway under it at a point where the street lighting was especially poor, only to feel the bayonet from a Soviet rifle poking into his left buttock. Wasn't that an evening to remember?

She, just twenty-five years old, marooned in the Western sector when the Wall went up, taking the phone call from her mother. "Your father's in jail, do something." And of course there wasn't anything to be done until that handsome young man had met her one afternoon in the Knesebeckstrasse and told her of a way out. "Help us," he'd said, "and we'll help your father. It's a good deal for you. You don't have to do anything for now, maybe never, maybe in twenty years. Just stay in the West and see what happens. If you'll agree, Dad can leave jail tomorrow. I gather he's quite a nice old stick, didn't really mean any harm, did he?"

To this day Martha could remember the joy in her mother's voice. Father was home, safe and in good health. And there was the magnificent feeling that they'd all gotten away with it. A feeling that had lasted some fifteen years, until she had joined an obscure subunit of British intelligence and the man from Berlin had called again.

He had known all about the unit, known where she lived, who she slept with. In fact, he'd confided, they had a picture book of her life since the day he'd first called her. And now was the time to return the favor, wasn't it?

Martha stared around the room, her eyes searching for the whiskey bottle.

9 _____

"Where's Martha?"

"I don't know. She hasn't been well lately."

"Oh dear." Cornish examined Tristram without much sympathy. He went over to the window, rubbed the dirty pane, and gazed out. "Not a very nice area this, is it?"

"I thought you knew that."

"We really must get you somewhere a little better." He turned back to the room. "I mean, of course, when all this is over."

"Quite."

Tristram picked up the file and opened it. Always the bloody preamble, the game, the nonsense. Always disguise the reason you've come even though you'll get to it in the end. Time killing, time wasting, that's why the empire went down the drain. If only they'd cut out all the crap, it would have saved fifty years. He pushed the file across to Cornish. "The man's ready to go."

"Is that so?" Cornish's thin lips smiled. He extracted a handkerchief from the left-hand sleeve of his jacket, dabbed his mouth, and replaced the linen square.

"In what way is he ready?"

"Everything." Tristram got up. "He was always ready. For God's sake, he almost wrote the book. He set up most of the networks in Poland. He speaks the language, knows the people, he should be teaching us."

"What did you do with him?"

"Upset him a little. . . ."

"Why so little?" Cornish's voice was quiet, insistent.

"Enough. Who knows?"

"And when he gets there?"

"He'll be met." Suddenly Tristram's voice sounded distant. "We've fixed that."

"I trust you've also fixed that this is an operation without further control from us. No case officer, no paperwork, no messages or cutouts. He's on his own."

"He knows that. I give him his last briefing tomorrow. He leaves Friday."

"Why then?" Cornish was already reaching for his coat.

"The border guards get pissed on Friday. They're tired, lazy. End of the week's shift. He'll stand the best chance."

"Think he'll make it?"

Careless, oh so careless, thought Tristram. Like inquiring about a horse in the three o'clock race. He looked at the floor, not answering. What did it matter about the odds? Garten was like all the other poor bastards. He either made it or he didn't.

* * *

With Passent gone, Dyadek sat without moving as the fire burned out in the grate. Only in the late afternoon did it die. By that time the vodka bottle was empty, the dog collar was on the floor, his shirt unbuttoned. He gazed at the shadows, his mood darkening.

It didn't matter that he had passed the word to Passent. At times he served the police, at others the underground. In the end it would even out and the ordinary people of Poland would be the winners. That was it, he told himself. That was why.

The prisoner he'd seen in Rakowiecka had whispered his confidence just as they were leaving the visitor's room. The little fellow had looked hard into Dyadek's eyes. "A man is coming. A friend is returning to help us fight. Any day now he'll be here." And Dyadek had seen the tear roll slowly down the man's cheek and onto the prison shirt and wondered at the sort of Messiah who could inspire such hope in such a place.

Maybe the prisoner had imagined it, confused rumor with fact. But Dyadek knew that the prison grapevine was the most accurate of them all. Information was the only thing that kept the inmates going. The underground fed them regularly.

But he minded breaking the trust. Of course he hadn't given it away for nothing.

Passent had been obliged to make a bargain. The release of a man in Mokotow, held for black-marketing, the son of a widow. The woman was dying and wanted to see the boy. Passent would fix it. The deal had been struck.

Dyadek heaved himself out of the armchair. For twenty years, he reflected, he had played both sides of the street, hated himself, hated Poland. He shivered. Sometimes he'd hated God. But he hadn't been alone. Others had done the same thing, made their accommodations with the Communists, tried to make a better life on the ground, supped with the devil because only the devil had food.

"You have to live life as it is," a bishop had once told him. "And in Poland there's nothing harder. The Communists are still the government. Even when they lost the elections, they were the government. They never gave up the instruments of power. Solidarity couldn't change that."

Dyadek recalled the little speech word for word. Over the years it had become almost a second catechism, a secret one, never recited in church.

When he thought about it the guilt would return and sit beside him. And now, as he stared hard into the fireplace, he could see a man on his way to Poland, a man with his head down, his face shielded from the cold, a man fearful and desperate. A man already sold and betrayed. He tried to find a prayer for him, but it wasn't there.

10

The British Airways DC-9 buffeted its way through the Berlin air corridor, the tiny wind tunnel that links the divided city to the West. It was the worst turbulence of the winter.

The aircrew had sought permission to change altitude but Soviet traffic controllers had refused. As the plane lurched and wheeled a woman had screamed once and all the passengers had gone silent.

Garten had felt no fear. It was only a machine, he reasoned. It either worked or it didn't. There was no evil intention. It was people you had to fear.

The Mercedes taxi had glided away from the airport, whispering over the cobbles, while the radio played those jaunty German tunes, all accordions and side drums. He had shut his eyes, feeling the pull back to Eastern Europe. By three-thirty it was getting dark. And then he remembered—darkness came more quickly in the East.

He slept for two hours. By the time the receptionist announced his "morning call" it was past six in the evening. Watch the time, he told himself. Ration it. And he had stepped outside the hotel and along the Ku-damm and turned left on Bleibtreustrasse for no better reason than because he liked the name—"Stay-true Street."

Garten enjoyed his dinner, stretching it deliberately, sitting down in the Kempinski at seven, knowing that he had till ten. Then a walk of eight minutes to the station beside the zoo, the train leaving at twenty past. It all looked fine.

On the table there had been smoked salmon and steak, strawberries from California, strong coffee and mints. "Would he like a slice of gâteau?" Yes he would, aware that he should take his pleasures on this side of the Wall because there weren't any on the other.

At the station Garten took the tickets and put the coins in his pocket. A white slip, a pink wagon-lit reservation bought at the last minute. Cash.

Up the stairs now and he could easily have turned around, gone back for a last evening, a fling in a bar, some company. But there had been enough last evenings. He had to face the days. Those ahead and those that had gone before.

You look in vain for a watcher if you look in a station. If they've got you there, Tristram had told him, they'll have you for the rest of your journey. You won't shake them.

The steam and the cold made Garten rub his eyes as he walked along the platform. And then they began slamming doors and all around him people were hugging each other. A foot away a family of four huddled in a multibody embrace. By their feet stood a small girl, strangely disconnected from the group. She peered around, thumb in mouth, her large spectacles pulling out the ears, giving her an owlish look. The expression seemed vacant, but as Garten climbed the steps to the train he could see tears behind the glasses and that didn't help at all. The kind of tears he had once helped dry for someone else—so many years before. He didn't want to see that now. Not for anything.

The carriage jerked into motion and the platform slipped by. West Berlin was shrinking, disappearing, the last Western outpost for 12,000 miles, the last one till you reached Alaska. He could feel the tickle down his spine, the cold finger. Five years since he'd passed this way, five years out of the zone. And how they had changed!

He remembered how good they'd been in 1961 when the wire had gone up overnight and the barrier had become a wall. Garten had been little more than a child, but his father had told him what was happening, pointed to the loudspeaker vans that stood in the Eastern sector screaming abuse at the American GIs.

Even then he had been staggered. For the East German guards had been shouting out the names of the troops, of their wives and children, their sweethearts for God's sake. And they had known the men by sight!

To this day he didn't know how they'd done it, could only guess at the extraordinary intelligence machine that openly flaunted such sophistication. But maybe now . . . Now there was free passage across the most hated border in the world. How long could it last? Thirty years of killing and desecration. Was it really over?

In East Berlin his passport was taken away by an officer with a leather satchel across his chest. It was standard procedure. If you were between twenty-five and forty, fit, male, and from a capitalist country, they would haul away your documents just to unsettle you, teach you a lesson. Some things never change.

It wouldn't matter, thought Garten. The passport was his, even if the nationality had been borrowed and the place of birth shifted westward across a few borders.

The man was back. His eyes held Garten's but his hand was outstretched. For a moment they stared at each other across the compartment.

"I believe this is yours." The hand held a blue British passport. Garten took it from him. Go on believing, he thought, and I'll live to be grateful.

As Garten's train stood still in East Berlin, Martha Cedar made her way to the telephone booth by the Elephant and Castle, a gaudy silk scarf over her head, coat buttoned to the neck. And no one saw her. It was late to be out. The South London traffic rolled past her. Partygoers, late diners, life's enjoyers on their way home. And none of them saw her.

She crossed the road. Easy now, she thought. Now that the decision had been made. It made the awful day a little better. The meeting in Harrods—nice touch, that one—the Russian, she had remembered from all those years ago, had carried a small bunch of anemones. A gift from her father, he had said. A quick smile and then an awful frown, as if to signpost the bad news.

She was in the alleyway now. Three phones at the end of it.

The Russian had made her sit in the coffee shop. The pig had ordered chocolate cake for both of them. She hadn't touched hers.

And then he had let it out. Poor Father was once again up to his tricks. Not his fault probably. Got in with the wrong sort of people. Anti-Socialist elements. That was it. The phrase they always used.

Twenty steps to the telephones. Maybe less.

Anyway, he needed her help. More to the point, if she could help him, he could go to his bosses and persuade them to let the old boy go with a warning. Let him go? Yes, sorry, didn't I say that? He's in Pankow jail, just across the Wall.

The light from an upstairs window shone suddenly across her path.

Of course the Russian had known someone was going in. Of course? All she had to do was supply a name and a time and her old father could be out by Monday. And Monday was a worker's holiday, so it would be something nice all around, wouldn't it? So casual. And she had made up her mind, not knowing where her father was, unable to trace him, unable to judge if the seedy little Russian was telling the truth —or half of it. Or any at all. But after so many years she couldn't leave it there, could she?

She opened the door of the telephone booth.

Martha had never used the number but it had stood ready in her memory, just in case, for well over a decade. Cornish's home number. It was late. Well past one.

She heard the cough, the throat clearing, and could picture the figure in his hallway in Stockwell, hair awry, the light on in the hall, the wife calling out in the background, the dressing gown over his shoulders. And then there was silence as he listened and she had said her final words.

"You must get him out, Mr. Cornish. Stop this madness. He must get out at once. He cannot survive."

"Where are you?" The voice hard, angry.

She replaced the receiver, not really believing there was any more to be said. All you had to do was retrace your footsteps up the alley, walk firmly, hold your head up, pull your shoulders back, and then you step right off the curb, hoping that the bus there will take your guilt away as well and that peace will come to all men and women, the way the churches always promised it would.

11 _____

From East Berlin it's only forty miles to the border with Poland, sitting unhappily where the Russians put it.

Garten felt the uneven rhythm, half sleeping between the stops and starts. And then, past one o'clock, the compartment door was opened and the cold air rushed in. And the light green uniforms had darkened, the accents thickened. And there was the language that came to him from his childhood—a young man with a mustache, a soldier of the Polish People's Republic, land of the eagle.

He'd taken the middle bunk, no two ways about that. Besides the two students wanted the top ones. An elderly couple from Lodz settled themselves below. "I can't climb," the old man told Garten, "my leg."

"No need," he had replied, "stay close to the homeland." And the fellow had chuckled, lain back, and wheezed his way to sleep.

Middle was good, though. Middle was neutral. Of course it had worked. One more quick look at his passport and the customs man had gone for the students. Hands into knapsacks. "What's this then?" to a packet of condoms. "Ah-ha" to some electric batteries. And the soldier had pointedly put the items in his pocket and stood up, daring them to object. "You don't mind, do you?" said the expression, but Garten could see that they did.

He turned out the reading light and then they'd really begun to move, rattling through the forests, flat countryside, past villages, silent in the mud and slush of winter. Poland, Poland, he whispered to himself, half expecting an echo, but it didn't come.

Instead in the broken minutes of sleep he could see the little girl, running down the street ahead of him, not fast because she had been only three, not yet steady on her feet. And she had stopped and turned, throwing back the tiny head with the blond curls and laughing with all the joy of the innocents. God in heaven!

How cold and stale it had become in the compartment. He pulled the blanket tighter around him. They were well into Poland. The fatherland— *Ojczyzna*, the hallowed word they never forgot. And the remorse hit him, for Zbig, for Grazyna, for little Maya Angelica. He pulled aside the curtain and stared out at the passing trees. "But I came back," he told them, "I'm back." He shook his head, trying to slow the runaway thoughts. All that mattered lay around him and at the end of his journey.

The lady who was to meet him had finished work at three that morning. It wasn't worth going to bed. She laughed to herself at the thought. After all, she'd spent most of the day in one bed or another. It was good to put the weight back on your feet.

Ania conducted most of her business at Warsaw's Victoria Hotel, as she had done for nearly seven years. It had served her well. The mixed sauna in the basement gave her the chance to display her assets. In the bedrooms, above, they were bought and sold. She now had her own chair in the foyer, a silver fox coat, and her own bronze Mercedes 230 coupe. In a kingdom of four walls and a mattress, she was the undisputed queen.

Ania put the car into gear and drove south toward Saska Kepa. There was time for some breakfast, a shower. It hadn't been a bad night, and she had even managed to pay her monthly dues. Half an hour with the hotel manager and twenty minutes with his assistant, a boy with pale skin and acne. And she could live to work again.

An old veteran across the street watched her arrive home. At times he thought of himself as her father, at others he envisaged a less platonic relationship. Either way he watched for her day and night. And she for him. He had been a courier for the underground long before Ania had been born. When her parents had lived in Warsaw he had been a friend of the family. He'd watched the little girl grow up bright and later beautiful. And one day he had introduced her to his friends, and she had stepped into the underground as he had stepped out.

She drank her coffee in the kitchen. In the mirror she could see the oval face framed by a thick blanket of raven hair. The eyes were tired and the lines around them more pronounced. She couldn't go on indefinitely with this kind of life. Something had to suffer.

Back outside in the car, the engine came instantly to life. It was her only love affair. The bronze creature that roared when she touched it, always there, always responsive.

Cornish ran a hand through his hair and sighed deeply. He was wedged tight between seat and table, watching Tristram eat breakfast. It was ten past eight in the Wimpy Bar on the Edgware Road and the rain spattered the windows.

"We washed them only yesterday," the waiter said miserably, and laid a coffee cup in front of Cornish.

Cornish said nothing, peering out, watching the traffic. Odd how bad news always arrived in the morning. Never at lunch or in the afternoon, rarely in the evening. Just served up in the early hours before daylight, cold and unadorned. They had called him even as the first of the Service teams had gone into Martha's flat, hauled her boyfriend into one of those little terraced houses in Maida Vale. Across London another team was sticking a red label on Martha's big toe, designating her a matter of national security and assuring her transfer to a very private mortuary in Kent.

Cornish took a sip of his coffee. "They'll want a session with you. In fact, they'll want a number of sessions with you."

"Why say it like that?"

"What d'you expect? You worked alongside her, related with her." He let the Service jargon hang in the air. "They'll want to know why you never saw the signs, read the tea leaves."

They glared at each other. Cornish broke the silence.

"So what now?"

"I told you. I sent the signal, not that it's my job, but that's what you wanted. If they got it, they'll have left Garten alone. He would have waited at the station and got back on the next train going the other way. He had a ticket. If they didn't, the underground will have met him, and I shouldn't be surprised if the SB have picked him up. From what you say, Martha seems to have been pretty specific to her Russian friend."

"She was." Cornish bit his lip. "Anything else?"

Tristram stopped eating and put a clenched fist on the table.

"What d'you think? You tell me what you want done. We wait. That's all we can do until he appears on the Polish news denouncing us, or else arrives in West Berlin and aborts the whole stupid mission. How the hell do I know?"

He looked back out at the street. The rain still hadn't eased. If it went on much longer, he thought, half London would have to go to work by boat.

Garten stepped down from the train into the gray light, laid his suitcase on the stone platform, and looked around him. It was the small station to the north of Warsaw, near Zoliborz. He saw the first of the morning trams on the railway bridge. The noise brought him back, as did the smell of cheap, low-octane fuel.

Ania spotted Garten well before he reached the exit, but she made no move toward him. As she waited on the adjacent platform her eyes scanned the people around and behind him, the railway bridge, the kiosk, the line of taxis.

There's no hurry, wait till you're sure, the young man had told her. And then he'd added, with a sly grin, "Don't be too eager, he's not a client." But the jokes didn't faze Ania. She wasn't ashamed of what she did. Bored, she told herself, lonely, but not ashamed. The job had its moments.

Garten was about fifty yards away now, crossing the tracks. The fox coat caught his eye, and not just his, and she wanted to reach out to him and take his arm. He looked young, she thought, younger than they'd said. Tired, disoriented. The kind of face she knew. I'll let him pass, let him out, she thought, take it as it comes. After all, this was a rush job, no time for fancy plans. No time for any plans at all.

He passed her. She noted the pigeon toes, the light sneakers, Reeboks, the kind she'd wanted herself. Pay attention. Concentrate. This one's serious. Aren't they all?

He was looking toward the taxis. He shouted something to one of the drivers but she couldn't hear it. Too far. One of them turned and smiled. They want dollars, she thought. They won't go for him, he looks too Polish.

And then she was just behind him and it seemed so natural just to start talking. Two travelers complaining about the taxis, the cold, the food. Ania knew all the lines. And she could see the flash of recognition in those serious gray eyes as she said the little phrase, the sudden flash that they can never hide, the one that says "You're my friend, take me inside, I'm scared." And his eyes said it for him.

She steered him toward the Mercedes, feeling the sudden resistance, the way she'd expected.

"Is that yours?" he pointed to the car.

"I'm sorry"—she smiled—"it was all they had in the shop."

He didn't return the smile. "You might as well have announced my arrival on Warsaw radio."

Ania opened the driver's door. "We thought of it," she said, "but then we realized there isn't anyone who'd care one way or the other. After all, five years is a long time. Welcome home, Comrade."

Garten got in the other side. She could see the words had stung him, but he'd been out for a long time and he might as well start with a taste of reality.

She was angry, sliding the gear lever into first, skidding on the ice, oblivious of the taxi that pulled out of the line and followed her north across the railway bridge.

12

"You'll be watching Tristram, I take it?"

The Director stared at the screen. Four-thirty in the Biograph cinema beside Victoria Station. Half-way through *Sins of Their Mothers*. He hadn't seen a film like that since he was sixteen, all sweaty palms and bulging eyes in the front row.

"We'll watch him from a distance." Cornish looked around the cinema. The old raincoat brigade was firmly ensconced in the front seats. At the back a girl was giggling. "He's too clever to put on a full group, even if we had the manpower, which MI5 assures me they haven't."

"So what then?"

"His mail, his calls, free time—all that."

"What does he do in his free time?"

"He goes dancing."

The Director snorted derisively. Two or three heads turned.

"Dancing," he whispered. "Good Lord!"

On the screen a woman began putting her clothes back on. The Director turned away.

"Let's push him a bit. After all, he knew Martha best, worked with the bloody woman for donkey's years." He looked back at the film. "Screwed her, I shouldn't wonder."

"He didn't."

"Didn't what?"

"Screw her." God, the noise was intolerable. "She had a boyfriend. You saw the file."

"Yes." The Director got up to leave.

"Sit down," someone said.

Cornish sniggered silently and stared straight ahead. It amused him to think of the Director of the Secret Intelligence Service being ordered about in a flea-pit cinema. And yet, he reflected, there was precious little to laugh about. Look at the Polish thing. You set the process in motion and it rolled on by itself, like a child's toy. Until someone stronger and more powerful came and took it from you.

13 _____

The note had been delivered to Passent by diplomatic messenger. An order not a request. They never picked the same spot. One day a café, next a stadium or bus station. Sometimes within the city, sometimes not. Strange, he thought, that the Russians behaved as if they were fugitives in an occupied country—when it was they who did the occupying.

As Passent drove he could hear the voice of the KGB officer all those years ago. The voice of such a small figure, badly dressed, sweating, yet oh so committed.

"Even when you go back to Poland you're our man, you understand, Emil?" It was the first time they'd used his Christian name.

"If you want to be a Communist, and we see that you do"—the arms had opened in a gesture of welcome—"there's only one kind. Forget the crap about sovereign states and different paths. You serve us or you don't serve at all."

Passent turned the Fiat onto Aleja Ujazdowskije. The Soviet Embassy lay a hundred yards down the hill, spanning both sides of the road. Left turn now toward the park.

With Moscow, of course, the choices were always stark—with or against, left or right. And you didn't stop to question. That wouldn't be clever. What had the man said?—"We always remember our friends and never forget our enemies."

A sobering thought at eight o'clock on a winter's morning when the summons arrives.

Inside the park the early snow lay thick along the pathways. But his were not the first footsteps. Passent counted three or four pairs and knew they were well ahead of him.

Only one man would show himself; the others would watch and monitor from the trees. He wouldn't see them because they'd be good. The best.

Passent had no eyes for the beauty of the park—the snow-covered palace, the stone statues, the frozen lake. Soon the children would arrive to skate and chase each other. But it was still too early for games.

He could see Klimov a long way away. And as he approached he made out the man's jaw. It had been carved with considerable genetic aggression, jutting out from the puffy face like a rock. The man stood still and silent against the palace wall.

"Comrade Emil!" The welcome was as warm as the lake.

"You said it was urgent." Passent stared hard at the trees. They were in among them somewhere. He knew it.

"We have to talk." Klimov wouldn't look at him directly. "You've had some information, I think, and so have we. It's time for us to exchange, cooperate."

A few yards away a rook took off from inside the trees, squawking, beating its wings violently for maximum lift. And then, just as it had cleared the forest, it swung back down toward the lake, dropping fast, pulling out at the last moment to land on the ice a few feet in front of the two men, as if offering itself in sacrifice.

"A man has arrived from London."

For a moment Passent didn't reply.

Ania drove fast, toward the Vistula. A gentle wind had dragged the mist eastward across the river, shrouding the far bank, shielding the drabness from Garten's eyes. On his left were the apartment blocks, the rows of tenth-rate rusting cars in front of them— to the right the Central Committee, its front portal wide enough to fit a tank. That, he recalled, had been foresight.

As they crossed the bridge the jumbled memories returned—an evening in the discotheque on the banks of the Vistula, hands held, hands locked, and then an early morning in the militia cells—hands beaten and cut. He rubbed them together. Rough hands that told the story of Poland.

Everything was where he'd left it. They had moved no monuments, no slogans, even the hands of a giant clock were stopped where they had been five years before. Only his pulse had quickened. Everywhere he went he'd be running. In crowded streets, on buses, driving as he was now. It would all be running, trying to stay ahead, to outthink the others. You lost a life each time you got away. In the end there were no lives left.

For a moment Garten settled back, bathing in the dry heat from the dashboard. On some of the street corners the face of his father would gaze at him from the mist, or Grazyna and the child—places where they'd dawdled or laughed or strolled. The events were there, but not the emotions, not anymore. Suddenly there was just the job to be done and a wife who could help him.

"Did you know my father?"

Ania pulled up hard at the traffic lights, the river behind them.

"I knew him, and I'm sorry."

He swung his head around to look at her profile.

"Yeah, well, everyone's sorry, aren't they? Only that's not enough."

Klimov retraced his footsteps. It was a narrow path that wound close to the shuttered, empty gazebo.

His security man had orders to follow Passent and make sure he had come alone. You could tolerate the Poles but there was no question of trust.

Without a sound the old figure emerged from behind the gaunt wooden structure and Klimov drew in his breath sharply.

"*Privyet*—greetings, my friend."

Klimov knew the voice even before his eyes registered the face. He took a step back but he wasn't alarmed, for the man with the blazing cheeks and dripping nose was no stranger, no surprise. The Russian from the dacha had long since shown how he could move through countries at will, could acquire personalities and passports denied to all others. Now

in the early morning, in a Polish park, he was doing
what all the years had taught him—making sure.

The two men turned back toward the lake, more
carefully now, more circumspect. For the park was
beginning to fill. A long line of schoolchildren had
been herded in for exercise. They looked pale and
miserable. Some were crying.

The Russian coughed and wiped his eyes with a
gloved hand. Klimov could see the uniform of a Soviet marshal below the coat. They moved out across
the ice. Risky ground, thought Klimov, but no more
than anywhere else.

"I've been inspecting our brave, fraternal forces,"
the Russian sniggered. "Lousy rabble. Couldn't fight
their way out of a paper bag. Anyway, I've been guz-
zling their vodka. What else? Oh, shooting some wild
boar, and then of course"—the Russian rubbed his
hands with delight—"we've had some entertainment."

Klimov knew all about the entertainment. For
years the Warsaw Pact commanders had distin-
guished themselves by serving up giant cakes at their
parties containing girls covered with chocolate sauce.
The cleaning-up operations had stretched many a su-
perior military mind. They'd also entered Eastern
Bloc legend.

"So tell me . . . what news of the little fellow
from London?" The Russian sniffed loudly.

"He's in. The dissidents have got him. Solidarity."

"Do the locals know that—the SB?"

"Yes, more's the pity. But I've told their man it's
our show and he's to stay out of it."

"How did he take that?"

"Badly."

The Russian stamped his feet and turned full circle. On the lake a skating child had fallen. The air was full of shrieks and cries of comfort. He sniffed again. It was time to exert control, to prod.

"The little fellow from London has a wife—doesn't he?"

"The SB have her stashed away down south. We expected a backlash after Lermontov's death. . . ."

"That, my dear friend, is the point. She can help the backlash. She will be angry, ready to do battle, help her husband." He wiped his nose. "See that she gets home and get her out without telling the Poles. She must be free to move without any of their incompetent thugs tripping all over her."

They made their way back to the cars in silence. The older man shook his head sadly. The park was beautiful. And yet, he reflected, it's only we Russians who appreciate nature. Of course there'd come a day when he'd settle back to life in the forest. Flowers in spring, mushrooms later in the year, the primeval grip of a Russian winter.

One day he'd be tired of all the cowards and traitors, the beating of heads. One day. He smiled to himself. But not yet.

14 _____

Two hundred feet above the chalet the soldier could look down through the trees and see a tiny billow of smoke from the single chimney. He lay still inside the arctic bivouac and searched the clearing with the binoculars. A cold country when you had to lie out all night, with a four-hour car journey and a six-hour hike behind you. Only that was the way they had wanted it.

Still a foreign country—Poland. And yet he had crossed no border. No one had checked his documents for he had none. There were countries where you carried papers and others where you carried a gun. Seldom were the two required together.

He had penetrated northeast of Lublin. The land had been flat, the ground soft, the moon hidden. And near the base he had cut the wire fence where the grass had grown long and unattended and he had stomach-crawled nearly half a mile till the copse gave him some cover.

And then, as he stood up and the strangled muscles stopped screaming, he had frozen where he was. In the distance he could make out the bobbing head-lights of a Polish border patrol, and his right hand had reached to the holster at the base of his spine. Just till they passed.

The car—his car—had been on the edge of the town beside a house that he had no orders to enter. A gray Trabant, East German and noisy. And his spirits dropped a little, for he had thought himself worth better.

He knew that the car was both transport and a signal. As he had driven it away into the darkness and cursed the broken heater, they would know that he was on course.

Now the soldier would watch the chalet and wait. He would move when he felt ready. It was the only thing Moscow had left up to him.

As the door closed Grazyna sensed the danger. The old woman had gone out, probably into town. Now she and Maya were left in the chalet and the pig was downstairs. The pig. She had called him that since the night he had appeared in their little room and leered down at her. The husband. The one who carried the gun.

In the days that followed that incident she had caught his eyes on her as they sat for meals, as they walked in the clearing. At times he had contrived to brush against her, not openly, not obviously, not so his wife would see, because he was scared of her snapping, her authority.

To Grazyna they were animals, both of them, living in a house of humiliation and despair.

Far below her a floorboard creaked.

She caught her breath. If he comes, she thought, I can fight him, scratch him, tear at his eyes. She looked around for a heavy object but there wasn't one. His gun, the revolver, I might get it off him. It's always on his belt. Worth a try. Please, God, is that my only hope?

She listened again but could hear nothing more than her own breathing. I'm imagining it, she thought, and she looked across the room at Maya, still asleep, still beautiful. The little nose turned up on the pillow, a blanket across the tiny figure, so thin, so pale. The child that had withdrawn into herself. The child that slept most of the day and cried late into the night. Her child.

And then she heard the footstep, the same way she'd heard it that first night.

The soldier had seen the old woman leave. What a cow! Waddling over the snow, fighting her way through the drifts, using an old walking stick for balance. A hag, but he'd let her go. Get in quickly and do the business. That's all they'd said. Nothing about the hag.

He slid out of the bivouac, gently, softly, the way he had been taught that year in Karelia, with nothing but the regiment and the bears for company. Fold it all away, down deep, packed into the ice, and they won't find a trace till spring. And then where will you be? Cuba? East Berlin?

For now it felt good to be on the mountainside with the downward climb, swift and simple, and nothing to think about except the stupid bastards who weren't expecting him.

As Grazyna got up from the bed she recalled a story told long ago by her father about a horseman who had ridden to Moscow, found a room at an inn, and discovered Death sitting in his chair beside the bed. He had gotten back on his horse and ridden to Kiev. Again Death sat waiting for him. At that he had ridden four days and nights without stopping, till he came to a little town on the Black Sea and Death lay waiting for him in his room. "Did you really think you could escape me by running?" Death had asked.

Grazyna knew he was outside the door, knew it because there are times when your mind can sense what your eyes can't see.

And suddenly the panic seemed to leave her and she realized what had to be done. Maya had to be saved. That was all that mattered. Funny how clear it all seemed when the lifeline ran out. How few the choices, how easily they were made. Even so, she shouted with fright as the door opened.

It could only have been a small cry, more animal than human, but the soldier heard it, like a stab in the head, a signal that time had run out.

It wasn't sympathy or human feeling that spurred him on, for he knew only that he would have to kill some and leave others alive. He had no personal feeling, just the orders. Orders that would separate the living from the dead.

Thirty yards from the chalet he began to run, his head down, the pistol and silencer in his right hand.

"I'll go downstairs." She spoke softly. And with that he had stepped out of the shadows on the landing and she could see the twisted face, half nerves, half aggression.

She could hear his breathing, his excitement, the heavy tread. Only now could she control him, lull him, then kill him when the chance arose. Beside the stove lay a bread knife, always there, always sharpened. She would reach for it when the time came.

The room was in semidarkness, a blind across the tiny window, and she sat on the sofa, wondering at her own voice, her own calm.

"Get ready. What are you waiting for?" That threw him. She could see the first doubts written across his ugly face. Maybe he couldn't, maybe he'd forgotten, maybe the old cow had made him lie in the corner on a rug like the dog he was.

But then he'd made his decision. A little cry of lust and he was heaving down his trousers and she knew then that he wouldn't stop for the world, that he could never have heard the shattering of the window-pane, could never have felt the blast of cold air of the silenced bullet that smashed open the back of his head, even as he fell upon her.

She must have blacked out. For there was the sensation that time had been wrenched painfully from her hands.

"Get up."

"You . . . he's . . ." And the scream was coming out of control.

"Get up." The soldier said it again quite quietly and then slapped her hard across the face.

As her eyes opened she could see the old man's body crumpled at her feet like a rug, irrelevant. And then the soldier's pistol hand was rising, the long snub silencer straight out like the arm of a robot. It was then that the scream broke loose.

"My daughter . . . my . . . daughter."

And he caught the trigger finger a split second away from the final pressure, seeing the thin face and the wispy blond hair through the banister, the eyes wide with fear and incomprehension, the woman pulling herself from the sofa, scooping the child into the air, burying her face in the little shoulder.

He could watch coldly as the panic turned to relief and a human being came back from the brink. The soldier smiled, not at a deed well done, but at the sheer exercise of his power. The woman and child would live or die by his hand. Only Moscow had decided they should live.

"You have two minutes to get your things, no more."

Grazyna wondered at the lilting Polish, but there was no time to trace it. He pointed a finger at her.

"We go now. I said now!"

Through the window he checked the clearing. And then the door was open and they were running through the thick drifts toward the trees, a practiced run, an anxious, hesitant stride behind it, and the little girl half dragged, half lifted across the snow.

They reached the first clump of trees. Grazyna felt her breath coming in short, painful jerks.

"Go on, go on, move it!" The soldier was waving them to push past him, deeper into the forest. She took the child in her arms and staggered on a few paces. And then something made her stop. As she looked back the man was kneeling in the snow, silent, unmoving, his eyes fixed back on the clearing.

She knew what it was, knew instantly, for it was a shape she could never forget. The old woman was trudging back to the chalet, cudgeling the snow with her walking stick. Maybe she'd forgotten something, maybe she'd completed her errand. Maybe . . . But Grazyna could see what was going to happen. She could see why the soldier had knelt so carefully, could see the gun in his hand and, instinctively, she pressed the child's head closer, blocking her vision. The woman seemed a long way away, thirty or forty yards, her back stooping, her dogged footsteps in and out of the drifts. . . . She will never know and I will never tell her. . . .

The bullet seemed to swing her around, the tough old body punched sideways, falling almost in slow motion to lie faceup, rigid, staring at the sky and the mountains and the birds that wheeled and cawed above it.

Grazyna knew the woman was dead, knew by the sudden emptiness that a dying spirit always leaves behind.

15 _____

They were well into the sprawl of eastern Warsaw when Ania pulled off the highway. Over the streetcar tracks, past a private market, and on the street corner was a gathering of dealers and scroungers. Poland at work.

The Mercedes stopped by an elderly block of flats, red brick, shabby.

"Follow me, quickly."

As Garten got out of the car he was hit by the noise from an industrial drill. Down the street a demolition team was attacking a ruined church. She pulled at his arm, and then they were inside, the door slamming shut behind them. Ania led the way down stone steps into darkness. Garten was aware only of a narrow corridor, its walls wet and jagged.

She unlocked a door and fumbled for a switch. A neon strip came on over the sink. Garten shivered. The damp was everywhere.

"What is this place?"

"Your home. Don't worry, you won't be here long.

Nor will the building. Anyway, we'll have to move you around."

"I want to see my family." His voice echoed around the bare room.

"I don't know anything about that. . . ."

"And I want to see Romek. I need to see him. Now —soon."

Ania's eyes flashed at him. "You'll see him when he's got time. He's not going to break cover just because you've rolled into town. No good coming back and telling me what you want. Things have changed around here."

"So I see." Garten put down his suitcase, suddenly aware that Ania was making for the door.

"Where you going?"

"Out. I'll be back later when I find out a few things."

"Wait." He tried to lighten up, tried to smile. The voice pleaded. "Didn't London tell you how important this is? Didn't they explain? I mean . . . I just don't have time—"

His arms caught hers, but she shook herself free, reaching for the door handle, pulling it toward her.

And then he lost his patience and the voice hardened, the fists clenched tight inside his pockets.

"Look, I haven't come here to sit in a basement and waste the days with a stupid bitch like you. Now get Romek and get him now."

She stopped then, stopped in her tracks, the door wide open, her face flushed. In the distance the noise of the drill died away.

She should have hit him. She knew that. But what good would it have done? Garten was tired and frightened. Garten was jumpy. Standing alone in that bare room with just a bed and chair, he would lash out at whoever crossed his path. She could see the determination, the set of the jaw. And yet that wasn't all she saw. As she slammed the door on him she was looking at the face of another fighter, another one of those Polish idealists who would stand smiling in the crowds, bracing for the water cannon, waiting for the riot police to club him down.

Garten would lose the way all the others had lost. Out on the streets. Where it always ended.

The child held them up, little Maya Angelica, her tiny fingers clutching her mother's coat, fearful and cold as they pushed their way through the forest. Once Grazyna cried out, setting the child down in the snow, her muscles pleading for rest, her feet in ice-cold agony.

The soldier forced her on, the lone thickset Russian in his arctic fatigues, swearing, cajoling, clawing his way through branches and undergrowth like an animal. And she knew the soldier would make it. The killer would make it. Others would die in the process, but he would come through. And she with him.

An hour, maybe two hours later, he made tea, holding a tiny kettle over a can of kerosene as the flame licked his fingers. Grazyna drank gratefully and closed her eyes while the warm liquid reached into her stomach.

"How much farther?" It was only now she could speak.

"An hour, maybe less. This part is easy, I . . ." And he turned away, suddenly remembering the rule of silence. Don't talk to them, don't fraternize with them. They're Poles, they're against us. Maybe we'll all go to Poland one day. That's what the colonel had said when he'd done the briefing.

They had come down from the mountain. Grazyna could see a wide valley and they were heading directly into the morning sun. Eastward. Toward Russia. She wouldn't cross that border whatever happened.

"Who are you?" she whispered suddenly.

The soldier turned. "Friend," he breathed and his finger pointed to the ridge and a narrow curving road that seemed to lose itself in the clouds.

Still they kept to the trees, all the time to the trees. And when they stopped the soldier's glasses ranged over the path ahead of them and the path behind. So careful, this one. So clever. And whose friend?

It was on the climb to the ridge that they heard the helicopter. He first and she a second later. For Maya Angelica had begun to cry with exhaustion and pain, and for a moment Grazyna failed to separate the sounds.

The machine seemed to come at them out of the sun, and if it carried markings, she couldn't see them. Fast and low it flew, its rotors pulling at the treetops, shaking the snow onto the paths below, shattering the peace of the mountains.

They stopped for a moment, but only the silence returned. And then they were on the narrow road and Grazyna and the child sank to their knees, gasping, crying out for air. But not the soldier. As Grazyna wiped the sweat away from her eyes she saw him half drag, half carry the little car from its hiding place. A woodcutter's barn, ramshackle and deserted in the shadow of the hills.

She sat in the back, the child on her knees, and the two-stroke engine burst into life, filling the air with noise and fumes, a flimsy, beige contraption with sloping hood and trunk—the tarnished pride of the East German car industry.

As they drove she and the soldier looked again for the helicopter but it had disappeared. For the pilot had no instructions to search, only to drop the team, cordon off the chalet, and return to the capital. That order had been specific. No flat local feet were to tread on this case. No reports to be written or sent. A murder in the Tatras and only one man in Warsaw to hear of it.

The heating had broken down that morning and Passent sat in his overcoat. It struck him that you could keep the climate at bay only so long. Sooner or later it came and got you.

He got up and tapped his finger on the windowpane. The temperature was the same on both sides.

He felt no pity for the murdered couple. They had wreaked enough violence of their own over the years. It was probably a fitting end.

And yet the shooting appalled him for a different reason. His operation, his people. His safe house, his prisoners. And now the whole framework had been torn apart. A standard assassination, not even an attempt at robbery. Someone had come for the two old people and dispatched them with a minimum of ceremony. A vendetta from the past? But why wait till now?

Passent went to the door and yelled for coffee. A moment later came an answering shout from one of the secretaries: *"Nie ma"*—There isn't any. It was Poland's daily cry for help—*nie ma*—but where had it all gone?

As he sat back in his chair he could see what had been too obvious even to acknowledge. Who else would have had the motive or the manpower? Who had warned him to stay out of their operation? Who would kill simply to reinforce the message?

For the first time in years Passent was taken aback by the ruthlessness of Moscow's men. The calculated bestiality, the disregard for life.

So shaken was he that he could barely move, sitting as he did on the edge of his chair, feeling the anger rising in his neck, the hot flush over his cheeks and forehead. The Russians looked on Poland as nothing more than a shooting ground. Now they were using the people as targets.

You couldn't allow that. Not even a Communist could let that go.

Passent put his head in his hands, realizing for the first time in his life that he was contemplating betrayal. The word had lodged inside his head like a cancer.

16 _____

It was the day of Martha's funeral in Willesden Green, bogged down in the suburbs of North London somewhere between the underground and the Main Line.

Why here? Tristram had asked. Martha wasn't from here. But then, he reflected, the Department had handled the whole thing. And if they'd lost Martha during her life, the bureaucratic hand was going to grab her back in death. The Department would chuck in the first clods of earth just to make sure she had really gone.

To Tristram it wasn't much of a send-off, even for a traitor. Cornish hadn't bothered with a black tie, still wearing the elegant speckled number.

The boyfriend, whose eyelids twitched uncontrollably, stood intoning, with half his trouser buttons undone. And then the little man from London Transport knelt and insisted on singing the Lord's Prayer. After all, it had been their bus that had sent her on her way, without even a skid. They wouldn't be writ-

ing that in the maker's brochure. Anyway, he was
awfully sorry, he said.

The vicar said good-bye at the graveside. He had to
go off and see someone. "Terrible business, wasn't
it?" His head nodded up and down, as if loosely connected to the neck. Cornish made a discreet coughing
noise. He took Tristram's arm, steering him toward
the station.

"D'you want a coffee?"

"No."

"Let's go in here." Cornish smiled indulgently and
held open the door of a little café. On the walls the
menus offered beans and fried eggs.

"I'm sorry, did you say yes to coffee?"

"I said no."

"Just one coffee, please." An Indian girl nodded
from behind the counter and disappeared to the
kitchen. Tristram took off his gloves.

"That's that, then."

"What?"

"Martha, I mean. They can keep her now." Cornish smoothed back his hair, straightened his tie.

"That's very gracious of you. The poor bitch was
used. You know that."

"Since when do you make excuses for traitors?"

For a moment Tristram didn't reply. He looked
around the café but there was no one sitting near
them.

"I told all this to the bloody team from Five, so I
might as well say it again. You're not dealing with
people who're born traitors. There's no type, no common profile. They all do it for different reasons.
That's what makes them hard to spot." He looked up

at Cornish. There was no discernible reaction. "And at the end of the day why shouldn't you feel sorry for a poor middle-aged German who walks under a bus because she can't stand living with herself and the things she's done?"

Cornish frowned. "I wouldn't blur the edges too much if I were you. She's blown Garten. The bastard's finished now."

"You don't know that."

"It's obvious." Cornish sat back. "They're just stringing him along, seeing where he leads."

"Wrong, Cornish." Tristram's cheeks were flushed. "They can't run the risk of losing him. The Russians are going to be all over Warsaw in a week's time. Besides, if the Poles netted someone as big as Garten, they'd be trumpeting it from every rooftop in the city just to show how clever they are."

The Indian girl brought coffee.

Tristram looked out the window. "There has to be another reason." Cornish cleared his throat.

"I'm afraid we no longer care about the reasons. Our instructions are to pull out of it altogether, cut our losses, write it off to experience. . . ."

"Instructions from whom?"

"The Director, and from me, of course. . . ."

"Of course."

"I realize this will be hard"—here it comes, thought Tristram, the conciliatory tone—"but we all feel this would be best. Garten knew the risks. Let's just leave it at that."

"More coffee?" The Indian girl leaned over the table. Cornish shook his head. He watched her go back to the counter.

"I'm still waiting."

"What for?" Tristram folded his hands on his lap.

"Your assurance that you will carry out my instructions and leave this business alone."

"I can't tell you that."

Neither had spoken after that. And long after Cornish had gone Tristram remained seated at the table staring out of the window. There was a tightness around his chest and his forehead felt cold and clammy. The same sensations he'd experienced that winter morning in Prague fifteen years earlier. Was it really that long? The warm little room at U Tri Pstrosu had felt so safe. Maybe he'd been tired, or maybe they'd been better than all the others. But he hadn't heard them till the door smashed open and the four of them, in hats and raincoats, lunged at him, destroying the stillness of the morning, pulling him downstairs into the cold, and only the start of a long journey to a tiny cell in Moscow, where he had seen no daylight, where the days and nights merged and lost each other in a world outside.

Tristram wiped his brow with a table napkin. He was shaking. But he knew he couldn't leave Garten to all that. Not without knowing. Not without a reason.

The Russian had been in Switzerland less than an hour. The taxi dropped him in the center of Montreux and he had checked the time by his wristwatch. Satisfied, he headed for the patisserie on the main square, anxious to mark his departure from Moscow with a coffee and an éclair. Pleasure, he decided, came in all sizes. And he thought again of the Warsaw Pact parties where the girls were covered with chocolate and the cakes with cream.

The warmth of the café made him sneeze and his nose blocked, denying him the rich taste of the pastry. With the beginnings of a searing headache, he made his way back into the darkening square.

He had barely pulled on his woolen ski hat when the snowball caught him in the center of his crown. Cursing quietly, he wiped the powdery snow from his face, scanning the crowd for the culprit. In the corner of the square a group of boys were running fast toward the lake. "I could tear out their fucking . . ." But he stopped himself, clenching his teeth in rage. If only they'd tried that in Moscow! By Christ, he'd have seen them crawl in their own blood. In days gone by he'd have rubbed their noses in it.

It took several minutes before the anger would subside, and then he fixed a pleasant smile on his face and helped an old woman to cross the road. "*Bon soir,*" he muttered.

"*Bon soir et merci,*" she whispered, heartened by the friendly gesture and the man's firm grip on her arm.

It was dark when the train dropped him in Blonay, leaving him to pick his way carefully through the unlit streets to the hotel. In his room the bed had been turned down and a sweet left enticingly on the pillow. He put the sweet in his pocket, pulled the curtains, and sat down to wait for the Englishman.

There were no pleasantries or exchange of greetings. They ordered mineral water sent up, but neither drank.

It didn't take long to identify the problem.

The Englishman took a black-and-white photograph from his briefcase, tossed it on the coffee table, and walked straight out of the hotel.

By nightfall the next day the photo was in Moscow, where it was compared with the original on file. The duty officer in archives remarked that James Tristram was probably a greedy son of a bitch since he'd put on so much weight.

17 _____

The sun set as the Trabant clattered over the hills, its engine flat out, the speed pitifully slow.

For long stretches they had the road to themselves, watching the stark, leafless trees—a straight road dotted with bus stops, piles of coal, a milk churn. Once Grazyna glimpsed a child sitting motionless on a gate, its hair standing in the wind. She felt the peace and the loneliness of the Polish countryside— the Slav lands, never peaceful for long.

Maya Angelica slept deeply, but her hands remained tight around her mother. The soldier was uncomfortable, his seat low and worn, his legs far too long for the pedals. At times he would swear at the little car. Grazyna heard it but felt no fear. The man had rescued her, she reasoned. He had killed to rescue her. Whoever he was, he would do her no harm. For almost an hour she dozed as the car joined the E8 transeuropean highway and changed direction.

The night was a jumble of impressions—the smell of the engine, the noise, and the discomfort. Once, out of the darkness, she saw the soldier's hand clutching a bottle, holding it over his shoulder, offering it to her. Without thinking, she grabbed at it, pouring the water into her throat, spilling it on the child's head. And then the sleep came again in tiny bouts and the unlit road led them north.

Hours later, it seemed, the soldier had stopped to relieve himself, but when he came back the army fatigues had gone and he was wearing a coarse woolen jacket and a fur cap with a wide peak.

At dawn they stopped again at a garage on the outskirts of Warsaw, just before the road runs down to the Vistula. The place was shut and the man had to bang on the door to wake the attendant. Grazyna watched them haggle over the price, felt the dryness in her throat and the emptiness of her stomach. And yet she knew that her own excitement would carry her on. She had escaped from captivity, she was alive, she was going home.

The soldier slipped into the office and used the telephone. He didn't call the embassy or the trade mission. He didn't wake any of the Soviet diplomats, still slumbering across the city. Instead he called a tie line, a local number with a permanent connection to Moscow.

He dropped Grazyna and her daughter on Nowy Swiat in the center of Warsaw, not saying anything, nodding shyly, waving them out onto the street. A man in a green loden coat came out of a milk bar and followed them, half lost among the morning shoppers.

The crowd paid no attention to the mother and her little girl, bruised and dirty as they were. The cold was an effective antidote to curiosity. No one hung about on the street corners. Heads bowed, hats pulled low, the people of Warsaw struggled in the wind like ships at sea.

Grazyna could have called and they'd have brought her in. But she didn't want to steal home like a casualty. Someone from the movement, she reasoned, had rescued her. It wouldn't do to fall at the last fence. Memories were long in Poland, and they'd remember for years to come that the two of them couldn't make it by themselves. Grazyna had to do it for both of them.

Even as she pushed open the door of the little cake shop, she knew they'd been recognized. But Maya Angelica was already rushing to the glass counter, pushing through the customers, pointing and crowing at the rows of pastries—"*vuzetki, kremowki*"—the sugar delights of children's Poland, as long as the sugar held.

Suddenly, Barbara, the younger of the two shopgirls, was lifting the child high into her arms: "Come with me, pretty one, and we'll find you something special, through here, that's it." She pulled aside a curtain: "Mum, you can come too. Come on, we've something special in here for the holidays."

The chatter was polished, oh so polished, and Grazyna couldn't help admiring the girl, her presence of mind, her intuition. A real Pole, she told herself. A real actress.

Barbara shut the door behind them and the smile left her face abruptly.

"I know you," she spoke in a hurried whisper. "I know you from the old days . . . a meeting with my mother. . . . Anyway, it's not important now. Did you have to come here?"

"There was no alternative. Besides, you are the contact point for my sector."

"I just wish it had been another time." The girl eyed them angrily. "They're starting the security blitz before the Russians arrive. You know, rounding up the dissidents, watching the old haunts, generally making trouble. We're trying to lie low for the moment. Anyway, what the hell. You're here." She looked down suddenly and saw Maya Angelica, the tears falling fast over her cheeks.

"My dear, I'm so sorry, I completely forgot." She turned back to a shelf, pulled down a box of cakes, and held it open in front of the child.

"Here, take one, go on. That's it, a big chocolate one."

And almost at once the little eyes dried and the child was smiling again.

Barbara pulled on her coat and opened the back door. It led into a school courtyard. The snow was falling again as the three of them passed the classroom window. On the blackboard Grazyna glimpsed a picture of Lenin.

I know more about him than any of you, she thought, looking at the children and starting to run. *You're only just beginning*.

After ten minutes in the snow the man in the green coat burst into the tiny shop and realized that he'd lost them.

18 _____

A mansion block. That's what the real estate agents called it. Apartments reached along stone walkways, boxes side by side with humans in them. Tristram heard his own footsteps, the echo of the East, and knew why Senya had chosen the place. A reminder of the life he had loathed but could never shake off. Here, beside King's Cross Station, Russia would hold him, grip him till the day he died.

"My friend, old friend." Senya stood looking at Tristram in surprise and delight, and then the bony arms reached forward to clasp him. He was as strong as ever, loyal, committed. Senya the brave, Senya the wise, Senya, who had shared his hope with them when their own had run out.

He pulled Tristram into the narrow hall and shut the door behind him. Quickly. Like the old days.

"My dear friend." He stepped back and they looked at each other smiling. "Another day survived." Senya shook his head.

"Another life," Tristram replied, completing the litany.

Senya led him to the little kitchen. "Sit here, sit here. I make tea. You eat something. Then we talk."

He opened the kitchen cupboard and Tristram could see the rows and rows of cans and jars, boxes and packets, piled to the ceiling. Senya had stockpiled for an army, part of him still back in the Russia of shortages and delays. There were habits none of them ever lost.

He put cold ham and cheese on the table, an oversized loaf, beer, gherkins. Beside the cutlery he set down two white napkins, starched and spotless.

They ate in silence, Senya filling his plate and licking it. Only those who've known real hunger do that, thought Tristram. I can remember that.

They went into the sitting room, long and narrow like a railway carriage, and Tristram was surprised by the array of paintings on every wall—a canopy of figures and colors. People and buildings represented in geometric shapes. The Leningrad school. Senya was still at work.

Tristram sat on a stool. "Something important has come up."

"I had thought so. You and I have no need to discuss the weather. Uh?"

Tristram hunched his shoulders and leaned forward.

"I sent a man in and he was betrayed. . . ."

"A short story, my friend. . . ."

"No, wait. . . . They know he's there but they don't pick him up. And yet they should do. He's big, and they need a big success."

"We are speaking of the Poles."

Tristram nodded. Senya knew the bloc like no one

else. The little straws, the shadows, the muffled, distant voices from across a continent. They all meant something to him. You couldn't buy experience like that. It wasn't for sale.

"What was this man going to do?" Senya closed his eyes, concentrating.

"Start something. . . ."

"How many knew of it?"

"Three of us, maybe four. . . ."

"And the man was free lance, I take it? How did you find him?"

"Coincidence. He was injured in a fight. They called me. He's a Polish defector. I was the one who debriefed him."

"And now?"

"Now they want to drop him, pull the plug, while he's still in there, before we know what's happened."

Tristram looked across at his friend. Senya was assembling the pieces, shifting them around, turning them this way and that. But he didn't like what he saw. Tristram felt the cold down his back. The room had grown quite dark and Senya seemed to have withdrawn into its shadows.

"You trust your own people?" His voice was a whisper.

"They got me out of Prague, remember. . . ."

"The world is changing, my dear friend. Inside the bloc, already things are different. New allegiances, new deals . . ." He sneered through a mouthful of gold teeth. "You know how they call all this reform in Moscow these days—new arses, old farts. Huh!" He laughed out loud, nodding his head up and down like a rag doll. And then the laughter died in his throat.

"My friend, everything around us has a past. It is the same with an operation. Everything leaves tracks, ripples in the water. Nothing passes in this world without a trace."

"I did the training as well, Senya. . . ." Tristram's voice was suddenly irritated.

"But how far back have you looked?" There was a gleam in the old man's eye that had not been there before. "What about your old inquiries—the Warsaw uprising, the suspicions about a British traitor?"

"We never pinned it down. You recall my contact in Prague. He said he had documents proving collusion between the British and Soviets. Said there was a British agent in Warsaw in 1944—someone who made the Poles believe Moscow would support the uprising."

"Did you ever see the documents?"

"You know I didn't. The Czechs arrested me in Prague shortly before I was to make a second contact. Since then no evidence—no trace of my contact."

"So the section dropped it."

Tristram nodded.

Without warning, Senya got to his feet.

"You should go now," he told Tristram.

"I . . . I don't understand."

"Go and do as they tell you. Forget this business." He was pulling Tristram's arm, shuffling down the corridor toward the hall. He stopped suddenly. "Listen to me. . . . I know how you feel . . . I know what you want to do. But I tell you—leave it alone, for yourself, for all of us."

Tristram felt a sudden draft beneath the front door. There were footsteps along the corridor outside.

"Tell me what you know, Senya. Tell me what all this means."

"I don't know. It's my stupid brain, a fairy tale."

"Say it."

"My friend, this is more than an operation that has gone wrong. This points toward you."

"What d'you mean?"

"Your defector, your section, you! Someone is beckoning you and you have no protection. More than that. There's an enemy close by. It is what I feel."

Tristram reached for the door handle, but Senya caught his arm.

"I'm serious. You cannot go in . . . the past . . . your work now. It cannot be. Not ever."

And then he looked into Tristram's face and read his own defeat. "You are a madman, my friend. . . ." He opened the door and pushed Tristram out into the night. "Like all of us."

Tristram didn't know what led him there, to the scrubbed schoolroom, to the seedy gushing couples, bored and unhappy, to the ancient gramophone with its needle scratching like a dogtooth across the records—all the princely inelegance, British, make-shift—damn cold.

Maybe it was his training. Whatever your mood, whatever the obstacles, see it through, something told him. Stick to routine.

And it couldn't have been worse. The night for Scottish reels, for whirling and prancing, for making what the man opposite called "a complete cock of yourself."

And there was June to grasp him gamely around the midriff, or what she could get at, smiling with her eyes, looking for an echo in his, set to climb another rung on the emotional ladder.

But he didn't want it. His mind fixed itself on the words and gestures of his Russian friend. And he lost the rhythm and the confidence.

"I'm sorry. It's not my night."

June smiled up at him. "Course it is. You're probably tired."

"Isn't everyone?" He looked around. The bank clerk was nuzzling the shop assistant like an anxious mare, the thin middle-aged artist was being led by his daughter, the resting actress and the butcher touched and giggled in expectation of not returning that night to their own homes and families.

It was, he decided, art in the loosest of senses.

"Skip to the left, boys turn, skip to the right . . ." The ancient piano teacher stood up in her carpet slippers, pawing the floor. "We really are a little ragged tonight, James, aren't we, all over the place, isn't that right?" She gave Tristram a pitying glance. "I'm relying on you, June, to keep him on course. Oh dear, I did think we were going to put on a little spurt before Christmas. After all, we've been doing these reels all year." She blinked at them like an old mouse, all bristles and teeth, her tiny nose twitching as if she wanted to sneeze.

It was another hour before she turned them out into the night. "Have a little practice at home, dear," she told Tristram. They all stood awkwardly on the pavement, not knowing what to say.

"Well, we better get going." The butcher gave them all an exaggerated wink.

"Me, too," said the bank clerk, and then they muttered their good nights, trying not to walk together, one or two hovering as if they were going another way, the little group lapsing back into shyness, anxious to retrieve their privacy.

June took Tristram's arm and held it all the way to the station, but she made no attempt to talk to him.

Her father had been like that, shut most days, open on just a few, like a business closing down. Deep and difficult, she used to call him. But then he'd had plenty of his own problems and she assumed Tristram did too. All the same, last time he'd wanted to kiss her and tonight she'd been determined to let him, because she was sure it would mean something to him, and he didn't seem the kind to do it every day.

Yet when they said good-bye he didn't move toward her and the smile came hesitantly and with evident pain.

"Will I see you on Tuesday?" The question seemed to pull Tristram back to the present.

"Yes, of course. I'm sorry I wasn't better company tonight."

He turned to go, but she reached up and kissed him on the cheek. A hedge against bad luck, she told herself. Because she had let her father leave once without giving him a kiss. And he had never come back.

It must have been close to eleven when Senya heard the knocking at the door. Soft, insistent. Odd that they hadn't rung the bell. And because all things odd carried potential danger, he tiptoed silently to the door and slipped on the chain. Anxiously he peered through the peephole but could see nothing and assumed that his eyes were simply playing tricks on him. There had to be someone out there. He was simply too blind to see them.

After a moment's hesitation he opened the door, just an inch, then another. It wasn't a large gap, but then it didn't need to be, for the muzzle and the silencer fit snugly between the door and its frame, and by the time Senya was aware of them, the bullet was already traveling toward his neck.

Back in his living room, Tristram turned on the lights—all of them. A desk lamp, candlelights beside the fireplace, a neon strip in the window—and the white walls shone back at him.

Home. Away from the shadows. It became a habit after they'd gotten him back from Prague. He couldn't bear the darkness. He would go to bed with the lights on and leave them burning when he got up. All around the house he had installed the brightest bulbs money could buy. In the shabby, narrow road the house stood out like a beacon.

They had told him to expect a reaction. "You won't be yourself, old man." The Service doctor had patted his shoulder. "It'll feel a bit funny for a while. Take some getting used to, I expect." He recalled all the vague predictions. But what did they mean? "Won't be yourself . . ." But who the hell would he be?

Then, gradually, as the months had passed, he had learned who he'd become—frightened by the oddest

things—the ring of a telephone, the click of the garden gate, loud voices in the underground. You never
knew what would trigger the fear.

But he knew now, sitting down on the white sofa,
hearing Senya's words—"an enemy close by . . ."—
the thick Georgian accent, half gasp, half whisper.
But how close?

He knew then that he couldn't return to the section. Already, perhaps, he was in danger. He got up
suddenly, turned off the lights, and moved on all
fours to the window. But there was nothing strange
on the street, no new cars or faces.

He switched the lights back on and sat there unable
to sleep, until the daylight took over and the sun
shone in through the dirty windows.

19 _____

"How much farther is it?"

Grazyna looked down at the tired face smeared with chocolate and realized the child had no sense of the danger. And as the streetcars swept past them over the icy streets, she marveled at the girl's resilience, her inner strength, the mental barrier that could block out the fear. Maya Angelica would eat, sleep, and recover. And she?

Grazyna felt the shopgirl pulling her arm. "Two streets from here. Hurry, it's not far."

They turned off the main square. The crowds were everywhere. At any hour people would leave their offices and wander out to shop, desperate to find food. Millions of man-hours were lost daily and the state was powerless, locked in a spiral of shortages and unpredictability. Even goods that were plentiful sold out within hours of hitting the streets, for no one trusted the system.

As they walked Grazyna could see that the militia patrols had multiplied. They moved now in fours, black leather jackets over the blue-gray uniforms, calf-length boots—the inquisitor's costume. Stopping to check documents, they would encircle the victim, jostle him, hold the identity card to the sky, letting the snow pour down on it, wetting the pages, smudging the ink. Tactics. Provocation. They knew just how far to go before the crowds would take no more.

Grazyna thought back over the day, trying to remember the faces she'd seen, the worried expressions, the rooms they'd sat in, the hurried departures, the move from one safe house to another. Only none were safe anymore. Transit points across an occupied city.

In a barely perceptible movement the shopgirl lengthened her stride and Grazyna and her daughter were left floundering among a hundred faces. And as the panic took hold of her Grazyna found herself being led by a man who had simply stepped in front of her, taking the woman's place, assuming the position of a guide.

He said nothing, made no gestures. But he didn't need to. She knew the technique, she'd used it herself. And so she began to feel more confident, drawing closer to him as they waited to cross the street. Not one of the usual crowd—not one of the young, anxious figures that had come to the little flat to talk to Jozef and Zbig. Not one of the regulars. Only when he half turned his head to check the road did she gasp with surprise, seeing his collar, realizing instantly that the man was a priest.

You wake suddenly. It could be day or night. There's no sense of time. Only your hands are shaking, you're sweating and you know the danger is close at hand. The way Garten knew it in the damp basement fifteen feet below the streets of Warsaw.

Maybe it's premonition, he told himself. The survival mechanism that all survivors create. For he had heard the footsteps where others might have missed them. Only they weren't that slow or quiet. By the time the padlock was forced from the door outside, and she had pushed her way in, he was standing there, already in his parka, suitcase in hand. For he knew they'd be leaving in a hurry. Once you've been on the streets, you don't forget them.

The Mercedes had gone. And they were across the road under a crescent moon.

They passed quickly down the street, but not too quickly. You don't ever run unless you have to. That was the rule. On their right the ruined church, half demolished, with its steeple still pointing into the clear night sky.

Inside the structure they heard a brick fall, maybe a stone, and Garten didn't look back, kept his eyes straight in front. Ania led.

They went on for half a mile, through the run-down streets, the three-, four-story blocks of flats with their leaning facades. Only a few lights burned, and when he looked at his watch it was past midnight.

They stopped beside a beige Polski Fiat, transport for the masses, and it took three attempts to start. "Blasted battery." She said it under her breath and Garten almost smiled. The little preoccupations of Poland. The little problems that added up to major problems. It was coming back to him as if he'd never left.

Ania drove with brutality, crunching the gears, wrenching at the wheel. They bumped dangerously over the cobbles, back across the river into the Old Town. Garten noticed the two mirrors on the windshield. One for the driver, one for the watcher. A car for business.

He wondered which procedure they'd use. Assemble at a safe house, come in from different directions, if things were bad establish a point and summon from there. Find a friend, find a comrade, borrow his room, sit in his chairs, drink his tea, then creep out again into the night when the meeting was over.

They'd play it that way. For them he was a major risk. Security would be the tightest.

Behind Nowy Swiat, Ania stopped the Fiat, got out, and crossed the narrow streets by the university. She didn't make a sound. They took the steep, stone stairs two at a time, panting with the effort.

Seven floors up and she touched his arm outside the door. "He's an old man, he's not expecting us, so play it gentle. Better not say anything. He's helped us before. I doubt he'll refuse this time."

She knocked twice quietly. Garten noticed the sudden stillness. A radio had been turned off. The sound of voices had stopped. Someone was listening.

She knocked again, a simple rhythm. An ancient face appeared at the door. The eyes blinked nervously. "It's you. What d'you want?"

"I want to come in."

"Later."

"Now!"

The man shut the door for a moment, and a few seconds later opened it and stood aside. A single light was on and Garten took in the disorder, the remains of a meal on the table, the sofa. He looked again. Under a blanket lay a young woman, no more than twenty. Golden blond hair, plump cheeks, flushed and healthy.

"My niece," mumbled the man, "staying with me." He fumbled with the cord of a dressing gown and rubbed a hand through tousled gray hair. He turned to Ania.

"It's late. Tell me what you want, then go."

"Listen, old friend"—she looked hard at the girl—"this'll take some time."

The niece had dressed and left. She wasn't a niece but nothing was said. Ania had made five phone calls, rapid, no more than a few seconds each. And now they waited, as if in prayer, the plan set in motion, nothing to stop it. And the city outside, asleep and unaware.

It must have been twenty minutes later when the door opened and the man who had eluded Polish security, and all the informers and cheats, all the liars and traitors of an entire Eastern Bloc country, stood in the doorway as if he could go where he pleased.

"Any coffee in this place?" The fellow smiled and took off an expensive sheepskin coat.

Garten got to his feet in amazement. They were two minutes walk from the Central Committee, a minute from the nearest militia station, and Romek was here. Now, Romek was back in Warsaw.

The "niece" hadn't wasted time. The thought flashed through Passent's mind as he ran for the car.

She must have telephoned headquarters straight after leaving the old fellow's room. What luck! And he had been thinking of canceling the surveillance on the old boy. Thank God for informers and thank God for this one.

Passent had made his own call. Two of the team would meet him at the gates of the Interior Ministry. They'd change cars and go from there. A small operation, minimum fuss, minimum noise. Quick and effective.

The two were already there when he drove up. And he left his own car in the drive and they were pulling away in the Mercedes even as he slammed the door. The car screamed down the empty street in second gear.

You can't beat the start of an operation, Passent mused, when you have it all at your fingertips, a place, a target. And you're on your way.

The girl hadn't known the identity of the old boy's visitors. But she was sure they were underground, possibly foreign, possibly illegals. Christ, he needed a catch, after Zbig and the disaster in the mountains.

The Old Town in Warsaw is crisscrossed with narrow cobbled streets. Some are one-way, others closed to traffic. The shortcut to the old Pole's flat led the wrong way down a tiny alley, and suddenly the three of them were yelling in unison as a black car slid from a courtyard to block their path.

Passent's driver hit the horn and the Mercedes's tires locked on the slippery surface. But the black car didn't move, just sat there motionless, the windows shaded.

Passent looked out, but could see no reason for the

obstruction. "Get out there"—he thumped the dashboard—"get rid of them now."

The driver was already running down the street, screaming and waving his arms. The night air filled with obscenities.

But in an instant he wasn't waving at all, and Passent saw him returning, head down, silent. He couldn't read the expression.

"What is it? Get them moving for Christsake. What the hell are you playing at?"

The man inclined his head to the window and lifted a steak-sized hand. "Hold it, chief, hold it. They want you. You'd better go."

"They . . . ?" Passent looked up, saw the man's face, read the resignation and the hatred. "They" always meant Russians. The car was a Volvo from the Soviet Embassy. Clearly the KGB station chief did work for himself. Klimov wound down his window.

"Sorry to hold you up." The light from the streetlamps glinted off Klimov's spectacles. "Something important has happened. One of our people . . . a potential embarrassment. We'll be gone in a moment."

"You'll go now. I'm in a hurry and my business can't wait. Back up—please." He hadn't wanted to add the final word but habit must have forced it out.

"I'm sorry, my friend. We must wait for a moment. . . ."

"That won't do. . . ." Passent was shouting.

"That will have to do."

For a moment they looked at each other in silence.

"Unless I'm mistaken, these are the streets of Warsaw and you exceed your authority—"

"And you forget yourself." Klimov turned away, as if tired by the conversation, then looked back at Passent. "You have a short memory, Comrade. You don't recall who taught you all your little tricks, got you your promotion, your apartment, and car, and all the other perks of the job. Uh"—he took off his glasses and sneered—"you and your kind make me sick, all of you. You're a disgrace to the Party . . . a disgrace to your own country. Go on, get out of here."

He wound up the window, leaving Passent to stare at the shaded glass. On both sides of the alley the tall medieval-style houses seemed to lean in on him. They'd all been built after the war—a gigantic effort to re-create past glory. A fake city, thought Passent angrily, and I'm part of it.

"I'll give you three minutes."

"How dare you . . ." Garten stood up in the tiny attic room, coming to within a few inches of Romek's face. And then it hit him . . . the memory of two dirty boys scrapping in the playground so many years before, the awful junior school out at Jelonki with its tired, bad-tempered teachers. He'd sorted out Romek then all right. Even now he could see the boy's bloody nose. It had felt so good.

He looked Romek up and down. "After all this time, my little friend, and still so rude . . ."

"I came, didn't I?"

"And how far d'you think I came?" Garten moved away and sat down.

"I'm asking myself the same question."

Garten looked around the room. Ania and the old man were in shadow. Behind them a tap dripped in the corner. It was just as Tristram had warned him, just as hostile. There'd be only one try.

"You know how my father died?"

Romek met his eyes.

"I know where he died and what went before. . . ."

"Then you know why I've come."

"Not so fast, my friend . . . we all knew Zbig and loved him. Now we mourn. What of it?"

"His death was an outrage and should be met with action. . . ."

"We're planning a service. St. Anne's . . ."

"A service is not enough."

"Then what would you have us do?" Romek got to his feet, flushed, angry. "You leave when you choose, return when you choose. By what right do you demand anything from us?"

"I want to see my wife and daughter."

"You don't need my permission."

"I need your help. . . ."

"We'll do what we can. I heard tonight that your wife is back in Warsaw."

"Where was she?"

"How should I know?" Romek looked at his watch. "One more minute for your business, my friend. Then I leave."

Garten rubbed his eyes. For a moment neither man spoke.

"How much do the British do for you?"

"I can't answer that." Romek looked away.

"Answer it!"

Romek shrugged. "Since you asked, they do a lot. Quiet, discreet. More reliable than the CIA. When

they promise they deliver. Mostly. It's their guilt after the war, not helping us. . . ."

"And if you lost their help . . ."

"What are you saying?"

"Answer me."

"If we lost help from London, I don't know. So
many funds, networks, the training . . . you know
all this, you know it would be a disaster."

"In that case, think carefully about what I tell
you."

By the time Passent reached the flat it had been
empty for well over five minutes. And yet he could
still feel the presence of those who had been there.
There was body warmth in the air and the room had
not yet settled, not yet quieted.

20 _____

Each weekday the black limousines of the Soviet leaders—the Zils—sprint along Moscow's Kutuzovsky Prospekt heading for the Kremlin. The route never varies. Each member of the Politburo, each Party secretary, travels in strict convoy, a black Volga in front and an outrider at the rear, covering the left flank.

On the sidewalks another group monitors the convoy, a dozen or so people staked out along the way, close to the supermarket, beside the Arbat restaurant and the House of Books, then on down to the hallowed columns of the Lenin library.

Whatever happens along that route is scrutinized and recorded. Passersby are watched, tourists are watched, and if anyone shows the slightest hostility, the watchers interpose themselves to guard the Zils.

It was eight-thirty in the morning and a sharp chill hung in the air along Kalinin Prospekt. The tops of the high-rise buildings were lost in the clouds. The General Secretary's convoy was level with the Melodiya record store when a muffled bang was heard, followed by the sound of a much larger explosion and the shattering of glass.

For a second, maybe longer, the cars halted in the center lane and an entire shopping precinct seemed to freeze in shock. Passersby said they saw signs of confusion in two of the vehicles. The occupants appeared to be gesturing wildly and shouting at each other. And then the cars shot off toward the Kremlin, leaving everyone on the street scratching their heads in disbelief.

In keeping with the new era of Glasnost, Tass later reported that the General Secretary's car had suffered a blowout and that ordinary citizens in the vicinity had at no time been in danger.

Tass did not mention that one of the General Secretary's closest bodyguards, seated opposite him in the car, had attempted to draw a pistol with something closely resembling hostile intent but had been overpowered by his colleagues, who had forced him to the floor, gripping him tightly around the neck.

Four minutes later, with the car inside the Kremlin and the General Secretary popping tranquilizers in his office, they had released their hold on the would-be assassin only to find that he had died of asphyxiation at their hands.

Tass did not mention any of that. But then no one had told them.

"Someone tried to clinch the deal ahead of time."

"My God!"

"It was indeed a stupid move. One of our salesmen became impatient."

"How will this affect our prospects for success?"

"There will, of course, be some nervousness, but things will go ahead."

"What about the salesman?"

"Fortunately one of our representatives was on hand, so we could terminate his employment immediately."

There was a loud cough and the tie line between Warsaw and Moscow went dead. Klimov leaned back in his chair, sighed with relief, and reached for the vodka bottle.

Outside in the parking lot he could hear the embassy children shouting at each other.

It had of course been a terrible business, but thank God the bodyguard was dead. He knew who it was. They'd recruited him three years earlier, the son of a regional Party secretary, sacked for incompetence on a particularly grand scale. There'd been plenty of resentment to build on, but clearly not enough intellect. The young man had understood only violence—the more subtle art of political manipulation had passed him by. How easy it was to put a bullet in a man's head. How much harder to destroy the man and his legacy together—the way they would do it to the General Secretary.

Klimov stood up and looked at himself in the mirror above the mantelpiece. Maybe, after all, it would work. His mind sorted through the details. Garten's wife had been safely delivered to Warsaw. Now she would help her husband, get him accepted back into the underground, get the operation started. Already Garten had met with Romek. He smiled. He had known Romek's whereabouts for more than a year.

Hadn't told the Poles. Why should he? It was a card to hold until needed. How well it had paid off!

He could picture the Russian back in Moscow with his sniveling nose and chronic sinuses. What a meticulous planner, what a survivor. How had he managed it for so long?

Klimov went back to his desk and sat down. Then it came to him—the key to the man's success, the key to his survival, his fruitful old age. Not one of his friends, not a single associate, he realized, with a shiver, had ever lived long enough to betray him.

21 _____

A single watcher can provide the key. Spot him and the rest fall into place. A point man, two loafers, a man eating lunch in a truck. Too many people doing far too little. And Tristram had seen them, taking the street from the top end, dropping letters to no one in the mailbox, returning slowly to stand in the shadow of King's Cross.

And that had been enough. You get out while you're still in that state of grace where you've fingered them and they've yet to finger you. Get out. And Tristram had crossed the Marylebone Road, the second and more tangible threat to his life, and found a pay phone. Quickly now, his heart already racing, the fear rising into his throat. Had he come too late to warn Senya? How long had they been watching him?

Senya's neighbor had been just a plate on a door he'd passed—J. Davies. He'd never met J. Davies but he got the number and dialed.

"Mr. Davies?"

"Who's asking?"

"I'm Detective Sergeant Anderson, Paddington CID. Er, it's about—"

"I know what it's about," said Davies. "I've told you buggers everything I know. Just because the old fellow's dead, there's no reason to make my life a misery, phoning at all hours. . . ."

And Tristram had carefully replaced the receiver and stood for a moment, lost in sadness, shrouded by the rush-hour crowd. Among all the people there was no one who could replace Senya. No one from Amersham or Kent or Birmingham who could know what Senya had known, see what Senya had seen, live through the torture and deprivation of those camps and then die beside King's Cross Station. Like Senya. The friend who had warned him. . . . *An enemy close by. It is what I feel.*

He pushed his way toward the escalator and down to the platform. A silver train waited.

I'm going away, he wanted to tell the passengers. I'm going farther than you. I'm not getting off at Boston Manor or Ealing or Earl's Court. I won't be walking the dog or cutting the hedge. I'm off to the bloc. Ever heard of it? Off to the bloc to find out why my friend had to die.

Funny thing about English trains. No one speaks out loud. And when the train stops even the babies cease crying. Plenty of peace on the London underground.

No one noticed him leave the carriage. It was Hounslow West Station, beside the highway, and the chubby middle-aged figure in the beige raincoat was of no interest to his fellow passengers. Had they been asked they would have suspected he lived in one of those endless "bunkers" laid out beneath the flight path of every jumbo jet, where the ceaseless noise jangles the nerves and the fumes kill off the grass in the backyard.

Tristram headed for the highway. Ten minutes later he was walking along the grass that borders the hard shoulder, and the cars droned past him. He alone was on foot, his mind in a city many hundreds of miles to the east, not wanting to arrive.

The traffic along the Edgware Road had eased. It was the little window between the morning rush hour and the insanity of lunchtime.

Even so the Pickford furniture van had to cruise awhile to find a parking space, and it was a tight squeeze outside the Patel newsagency. So tight in fact that the driver knocked over the Patel motorcycle and the distraught Indian rushed out in his shirt-sleeves, shouting and waving his arms. He stopped suddenly in surprise as the cab door opened. His mouth attempted a smile.

"Mr. Cornish . . . Mr. Cornish . . . I . . . I was not expecting you."

"Sorry about the bike, Patel." Cornish walked around to the front of the van and inspected the object, now lying in a puddle. "Nothing serious."

"No, no, nothing serious at all." Patel followed a few paces behind.

"We've come to collect a few things for Mr. Tristram. He won't be here for a little while."

"Yes, yes of course."

It took three men until the late afternoon to clean out the rooms. Without Patel they could have done it in an hour. But the young Indian insisted on cluttering up the staircase, producing first one child then another for the men's inspection, stuttering with pride over their life histories and achievements.

The filing cabinets were the last to go. And try as he might Patel couldn't understand why one of the men seemed to stand guard as they were carried out. Such shabby old objects. Probably junk, he reasoned. In any case, they wouldn't get much for them on the market.

For a moment the Indian stood in the doorway, trying to collect his thoughts. The removal men were locking the back of the truck. Cornish gave a cheery wave and swung himself up into the cab. And it was then that Patel took his courage in both hands and ran to the edge of the pavement.

He tapped on the window, but Cornish wouldn't look around. The driver turned on the ignition and Patel tapped again. And it was probably Cornish's dismissive flick of the hand and his expression of annoyance that made even the genial Indian step back and let them go.

He would have told them if only they'd waited, told them of the package that Mr. Tristram had left in his care long ago, with special instructions. And what should he do with it now? It was really too bad the way these people behaved.

The truck had gone and he moved back to the curb to inspect his motorcycle. Some of the glossy paint had been scraped off the side. The rear mudguard was dented. Bugger them all, he thought unkindly. He'd hang on to the package just to show them, and no one would have it. He grinned a set of black-and-gold teeth and hurried back to his shop. It would be his secret.

Less than an hour later, feeling cheated and deprived, Patel relinquished the "secret" to the taxi driver who had brought him Tristram's note. Thank you for your help, it said, thank you for your friendship. I'll be back in a few weeks and will reward you handsomely for your trouble.

He threw the note in the wastepaper basket, reached for a little jar of paint, and went outside to touch up the motorbike. A handsome reward! He didn't believe a word of it.

The taxi took the package to London airport's Post House Hotel. And when he got it James Tristram made his second call. He dialed Cornish's direct line.

The number rang only once.

"Hello."

Tristram knew the accent—South Middlesex, major's daughter, he assumed, cleared to the lowest of the levels, and not one of the brightest.

And instantly he understood. This was no longer Cornish's number. The call had been routed to a "siding"—a substitute number held open for two or three months after the Service disconnects the original. Normally they kept on a single operator around the clock, just to see who called.

"Hello." The voice became most insistent.

"I'd like to speak to Mr. Cornish."

"I'm sorry, there's no one of that name here. Can I help you?"

Tristram had heard it before. The girl was probably nervous—first caller, didn't want to lose him.

Sometimes, he knew, the sidings were useful. Often they yielded nothing. He recalled one operation where a heavy breather had latched on to the number and another little girl from South Middlesex had become extremely upset. In the end they'd had to disconnect that number as well and the fun had stopped for everyone.

He replaced the receiver. So they'd set up a siding that quickly. Usually it took a day or two just to fill in the forms. Not this time. Someone inside the Service had the power to cut him out, excise him. For a moment he thought of running to the office in Curzon Street, showing his pass, demanding entry. But that would be offering his body on a plate.

"Can you trust your own people?" He could hear Senya's words as if he were there beside him. Senya had known.

He opened the package and took out a brown envelope. It wasn't much—a few traveler's checks, a second passport, a couple of press cards acquired at trade fairs in the Eastern Bloc. And in among them the little blue identity card from Romania, where Britons, he knew, could obtain visas on arrival. A key. If only it still fit.

But don't think about what lies ahead of you, don't concern yourself with the odds or the notion of failure. You've known it already. There's nothing more they can do to you, no pain or fear that you haven't already suffered. It's easy now. You know how they take your mind and use it against you. Play on your fears, different ones at different times, like piano keys. And they know all the tunes, all the tunes that you've ever played. Whatever went into your life they can take out, whatever mattered and shone they can diminish and sully. You know that, you can fight it. This time you're stronger.

And even as he burned the cards and papers he wouldn't need, checked the suitcase, James Tristram felt the blows to his body in the little cell in Moscow, felt the parched throat and the agony of sleeplessness and exhaustion.

It went with him, all of it, as he made for the airport, as he sat in the departure lounge, as he drank the milky tea, passed through immigration control and on to the evening flight to Bucharest, concrete capital of Romania.

As the plane jerked off the runway and headed into darkness, Tristram tried to remember his last day in the Eastern zone, at the transit point between West Germany and Czechoslovakia, on the coldest day of his life. And he'd done what they'd told him never to do. He'd looked back while crossing the border, before the swap had been finalized, seconds after the man from Moscow had pushed him toward the West, the hatred and anger in his voice at a prisoner taken from him, and the warning: Never on any account to return.

They had met again beside the Embankment so that Cornish should be reminded that this was unofficial, high-risk—the kind where you could lose your pension and no one would ever know why.

The Director spoke first.

"Sorry about the theatricals."

"I quite understand. You should know Tristram has gone."

"Bad business. Do we know where?"

"Not yet."

"You've closed down his section, I take it?"

"Of course."

"If he's gone abroad, he could be a major embarrassment."

"We'll have to hope that he hasn't."

"Indeed."

The two men walked off in separate directions. Neither was in a hurry. And yet both experienced a feeling of urgency, carrying their anxieties across the city, each sensing a threat but for different reasons.

22 _____

It was the third raid that day. Sudden, public, high-profile. The kind that contains a message for everyone.

The cars had drawn up on the main street opposite the Palace of Culture and the militia had struck out with a vengeance. They were psyched up for it, pushing their way through the shoppers, kicking over a bicycle, the truncheons in their hands, straight into the restaurant, for they knew exactly where to go. Table by the window, three men halfway through their mushrooms and sour cream, meat and potatoes ordered and on the way.

They were grabbed from behind, one of them already on his feet, the bag in his hand, the envelopes cascading onto the floor and all the close-typed leaflets spilling out under the black boots.

The men had no time to struggle, and yet the patrons of the restaurant couldn't let it go at that. Not there in Warsaw, not after the Nazi occupation, not after the black years of Stalin.

And so they stood up, fifty or sixty of them, many

with their napkins around their necks. A few held their glasses, the talking stopped, and a sudden silence fell over the dining room. The traditional mark of hatred, more powerful than a fist or a gun.

It wasn't lost on the militia, forcing them to bow their heads in shame as they pushed their prisoners into the street. Only the last of the officers caught the low whisper, caught the threat, the promise that their faces had been marked and identified and wouldn't be forgotten.

Passent watched from across the street, but he didn't watch the militia. For them it was routine—clearing up the troublemakers before an important visit. But sometimes it paid to study the crowd around the action. There were times when you could gauge their responses and their loyalties. Moscow had taught him that. "Look carefully," went the lesson. See who stops and who runs. A guilty conscience can stand out even in a crowd.

He had watched the girl with the raven hair, admiring first the legs, then the fur coat. The raid had taken place just a few feet from her but she hadn't reacted like the others. Some had screamed, others ran away, a few shouted obscenities at the militia. Not she. She had continued down the street as if nothing was happening. That took nerve and practice.

She was quick on her feet. Elegant platform shoes, the hint of a blue dress below the coat. He took it all in as he crossed the road, falling in behind her.

He could have been wrong, he told himself, quite wrong. But you get to know when the odds are with you, when intuition and circumstance bond you together and make a fact.

As the girl reached the end of the street and turned to take a final look at the commotion, Passent knew exactly who she was.

He followed her to an apartment block on the site of the old Jewish ghetto, where the vast marble statue stands up and cries against the atrocities of the Second World War.

He watched her go in, swinging her little plastic bag, not happy, not jaunty, but preoccupied, on her way to do business.

Passent remained outside. In the gathering darkness he could see one or two elderly figures close to the statue. A couple sat on a bench staring at the ground in front of them. A man with a beard paced up and down, dragging his feet. In the still cold an almost unbearable sadness seemed to settle over the square. All around him were modern buildings, new buildings, and yet, Passent reflected, there was no shifting history. Wherever you looked the old Nazi killing ground lay beneath your feet.

"I've brought you some food."

Garten turned and took the bag from Ania. He, too, had been looking out over the ghetto.

"What now?" he asked.

"We wait. The union is meeting. The full committee will have to make the decision."

"How d'you think it'll go?"

"Romek is against it. You should know that. You

bullied him. Anyway"—she looked away—"he's always hated you. Even at school."

"And the others?"

"The others are hotheads. Many of them. They were always more interested in hanging the government from lampposts than talking to them." She took her coat off and hung it on the front door. "Why don't you eat what I brought you? They'll call us when there's a decision."

Romek sat despondently in the back of the car. The driver read his mood and said nothing. He was a student, used only intermittently—when he had time and they were short. Plenty of the spiv in him, with his dangling cigarette and dangling medallion. But he was good with cars, drove fast, and knew how to fix them when they wouldn't drive at all.

South they traveled to the meeting—skirting the little villages, down to Katowice, city of mines and filth.

They stopped in the center, where the giant colliery wheels stand hard against the blocks of flats. Romek stepped out onto the cracked, uneven cobbles, tasting the acid on his chin. Acid pollution, the city and its people enveloped in a cloud.

As he walked he recalled the days before martial law. Solidarity had declared the region a disaster area. Doctors and scientists had been called in to investigate. And they had found all the contaminated food, the high rates of infant mortality, the sun that seemed to set early in protest.

The tanks had settled the issue. The disaster declaration had been torn up. Only the disaster itself remained.

Romek bought food from a small shop—bread and cheese, some mineral water. The miners always had food, he recalled. At any rate, it brightened his mood.

The student, too, seemed more cheerful, humming a tune as he drove. They'd told him to take it carefully. No—more than carefully, they had said. Like a monk through a convent of sleeping nuns. Raise no eyebrows.

But they didn't want to be late for the meeting. For the issue was vital, the most vital in years.

Romek had made up his mind before they'd left Warsaw. And he'd told them, hadn't he? It was imperative to turn Garten down. The British plan was reckless, outlandish even. They would be used as cannon fodder, trying to test the limits of tolerance within the bloc. He couldn't buy that at any price. He sat back and shook his head at the passing countryside.

They both saw the sign to the town of Oswiecim.

Romek had gone there first with his father, who had wanted to revisit the place after the war. The old man had looked about, not saying a word, gone away, and never returned. Twice is enough, he had murmured on the way home. Twice is enough for anyone.

Now, Romek reflected, the underground had made it *their* place—late at night when the locals passed hurriedly by, long after the day staff had left.

They rounded a bend and suddenly the student was cursing out loud. Thirty yards ahead they saw a uniformed militiaman step from behind a car concealed in an emergency pullover. The man held a lighted stick with a radar gun.

"Fuck!" Romek sat up. "What is this? Were you speeding? Christ, this is all we need."

The student stepped hard on the brake and the car stopped a few feet past the officer. The boy wound down the window. So it seemed natural for the figure in uniform to lean his elbow on the sill, rest the radar gun, and ask for the men's identity cards. And as the two of them felt in their pockets, there was no way they could see the front of the gun open and the tiny barrel push its way forward.

Romek felt nothing at all when the silenced bullet smashed his forehead, and the student had time only for a cry of surprise as the militiaman stepped back into the rushes by the side of the road and fired again.

The man left the bodies where they were and changed clothes in the semidarkness, three miles from the town of Oswiecim, or as the Germans and the rest of the world will always know it—Auschwitz.

"It's been three hours since they met. Why does no one call?"

Ania awoke with a start. As she opened her eyes she could see past the angry face of Garten to a crescent moon.

"How quickly you forget their ways." She rubbed her eyes. "You don't remember how they shout and squabble, even when there's nothing to squabble about. Once they took three days to agree on the number of toilets in a steel plant. What did you imagine? That Romek would wave a magic wand?"

"You're soft, all of you, naive, still pissing yourselves behind trees. Don't you know the world's moved on?"

Her face told him he'd hit home. But, God, they were slow, backward, still blaming the Russians for everything. Garten turned back to the window. This time they'd have to show the world they could do it right. Stop the recriminations, the bickering, the excuses about getting left in the lurch. Poland, as his mother used to say, would have to change its own diapers.

The knock at the door caught them both by surprise, and Garten was to remember only that it had opened before Ania could reach it, a gun in her hand, but too slow, way too slow. *A terrible breach of security* —his first thought, staring at the woman and child, weary and bedraggled on the doorstep, a priest behind them, the wetness coming involuntarily to his eyes as the years of loneliness ran away and the child rushed headlong toward him.

From inside the doorway Passent had seen the three figures enter the apartment block across the square. A priest, a child, and a woman, and even in the blue-white light from the streetlamps he knew them, knew their intentions.

So this was where they would tie the knot, where the old agents and couriers, where the man from London would gather. Follow a whore, he thought, and she'll lead to a prince.

He forgot about the cold. But somewhere deep in

his mind he felt the stirring of a conditioned reflex. Ring headquarters, get reinforcements, tell KGB liaison. You could round them all up in an hour. Be a hero. Win a medal.

But he couldn't move. Not this time, couldn't take his eyes off the apartment block and the lighted windows. No ordinary operation, this one. Protected, nurtured by the Russians. Klimov and his crowd. Wrong somehow. Wrong and dangerous.

Maya Angelica had not hesitated. All those years she had kept alive the image of her father, far away and out of sight, and to her there was no concept of lost time. Time was what you held in your hand. And that was why she ran to her father and held him.

Grazyna steadied herself against the wall. She was aware suddenly that the three of them were alone. The priest and the woman courier had gone into the kitchen. Outside the wind had dropped and snow fell in thick, large flakes. And Jozef Garten, the man she had loved, then hated, then shut out of her mind forever, had returned. She couldn't cry, couldn't approach him. It felt as if she were somewhere else—a distant observer as her own life passed in front of her. Two or three minutes went by before she could speak.

"I don't know what to say to you, Jozef. I don't know why you've come or what you're doing." She shook her head in disbelief. He hadn't changed. She could see that. Still the same prepackaged revolutionary in his sneakers and jeans, the face unshaven, the features pointed and anxious. And he didn't know what to say to her. She could sense his awkwardness as he held the child, his eyes tight shut.

Far away it seemed the telephone was ringing. Long, slow tones but Grazyna knew it had been answered in the room next to them. She could hear the woman's voice, single words, questions, but she couldn't make them out.

"I want to tell you . . ." Garten moved toward her, but then the door to the kitchen opened and Ania was hurrying in with the priest behind her.

"What is it?" Garten swung around, the little girl still clutching his legs. But Ania had turned to Grazyna.

"They want you."

Grazyna looked puzzled.

"Go on, pick it up."

She went into the kitchen but didn't shut the door. She listened for a moment, then spoke two sentences and replaced the receiver.

No one said anything but their eyes asked the question.

Grazyna returned to the living room.

"Romek is dead," she said quietly, "and the coordinating committee has therefore approved your plan in his absence." She looked hard at Garten. "Now I know the reason for your return," she told him, "the rest can wait. At this time the movement is on a war footing." Her face was flushed with excitement. "And by a vote, just an hour ago, I myself am asked to lead the operation."

Maya Angelica detached herself from Garten and ran back to her mother.

23 _____

The Romanian airlines plane had screamed in over the city, breaking cloud at a little over a hundred feet. Fast, unstable, using too much throttle. Tristram found himself clutching the armrest, choking back the sickness.

Immigration now. And he had loosened his tie and played clueless. Not hard, was it? Heavy, sweating face, hot and bothered. What a sight! They must have thought—one more baggy-trousered Brit, for they had demanded nothing more than nine pounds for a transit visa. And he had climbed into an ancient Renault taxi that smelled of cheap cigarettes and rattled its way uncomfortably over the plains of south Central Europe.

They drove through unlighted streets. Tristram could barely make out the few gray shapes moving silently along the pavements. Here and there a candle burned in a shop window. Once a police car flashed past them—all lights and sirens—but the blackness hung like fog over the city, witness to an energy crisis that had broken the fragile economy and scattered its pieces.

I'd forgotten the poverty, he thought, *forgotten the dark, forgotten what it's like to be a thousand miles from anywhere you want to be. Even after the revolution.*

Inside the hotel a kerosene lantern glowed forlornly on the reception desk. A dark-haired woman sat on a stool.

"Evening." Tristram undid the top two buttons of his coat. "I have a transit visa—"

"It is not necessary to explain. Fill in the form."

She slid a questionnaire across the desk.

"Are your telephones working?" Tristram saw the bored eyes sharpen.

"Our telephones always work. Why do you ask?"

"I wish to call a friend."

"The friend is in Bucharest?"

Tristram nodded.

"There will be no problem."

Up in the room he dialed the first of two numbers he had memorized. Andrew Milton, number two at the British Embassy. By chance Tristram had checked his file a year earlier. In the London archives embassy staff were labeled as angels or devils, according to whether they had covert status. Milton, he recalled, had no intelligence classification. MI6 had never even invited him to tea. Milton was a cherub.

"I can't really invite you over." The voice was Cambridge, not overprivileged, but not overpolite. "We've got a do on. Why don't you come by in the morning?"

Tristram smiled into the receiver. "No time, sorry. The plane leaves for Warsaw at eleven. Just time to get my visa from the Polish Embassy. I was just wondering if you knew who the consul was. Always helps to know a chap by name."

"Lord. Haven't got a clue, I'm afraid. We don't really talk to the Poles much these days." Tristram could hear voices in the background. "Look, I'm sorry, I better go." Milton sounded flustered. "If there's a problem, give us a call, all right? 'Bye."

Tristram got up and went over to the window, but all he could see was his own reflection. It had been a pointless call to a clueless British diplomat, but maybe enough to confirm his cover story if hotel security was listening. The new security—every bit as good as the old.

He went back to the phone, dialed again, and held his breath, because this was the only call that mattered, this was the only man who could help.

"May I come in?" Cornish hadn't expected the woman to be so small. He angled his head down toward the curly black hair and glasses and offered a practiced smile.

"You'd better." She moved aside. "Here in the front room, if you don't mind."

It was a spartan little box, thought Cornish. "Somewhere in Catford" was how his secretary had described the terraced house that collected dirt and fumes and propped up its neighbors along the periphery of South London. Cornish sat on a foam rubber chair in the window.

"I gather you teach physics."

"That's right."

"Never much good at it myself, I'm afraid."

"Oh dear." She looked up at him with vague amusement. She wasn't nervous, wasn't concerned.

"You said you're from . . ."

"Social Security." Cornish reached for his briefcase.

"I see."

"I'm sorry to bother you, but I need help with something." He detached two or three sheets of paper from a manila file. "Here it is." He frowned at the typewritten screed. "D'you know anything of a man called James Tristram? The only reason I ask is that he appears to have gone missing."

She sat and looked at him for a moment and then made the kind of decision she had promised she never would. It went against her education, her mother's strict precepts, and her natural uncomplicated attitude to life. But then she hadn't taken kindly to Cornish, his air of condescension, his transparent dishonesty. It was as if he were saying to her, I'm lying, but that's because I'm important. So play the game.

He was, she decided, quite unlike Tristram in almost every way. James had been closed, but vulnerable, caring. And if he'd disappeared from men like this, he must have had his reasons. All the same, both she and Cornish were genuinely surprised when she confessed she had never set eyes on James Tristram in her entire life.

It was, of course, silly going to the dance class, knowing that he wouldn't be there, but hurriedly glancing around the door, ready to be surprised. Just in case.

"Hello, dear. D'you know where Mr. Tristram's

got to?" The dancing teacher, shuffling up to her in those old carpet slippers, the others leering at her, sensing a scandal. A few whispers . . . had she? Had they? It was surprising how little it took to get them all talking.

"No idea," she responded, and wished she hadn't come, because she couldn't leave now, couldn't let them think she'd made the journey just to see him. She took off her coat.

"Sorry I'm late."

A new man came up to her. Julian, he said, and smelled of eau de Cologne. What about a whirl? He had pushed too close, held her too long, sloping long fingers around her back, over her bra strap. That had been too much to take.

"I'll sit this one out, if you don't mind."

"Please yourself." Julian moved quickly away and began eyeing the other possibilities. She sat down on a school bench as the piano rumbled and thumped with the heavy-handed rhythms. She wouldn't come here again, she told herself, and it had once seemed like such a good idea, such a wonderful chance to meet and make friends. But she had always prided herself on clear thinking and logic, and she knew it was over.

On the street outside the hotel Tristram sucked in the cold, damp air and waited for the man. Eric had understood the call. After all these years Eric was really good, really sharp. Just the way he was listed in the Service file. There had been only the slightest hesitation in his voice, and then the deep Welsh baritone exploded in laughter. Of course he remembered

Mr. Tristram and Mr. Tristram's family, and the school up the road, and how were things these days in Wales, and what a lovely surprise to hear from him again.

Tristram's heart had begun racing with excitement, because Eric had remembered the code, the recognition signal, and had acted his part as if he'd acted it for a lifetime.

He looked up and down the street, but there was no one there. The last buses had creaked and rattled their way into the suburbs, overloaded, leaning crazily, like giant caterpillars. If there'd been any fun, it was over.

But even in this black hole Tristram could feel the old exhilaration. He was back in the field, operational, alive, the first contact made, way out on a high. It wouldn't last. He knew the pattern. In a matter of hours the desperation would set in, the loneliness and fear. And then he'd be running, hiding and dying a little each time a shadow crossed his own. But just for a few moments he would feel good, feel safe, build morale for the days ahead.

The sudden noise of the little car shattered the stillness around him. He saw the headlights and the little white Fiat and the two figures inside. He stepped onto the curb.

"Get in, get in." Eric had pushed open the door and Tristram glimpsed the swarthy, bearded figure and the long hair and realized that the other passenger was a dog. He slammed the door behind him. The car moved off, its engine sounding like an angry sewing machine.

Eric drove erratically and with little skill, and Tristram became aware that he was not the only anxious passenger. He could feel the dog's hot breath on the back of his neck.

He turned and looked at Eric's profile.

"Nice dog."

Eric roared with laughter. "Nice dog," he mimicked, "you think so. I tell you my friend, this is not a nice dog, he's a horrible dog, the worst dog in the world. I hate him." The car screeched around a corner. Eric struggled with the steering wheel. "But he's useful. You have a dog in your car—you must be legitimate. Nobody questions a man with an animal. It's like you're wearing a sign saying 'Nice Guy.' It's true. But this dog, he's a pain in the arse, always hungry, wanting meat. You know half the food shortages in the city would disappear if this creature stopped eating. Yes, you, greedy fucker." He put a hand back and tickled the animal's chin.

Tristram stared straight ahead but he could see no landmark, no sign, not even a lighted window. It was as if the city were at war, and he pictured the people lying asleep, nervous and fitful, afraid of what the morning might bring.

Andrew Milton hurried from the apartment block and headed for the embassy, three streets away. His wife had not been happy about the disrupted dinner, nor had her parents—frightful busybodies, out on a week's visit, plonking themselves in the flat to make sure their daughter was being properly treated, bringing their bloody jam and sausages out from London and then eating it all themselves.

"Stay at least until coffee, darling," Melissa had

said. But he couldn't, could he? Because when the
security officer says there's a message for you, then
you have to go. And the coffee would get cold and the
ice cake would melt and Melissa would be in a foul
mood when he got home. And that would be that for
another night.

Of course he should never have taken on the added
responsibilities. But when the head of Chancery had
been injured last year in a road accident, the Service
had gone to him and asked if he wouldn't mind filling
in. Just for a while. Just till they got someone else out.
Someone with the language. And after all, it was only
Romania, so there wasn't much to do. Not as if it
were Moscow.

Milton reached the embassy gate, climbed the
steps, and banged on the door.

"Glad you're here, sir." The security man let him
into the narrow hallway.

"Well, I'm not," Milton replied.

The guard ignored him. "Machines have been going crazy last half hour. Bells all over the place."

"All right, all right, let's see what the fuss is
about."

They made their way to the communications room
on the top floor. "Right, I'll take it from here."
Milton put his key in the door and marched rudely
inside, slamming it behind him.

"Pompous little shit," muttered the guard, and he
stamped downstairs, planning petty revenge.

"You want a drink?" Eric placed a bottle and two
glasses on the table.

Tristram looked around him. They were in a

kitchen in an apartment block, somewhere outside Bucharest. Gray walls and grease, some cracked linoleum, a cupboard door hanging crazily from a single hinge. Opposite him sat a stranger and a dog, holding his safety between them.

"Can we talk?"

"Of course we can talk. They can't even afford microphones to bug the hotels." Eric poured himself a drink.

Tristram said a silent prayer. "I need a visa into Poland by tomorrow." He looked at his watch. "Make that today. I'm sorry to come like this. There was really no choice."

For a moment the Welshman didn't reply, but Tristram could see the geniality drain from his face, the black eyes darken.

Eric had a large, hooked nose that glistened in the neon light.

"When did you get here?" he asked quickly, quietly.

"Tonight. Came in from London."

"Why didn't you get the visa there?"

"Dangerous." Tristram could feel Eric's eyes dissecting his thoughts. "Something's wrong in London," he added. "Seemed safer to come here."

"Huh!" Eric snorted derisively. "Since when is it safer to walk into this snake pit? Things must be pretty bad in London if you've got to start booking your holidays over here." He picked up the bottle and carelessly poured another glass. "Why should I trust you?"

The dog sighed loudly, raised his head off the floor, and laid it on Eric's feet.

"Because if I were from Romanian security, we wouldn't bother playing games with you. You know that. They get their pleasure in other ways."

"True." Eric sat back and appeared to make up his mind. He got to his feet. "Give me your passport." He didn't say anything else, didn't say yes or no, didn't need to, thought Tristram. For the face was once again puckish, confident. And Eric and the dog were hurrying through the door, down the steps and out into the city.

Tristram felt the loneliness settle around him. Looking at the dirty kitchen, he imagined Eric must have lived in similar squalor during his early life back in Wales. It had all been on file—the mining family, the red-brick hovel beneath the highway, the sickly sister, and it hadn't taken Eric long to realize that life came in bigger sizes and a prettier package elsewhere.

Eric, he recalled, had been lucky. Cocky and lucky. The kind, they said, that always swung the world by the tail. So he'd got a place at the local polytechnic to be an engineer and had promised his friends he'd someday build himself a ladder and climb out of South Wales once and for all.

One summer a fellow student had suggested a holiday in Romania—really cheap, buddy, terrific bargain. So Eric and a party of friends had gone off for two weeks to the Black Sea, where it hadn't rained once and the girls would do it just for a rayon shirt and a razor blade for their legs. Paradise.

Somewhere far down the corridor Tristram heard shouting. But it wasn't Eric. Not yet. Give him time.

Of course when he thought about that trip to

Romania, the local talent spotters would have been all over those students, sorting the bright from the hopeless and really letting fly with the Georgian brandy. And Eric would have stood out, with his large frame and his ill-fitting clothes, the gentle giant from the valleys, his eyes just beginning to open.

When the two-week holiday was over he had been offered a job on the English-language service of Radio Bucharest, beaming out dismal stories of Western injustice and eulogies about workers' cooperatives. He was to have an apartment and a car—what a lark!—one of those ass-in-the-air Renaults that the French no longer wanted. But to Eric it signaled riches and fame, fame and riches. He hadn't thought about it, just said yes then and there.

Tristram wondered when Eric had begun to see through it. Maybe he had just grown tired of the lying and fawning, cold food, no meat, a sense of fun, like Dachau on a wet afternoon. In any case, somewhere along the line he had lost the joy of it all and the Service had spotted him like a lighthouse in a sea of gray. When the revolution came in '89, he had lain out of sight, and thank God for that.

A half hour went by, forty minutes, and something made Tristram look up. Eric was standing in the doorway watching him.

It took Andrew Milton longer than it should have to decipher the message. And when he'd finished he was sweating with anxiety.

First time he'd had a snap from London. First time they'd dropped him in it. And they really had this time, because he didn't know the procedure. Not properly. Just from the course. Six weeks last summer and a hundred warnings about not fucking it up.

He read the tape a second time. Quite specific for them. No woolly nuances. Just get on with it.

Someone from London had gone over. Might pass your way. Warn assets against any direct approach.

Milton unlocked the safe, took out a book, and leafed through it.

Later, much later, he knew he shouldn't have done it, shouldn't have called, shouldn't have pressed the panic button. But he didn't know what else to do. And when it all came down to it, he didn't know the man, hadn't ever seen the new Romanian security police in action, and he wanted to finish it quickly because Melissa was such a difficult bloody woman, she and her parents.

Eric reached for the phone, held it a moment, and then replaced the receiver. He didn't take his eyes off Tristram.

"Phantom caller." Eric made a face and pulled the British passport from his jacket. "See this. A gift from Uncle Eric . . ."

The phone rang again and they both froze, standing there in the kitchen with the neon light starting to flicker and the dog in his basket in the corner. Eric was counting. Four rings. Then it stopped.

"Right, that's it." And the look said it even before the words. "We'd better get you out of here."* Suddenly he was moving rapidly and Tristram felt the panic like a jab in the chest, the dryness in his throat.

* That's a signal: "Break all contact."

"What is it? What's going on?"

"Move man, move, I said. That was trouble. Have you left nothing behind?"

"Nothing."

They were through the door, two men and a sleepy dog, and Eric wasn't waiting for the elevator—taking the stone stairs in great bounds and the dog scampering ahead of them. Tristram was out of breath. He was slow, but he made it out of the building, tripping once on the ice, just in time to see the moon rise over the clouds, lighting his way to the little car.

They had all gone to bed by the time Milton made it back to the flat. There was a note on the kitchen table: "I do think you might have come back earlier. Mum and Dad were jolly upset. Daddy wanted to talk to you about your investments, and they're going on Thursday. Don't forget the milk if you're out early."

He sat down and thought it over. Could he have done it differently? What were the other options? Of course there was all the nonsense about chalk marks and stickers on park benches, a certain kind of scratch on a car door, a newspaper through the mailbox, but all that took time. And London had said urgent. No delays. But he knew the risk.

He tiptoed into the bedroom and slid soundlessly under the comforter. But Melissa was such a light sleeper. "Why d'you have to wake me up?" The muffled voice was sleepy but annoyed.

"I've been here for hours," he whispered. "Just went out to the bathroom."

"Liar."
She turned over and wrenched the covers off him.

By the time Milton fell asleep Romanian security had checked Eric's phone and they knew where the calls had come from. Both of them. And in a hurried meeting at headquarters they decided, in view of everything, that Eric was worth a much closer look.

So while Milton was sipping coffee and reading a five-day-old copy of *The Times* in the British Embassy, they had the cars out, cruising quietly into the southern suburbs, nothing noisy, not that anyone had the power to stop them or run. Quietly the new security machine had taken its place in a government too split and weak to stand up to it.

They took Eric across town and didn't bother to chat at all until he was spitting blood into a bowl and his wrist had been fractured behind his neck.

And all he could think about was the stupidity that had brought him there in the first place and the holiday in Romania, and the little Welsh family, who, even as he sat there taking the punches, would be eating breakfast beneath the highway—fried bread and cereal. And it was probably drizzling, the way it mostly did in South Wales.

Remarkably he kept his thoughts off the questions they were asking, the inconsistencies, the meetings and encounters that they'd known about for months, the conversations they'd bugged.

They really did have most of it, he decided, but it was worth giving Tristram a chance—that funny middle-aged creature who'd mouthed a shy "Bless you" as he was dropped at his hotel, waving good-bye in the light of the city dawn.

In the late afternoon they brought Eric the remains of his dog that they had assiduously run over with a truck and dumped in a plastic container. It was only then that he broke down and told them everything.

By which time James Tristram had landed in Warsaw.

"Why did you lie?" Cornish had stepped suddenly from an alcove along Hungerford Bridge, taking her arm, matching her pace. By the time she struggled he was gripping her. There was nowhere to go. Only forward.

"I didn't lie." She pulled away, but didn't run.

"You're not stupid, Jane. Don't try and act a part."

"My name's June." She turned and looked at him straight-on. It occurred to her that in other circumstances she might have laughed. But not here on the bridge, beside the waters of the Thames with no one to help her.

"I'll ask you again—why did you lie?"

They reached the end of the bridge before she spoke, taking the steps to the side, wending their way carefully down toward the Embankment.

"I lied because you lied to me." She tossed her head at him. "I know who you are."

"Who am I?"

"You're some sort of government man, something secret I s'pose. But it doesn't really matter. You tried to deceive me. And I've never liked that sort of thing."

"And now that you know?"

She crossed the road ahead of him.

"I still can't help you. And even if I could, I'm not sure I would."

"You might be able to help your friend." Cornish fell in beside her.

"You don't really believe that, do you?"

He didn't answer.

"You see I have this feeling that neither of us can really help him now. Not you, not me. I was thinking of that tonight at the dance class. Perhaps there was nothing any of us could do."

"Why do you say that?"

"Just a feeling. Some of us have to carry our own crosses. Maybe he was one of those."

"Was?"

"Just a word. You see, neither of us know, do we?"

They walked on for a moment, like a long-married couple, not holding, not talking.

"I supposed you loved him." Cornish hadn't planned to ask but he couldn't help it.

June stopped walking. "No, but I might have, if there'd been time. You sort of know these things, don't you?"

She went on but Cornish didn't follow. Odd, he thought, to have delved into the private life of James Tristram. Odd, because for fifteen years or so he hadn't really had one. There had been little enough to put in his file—except the dancing. And now his partner had decided that he wouldn't be coming home. And she wasn't alone in that.

In the distance he could see the small figure climbing back onto the bridge, losing herself in the crowd.

24 _____

The wind had sketched patterns in ice across the glass and for a moment Passent couldn't be sure. Carefully he eased open the door and stared out into the square. The briefest glimmer of light fell across the gray fur coat and he knew Ania was on the move. But God, she was confident, taking the street slowly and thoughtfully, dressed in her finery, like an invitation to a mugging.

Not too close though. Don't frighten the little tart away. See where she takes her secrets, follow the chain link by link. She had to be mad, though, with heels like that on the ice. A miracle she hadn't broken a leg. Nice legs too. Plenty of comfort from them on a winter's night.

Of course he could have taken her now. But what could he do with her when there's no help, not even a car? And the odds are bad with a single watcher, the odds are terrible, the risk enormous.

For the victim need turn only once, hearing a footstep, seeing a shadow, sensing an unwelcome and hostile presence, and you're blown right out of it.

From a distance of a hundred yards Passent could
see she had picked up speed and was onto the main
road before he'd realized it, stepping out into the oncoming cars. The little Fiat stopped to pick her up
way before he could get there. But he did see the
taillights moving south and the indicator flashing left
at the next junction. And then he smiled to himself.
Ania was returning to the Victoria Hotel, back to
work. He'd know where to find her. Of course he
would. Not tonight, while she was pleased with herself and confident, but later, when her guard was
down.

Despite the cold, Passent decided to walk home. He
rented a large prewar apartment just across from the
Central Railway Station—plenty of dark wood paneling and hardwood floors. But it was bare and antisep-
tic. Even the cockroaches had left. And the drink
didn't help. After his third glass of brandy he still
had no idea what he would say to Ania, how he
would handle it when he finally crossed her path, and
whether his courage or his hatred would see him
through.

They had watched as Ania hit the street. Grazyna
had seen the shadow fall in beside her. Coincidence?
The stab of doubt that can force the reappraisal of an
entire operation. Only this time there was no leeway,
no exit.

Maybe, she thought, the watcher was alone. But
why would they do that? Eyes traveled in pairs.
There was nothing for it. They'd have to split and
take separate routes. Rendezvous in the south in

twenty-four hours, and then move it, for the days were running short.

"You know where to go?" She turned to Garten. They had dimmed the lights. His face was in shadow.

"The old place?"

"You sound surprised."

"I am—surprised no one betrayed it. After all, a lot of other things went down the drain."

"Yeah . . . and people." She looked into those green eyes of his. She hadn't forgotten how angry they could be. Not even after all these years . . .

"I wasn't trying to—"

"Stop it, Jozef."

As she said it she could hear the echo of a thousand past squabbles, his naiveté, his idealism—and she like an immovable brick wall, both feet on the ground, always barring his path. Drop it, Jozef. Drop it then, drop it now. Don't come back into my life and fill space.

"Perhaps I should go first." Said so quietly. They both turned from the window, remembering that Dyadek was still standing shyly by the door. Beside him Maya Angelica slept with a blanket wrapped around her.

"If I go now, you'll know one way or the other. It won't matter if I'm seen. I could have been in one of a hundred flats."

"You'll warn Ania, then?" Grazyna went over to the priest and took hold of his hand.

He nodded, letting himself out, easing the door shut behind him, practiced and silent.

Again they looked down into the square, but no one appeared behind Dyadek. The area was deserted.

In the distance, beyond the rooftops, a reddish hue hung over the city.

"Is the priest going down as well?" Garten was tense, excited. She could almost feel his pulse.

"No, he stays here. He doesn't take part in any decisions."

"Which leaves just you and me."

"I make those decisions, Jozef. Me. The ex-wife. Got it?"

You're tough, he thought suddenly. Much tougher and more attractive than you used to be. But then what did I expect?

"What d'you want me to do?" he asked. Docile, suddenly, obliging. He could see only her profile, the fuller figure against the window.

"Steal a car. Make your own way down there. It'll be light in a few hours."

"And you two?" He gestured toward the girl.

"We go another way."

"We could go together."

"Not anymore, Jozef. Not anymore."

It was many hours later when Dyadek saw his bed. He had returned to find a fifteen-year-old girl crying outside the door of his apartment. He had carried her inside, given her tea by the fire, and learned that her father had died that night in the hospital.

He had known her from birth, baptized her, he recalled, watching as the words jumbled with the tears, the little head jerking in anguish and pain.

For the rest of that night he had forgotten the underground, forgotten the subterfuge and deceit and thought only of the mission for which he had been ordained. The simplicity of it, the beauty of providing warmth and caring, solace for the bereaved.

He returned again to his apartment, sucking the cold morning air through his teeth. Only a few people were about. His people, he told himself, his flock. For that night, surely, he had been a shepherd.

And he thought again of the girl, the advice and sympathy he had given, how the church would help her, the kindnesses she would receive from the parish. She would not have to face the world alone. He would see to it himself.

As he lay on the rough pillow he felt somehow cleansed, regenerated. Maybe God would give him new strength, maybe the double life could end. Someday, he felt sure, there would be peace and security for all.

25 _____

The daylight is no friend to Auschwitz, to the barbed-wire fences, to the watch towers, to the railway tracks and sprawling prison blocks. Even the stark countryside around it seems diseased and disfigured.

Above the main entrance to the camp hangs the wrought-iron inscription *"Arbeit Macht Frei"*—Freedom Through Work—one of history's more grotesque calumnies.

Mostly it's the foreign tourists who come to stare, often in silence, as they visit the cells and bunkers and examine the instruments of death. But sometimes a former inmate will return, driven by the need to purge his nightmares, to free the faces of the dead and the dying from his memory.

Year after year the relatives of the victims still come. They bring flowers and stay close to one another, often covering their faces with handkerchiefs, lost in grief. The guides and caretakers recognize them and leave them in peace. Only at night do they move them gently toward the exit, taking care not to hustle or offend.

And then there's the peace of Auschwitz, won out of the suffering of hundreds of thousands, brought here in cattle cars to die of cold or malnutrition or murder, their shouts, their anger carried away by the winds that sweep westward across the plains of Central Europe.

To that place came the leaders of the underground, some in groups, men and women, a child or two with them, as the late afternoon sun headed for the horizon across the border in East Germany.

They had all noticed Grazyna, the long blond hair bound beneath a black woolen cap, the little girl beside her, but they gave no sign of recognition. In the chilly air they stopped and listened, talked among themselves, straggled slowly. There was nothing to tell them apart from the other visitors, twenty of them summoned from all parts of the country, from the mining areas of Silesia, from the tri-city of Gdansk, from the lakes and the mountains, they had heard the call and answered.

They all shared the knowledge. Each had memorized the number of the old cell block, the nineteen steps to the basement, the lavatory door where there was no lavatory. Just a table and chairs, a bare light bulb, bare floors, and the business to transact.

From her place at the head of the table, Grazyna eyed them one by one. They offered no greetings, rough men and women with hard bony faces. Behind them the years of sacrifice and struggle. Such people, she observed, held no comfortable philosophies, possessed no charm or grace. With each morning came the cheerless decision to obstruct the government that ruled their lives, to undermine its security, and in the end to smash it. There would be no small talk here, no time wasting.

In the corner the coats had been piled on the floor, sheepskins and woolen greatcoats, an army uniform, a mound of fur hats. And now they sat in their cardigans and jackets, in overalls and shirt-sleeves, the secret representatives of a country that they had declared to be at war.

Truly, thought Grazyna, looking at them through the cigarette smoke, hearing the silence echo around her, you hold our future in your hands.

Garten had been the last to arrive. She'd known he would be. Jozef would make an entrance, cut a figure. Jozef would seize the dramatic, exploit it, make it his own.

He had swung almost silently through the door, shutting it behind him and then turning to face the group, without even a word, meeting each pair of eyes, not flinching. A silent pledge of strength.

And the sheep had gone for it, hadn't they? The return of the prodigal Pole had proved too much. Grazyna could see a tear on a few rough cheeks; one or two shook their heads in disbelief. And they had risen to applaud him, and welcome him in, to hug the slight figure in the blue parka, Zbig's son, come home to fight.

She alone had remained seated, and they hadn't liked that. She read the set of their chins, the clenched jaws, the resentment just below the surface.

Of course they didn't give a damn about her reasons, her daughter, the man who had turned his back on them, the agony of desertion. All they cared about was the operation. And they'd bought it without even removing the wrapper. Just like the old days. If it sounded right, then it was.

Jozef, you're so cunning, she thought. But you were never this good. Who taught you? Who trained you? And the professional in her began to applaud. But not the woman, not her. She could see through the fancy phrases, the come-with-me-and-we'll-triumph song, the patriotism, the Church, the Russians. Jozef was pressing all the buttons that counted, winding the people up, blurring the line between reality and dreams.

We Slavs, she reflected. We're so easy. Give us a cause and a fairy tale and we'll die for both of them. We can't resist a pull like that.

Almost imperceptibly Garten took control of the little gathering. Gradually they had shifted in their chairs, away from Grazyna toward him. Nothing was said or decided, but she had lost control all the same. She felt the despair creep into the room and stand beside her.

When it was over they began to make pledges of their own—full support in the mines, factories, and shipyards. A strike, then a demonstration, a street battle and the sacking of public buildings. And then?

The question had come from a thin, almost skeletal figure near the center of the room. And then?

Garten was on his feet. "We'll have shown the world there can be no deals with the Communists."

And then? The voice sounded bored but persistent.

"They'll back down. Force them out of the coalition."

And then? The rest of the room had fallen silent. The two men held the stage between them.

"We show them we won't be fobbed off like all the other times."

And then? The voice was rising now to a climax.

"My friend"—Garten moved away from his place and began to walk the length of the table—"what is it you want? A fight with me or with our enemies? If we do something now, we stand a chance of settling the score finally, for the sake of everyone."

Now the man got to his feet—a farmer, before that a fighter in the army. He didn't know what an easy life was.

"I don't believe you." He looked around, savoring his moment, buttoning the green cardigan. "I don't believe any of it. I say we're being used. I say you've come back from the West wanting us to stick our necks out only to get them chopped off. I say you're going to get us all killed." He paused. His cheeks were flushed. "I say that instead of winning, we're going to see the worst repression here since Stalin. Look, for the first time since the war we have something close to democracy. Not everything, but better than it was. But you want to see it all go to hell. You want to know what I think? I think you're all mad."

For a moment he stood there like a fox at bay, and the long faces at the table told him he'd found no support. Awkward, angry, he made for the door, but Garten's voice seemed to catch him by the shoulder, spinning him around.

"Be careful, friend." The man picked up his coat and kept on walking. "I said be careful. Think what you want, but don't go spreading your thoughts around. You're a Pole, friend. Not just any old trash. Think very hard."

They had wandered out of the airless, poky basement, no longer tidy and sterile, but left carelessly, like an unmade bed. Just the two of them remained. Grazyna looked down the table to Garten.

He couldn't keep that smile off his face, that red face tinted with victory. Slick and confident, that one. Had them eating out of his hand. A few clever epithets and a bit of the old magic, his father's magic. And that's all it had taken. Especially now, after years of boredom, years without a proper fight. That's what they wanted, all of them. Give them heads to bash and cops to kick and they'd be happy all day. And Garten would make them happy. How little it took, she reflected. Far, far less than she'd ever imagined.

He got up from the table. "Look, I'm sorry about the meeting—"

"You shit!"

"They didn't give me a choice—"

"Choice! You didn't want a choice. It's what you came back for. Man with a mission—that's what you wanted."

"I did what was best. What d'you think I came back for?"

"I . . . D'you know something, Jozef? I don't even care what you came back for. Not now. There were times when it might have mattered, in the early days, just after you left. I might have cared then. But you didn't have any place for us, we weren't included in your little plans, were we?" The voice rose in a shriek. "We didn't even know if you were alive or dead. D'you know how that feels?" Grazyna turned away from him, leaning her head against the wall. The tiredness came suddenly and for a moment she seemed to sway.

"You know something, Jozef? I've been thinking about this for a long time, and I know what you are now. I really do. You're one of those cowards who thinks he's a brave man. And d'you know something else? . . . They're the most dangerous of all."

In the dacha outside Moscow the Russian, barely able to contain his excitement, had seen off his visitors. A collection of ponderous old crows, he told himself, apparatchiks and fawners, the men who now surrounded the new General Secretary and were charged with his security.

Security. What a joke. They couldn't arrange security for a teacup, and so they had come to him for advice, wanting to tap his experience. And he had given them that. Oh most willingly, most happily. How good of you to come, how kind of you to ask. Have some more tea. Indian tea, of course. And some biscuits. They're called shortbread. I get them from an old contact in Scotland. A wink and a nod. And the four most respected envoys from the proletarian state of Lenin had supped and gorged themselves as greedily as they knew how. Glorious indeed to be one of the "haves" and be surrounded by the "have-nots."

He had shared with them a few memories from the

old days, from inside the Lubyanka, when they hadn't been too careful about the ways they'd gotten information, nor too careful about the bodies they'd disposed of. But he could see they had no appetite for that. One had even choked up half his tea, the wasteful devil. But they were the new breed, no stomach for anything except selling out the creed.

They had asked about crowd control. He'd nearly laughed out loud at that one. In the old days the crowds hadn't needed controlling. You merely manipulated them, fed them on promises and propaganda, and they would lie down in their baskets like the fools they were. Crowd control!

And as for the trip to Warsaw, he had lied through his teeth about that. No need for excessive measures, he'd assured them. The Poles have changed, they like us these days. They like the General Secretary. They admire the new openness in our society. We're friends again. You won't get any trouble from them.

And they'd gobbled that up as well, as the housekeeper had brought the cold meats and vodka, the French champagne to be served in the Waterford crystal—and then they had toasted the success of everything. The traditional fat cat's toast, the best of everything for the world, and the best of all that for us.

After that it had taken them nearly an hour to get their coats back on, falling over each other and giggling like babies. And to end the disgusting spectacle he had helped them out to the cars himself, anxious to get rid of the great useless hulks.

It was only then that the telephone had rung. Only

then that he had heard the low, dull voice from Poland and the news for which he had waited.

London's agent, Garten, was in place and had taken over the underground. And now, inexorably, the operation would go forward into its final phase.

For almost an hour he paced through the dacha, moving soundlessly from room to room. *Just a few more steps*, he thought to himself, *and I'll be there*.

26 _____

The thin farmer had pulled his sheepskin tight about him and left Auschwitz in a hurry. Standing ankle deep in the snow, he had hitched a lift from a truck driver and they'd hit Warsaw well after dark. Two buses and a taxi had completed the journey, and shortly before midnight he had reached a small farming hamlet northeast of the capital.

Worn out by the journey, he slept until late the next day. There was little to be done on the farm. His wife had fed the six pigs they owned, the hens squawked inside the barn, two old cart horses dozed in their makeshift stable. It was the worst of the winter and they would all sleep through it. Just as they did every year.

On Monday morning he walked his seven-year-old son to school across frozen fields, where the stick trees grew out of the snow gaunt and ugly. More snow and then more snow would come, and only when it had exhausted them, left them pale and depressed, would the sun break through the clouds and release the spring.

It didn't help the little boy. His asthma had worsened, and the doctor who'd come out once from Warsaw had not been helpful.

"Take him to the sun."

The farmer laughed. "Yes, of course, how stupid of me. The Riviera? California?"

And they hadn't raised the subject again. There was nowhere to go and never would be.

Yet it hurt him to hear the boy coughing away at night, struggling to breathe, the pallid, shy creature who walked beside him, afraid of strangers, afraid of his teachers, afraid of his shadow.

Not that there hadn't been reason for fear. You only had to think back to the old days of the farmers' unions, when hordes of those burly, rough-coated fellows had wandered through his kitchen at all hours of the day and night. And they hadn't been the only ones to wander. He hadn't forgotten the little gray Fiats that used to wait at the bottom of the drive, with men who never spoke, never wound down their windows, just whispered into their radios and sat there day after day.

He couldn't go through that again.

They had reached the school and he bent down to kiss the boy on his cheek, watching him go in without a word, without a backward glance.

Those days, he reflected. All the shouting with his wife, her fear, his panic, the boy's illness. Sometimes he hadn't known how to contain it all. And it wasn't until that day in December 1981 when they'd declared martial law, taken him away, with all his workers and friends, locked them up in an internment camp, shattered their Christmas, that he'd realized they'd wasted their time.

You couldn't change this system, you couldn't even make a dent in it. You could never find the people who ran it, the faceless bureaucrats in the bowels of the Central Committee. The people who really ran it. They'd been cemented in during the Stalin times and they never came out.

As he neared the farm he could see a car about a hundred yards down the road. It must have been parked, for even at that distance he heard the engine start. Too far to see a license plate, too far to see a face. And he knew most of the cars in the area, but he didn't know that one.

As the day passed he thought no more about it. His wife had gone to see relatives in Warsaw, two of the farmhands fed the animals and led the cart horses out for exercise, hay was fetched from the loft in the barn. And for a long time he gazed out of the kitchen window at the snowscape, thinking of the meeting, thinking of what to tell the other farmers when they came that night.

At three o'clock the sun was low in the sky and he tramped his way back to the village school, nodding to the mothers and fathers, the little gaggle of children that shot out as the doors were opened.

The boy said nothing on the walk home, and it was only when he'd eaten his tea, some bread and cheese, milk and an apple, that he produced a crumpled letter from his pocket.

"I found this. It's for you."

His father sat up. "What d'you mean you found it?"

"It was lying on my desk. Has your name on it. The teacher didn't know where it came from."

The man picked it up, seeing the letters stamped hard on the envelope with a ballpoint.

He opened it up and read it, and his expression must have altered quite suddenly, for the boy put down his apple and bent forward to touch his father's arm.

"Dad, what is it?"

The man got up and went to the window.

"Dad!"

"It's all right." He wouldn't turn around. "Just have to think of something. It's all right."

He didn't want the boy to see his fear, didn't want him to see the shaking hand. After a few moments he snatched up the letter and threw it in the fire, and yet he couldn't forget the wording.

I'm bringing this home, it had said, *to ask you to think of your loyalties as a Pole. If you don't, there'll be another letter, but I won't be able to bring it.*

He looked hard at the boy's anxious face. The child had no clue as to what he had delivered.

27 _____

Along the Arbat, even in the cold, thirty or forty people had gathered beneath the clustered street-lamps. It's the fashionable stretch of central Moscow —the pedestrian precinct, with its antiquarian bookstores and picture shops, now dark and shuttered for the night.

And yet among the students and actors there was laughter and the music of a guitar—the twin sounds of thawing politics. Only the winter was locked in steadfastly.

The Russian moved silently among the people, the two younger officers at his elbow. A surprise, they had promised him, a little relaxation after business. He dabbed unenthusiastically at his nose. In the cold it dripped interminably.

A sudden tug on his arm and the three of them turned right under an archway into a courtyard, then a second courtyard, and an old double door opened in front of them.

Even as it swung toward them the Russian could hear the sounds of animated conversation, of singing,

of cutlery on plates. A uniformed guard appeared in
the hallway and it was then that he heard a thousand
warning bells, loud and clear. Without waiting, he
turned on his heel, half dragging the two men with
him, pulling them out into the darkness, apologizing
in a loud, drunken dialect, accelerating away from
the door. The guard shouted and slammed the door
behind them, but the Russian didn't stop until he was
back on the Arbat, way down toward the inner ring.

"What the . . . ?" One of the officers wrenched his
arm free. The Russian swung toward him.

"Fools, both of you! What in the name of Christ
were you taking me there for? That KGB whore-
house is for ignorant scum, for drunks, for the clap-
ridden sons and daughters of our officers. I'd almost
forgotten it existed. Fucking idiots!" He cuffed one of
the men around the face, and for an instant the three
of them stood in the doorway of a shop, their breath
coming fast and loud, the shadows merging against
the old cracked walls of the houses.

"Comrade, I fail to understand your concern. The
place is secure." The older of the two officers glared
at the Russian.

"Then you understand nothing. A public lavatory
is more secure than that house of reptiles."

"But surely, Comrade, it is good that we are seen in
public together, then there can be no suspicions."

The Russian gripped him by his lapels. "You stupid
lump of shit. Don't play games with these people,
don't try to bluff them. If you have something to
hide, then hide it, *and* yourself. You will not survive
long if you forget that."

The two KGB men lapsed into silence. Even in

civilian clothes they wore their rank and their arrogance. The one who had spoken had pale cheeks,
pockmarked from acne. In the street lighting his face
held the texture of a gravel driveway. He lapsed into
a sullen, oafish mood.

They walked in silence toward Kalinin Prospekt.
The Russian decided to ease the atmosphere.

"What time does your flight leave?"

"Five-thirty in the morning, Comrade."

"Breakfast in Warsaw, then. You anticipate no
problem with the security arrangements?"

"None at all." The pockmarked face swiveled toward the Russian. "All the arrangements for the
General Secretary's visit should have been completed. We make the final checks and report back."

"To me."

"To you, Comrade." There was the briefest of
pauses. "And to others."

"Of course." The Russian returned the man's
glance. Cheeky boy, he thought, but don't play games
with me, my little dove, because I was cheating long
before you even learned the rules.

"We meet then in three days." His look took in the
two of them, savoring the final sting. "Give my best
wishes to your wives and families."

In that instant, before the men turned away, their
eyes registered the threat and the warning and understood them. The Russian was quite certain of it.

At dawn he picked up the tie line to Warsaw.
There was no routing through the international exchange. Channels within channels, the Russian reflected. Set up with KGB equipment and resources

and yet the KGB had no record of it. Friends were useful while you had them or had a hold on them. He remembered what an American president had said about his hometown! If you want a friend here, buy a dog. It certainly held good for Moscow.

"Our two lovers are on their way."

"Uh?" It took Klimov a moment to wake. His wife turned over in bed and kicked him angrily on the kneecap. "Yes, yes, of course. I understand."

"You may possibly have another guest."

"I see." Klimov sat up. "It would have been better if we had alerted our friends here to help us."

"From what you were telling me earlier, we have precious few friends in that direction. . . ."

"But . . ."

"I will handle it personally. This one is mine."

Klimov heard the phone go dead. As he got up his wife kicked him again.

28 _____

So many times Tristram had wanted to chuck it in, even give himself up. He remembered when they'd come for him in Prague. There had been the sneaking, insidious comfort in knowing the whole thing was over. No choices left. Nothing you can do, old chap. Just lie in your cell and talk to the funny man in uniform with the bright lights.

And for a time it would have been so easy, because then they let you sleep, leave you alone, even feed you. If you cooperate.

Ten years since he'd last stepped into Poland as part of a trade delegation that wasn't, as a trade delegate who wasn't, as an agent looking for potential recruits. And that's the way it had been. A fishing trip, make friends, buy a few too many vodkas, flash the legal tender, hint, hint, hint, and maybe a shadow would cross yours.

Different now. No safety net, no colleagues, a false visa. He couldn't even check into a hotel. So it had been straight to the station in a taxi. The suitcase had to go. Into the station checkroom, and it wouldn't be coming out again. You can't roam the streets with a bloody suitcase, like some stranded tourist.

Leaving it was a liberation. Back on the street with your wits and nothing else. Shirt and underwear washed each night and hung on a radiator. That's how it would be. His mind began feeding him the details, some good, some bad. The sun was shining high in the sky as he headed toward the Old Town, stopping for a freshly blackened pizza, eating while he walked, as light-headed as if he were somewhere else.

Garten would have felt the same, he reflected. And now the two of them were back East. He'd have to find the man and get him out. He'd made that decision. Somehow the operation had been hijacked. He didn't know how—but Garten was now working unknowingly for the Russians' cause. He had to be stopped, found and stopped.

Outside St. Anne's Cathedral the police stood guard beside an old Solidarity monument, their aim to prevent any antigovernment demonstrations nearby. How weak and insecure they must be, thought Tristram, to be scared of a stone symbol. How quickly the mood had changed.

He mingled with the tourists in the Castle Square, all cameras and hand in hand. The groups, the couples, the students, and then he was in the narrow lane outside the cathedral. And this was where it would happen. Not for nothing had he sat in London year after year reading all the underground reports, knowing who was who, where they hung out, the escape lines, the courier networks, the informers in the police and army. Well, this is the day, James Tristram, when you carry all that to the bank and cash it in.

Strange thoughts to take into a cathedral. And Tristram's flabby face was red from the cold and from the excitement that rose inside him. Flustered, suddenly, he stopped just inside the great doorway, looking down toward the altar.

Without thinking, he crossed himself. Did I do that? Never happened before. But you have to act the part, you've got to blend in. Anyway, a prayer can't hurt. And I of all people, I need a prayer.

Around him he could hear the soft whispers, tiny echoes from the vast ornate ceiling, from the pillars and stone walls. Centuries of hushed words and suffering seemed to hang in the air. He made his way quietly to the left, to the curtains that cordoned off the vestry, away from the old men and women who sat thinking, the army recruit in uniform, Poles and foreigners. Friends and more friends, friends and enemies.

I could sit for a while, he thought. Two minutes won't make a difference. And it was only when he sank into a pew that the tiredness hit him. It was cold there. You took God's climate as you found it. No concessions to that. And he pulled his coat tighter around him. And then his eyes really wanted to close. In the old days he wouldn't have done it, but the self-control had gone. Fear is exhausting, it paralyzes all your functions, digs deep into your daily life, finds the moments of weakness. Thirty years since he'd been trained, ten years since he'd screwed it all up and come apart like a broken reed. Easy to do, of course. Agents are the most volatile of all, like drug

addicts. Some adjust for a while and enjoy it, others
go sick the moment they begin. Unless you come out
of it quickly, it will always end one way. Always.

Tristram remembered thinking that was just a sob
story and he wasn't going to buy into that one. He
didn't remember anything else before sleep arrived.

The commotion at the back of the cathedral shook
him awake. A sudden scream, then crying, and a
sharp wailing sound that echoed backward and forward through the building. And he knew where to
look—not for the source of the noise but for the action close by. Only the uninvolved scream, the by-
standers, the chance onlookers who come upon something that shocks them. The involved never scream,
never have time. As his eyes adjusted from sleep Tristram saw a man being held facedown on the flagstones. Three others had forced him to his stomach—
plainclothes agents, you could see that. The practiced
brutality, fingers on the pressure points, a knee in the
back. Textbook.

A clergyman had begun to remonstrate with them
and a crowd of worshipers gathered in a semicircle.
Three thugs in black leather coats, young and rough,
getting paid for what they liked doing best. And you
could see in their eyes, they couldn't believe their
luck. Tristram watched the face of the senior man—
the little smile at the corner, the smile of triumph, the
sweet exercise of power over the powerless. They
dragged the man to his feet, pushing him before them
out into the street, the priest left standing, his arms
outstretched in a gesture of helplessness, murmurs
rising from the little crowd. Tristram heard the word

Lapanki—raids, the same word used for the Nazi swoops during the occupation of Warsaw. He shrank back to his pew. So this was the city he'd arrived in. He should have expected it, random arrests, quick surgical strikes in public, a whole range of security restrictions slammed into effect before the sensitive visitors arrived.

And the Russian was really sensitive. This reforming Russian, setting nerves on edge throughout the Eastern Bloc, jangling alarm bells among all the cliques and party elites from East Berlin to Sofia. Tristram smiled to himself. The old foxes wouldn't have had a good night's sleep since the man had come to power. And now?

Now wasn't the time to hang around. If they were taking people from the churches, they were really worried. Best thing was to get out, stick to the open streets, return after dark for the evening service. Of course they'd be waiting, scouring the crowd. And yet he had to get in and make contact with the priest. Otherwise when night came he'd be alone on the streets, friendless and frozen. And they'd hunt him, corner him, cut him down where he stood.

The traffic had been halted in the morning rush hour and Ania could see the convoy in her rearview mirror. They were coming up fast behind her, the armored personnel carriers, jeeps, a few water cannon. And she lost count of the olive-green transporters droning past, snaking their way through the city. They were heading eastward to their barracks. Reinforcements. For days they had been streaming in from across the country. But why so many?

And yet she knew it had started. Really started. Not just the vague unchanneled plans that they'd kicked around late at night in apartments all over Warsaw. But an operation.

A militiaman waved her forward. Hard to keep to the speed limit. She could feel the tension forcing down her right foot. But play it carefully. No sudden moves. This is what you wanted.

It was a sixties terraced house, nice neighborhood, plenty of diplomats, a doctor, ministry men—and they didn't know who came to stay behind the pink walls. They assumed simply that it was a good Catholic, blessed with a large family—cousins, nieces, uncles, sisters. He said. They were there that afternoon as Ania rang the doorbell.

It was a shock, seeing the guns handed out, switchblade knives, too, a few rounds of ammunition, and yet she had known what would happen. The game stops here, she thought. Maybe it should have stopped a long time ago.

She wasn't the only one to think it. Standing there in the windowless basement, she realized that there was none of the usual banter or jokes. Like a love affair—the more serious it got, the less they talked. A young man nudged her. She knew him only by sight. "I never thought we'd see this day," he muttered.

"Nor did I."

They didn't speak again. And yet Ania felt a warmth between them. They would marry their destinies and in the streets of Warsaw they would rise up or fall together.

29 _____

The two KGB officers hadn't enjoyed the flight from Moscow. It was an army plane and the army doesn't like the security services. Their food packets had been stolen. No, there were no extras. Very sorry, Comrades. And the sergeant had burst out laughing and the savage, underheated transport plane had rocked to the sound of mirth.

A staff car had met the two of them in Warsaw, the pockmarked senior and his deputy, all quiet and keen and overawed, and they had driven northeast till they had put the confines of the city behind them.

In a disused barn they had stopped and changed clothes—new khaki, new shoulder insignia, brown boots, and the cap, so different from their own. And then back in the car, the new uniforms rough and tight against the skin. Polish uniforms, the way it had been planned. Now they would speak only Polish, a coarser, less melodic Slav than their own. But it was the language their families had spoken when they'd lived in the Western territories, before the forcible induction into the Soviet Union. Only these men were loyal, and that's why they had been chosen.

They got back on the road, but the going was hard. The temperature had risen a little and turned the icy road to slush. The Volga skittered and lurched from ditch to pothole.

They hated Poland. Not even a proper winter, said the senior man. Not even a proper country, came the response.

"Talk about opening the borders, don't they?"

"Talk too much if you ask me."

"Where will it all end?"

They both laughed at that. A secret, shared and enjoyed. And, God, wouldn't they show the bastard Poles what was what, reteach some discipline, bark them back into line like the sheep they were.

Of course they'd always be second rate, the Poles. The senior officer stretched languidly in the front of the car. It was all their old-fashioned nonsense about heroism. They weren't even clever enough to kick when their opponents were down, still imagined you could fight in a clean shirt and polished shoes. They didn't realize you had to get down in the gutter and claw your victim to death. No friendly fights. No exhibitions.

They turned off the main road. The track was a single lane that dipped down into a long, wooded valley. They were under the trees now. Branches scraped at the Volga, tore at the side-view mirrors, but the noise of the wheels had changed. The car was clanking along on metal tracks laid out like a railway line. It was designed, they guessed, for heavy trucks and armored vehicles. And suddenly they were in a clearing and they could see where the narrow road ended. Ahead of them, a canvas encampment that appeared to stretch away into the depths of the forest. White igloos had been erected around a central command post—a large square tent, with an array of radio antennas behind it. Groups of soldiers were eating on wooden benches.

The senior officer left the car and looked back the way they'd come. In a trench alongside the metal tracks he could see a machine-gun emplacement that hadn't been visible from the vehicle. No strangers would make it to the camp on that road. He was sure of it.

"Comrade Major."

A red-faced lieutenant saluted smartly. Polish uniform.

"Follow me."

The KGB officer knew where he was going. They'd prepared him a tent and would expect him to sit in it. Typical army—stall, delay, make excuses. He looked around him. In one corner a group of soldiers in arctic gear lounged against a truck, their caps pulled haphazardly onto the back of their heads, cigarettes dangling from mouths. Stretched out between two trees a row of underwear dangled on a makeshift washing line. Polish underwear.

His boots slithered through the slush. Angrily, he turned away from the soldiers.

"Where's your commanding officer?"

"He'll be with you shortly, Comrade Major. He asked me to make you comfortable."

The lieutenant gestured to one of the larger igloos, unzipping the canvas doorway.

"If there is anything you need, Comrade . . ."

"I shall summon you."

He looked about him. His junior officer had been shown to a similar tent some fifty yards away. Christ, what a setup. The place should have been buzzing, and all he could see were ill-dressed louts, heavy equipment idle and mud-bound, a row of T-62 tanks unattended, the crews nowhere in sight. Since when did those machines work by themselves? The men should have been maintaining, servicing them, not pissing about chatting.

He swung his bag into the tent. He knew then that it wouldn't do. Out of all the strike units, this was the most important. The whole plan hinged on it. Once the street violence got under way in the capital, this unit would have to move in and crush it.

Not in a hurry. They would first let the underground have its day. But then, with measured and progressive viciousness, they would clean them off the streets like the filth they were. A punitive operation against civilian targets. Routine procedure. God alone knew—they'd done it enough times in Russia. The mining strikes in the Donbass, the awful riot in Novocherkassk, and a hundred and one different occasions of which the West had never learned.

But this unit was a disgrace.

On impulse he zipped up the door of his tent and began walking. He needed to get his bearings, cover all the exits.

It took him no more than three or four minutes to reach the edge of the trees. A light breeze rustled them, swirling the snow from the surrounding fields. If anything, the clouds had sunk lower and visibility was getting worse. Tonight, most likely, they'd be fogged in.

He reached into his parka and brought out a pair of field glasses. In the poor light they were almost useless. But as he strained his eyes he could just make out a shape on the north side of the valley. What was it? For a moment the wind must have shifted, for suddenly the shape came clearly into view. A tiny farmhouse, some outbuildings, smoke rising from the chimney.

The KGB major examined it all carefully and replaced his binoculars.

Tristram had wandered into a supermarket, hoping to kill time, but the bare shelves and shoddy products repelled him, just as they always had. Piles of brown paper bags had been stacked in a corner. There was no attempt to package or attract. No bright colors. Instead the state was offering its people rationed fatty meat, mineral water, pickled vegetables, and canned tomatoes. It angered him. People weren't just sinking into poverty, they were having it thrust upon them.

A woman shop assistant shouted at him because he hadn't taken a wire basket. He said nothing. There was no shortage of rules, no shortage of people to enforce them. Like living in a zoo.

Finally, tired and unhappy, he made his way to the Victoria Hotel, knowing there was a coffee bar on the first floor.

If it hadn't been for the coat, he would never have raised his eyes. But the gray fox reminded him so much of his mother, the rich flamboyant lady who had in the end accumulated a string of husbands and an entire library of their check books.

Dear Mum, what a flirt you were. And as he looked up into the cool brown eyes and the black hair that encircled them—she smiled at him. Just a little too quickly, so that he knew she wasn't there for the coffee. He watched her go through the act, crossing the legs, the tongue tracing a line across the dark lipstick, a toss of the head to say she would take it or leave it, whatever happened.

He picked up his cup, and her movement was so rapid, so well executed that she was sitting opposite him at the table almost before he realized it. The smile had broadened, but she wasn't going to speak first. Let the client do the introductions. He knew how the professionals played it.

"I . . . I'm sorry. Good afternoon."

"Good afternoon." She sat back pleased with her English. The first potential customer all day and they'd told her to keep up appearances. The legs crossed again.

"Perhaps you'll join me in a cup of coffee?" Damn her.

"That would be nice."

A waitress brought another cup, and he poured from the silver pot.

"Are you staying here?" he asked.

"No, not really."

"Just come for tea?"

"Yes, that is correct. And you, Mr. . . . ?"

"James."

"And I am Ania. What are you doing in Warsaw?" Her hands locked slowly together.

Tristram examined her carefully. Eastern Bloc whores rarely worked for mere money alone. Was she asking questions or holding an interrogation?

He groped for his watch. "Look, I'm really sorry. I have to be going."

"You seem to be sorry all the time. Anyway, you haven't finished your coffee."

"No, but I'm meeting someone. . . ."

"Not a girl, I hope. If it's a girl, you're wasting your time or your money. . . ."

They both laughed together. "No, it's not a girl."

"Perhaps we shall see each other again." She passed him a little card. On it was a handwritten number. "You see, Mr. James, I have so little conversation, you understand?"

Tristram thought he saw the eyes darken. She tossed her head again. "What does it matter, anyway? I just thought we might have talked . . . so long since I did that. Please take this and call me. It's possible I can be helpful."

Helpful. The word stuck in Tristram's mind as he nodded and turned to go. Not a word most whores would use. Hardly a concept that applied to their function.

He hurried through the crowded lobby and out into Victory Square. Dusk and darkness were merging. A long line of taxis stretched outside the hotel, and the beautiful people of Warsaw were arriving for a reception.

Helpful, she had said. He walked swiftly past the Bristol Hotel, on toward the darkness of the Old Town. He might need someone helpful before too long.

30

The forest is never quiet. Animals seek out their prey, slithering, stalking, pursuing. By night they can use their extra senses, their radar, hiding their actions in the darkness. But day or night, all eaters are killers.

The KGB major heard the shouting as if in a dream, and then his tent was opened and a hand shook him roughly.

"Comrade Major, quickly. We need your help."

He pulled himself from the sleeping bag, drawing in his breath sharply as the wind attacked him, sucking out the warmth.

"What the fuck's going on?"

No answer.

Boots next, and the parka, zipping in one movement all the way to the fur-lined hood. And he was running along the tracks to the command center, three men around a jeep, lanterns in their hands, the engine running noisily, soldiers in battle capes falling in around them, the trees a dark shroud against the sky.

"Major, we have no time to waste. Let's go."

"Go where?"

"I'll explain. Get in."

They swung into the jeep. In an instant twigs and leaves were scratching his face, the cold wind numbing his senses. He snatched at the driver's shoulder.

"What is all this?"

The man turned for a split second. "Two of our lookouts, young fools, got themselves pissed, then went for a walk." He swerved to avoid a branch. Darkness on all sides. Only the headlights picking out a narrow trail. "Anyway, these bastards blundered into a farm, up on the ridge, started shooting the windows. We've surrounded them, but we need someone with perfect Polish to talk to the farmer. They mustn't know who we are. And they mustn't hear Russian spoken. That's where you come in. Talk to them, pacify them, while we flush out these two scum. If we don't do it quickly, we'll have the whole town out and then we'll be blown. We don't have a choice. You speak the best Polish. . . ."

The major cursed them under his breath, cursed them to hell and back again, as the jeep fought to stay on the tracks.

They had begun to emerge from the forest. He could see the hill in front of them, a streak or two of light in the sky, the dawn an hour away.

The farmer crouched with his wife and son in the basement, his heart racing. In the darkness he could hear the woman sobbing uncontrollably. He held the boy on his lap, gripping him tightly, pressing the terrified face into his shoulder.

He blessed his foresight in fixing a lock on the inside of the cellar door. But how long would it hold? How much pressure could it sustain?

As he crouched on the stone floor his mind went over the jumbled events, the dogs barking in the yard, the panic that had stabbed him into wakefulness, pulling his wife from the bed, running to the attic room where the boy slept as the first of the shots had smashed into the ground-floor windows. Automatic rifle fire. He could recognize the sounds. He'd trained on the weapons, knew their range and capability.

They had half fallen down the narrow staircase and he remembered noticing that the dogs had stopped barking, but then a second volley had come in and he could hear slates peeling back off the roof and the gush of water, and he knew then that the tank had been punctured. But who in hell was it?

The dogs were still silent. Beside him his wife was intoning a prayer in a thin, wailing voice. He reached over and shook her hard by the shoulder.

"Quiet, woman! Let me think!" He tried to recall the warning from the underground, but it made no sense. Would the underground go this far? It was then that he heard the vehicle pull to a halt outside, the boots running over the icy courtyard, and the bang of his door as it was wrenched open.

The major had seen the troops move forward. It hadn't been hard. Once they'd located the two soldiers, a squad had gone in with stun grenades and blown the bastards unconscious. Not a problem in getting them, but a big problem in mopping up.

As he looked about him he could see the damage.

The two dogs lay side by side in the slush—one of the heads had been half blown away. Over in the stables the horses were stamping their hooves, neighing, kicking at the stalls. As for the house—pipes were leaking, part of the roof had been punctured and a large number of windowpanes had been shot out. There'd be damage inside too—furniture ruined, crockery. Not bad for a night's work. He looked around again. The smell of cordite lingered over the courtyard. Now he'd have to be nice to the fucking people.

The lights inside were working as he pushed his way into the kitchen. Bullets had torn the plaster off the wall in long gouges. They hadn't been short of ammunition.

"*Czy ktos jest?* Is anyone here?" he shouted. "It's safe. I'm a Polish officer, Sixteenth District garrison." The voice seemed to echo through the house.

He hadn't heard the footsteps, nothing, but he turned quickly as the basement door opened and a thin figure in a nightshirt stumbled, blinking and unsteady, into the kitchen. The major could see that his hair was awry, his hands were twitching, gray stubble lined his cheeks, and it was a while before the man could speak coherently, a while before he could sit still and think.

At first light the major left the house. The wife had emerged with the boy and they had sat, all four of them, in the kitchen, with coffee and some ancient evil-smelling brandy. And the man had understood. Two drunken soldiers, a court-martial would be prepared. A matter of the utmost seriousness, and a team of engineers would make repairs in the morning. Could they move out for a day while the work was completed? A visit to a relative in Torun? That would be ideal. Humble and sincere apologies. A terrible incident, but if the family could keep it to themselves. After all, the reputation of the Polish soldier was at stake and the whole unit would have to suffer if news got out.

They had smoked a cigarette or two and the major had gotten up and left the pack. The jeep had returned him to the forest, and as he reached the command post the young lieutenant had been waiting for him.

"The commander wishes to thank you personally for your assistance."

"Tell the commander it can wait till the morning. I will then expect to take part in the disciplinary proceedings. A full report is necessary."

"That will not be required, Comrade Major."

He turned sharply. "And why is that?"

"The men were executed twenty minutes ago. It was in strict accordance with military code." The young face showed no emotion as the first glimmer of daylight shone down on it through the trees.

They boarded up the bedroom window and tried to sleep. Fear brings a tiredness all of its own, and yet the farmer couldn't rest, couldn't settle. The night had been shattered, the stillness of the farm, and he was much saddened by the loss of his dogs. The boy would miss them terribly. He hadn't told him. That would have to wait till morning.

But there was something else that nagged at him.

Perhaps it was the shouts of the soldiers, and yet they had been drunk and he had been half asleep and it hadn't been possible to make out what they were saying. A court-martial, the major had promised them. He wouldn't like to be in their shoes. And the major? Funny type, that one. Cold, blond, almost Scandinavian. And yet a lot of Poles looked like that. But the voice had been strange. Some odd expressions, sort of old-fashioned. Not the new Polish, full of slang and Westernisms, but formal, stilted. He'd heard that accent before, somewhere, but he couldn't place it.

He wanted to sleep, and was about to climb the stairs when he thought of the cigarettes he'd left on the table. Just one and then he'd sleep well. Today was Sunday, the workers were off, nothing else would happen, would it? And if he missed church that day, he could live with the frowns and the guilt, and the priest who would visit during the week asking why he had not brought the boy. They didn't care about him or the wife, but they really wanted the boy, wanted all the young children before the state got its claws into them.

He picked up the cigarette pack, toying with it, turning it over and over. Several minutes went by before he noticed it was a Russian pack, with Russian army markings. It took his breath away, for in that instant he knew where he'd heard that accent, knew where it came from, and his lip began to quiver as he realized the full extent of the danger.

Two hours later he packed his wife and son off to Torun as planned. As for himself, he walked two miles to the village, borrowed a motorcycle, and headed for the capital as fast as he could.

31 _____

His feet had begun to hurt, cold feet, dragging along the rough cobbles, through the gray streets, through the postwar reincarnation of the city of Warsaw. Tristram thought of Zbig, Zbig's city, uprooted, torn apart building by building by the Nazis, its heart removed and smashed, the golden youth and the golden culture consumed by the flame throwers, trampled by the tanks.

He knew Zbig's story, knew he had survived the hellish uprising in 1944, the street fighting and the terrible retribution that had followed.

Zbig had risen fast through the underground—a young man, barely out of the university, so tall, much taller than all the others. At the age of twenty-three he found himself in a resistance army that had literally died around him. One day he had awakened to find himself leading it, because there was no one else.

He had learned quickly. Tristram remembered the detailed researches he had made into the life and times of Zbig, researches that had never been completed, and now never would be. Zbig, who had led his war through the city sewers, through bombed-out buildings, through hideouts in the rubble. And even as the destruction had raged about him, still found safety below ground, often leading no more than a teenage rabble, a string of malnourished diehards to whom reaching the age of sixteen meant long life.

When the Russians had finally entered the city, after watching its annihilation from the safety of the eastern bank, Zbig had left. As he walked out thousands of wounded and homeless flocked back in.

Somehow in the confusion he wandered off across Europe and eventually hit an American unit in Germany. He was dazed, shell-shocked—and unable to talk.

By then Allied intelligence was fully aware of the Soviet strategy. They knew that in 1944 the underground had been told to rise up, promised Soviet support, but it had never materialized. Why, they wondered, had the underground believed Moscow in the first place? They counted on the young giant in the field hospital near Munich to fill in the gaps.

There were weeks of silence, and then on a warm June afternoon a few moments of golden clarity. Zbig had told them of the underground's doubts. They knew the Soviets were unreliable. But the voice of one man had been decisive. Zbig had rubbed his eyes and stared out of the window.

The American intelligence officer had touched his arm, trying to prompt him.

Zbig had coughed. They could see that sweat had broken out on his forehead.

"He was so persuasive."

"Who?"

"The Englishman." Zbig had paused. "Young man, he was, like all of us. Young and very, very brave. All the teenagers wanted to go with him on ambushes because he always came back. Such hope he inspired. You know, even with all the killings and executions, he could still make us laugh. There was joy in him, life in him, and nothing, it seemed, could take them away."

Again Zbig had stopped. A nurse had wiped his brow. There had been three of them in the room listening to him, silent because somewhere in his mind Zbig held a piece of history, vital, priceless.

"And then one day he went missing for about ten hours. No one knew what had happened. We were in despair. I even sent some people to try to find him, bring his body back if he was dead. Maybe he was wounded. How could we know? And it was late in the evening when he returned, bruised, tired, his clothes torn. But he said he had information . . . something like that . . . just information."

"What kind?" The intelligence officer had stepped forward.

"He . . . he said he knew for a fact that this time the Soviets would help us. This time it would work. We were to trust Moscow, and when they gave the order to start the uprising, we were to follow it. When we rose up they would push across the Vistula and drive the Nazis out."

Zbig's hands were shaking. The nurse gestured to the intelligence officer to leave. He stood his ground.

"You have to tell me who it was."

"Major, I must insist you leave." The nurse tried to pull him away.

"I can't leave." And the major was beside Zbig, crouching by the chair, gripping his arm. And now Zbig was shaking all over, and the sweat was across his face.

It was then that the nurse had returned with a doctor and a sergeant, and between them the major was dragged out into the corridor.

In the days that followed Zbig had suffered a relapse, and it was many weeks before he had been fit enough to return to his home, return to Warsaw.

Of course Tristram recalled that the U.S. intelligence officer had seen him before he left, attempted to extract the information, but Zbig's memory had gone. Retreated, the doctors had said, retreated to somewhere safe in its own recesses. The information would most likely remain unattainable for the rest of his life.

They had been right. Tristram stopped for a moment. On the street corner was a plaque to the victims of a Nazi execution. On the flagstones burned a small candle. Beside it some flowers.

None for Zbig, he thought. None for the man who had taken his secret with him.

He was near the cathedral now. The crowds were thick. And then he saw them—the Solidarity posters were beginning to appear. Christ! A bloody demonstration and he'd be in the middle of it. Everywhere around him he could see the excited faces of the people, and then the chanting broke out close by. "*Solidarnosc, solidarnosc*"—on and on. Tristram hurried through the people to the cathedral.

He was on the steps when he felt a shove, heard his name spoken softly. He turned around with some effort because the crowd was packing tight around him, surging through the doorway. Behind him stood a swarthy figure, late thirties, in a black leather coat. "Mr. Tristram"—he was having to shout—"Mr. Tristram, please to come with me." As he looked down he could see the long thin shape in the man's hand. The gun had been wrapped in newspaper but he knew what it was. No mistaking that. And it was then, as the crowd surged again, that hell itself seemed to break upon him.

Suddenly Tristram felt himself thrown forward, his balance gone, and as he looked behind him the man in the black leather coat had gone.

He didn't stop to think. Now inside the cathedral, he shook himself free of those nearest to him and dashed for the side entrance. On instinct the crowd parted to let him through. Only in Poland can they sense immediately that a man is on the run, only there is it a national phenomenon, only there can you rely on a stranger.

Almost immediately he felt the people close ranks behind him, and then he was through into a narrow stone corridor. Left side, a black curtain. He pushed through it, seeing the priests half dressed in their cassocks, and he had found the Polish without searching for it. *"Pomoc! Muse wyszcz"*—Help me. I have to get out. Suddenly a young deacon was running in front of him, pushing open doors as he went, commotion everywhere. And you never knew you could run so fast until you had to. Never knew that the mind could connect to the legs. Go on, push it. You have to make it for all our sakes. Who had told him that?

Last door, and Tristram was out in the street. A back entrance, a side entrance, it didn't matter. All that mattered was that he caught the words of the young priest—third door right. Open it. Quickly.

Down the cobbles. Dark suddenly, maybe it was dark all the time. Third door, was this it? Looks like a shop. The handle gave almost as he touched it, and all around him he could see shards of light reflected in a hundred different directions. A glass shop, an artisan's place. Tristram froze for a moment. Don't break anything. No hurried movements, no noise. Even when you're running, they'd told him once, a second or two of thought can save your life. Keep the mind going. Don't, for God's sake, switch off. Easy to say, he thought, his breath rasping from his throat, his heart protesting wildly.

"Don't be afraid."

It was the voice of an old woman, but it shook him to the core. Tristram swung around. He couldn't see her. There had to be a door to an inner office, but she had stayed well back in the shadows.

"You have nothing to fear from me." This time he caught the movement. White hair in the darkness. "Come with me, young man. Let me see your face."

Tristram moved toward her, shocked by how small she was. To his surprise, a bony hand touched his face. "Let's go in here."

She led him into deeper darkness and shut a door behind him. Only then did the light come on, not a bright one, and he could see the woman before him. She would have to be eighty, he told himself, for there was no fear or excitement in her demeanor.

Life would hold no new surprises for her. She was at peace with whatever it sent.

She was dressed in a long black frock that hung from the thin body nearly to the ground. Her hair had been tied fast to the back of her head. On her shoulders a white cardigan. And within the deep lines of the face, sharp blue eyes gazed unflinchingly across the room. Tristram had never seen someone so self-possessed, so much in control.

"I am sorry to come like this."

"How else would you come?" She gestured for him to sit on a sofa. "Besides, you have come a long way, I think."

"Look, I won't stay long. Don't worry. A moment or two and then I'll go."

"My dear young friend, you must stay as long as you would like. I have lived through the Nazi occupation. They could not move me. I have lived through the Stalinists, and they couldn't move me either. D'you think these boys in their silly uniforms can frighten me?" The gentle eyes glinted with a sense of fun.

Tristram looked at her, and she must have seen his gratitude, his concern.

"Sit here for a while," she told him. "You are tired and I will bring you something to eat."

As she made for the door he could feel the emotions building inside him. The sudden fear, then the sudden relief, people to kill you, people to help you. Hot and cold. Deadly and safe. You couldn't live long between those extremes. He knew that. The mind wouldn't take it.

* * *

Garten had watched the farmer enter the auditorium, watched him look anxiously around, fiddling with his fur hat, the eyes darting in all directions. My friend, you're a fool, he thought silently. You're a police agent's gift. Even at fifty yards they can smell the guilt rising from you.

All around him people sat huddled in their coats. In the old days they had left them in the garderobe. But now there was no heating. He imagined it was the only country in the world where people put on clothes to watch a film instead of taking them off.

The Moskwa cinema was crowded, as he knew it would be. They were showing a seventies American film, *An Unmarried Woman*, a welcome change from the old diet of Soviet pictures, which were cheap to buy and kept the Russian Embassy quiet.

It was to be the last Western film for a while. The arrival of the Russian leader would herald the showing of all sorts of Soviet kitsch—*Love in the Tractor Plant*, *Fraternal Help to the Afghans*, you name it, he thought, and the Poles would roll it. They would stop short only at the Second World War. And here, of all places, there would be no tributes to the glorious Soviet assistance, no eulogies about Yalta. The authorities knew just how much they could get away with.

He watched as they rolled the opening titles. The farmer's call had unsettled him, caught him unawares. The message had taken a day to reach him, another day to be returned. Throughout Warsaw as many as ten people would have been involved as mailmen. Extra measures were being implemented, extra precautions, because they were getting to the

critical stage. And you couldn't risk betrayal now. A
war footing, they had called it. And a war footing it
would be.

An hour and a half he waited in the side seats, letting the American accents wash over him, understanding much but not all. One by one they flashed
up the subtitles, a monotonous, killing procedure, but
his eyes never left the farmer for long, the thinnish
black hair, the white scarf he'd been instructed to
wear.

As they began leaving their seats he had moved,
quickly weaving his way through the people before
the tide turned toward the exits, catching the man by
his arm, seeing the look of surprise and the instant
relief.

"Walk with me, my friend, my dear friend," Garten had whispered, and they had blended naturally
into the crowd, two comrades smiling after an evening of entertainment, a joke about the characters,
and out of the main exit and right toward the city
center. Always a militia patrol outside, always they
would watch the crowds. The wind hit them hard as
they turned into it, swiping at their faces, blowing
their coats this way and that. Past the East German
Embassy, past the Foreign Ministry, and across the
highway bridge. And now you can tell me, now you
can talk. The farmer rubbed his frozen jaw as if it
might help him recall what he'd seen.

She watched Tristram as he ate, slowly at first,
then ravenously, tearing into the sweet, brown bread,
the sausage, swallowing it whole. His breathing came

rapidly as he forced the food wholesale down his throat.

"Steady, young man." She looked at him kindly. "The train will wait."

He stopped for a moment, not knowing what to say. There was peace in the room. Around the woman were the ornaments and possessions of a tidy person, but there was warmth and humanity—a child's rocking horse in one corner, a picture of a sunflower on the wall, a collection of black-and-white photos of smiling faces—the people she had touched in a lifetime of love and caring. But she had known more sadness than laughter. Tristram could read the lines in that old pale forehead. Character lines, suffering channeled into strength. The kind of courage no man could shake.

"I think we will listen to some music." She got up and went over to an old record player, a mahogany box with the twisted silver arm that ended in a needle. She wound the spring with a handle. And Tristram had known it would be Chopin, pride of the Polish nation, and the music lifted his spirits as she had known it would. He pushed his chair back from the table, and his lazy, rounded figure seemed to slump a little. How strange, he thought, to be sitting in the middle of Eastern Europe, listening to music, with the secret police outside on the streets trying to hunt him down. He shut his eyes tightly, thinking only of the music and the old lady and the peace of God that could reach you in any corner, however dark.

32 _____

"I should leave now." Tristram looked into her eyes and saw the anxiety for the first time. The record had ended. It was midnight. He had to assume that the patrols were on the street, but he couldn't leave it till daylight. The woman would be finished if he was caught with her. There was one chance and even that was doubtful.

"D'you have a telephone?"

The old lady nodded. "But you must remember that calls are often monitored."

For a moment he couldn't find the tiny card, searching as he did from pocket to pocket. Finally he located it in his wallet. He didn't remember putting it there.

Tristram dialed and leaned against the wall. Two rings, three rings. That's it, she's not there. Four rings, five rings. And I'll let it go till ten. Suddenly there was a sleepy noise at the end of the line. And it was her. Relief coursed through him.

"Hello, hello. I . . . I'm sorry, it's James from,

from the hotel. We met this afternoon. I'm . . . sorry
to call you so late."

"D'you want to meet?" The voice instantly awake.

"Yes . . . yes, I do." Her tone surprised him. Businesslike suddenly, taut. Not the way a whore plies
her trade.

"Where are you?"

"Old Town."

"D'you know Nowy Swiat? . . . Meet you at the
corner, by the Central Committee, in fifteen minutes."

Christ! He didn't have long. The old lady had
sensed his urgency and was already on her feet.

"Wait two seconds," she told him, and hurried out
of the room. Less than a minute later she was back
with a coat over her arm.

"Put this on quickly. It was my husband's—an
army coat. And the hat too. They won't stop you in
this. You're an officer. That means you're a Party
member. They'll leave you alone. It's your best
hope."

She gripped his hands. The strength was incredi-
ble.

"Hold yourself strong, young one. Don't let them
scare you." She pulled his head down and kissed him
suddenly on the forehead.

"When you've done what you must do, bring me
back the coat. Now go! Go."

He looked back only once, catching sight of the
white hair in the shop window, the tiny face taut and
anxious. She didn't wave. When everything's been
said, there's somehow little point.

* * *

"You did right to tell me."

For a moment the farmer appeared consoled. Garten patted him on the back as they made their way through the dimly lit streets. The man was clearly in a state of some anxiety.

"The best thing, my friend, is for you to return home and try to monitor their movements. We all know there are joint training exercises from time to time and the Russians crawl around far more often than they tell us. Maybe it's all routine."

"It's not routine for them to wear Polish uniforms." The farmer shook his head. "I tell you there is something seriously wrong." They had stopped in the doorway of a church.

"Look—what the hell d'you think we can do? Even if they're not routine, are we supposed to take on an entire regiment of KGB troops?" Garten paused, exasperated. "We have no choice but to watch them and try to give warning if they move."

"I don't like it. It's the way they did it in '81, moving in communications and troops, surrounding the city, then declaring martial law. Now they suspect something else is going to happen. And why do they expect that? They expect it because there's been a fucking leak. That's why!"

"For the love of God, keep your voice down!" Ahead of them in the square Garten had glimpsed the yellow patrol car. Militia. They were all over the city, just as if there were a curfew. No one was safe. The car coasted down a side street and Garten breathed again.

"Go home and leave it with me. I have an idea."

"What idea?" The farmer sounded skeptical.

"You listen to the foreign radio stations?"

"Of course I do. Doesn't everyone?"

"If all goes well, you will hear a report in a few days time about Soviet units sighted in Poland in greater numbers than usual."

He grinned. "That should stir them up one way or another. It may also force the West to put some pressure on our government here."

The farmer looked unconvinced.

"It's the best we can do, my friend." He patted the man on the shoulder. "It's all we can do."

At fifty-five the human body has few extras available. For Tristram the exhaustion was beginning to tell. All the symptoms came together, the heat, the cold, the shaking, and the legs that screamed out in agony. Ten years out of training, ten years as a deskman, and you lost the feel of the streets, lost your edge. Unless the killer instinct is fed constantly, it will lie down and go to sleep.

The car came at him from nowhere as he crossed from Nowy Swiat. He didn't know how it missed him. The beige Polski Fiat had gone into a four-wheel skid and pulled up an inch away. And he put out his hand to steady himself against the door, seeing the window open, surprised that it was Ania in the driver's seat, the quizzical smile unshaken, a fox cap pulled tight over her head.

"Get in, get in. You want a lift from me or the militia?"

It was a tight fit in the car, but Tristram didn't care. She moved rapidly across the streetcar tracks.

"And this uniform"—she turned slightly and pulled at the greatcoat—"I hardly recognized you."

"Good."

"It would not have been so good if I had driven past. Uh?"

And then the doubts began to hit him like sledgehammers as they drove fast over the potholes and the cobbles, bumping from street to street across the darkened city. What if she was an informer? Christ, they'd all die laughing, and who could blame them? He felt the anger and uncertainty that comes from knowing you're powerless.

She must have read his thoughts, because he couldn't hide them the way he once had.

"I don't often do a pickup service as well." She smiled.

"Is that so?"

And that seemed to pull a trigger. All at once she pulled into the curb. The easy smile, the pleasant manner had gone.

"Let's get one thing agreed now, okay? You called me. You want to meet, so we're meeting. I don't make any secret about my business, but you don't seem interested in anything like that. So tell me, what is it you want?" She didn't switch off the engine, just turned halfway around in her seat and watched him. Maybe, he thought, he should have packaged it up, disguised things better. But there are only so many roads to take, only so many games to play before you end up playing against yourself.

"I need somewhere to stay tonight. . . ."

"We have hotels. . . ."

"I can't register in a hotel. I have to find somewhere else." He was watching her eyes, but they didn't flinch. "People are after me. I need to find my friends. It's complicated." Watch her look for the slightest sign.

But she didn't move, sitting in the tiny car by the roadside, staring into his face, round and anxious.

"Why should I help you? You're a foreigner. God knows what you're doing here."

Ania turned and looked at the empty road. They were on a bridge overlooking a four-lane highway. No traffic now, with the light, flaky snow falling around them.

"Will you help me?"

"That depends."

"I should warn you . . ." And he never finished the sentence. All the time they'd talked she must have been reaching for the knife under the car seat. For he caught the flash of the long, stiletto blade in the street lighting as she swung it to within an inch of his chin.

"You don't warn me, my friend. You don't ever warn me. . . ."

All he could think was how slow he'd become, reflexes all gone to hell, and how easily she could have nailed him.

She put the car into gear and moved off.

"Let me give you a warning," she whispered. "If you aren't who you say you are, I'll kill you with my own hands." He could see her slipping the knife back under her seat as they drove east across the Vistula. The night was jet black, but Tristram's heart was singing.

33 _____

To all the people who've spent a winter Sunday in Brighton, to all the lonely day-trippers who claw their way over the pebbles to stand in driving rain, gazing vaguely toward France—Cornish bequeathed his own dismal thoughts.

As he drove along the front each shuttered shop window seemed to add to his gloom. It was, he concluded, the sense of being in the wrong place at the wrong time, the sudden realization that life must be somewhere else.

A motorcycle dispatch rider had brought the overnight message from Warsaw, and he had telephoned the Director, who thought it would be "grand" if Cornish could come down for tea. And so he had left the boys with their university studies, left his wife with the makings of a bonfire—"Well, someone's got to get rid of these leaves, haven't they?"—put the new Honda into drive, and taken the superhighway to the coast. As the sun flashed in and out of the clouds, Radio Three had sent him, it seemed, all the funeral dirges Albinoni had ever composed. And it didn't look "grand"—any of it.

Drive west along the seafront and the road carries you into Hove, which is quieter than Brighton and was never invaded by the scooter gangs of the sixties. The Director lived in Courtenay Gate—a square 1930's hulk about three feet from the beach. Cornish had been buzzed through the main door, but the Director wasn't going to let him into the flat.

"I think we'll go out for tea. 'Bye, dear," he shouted over his shoulder, opening the door a crack, striding through it, slamming it behind him. It struck Cornish that perhaps there was no one inside the apartment at all—the Director was simply being unsociable. For the man already had his coat on, a short blue-gray car coat and a dark green felt hat. Cornish had never seen him at weekends, never set eyes on the Sunday uniform—brown shoes instead of black, checked shirt instead of stripes, cravat to replace the necktie. The result was still the same: a short, wiry figure, upright and stiff, a man not overexposed to the social graces. In his class, thought Cornish, it wouldn't have mattered. Most people would have said he was shy or reserved or just a touch eccentric —anything rather than admit that the man was rude. But to Cornish he *was* rude just the same.

"Why don't you drive for a bit?"

Cornish nodded. They got in the car, and as they headed toward Newhaven the rain fell away. Over toward the Downs, Cornish glimpsed a rainbow, faint and fragile. A few minutes later, when he looked again, it had gone.

At Rottingdean they left the car and tramped along

the winding concrete path that hugs the coastline beneath the cliffs. The sea had dumped great piles of shingle onto it; pools of water had accumulated in the potholes. An outdoor swimming pool appeared to have taken the brunt of some subsidence from the cliff. The walkway was deserted. Only the sea gulls followed the two figures, cawing and wheeling high above them, squawking noisily, then darting out over the rough, foamy waters.

"Why the message?" The Director picked up a pebble and threw it far out to sea.

"I don't have any problem with why the message was sent. I would have thought the contents were quite disturbing in themselves."

"We'll get to that in a moment." The Director seemed impatient. "I was under the impression that Garten went over there deaf and dumb. That is to say he would receive no messages and send none."

"That was the understanding. Things of course have moved on a bit since then. For one thing, I'm not at all sure why they haven't picked him up after Martha was good enough to tell them of his arrival."

The Director stopped and looked back the way they had come. A straggling family had come into view, a child on a tricycle, plastic raincoats, a picnic basket, and the tears and dark looks indicating the progress of a full-scale Sunday row.

He waited till they'd passed. "I must say I wouldn't set too much store by this report of Soviet divisions skulking around in Poland. What did the thing say? Polish uniforms, mmm? Sounds pretty routine to me."

"Why not mention it in the intelligence digest to Number 10 and let them sort it out?"

"I don't think I want to go that far, thank you so much." The Director turned and began to retrace his steps. "Why don't we get some tea?"

The café had, it seemed, opened its doors for an airing. The place was hot and sleepy, like a hibernating animal that awakes too soon.

An elderly man in a cardigan sidled over to them. "We're closed. Come back in a month."

They retraced their steps onto the promenade.

"There remains, of course, the question of Tristram." The Director looked profoundly unhappy.

"Nothing. At least nothing since that thing in Romania. It's possible he's in Poland, but we have no idea what he's doing. . . ."

"Or for whom he's doing it." The Director stopped and looked out to sea. The clouds had drawn in over the English Channel. The sea had calmed. A ship close to the shoreline was barely in motion.

"I should be telling you to clean up this mess"—he looked hard at Cornish—"but for the moment it appears to be out of our hands."

34

She made him sit at the kitchen table while she prepared coffee, uncertain whether to trust him, uncertain of his motives. *And I know men*, Ania thought to herself. *I've known them shy and diffident like this one, pissing in their pants with excitement, unable even to take them off when the time came for it.*

But this one had strength. Below the surface, the balding head, the flabby body, this man was no amateur. She had seen him get out of the car, taking in the street at a glance, memorizing the name of it, the house number, the license plate on her Fiat. All the details stored in the bank. So easy, so automatic. Maybe he was out of practice, but he'd been there. Sometime in his life he had been there.

Tristram sat awkwardly on a wooden stool. He hadn't taken off his coat and he was sweating profusely. And yet she knew he wasn't frightened. Not the way Garten had been. This one was thorough, painstaking. Step by step, he would take it.

She removed the saucepan from the stove and poured hot water into the cups.

"Black, please," he told her.

She sat down opposite him. It was, she thought, only a matter of time before they reached the crucial stage. And then you take a gamble and slowly, carefully, you bring out your secret and unwrap it piece by piece in front of a stranger. You take all the precautions you can, or else you guess and guess fast, but either way you'll be taking a risk, because that's the nature of the business.

So offer your trust, she thought, a little at a time. Ration it out. If you're wrong, there's still the knife and the automatic in the drawer. And she knew she could use them, not because she had, but because the prospect held no horror for her.

"Why don't we go somewhere more comfortable?" Ania led the way to a sitting room with low square sofas. The house had been modeled on a mountain chalet and a large wide chimney swept down into the room from the ceiling. Outside, a wooden terrace overlooked the garden.

She caught his eyes absorbing the room. "I rent it from a diplomat who's working in Paris. It's cheap if you pay in dollars."

"Yes, of course."

A single light burned from a lamp on the coffee table. Tristram took off his coat and laid it on the back of the sofa. To both of them it seemed they were standing on a cliff, waiting to jump.

They had talked for an hour and now they were silent. She had talked. But how she had wanted to! It was an amazing relief to share a secret, and now it hardly mattered whether her confidant was genuine

or not. For the first time in her life she had stood
naked in front of a man. Not that way, she told herself. But with her fears and her weaknesses on show,
the quiet lonely moments that a soul retains for itself,
the inner grief, the guilt, the regret, the wreckage
that even the quietest of human beings leave in their
wake.

She had told of her first steps into the secret world.
A child inducted into espionage without pain and
without even the knowledge. As early as she could
remember Ania had left messages in baskets, entered
buildings where her parents would shy away, traveled right across the country, sat in cars on unknown
roads, lending legitimacy and innocence to a movement that had taken her without ever asking.

There were times, she said, when the bitterness
was unbearable. Friends had gotten jobs as doctors,
or scientists, or teachers—and she had two jobs that
were not fit for public discussion. To those that
asked, she was a translator. To those that suspected,
she said nothing at all.

You could survive that way because in Poland there
were still people who would say nothing, see nothing, turn away from dark encounters in streets or
cars, forget the irregular absences, the comings and
goings that were never explained. And yet there were
mornings when paradise itself would seem to be a
normal life. A life without fear. Dates she could
make, pleasures she could enjoy.

Years ago, she told him, there had been a boyfriend,
serious fellow from the university. He had known
nothing of her work in the underground. At first that
had liberated her. In the end it had trapped her,

bored her, infuriated her. A man who worried about an apartment and a car, food for his parents, prospects on the social ladder of this Communist establishment. All this while she was undermining the system below the surface, quietly trying to pull out the rug, unconcerned by the trivia of daily life.

They had parted company without him ever knowing why. No one since then, she had said. Never the man nor the opportunity.

"You're like that," she told him. "Yes, you are. Look at your clothes, your mannerisms. You're not used to bothering or taking care of yourself, or of anyone else for that matter. A selfish life, you and me. We go where we want, come home when we want, and fight any little battle that we want. Dressed in our secret costumes, we're like actors, only there's no audience. How d'you like that, Mr. James?"

He didn't answer because he didn't like it—much.

"How long is it since you loved someone?"

That was even harder to answer, thinking as he was, back through the shy years of Oxford, one or two shy years in the city—not with much of an end in view—and then the perfect home for shy people— the Secret Intelligence Service, where you didn't have to talk to anyone unless it was essential and you could pace the linoleum corridors staring at the ground—if you wanted. It was almost encouraged. But love someone?

"You see," she went on, "it is different here, but the result is the same. We think we are direct people here, us Poles. If I hate you, then I spit in your face—that sort of thing. But it's not true. We always look over our shoulders, thinking someone's listening, being nice to people we loathe. So we walk straight into *zasadski*—traps, brick walls. We're so used to hating people, we've forgotten how to love. And me? Well, in my case, what would be the point after all?"

The bright, assured facade, the bravado, seemed to have come off the pale cheeks like so much makeup. Ania brought out a handkerchief and dabbed at her eyes. "Look what you made me do. I've started to feel sorry for myself. My God, what a disgusting spectacle!"

She got up, lifting the two coffee cups, stumbling slightly, tripping heavily on the low table. As she leaned over him Tristram was suddenly driven to reach out and pull her toward him. She sat down heavily on his lap, but made no move to get away, and he put both arms around her, feeling his body start to shake uncontrollably, although he couldn't have been cold, not there beside the fire that burned so brightly, keeping the winter at bay.

"You lost him, then?"

"He lost himself. It was in a crowd. Just bad luck." Klimov wished suddenly that he hadn't said that, watching the color rise in the Russian's cheeks, the portent of bad things for those around him.

The two men had met in the Dzik café, near the central railway station, crowded and overheated. A waiter offered menus but they declined them. To Klimov, Polish menus were like history books, reminders of what had once been but was no longer.

"*Co jest, co nie ma*"—What have you got—what haven't you got?

He could see the waiter was brash, cheeky, probably an overpampered student. His own son was at the university and he loathed the boy.

The waiter spread his hands. "What you see is what you get."

"We don't want your jokes, prick. Tell us what filth you've got in your kitchens." The Russian had sat up, his eyes blazing. Klimov could see the knuckles clenched tight on the table. The boy had noticed too.

"We have some ham today or hare in cream sauce." He was stammering, glancing sideways. "Bread, butter, fruit drink."

"Bring it."

The boy looked uneasy. "Bring what?"

"Everything." The voice rose. "Now!"

It was a few moments before the Russian could speak again, the anger draining away from his face, the breathing slowing down.

"The little man Tristram has gone to ground." He looked around the restaurant. "Where will he go? Is he a coward or a fighter? Does he run from us or accept the chase?"

Klimov leaned forward. "You've read the archive papers. When he was arrested there was a full psychological profile. . . ."

"Regrettably it was not full. It was pathetic. In those days our so-called psychologists were more frightened of us than the prisoners had ever been. They wrote what we wanted to hear. Pages of nonsense about psychotic tendencies, paranoia, schizophrenia. Most of them had never seen the illnesses they were diagnosing. They simply flung the words in the air and we caught them." He rubbed his eyes and coughed, trying to clear the phlegm from his throat. "Of course there had to be fear. They should have been frightened of us. Fear is the only way. But in this case it worked against us." He shook his head gravely. "I will admit that."

"But something must have emerged."

"The man is not what he seems. He looks like an idiot. Fat, bloated, the body of a woman. No self-respect. But his mind is something else. Even those idiots in the Lubyanka never pretended to understand him. He never gave them anything."

"What do you want me to do?"

"You?" The Russian looked at him with contempt. "I will find him. I will get to him. If he reaches Garten, the whole thing is finished."

The waiter slammed a tray of food on the table. His absence seemed to have emboldened him. The Russian looked thoughtful.

"You know, Klimov—we have to look at the pressure points, his vanities, the people he might care about." He picked at the plate in front of him, slowly at first, then more rapidly, his greed and his hunger intensifying.

35 _____

In London the days had become so short that lunchtime seemed almost to mark the end of them. There
remained, at most, a couple of hours of daylight, during which the schoolchildren picked their noses or
talked or even slept through the lessons before burst-
ing out into the darkness and the drizzle and tearing
home.

June had tried all the tricks she knew, setting up
models and demonstrations, using little carts and
ticker-tape machines and all the paraphernalia of a
junior science course. But at four-thirty, with even
her good humor on the wane, she had admitted defeat. Physics on a Friday afternoon was like trying to
resurrect the dead.

The school had been quickly deserted. And she had
sat in the empty classroom as a single winter fly
buzzed around the neon light and the car doors had
slammed shut outside, and the scuffing of shoes and
the schoolboy taunts had become lost in the rush-
hour traffic.

Normally (whatever that meant), she would have

stayed on for the dance class or gone home and done her hair, changed into the dark blue frock, and come back a bit later. But she no longer had any enthusiasm for it and the dances themselves seemed dull and mundane. A succession of new partners had come and gone—a widower in his late sixties, a salesman recovering from a road accident, a hairdresser who had known he was handsome and had wanted her to know it too. June kept thinking that James Tristram would shamble back into the classroom, pulling up his trousers—and from out of the darkness she would have a friend.

She got up and put the pile of exercise books into her basket. In the corridor the cleaners had begun washing down the floor, two West Indians, she thought, noticing the overalls and long shirts, not the usual people. She said good night but they didn't answer. As she passed by she could hear them set down the mops and pails and she was convinced they were watching her, although she wouldn't look back, hurrying along the linoleum, fearful suddenly without knowing why.

Outside, the traffic had clogged solid. Walk, she thought. That's what you need. Clear your head. Stop imagining things. Forget about James Tristram and throw away the fairy tales. Real life is about facts. Not maybes or dreams. Hard facts—the kind she taught in physics.

She tried walking slowly, thinking of the weekend, a trip to the shops, phoning mother, writing some letters—but the anxiety wouldn't go away. People seemed to be looking at her. She stopped by a shop window, trying to watch the crowd in the reflection.

Was there a man on the other side of the street? He could have been West Indian. One of the cleaners maybe, but he was too far away. This is crazy, she thought, I must be mad.

She went into a bookstore, fighting to clear her mind. What about the elderly man who had come to her house and questioned her?

He had left her alone. Was this connected? Was what connected? All around her people were browsing in silence.

June went to the window and looked out. She was resolved to forget the whole thing, to go home and have a bath, supper, a book in bed. The sight of the man in the overalls by the bus stop made her change those plans abruptly, made her draw in her breath sharply, made her heart beat double and the blood rush to her cheeks. Now that she knew she was in danger, she could think, clearly and easily. Her mother had always told her she was sensible. This was the time to prove it.

36

Half a mile from the Warsaw steel plant they climbed the block of twelve-story apartments and got out onto the flat roof. From among the mass of pipes and lightning conductors they could see the factory, lit up by arc lights, smoke rising in clouds from its chimney stacks.

Garten had led, Grazyna had followed, and with them were the two drivers who would steal them away on separate routes to separate suburbs when it was all over.

Grazyna began to clear the ice and snow from a small square on the roof, and from two shoulder bags they carefully lifted out the equipment and laid it there. The drivers hooked up the wires, stretching some of them out across the surface of the roof, carefully because the wind was gusting hard, threatening to blow them off the top of the building.

Five minutes later they were ready, and Garten held in his hand the loudspeaker for a small medium-wave transmitter.

"You've got the tape?"

She flushed angrily. Did he really think she would come all this way without it?

"Did you bring your brains?" she snapped back.

"My wife." He shrugged at the two drivers and gave an exaggerated wink. "Bit moody this time of year." He laughed and they chuckled. And when she looked back, much later, it was at that moment that she knew she hated him—the cocky little figure in his sneakers and parka, the arrogance of the pampered revolutionary who wants his victory and wants the whole world as well—the man who takes, not because he has to, but because he hasn't the manners to ask.

They looked at their watches. It was a minute to midnight. Garten inserted the tape into a recorder. "Don't forget what I said. Once it's gone, we have to hurry. Jas—you get the wires rolled up. Karol, help me stow the equipment. Two minutes to get down to the cars and that's it. And you take it slow all the way. They'll have the detection vans out as well as security." He checked his watch again and pressed the button. And suddenly the cracked, tinny music was blaring out over the rooftop, and there was a voice they knew instantly. Grazyna began mouthing the words of the man who had awakened Poland, who had sent the nation his strength and his caring, the one standard bearer who traveled the world but left his heart in Poland—John Paul II, the Polish Pope.

It was as if, she thought, he was out there on the rooftop with them, taking the coded message into every mine and shipyard, into every farm, to every fisherman or sailor. She tried to picture her countrymen sitting nervously in kitchens or basements, in cars, or in chalets high in the mountains. Would they hear the signal and heed it?

Before she knew it Garten was shutting off the machines and they were moving quickly through the routine, the wires disappearing, the bags on shoulders, and down the fire escape to the parking lot. Slick work, she thought. We're still good, all of us. We still have something to show them.

She was already in the first car when he grabbed her hand. "Why don't you come with me? We could talk."

She pulled her hand free. "We have nothing to talk about. Those days are long over. When will you realize it?"

The driver let in the clutch and the white Mercedes taxi rolled out over the soft snow. As they headed away from the steelworks she could see him, silhouetted against the arc lights, gazing after her, motionless. Perhaps, she reflected, he had never been right. Perhaps it had just been chance or convenience that had brought them together. And now it wasn't convenient any longer. Not to her. Not to her daughter. Not to anyone who counted.

The driver turned and looked at her. "What was all that about? I mean the Pope's speech?"

"They've made a code from a sermon he gave in Krakow. Different parts mean different things, according to the time and date of transmission. This was a dress rehearsal. When we launch the uprising it'll be done this way and there'll be one more code."

"Why are you telling me this? Isn't it supposed to be secret?"

She didn't answer immediately. They were now

into the southern suburbs, the off-white blocks gleaming out in the night. "I just thought you ought to know something. These are going to be difficult times from now on. Dangerous, possibly for you, possibly for all of us."

"I know that."

Suddenly she could see how young he was and how little it mattered to him, and how deep his hatred and frustration must be to drive him so far along such a dark road.

They had slept on the sofas, apart yet still together. Each had wakened separately but their thoughts ran in parallel, a new trust built and established between them.

Ania sat up, pulling a blanket tightly around her. The room had grown cold. It reminded Tristram of mornings long ago in Oxford, many hours after the party had ended, and you couldn't remember if you'd behaved like a gentleman or not.

"Garten will be hard to find." She lay back among the cushions.

"Why's that?"

"He's gone down the line. That's the rule. I see him in, I baby-sit him for the first forty-eight hours, then he goes to another sector. I go back to my duties. No further contact. He can't speak to me, I can't speak to him. Very safe."

"And all this is part of your special security?"

Ania kicked at the cushions. "I told you this. A war footing. That's what they said. First time in forty years. This one is big. Our whole future, the future of

Poland, is at stake. And you know what else?" She turned onto her stomach and gazed across at·him. "If we have to kill to protect the operation, then we kill."

"It sounds a little drastic."

"What do you mean—drastic? You don't think that forty years of Communist rule was also a little drastic, uh? That the killing of our officers in Katyn was not a little drastic, and that this, our last chance to get out through the bars and show the world we can win —is not that a little drastic?"

Tristram got to his feet. My God, he thought, how well you did the job. Garten coming here, brainwashing the movement, and here she is reciting the phrases you taught *him* in London. Only now you have to stop him, stop them all.

As he looked out of the window Tristram could see the plan with terrible clarity. The Polish underground would rise up against the General Secretary, would humiliate him, and all the moves toward reform, and would be crushed once and for all.

A second uprising would be betrayed just as the first one had been all those years ago in 1944.

But he wouldn't tell that to Ania. Once she had helped him to find Garten, he would have to do it by himself. But could she help him?

Take a look at her lying there in luxury, relaxed, and yes, you can think it—beautiful. At that moment she looked up into his eyes and smiled.

"You know, my friend, there are just three days left before the Russian arrives."

"I have to see Garten before then. He must get the information I have for him."

Ania got up off the sofa and the blanket fell away from her. The woolen dress she had worn was crumpled. She hunted on the floor for her shoes.

"In that case," she said, "I shall have to find him."

37 _____

Most people never know what it's like to face danger —real danger. But you, June—you know, taking a handkerchief from your bag, wiping your face, moving back through the store away from the window.

You know he's seen you, and your only safety is to stay with the crowd, not face him on your own at the end of a darkened street.

Force yourself to go outside, only don't run. If you take it slowly, and easily, walk with the crowd, there's nothing he can do.

Out of the shop and into the street now, turn right and you keep your eyes on the ground. And you caught the flicker of movement at the side of your vision. Steady. Look where you're going.

She crossed the street, one boutique after another, late shopping and all the weekend money to burn. Everywhere you look the shopping bags are waving and half the world is chucking away its money and you've got to think of saving your life. This morning it looked so dull. Don't ever say that again.

"Watch it, love!" You didn't see him, did you? A

man with a sandwich board, proclaiming quotes from the Bible. Oh God, strains from a band, must be the Salvation Army. Didn't know we were a religious country.

Down the high street she walked and you wouldn't have given her a second glance. Thin, short, pale, and anxious, a concerned, committed Briton of the eighties. Not the nouveau, happy type at all, more interested in halting the seal cull and fox hunting than a beer in the pub. Not an elegant tread, but dogged, determined, she would get where she was going.

There's a blue light down on the far side of the road, and you daren't hope. Go a little nearer, wipe your eyes, and it really is—isn't it? The police station that you'd known all along was there, you really had, but you'd forgotten. That of all things at a time like this.

It seemed such an effort—the last few steps, through the swing doors, and at the front desk all the urgency of a Sunday tea party. "And what can we do for you then, miss, what seems to be the trouble?" Uncle and nurse in a blue uniform peering across the counter with the big book of lost-and-found open in front of him.

"I don't want to be dramatic about this, but I think my life is in danger. And it could be a matter of national security."

"I see."

He didn't. The thin smirk that said *I've met your type before, heard it all before, seen it all before, and there isn't a crime you can tell me about that I haven't already solved with my smug little brain from Sevenoaks.* Oh dear, it would be him. But not for long. For her quiet insistence brought the inspector, which brought the superintendent and a phone call to Special Branch, and another one that nobody in Britain could ever have traced. But perhaps, after all the long lines of communication, there was just one thing that swung it in June's favor. "Tell them I'm a friend of James Tristram," she whispered to the detective, and then it all began to happen.

Cup of tea, madam. I'm sure we've got a biscuit here somewhere. So sorry about the wait, but you know what it's like, security and all that. Bit cloak and daggerish for my liking. Mine, too, she thought.

A car was on its way, they said, as if a car meant very important person. And when it arrived she could see it all the way down the corridor, black and square and shiny, with the rear passenger door already open for her.

"Look, sorry again about all this." The superintendent didn't want to wait around, clunked the door on her, and she settled into the soft, springy seat.

"Where are we going?"

And it was only then that the driver turned and smiled at her. And she thinks she may have screamed, but in the hours and days of semiconsciousness that followed, she couldn't ever be certain.

They made her sit on a metal chair and from the photograph you couldn't have told where she was. A rough stone wall rose up behind her. She was conscious, it seemed, still dressed in a dark raincoat, dark clothes beneath it, a dark, distant look.

Six feet in front of her they set up a television camera on a tripod, professional equipment, lights, the full rig, and then threw questions at her in a language that she neither spoke nor understood. The rhythm was gentle, unhurried, and through it all she nodded vacantly, her eyes fixed on the stone floor beneath her. When they turned off the lights she was still nodding as they lifted her from the chair.

Less than an hour later they wired the photograph along a telephone line. Next morning a videocassette was put aboard the LOT flight to Warsaw. A man in a black leather coat took the package directly from the pilot as the plane sat on the tarmac and a batch of fresh Polish snow began to fall.

It took less than fifteen minutes to reach the television station on Woronicza. The man showed a pass at the gate and headed for the farthest entrance. There were three of them waiting for him in a room at the top of the staircase. A picture editor, a director, and a man who didn't identify himself. But they were used to that. This was Poland. They didn't need to look at the map.

They titled the package "An Interview" and ran forty seconds of it in the main evening news that night. The stern announcer with the hollow-sounding microphone declared that a female agent from an unnamed Western power had been apprehended within Poland's borders. She had confessed to espionage. In the picture you could see her nodding. The state prosecutor, they said, would prepare the case for trial. The proper organs were continuing to investigate. But for now a major spy ring had been broken. More arrests were imminent.

Pause, head up, smile.

A group of Soviet musicians had arrived . . . and the announcer droned on endlessly.

Inside the British Embassy the head of the economics section turned off his set, stopped the recorder, and sat back thoughtfully in his chair. He'd send a flash, although the monitoring service in Cheltenham would have picked up the broadcast and would be running a rapid translation. He didn't know who the woman was. He just sensed she was trouble.

The next morning when he opened his copy of the Party newspaper, *Trybuna Ludu*, and saw her front-page picture, he was certain of it.

Four floors below the Director's office Cornish saw the message warning on his computer screen. He knew the main data bank deep inside the building would record the display along with at least a thousand others. Under new security regulations nothing could be erased for at least twenty years. Even if you specifically ordered the destruction of a file, it would wipe it only from the catalog. Someone, at some time, would be able to recall it. And then, if a traitor were uncovered, piece by piece the entire jigsaw of his activities, the files he had seen, the reports he had written could be reconstructed.

It was another insurance policy, useless and expensive, until the inevitable day when it would be needed.

The message had been fed in by telephone, but that did not disguise its origin. The Director had accessed the computer with his own personal code, without which it would have barred entry to the system. But what it could not do was give his location. He could have been inside the country or out of it, on a plane or in a car, and Cornish didn't waste time on speculation. These days the man was constantly away from his desk, constantly out of the building. Sometimes at home, sometimes not. In his absence the Service was run by a triumvirate of departmental chiefs who executed the British government's secret policy directives right across the world.

The Director had set the rendezvous at a tearoom in Golders Green. As Cornish entered he was aware of the foreign languages thickening the air around him. As he passed the tables, rammed tight against one another, he could identify German and Yiddish, the lingua franca of the plump, elderly women with their fur coats and expensive jewelry. They didn't stop talking, but he could see the eyes watching him, assessing him. Back in their own countries they would have lived and survived by their wits alone. They hadn't lost the old habits.

Right at the back of the room, the Director had ordered tea for himself, but he motioned the waitress away as Cornish sat down.

Cornish looked annoyed. "I thought I might at least have a cup of coffee. It's taken an hour to get here through the traffic."

"This isn't a party. Just sit and listen." Cornish could see how tired the man had become. The dark circles had expanded under his eyes, which were puffy and bloodshot.

"I've had enough of this nonsense in Poland. Why was this June creature not being watched?"

"I myself saw her twice." Cornish felt the flush rising up his neck. "She was of no value, obviously liked Tristram, but it was hardly the love affair of the century."

"Didn't need to be, did it?" The Director took out a handkerchief and wiped his mouth. "How fond was he of this woman?"

"I don't know, we never asked him. He seemed to like her, that's all. He isn't someone who wears his heart on his sleeve."

They stopped talking and it occurred to Cornish that this had been a bad place to meet. Very few men around, he observed. Most likely they'd all been driven to death by the old women chattering away nineteen to the dozen.

The Director moved his cup into the center of the table. "I've decided to break through the apparent wall of ignorance that seems to surround your operation." Cornish raised an eyebrow. "We're going to finish this once and for all. I've had enough of the Poles making stupid bastards out of us. Maybe they have this woman in Poland, maybe they don't, maybe they have Garten and maybe they don't. And who the hell knows what Tristram is playing at." He wiped his mouth again. "End it now. Terminate the entire farce and all the players in it. If you can't bring them home, leave them where they are."

Cornish shook his head. "It may be too late."

The Director was on his feet, barely audible above the teatime chatter. "You'd better hope," he said, "that it isn't."

38 _____

Passent had thought it all through. For a day and a half he had lain in his apartment near the central railway station, hearing the traffic, watching the sky go from gray to black to gray again. Bit by bit they had chipped away at his confidence and his position. The operation in the Tatras, the blocked road in the Old Town, the total disregard for Polish authority. He shut his eyes and listened to the traffic.

It was good to be away from the office, from the petty spying and informing that filled the daily routine. Whatever skills the security personnel employed on the street they brought back with them into the building, using them on colleagues, on rivals, even friends. No longer did anyone think about right and wrong, good or bad. The aim was manipulation. If you could do it, you did it.

Passent well remembered how two agents had vied for a senior job the year before. One had gone so far as to put surveillance on his rival's teenage daughter. The girl was found to have had an affair with a former Solidarity adviser. In small-town Poland such things were inevitable. People walked the same side of the street because there was only one side to walk on.

All the same an unsigned report had found its way to the departmental head. And guess who hadn't got the job when the time had come to choose.

He lay back on his bed, a can of beer in one hand, the remains of some bread and cheese beside him. How quickly it had all changed. And yet, he reflected, it was probably inevitable. As a child his family had done a good job trying to make him Polish and proud, taking him to church, teaching him the truth when the schools had offered half-truths and distortions. And some of it had stuck, hadn't it? Despite the Soviet training, the indoctrination, despite the desperate, clawing ambition they had nurtured inside him, he was still a Pole—not a Russian. And if he had sold out in the past, he would do what it took to buy himself back.

Slowly he got dressed and stood looking in the mirror. He would find Ania and help her. He would throw in his lot with the underground. He should, he told himself, have done it long ago.

In the chill of the late afternoon she made her way into town, the Mercedes purring through the rough streets, shimmering past the dirty trucks and buses and the struggling Fiats.

At the Victoria Hotel she got out, pulling the gray fox coat tightly around her and picking her way in the high black boots across the parking lot. Like three sisters, the regulars stood on duty beside the elevators, hair sleek, shoulders back. Ania knew them all, a part-time nurse who earned more in an afternoon than she did in a month at the hospital, a student, and a part-time shop assistant. They all looked glossy, heavy-busted, a direct assault on the senses of the traveling male. And they did well in the hotel, picking the rich businessmen and the errant tourists anxious to sample the only plentiful commodity left in the People's Republic of Poland.

In the lobby business was poor—eyes turned toward them but the feet kept on walking. A few times smiles were answered, a head shook in silent appreciation, but no offers were made, no deals clinched.

Together they watched as a government delegation marched purposefully inside on its way to an official reception. In front the security men, behind them the sycophants. In the middle the chunky, more confident figures with the cleaner shoes and the better-fitting suits. Tailor's dummies, thought Ania. Molded by Moscow.

She remembered what a friend in the underground had told her—they're all little men, he would say, all fresh from the provinces, with their small-town attitudes and allegiances.

They grew big in little places, learned small lies before big ones, learned the giving and returning of favors, the patronage that would help them into power and keep them there. And inside they're nervous, she thought. They relied on cunning, not intellect, not on people to elect them, but on friends to protect them. Who knew whether a friend was not simply an enemy wearing a smile?

She turned to go back to the lobby, but a hand caught at her shoulder.

"You have a moment, darling?"

Her heel caught and she stumbled.

"God, it's you." And the manager stood there, grinning a fat little smile, a layer of sweat glistening on his forehead. The runt, she thought, looking down at him. Not enough to climb on top of his piglike wife on a Saturday night, he wants extra.

"You've had yours this month." She turned away and began climbing the stairs to the coffee shop.

"Just a chat, darling, little drinkie maybe. Marek only wants to talk to his baby." She cringed. The little boy whine, the same whine as when he took off his pants and began playing the silly games.

"Marek can have two minutes if he's a good little boy." She patted him on the head.

The manager had an office on the first floor, overlooking the square, but the view was inside. Ania imagined it was how Paris brothels had looked in the nineteenth century—tasteless and exaggerated. A white shag pile carpet shared the floor with an imitation leopard rug. Sofas, with seaside motifs, had been fashioned in the shape of boats. The room was in virtual darkness, save for a miniature spotlight that pointed at the ceiling.

"Sit down, darling." His digital watch began to bleep wildly. For a moment Ania wanted to laugh.

"What is it, Marek?" She pulled her fingers through her hair. "Trouble at home, none of the maids coming across?"

Marek sat disconsolately at his desk. "You know, darling, I've said it before and I say it again. You and me . . . we could have . . . I mean I would have left the old fool . . ."

"Poor baby!" The voice mocked him without mercy. "Want a cuddle do we? Feeling the cold on our bottom?" The smile died. "Enough of this nonsense. I've got more important things to do than listen to you."

He got up from the desk. "Ah-ha, but you haven't, you see, my clever little whore. Because you don't know what I know. You get all the gruntings and groanings and I get the secrets. All of them, whispered around my comfy hotel, with all those sensitive microphones that everyone was kind enough to lend me. See? See? So what will little Ania give me if I tell her?" He tiptoed around behind the sofa, and she felt his hand massaging her neck. "I don't want much, my dear."

"Perfect. Then you won't be disappointed."

"Bitch!" Marek went back to his desk.

Ania smiled her sweetest smile. "It was last night"—his voice lowered—"one of the rooms at the back, the ones we give to the Russians 'cause they can't afford to pay. Anyway, the place is crawling with them. You know—the new leader's coming in from Moscow."

"I know, I know."

"So what d'you know, uh? This man, maybe he's security, maybe KGB. You know they don't exactly talk—these people. Well, I'm listening to the tape, and suddenly he says to his friend, 'Good riddance to the fucker'—the General Secretary, they mean. And the other one says, 'Yeah, it's time we had a real government, time we kicked arse.' And the first man says, 'Yeah, well, don't worry, my friend, you'll get your chance sooner than you think.' You see? First time in all these years. Normally these people—they're so busy clenching their buttocks, you couldn't even hear them fart. Now this. What d'you think?"

Ania got to her feet. She was shaking suddenly, she didn't know why. It wasn't Marek. She never shook when she was with him.

"I think you're a very clever boy." She wasn't teasing any longer, kissing him on the forehead, frightened suddenly by what she'd heard, uncertain what it meant.

Passent almost missed her. She had crossed the driveway, head down, almost crestfallen. It didn't look like the Ania he had seen before. Bouncy, blousy, tarty. She wasn't heading for the Mercedes. He could see her moving quietly toward the tomb of the unknown soldier, through the park, losing herself among the trees and shadows.

Aren't we busy, he thought, surveying the street, counting the straggling figures, a drunk or two, a man carrying a sleeping child on his shoulder. Not much in the way of cover. He looked up at the red hue over the city and felt the temperature falling around him.

The anger rose deep inside Tristram in a way he had not known for years. For an hour, maybe longer, he sat in the house banging his fists against his temples till his whole head was throbbing. It was the one possibility he had not even considered—and they had taken her, violated his life, intruded into the tiny private sector where daylight so rarely fell.

He had seen the television news, watched the film

clip with horror, the flush spreading across his forehead, his heart jolting and jarring in his chest.

And they had known their business, known the
theory of pressure. So clever they'd been, because
you never needed to use the family or the loved ones.
Any acquaintance would do, and sometimes the more
detached, the better, the more uninvolved, the better.
Because then the victim would feel guilt and revul-
sion at the taking of an innocent. And June was truly
an innocent.

He shook his head in horrible admiration. How
quickly they had found her! Little June, unassuming
June, small and not really attractive, but fun and
bright, and there had been promise in that smile.

Tristram got up and paced the room. He could feel
the unseen hand, could see the hands beckoning him,
the art of the distant manipulator drawing in his
prey, but from a distance, well out of range.

They had known how he would feel. Maybe they'd
looked up the file in the Lubyanka, and suddenly he
could remember the interrogation, the one where
they'd asked about love and girlfriends. It had seemed
such an odd question, and so surprised had he been
that he had loosened just for a moment, let down his
guard, spoken of a love that had once flowered and
died, more to rekindle the warmth of it in the prison
than to give away information. But from that day
they would have known that he had once cared, that
he could care. And they'd have calculated that even
the most fragile of relationships would matter.

He hated them for that, the way they had broken
him all those years ago, the way they could do it
again from a distance. And yet he wasn't in a cell.

Not this time. And if you fought them, if you lashed back at the moment when they thought they had gotten you, then there was a chance. Just a small one.

Tristram went out into the hall and reached for his coat, the anger channeled, his breathing calmer.

It was on impulse that he returned to the living room and picked up Ania's handbag, lying by the fireplace on the floor. Maybe she had forgotten it, maybe she had left it on purpose. But Tristram knew, simply by the weight of it, that there was a gun inside, bulky, cold, and fully loaded.

Grazyna tried to stop herself sleeping, but the excitement and exhaustion were a powerful mixture.

In the apartment overlooking the ghetto monument, she could have slept the day away. Maya Angelica had been taken to stay with her cousin. That had been a relief. Vital to get the girl out of Warsaw. Too many things were happening, there was too much danger. Out of all the crises that Poland had suffered since the war, surely this would be the most decisive.

She stood by the window and looked at the darkening square. It was almost over. For a week now she had played her part, carried out the mission, met and coordinated, and the underground would be ready. Perhaps they had been ready all the time. Millions of them, eking out their lives, waiting for nothing more than a signal.

It had been dangerous work but strangely rewarding. For she had traveled from workshop to factory, from shipyard to mine, and all across the country she had seen eyes that gleamed, clasped hands that were strong and cold, looked into souls that were un-shakable in their resolve. No shortage of them.

She remembered visiting an old streetcar driver, retired, but still a link man in the local union, the one who reported the workers' mood. The short gray hair had stood up from a scalp that seemed crafted from stone and the rasping voice had wavered. "I had given up hope." His old brown eyes had looked down at the table as they had sat in his tiny kitchen in Mokotow. "All the ones I had fought with are dead. And the young ones . . . I didn't know them. But we should be proud of you." He had coughed pain-fully. "Lies are ancient, but truth is eternal." His hand had touched hers. "I have no doubt that you will succeed."

Ania had turned only once, and she had known she was watched. It was instinct, not observation. The wrong configuration of people on the street, the wrong clothes, the wrong walk. After all the years she had lived in Poland her mind would automati-cally register an alarm.

But it wasn't the time to lose an enemy. That's what they had told her. When things are moving, and the end's in sight, you can't let your enemy go. You pull him to you, hug him tight, bring him in, because you can't let him out of your sight. The victim must become the attacker.

She had reached the main road. One more military column was passing in front of her, soldiers being bused in as if Warsaw were the front line. At each end she glimpsed armored personnel carriers, several water cannon. The city was being turned into an arsenal. All this for the Russians, or was there more?

Ania crossed at the lights. She had been heading for Grazyna's flat, the safe house. *Don't go too close. Lead him on, but leave no clues. If it goes wrong, he mustn't know your destination.*

He was closer now. And maybe, just maybe, he would make it easy for her. Maybe he was one of the cocky ones, maybe he fancied her, maybe he had been sent to bring her in.

She was moving north along the main highway, wide pavements, some winter trees. *And you'll have to get onto a side road, a dark road, take him on, find out his motives, what he knows, what he doesn't know.*

Of course it could be innocent. Clients follow whores. Sometimes. One man had followed her—an American. Nothing malicious, but a small-town kid, working for a U.S. network, first time abroad, away from his wife, and his eyes so wide open with excitement. All he knew was that Communist countries were bad. He had looked at her body in amazement, as if it were out of place in such an evil society. But he had followed her, all dopey and drippy and full of silliness. And she had gotten rid of him by promising a meeting in a week's time, when she knew she'd be away, out of Warsaw and somewhere he'd never find her. It could be someone like that. She looked behind her and started suddenly because he wasn't where he had been. The street was almost empty. She knew it was the most dangerous time of all. And as she turned around she put her hand in her coat pocket and felt the knife, the long thin steel blade on which, she was certain, her future depended.

He had to have crossed the street in front of her. That was the only explanation. The thin figure stood before her, his coat open and flapping in the wind. Somehow he seemed vulnerable. And yet she knew that face, the official white shirt and the cheap rayon tie. Somewhere it seemed on a far-off summer's day she had seen him. Where had it been? A march or a church service, a photograph or even another life.

He didn't approach her, just stood stock-still ten feet away.

"I'm Passent." The voice was matter-of-fact. And yet she could see that he wasn't sure, wasn't on safe ground.

"Who's Passent?" She took a step forward.

"Someone who wants a talk." He tried to smile.

"Do I know you?"

"I don't think so. But it's possible. I sometimes forget faces."

"Why d'you want to talk?"

"I could help. I want to help."

Careful, she thought. You're too quick, my friend, too eager. And I know where you come from. She looked down at the stay-pressed trousers and the lace-up boots. And she remembered what a friend had told her about recognizing policemen. They're just like criminals only better dressed. Their eyes dart about when you talk to them. They're always looking over your shoulder, and they're at their most dangerous when they smile. Like reptiles.

And there before her was a perfect specimen. King of the reptiles. And she knew what she had to do.

"Why don't we walk a moment?" She moved toward him, passing him by on the outside, strolling out in front, the hips swaying. "It's not a bad night."

Passent looked surprised. "I have something to tell you."

Classic, she thought. Classic. The infiltrator always bears a gift, a symbol of goodwill and sincerity. But we'll play it my way.

They began to walk side by side. She turned them right, then left, and the road was darker, the streetlamps farther apart.

"Do you know my name, Passent? Or am I just a file? A number?"

"Your name, I know your name." He didn't deny the existence of a file.

"And you know what I do." Statement. Not a question.

"Yes."

Into the alley now, nice and gentle. "And what's it to be tonight, darling?" Soft and throaty, the come-on, the way they liked it, all of them.

He looked embarrassed, wrong-footed, hadn't done this sort of thing before, not a strayer, not the imagination for it, she thought. Not a gambler like the ones I've known. And yet deep down, when you took away the game and the job, he wanted it. She saw him lick dry chapped lips. You want it, don't you? And she knew she was right even before he opened his mouth.

"You do this often?"

Pig, she thought, you know how often I do it. They had stopped and she moved in closer.

"Three times a week, darling, twice for money. Once for love." She smiled and her hand went into her pocket.

"And which is it tonight?"

Oh, you do want it, don't you, my little one? You want it so badly.

"It's love, darling." And her hand came out with the stiletto, so fast that she wasn't even sure it belonged to her, fast and straight, through his shirt, up under the ribs and into the heart, just as they had done it to the Germans all those years ago when they had occupied the city and turned it into a slaughterhouse.

Passent looked at her without a sound, the shock opening his eyes wide, but his mouth unable to speak.

"It's love," she repeated softly, and left the stiletto where it was, feeling the body, warm and falling, turning back the way she had come, starting to run over the cobbles. A killer, she told herself. I'm a killer, and the horror and the excitement drove her headlong over the empty pavements, out of the shadows and into the square.

Grazyna didn't know what made her look out. Maybe it was the dismal stillness, the boredom that weighed so heavily in the tiny apartment. At any rate there was nothing to distance her from the little figure, twelve stories below, that tore toward the ghetto monument, across the flagstones covered lightly with snow, just a dark shape, but the wind was with her, fear was with her, and you could tell it all from a distance, that this was a human being on the brink.

Grazyna stood transfixed, but her fingers had tightened white against the windowsill. And now there were the beginnings of light in the square, a headlight wavering up and down from the southern end. A car was coming fast. And a cold chill seemed to break into the room. Two objects were converging, a primeval pull, mankind rushing toward the light, and the car unseeing, unaware.

There was a moment when the scene stood still. The figure had left the central square, diving, it seemed, into the road, and the car was rounding the corner. Too far away to make out what it was. Grazyna put her fingers in her mouth, but nothing had happened to slow the collision. Nothing could stop the final lurch, the car skidding and turning, juddering to a halt. Suddenly there was no movement, no sign of life. The dark figure lay in the road and the headlights were fixed and still.

Grazyna didn't think, didn't bother with a coat. She took the stairs, silent almost in her slippers, running, tripping. Down, down, driven toward the horror of the night.

As she left the block she could see others emerge, drawn perhaps by a noise too distant for her to hear. Some flashlights, another car had appeared, and she didn't stop, for thirty yards away, stretched out in the dirt and snow, she could make out the fox fur coat, the height of luxury, a coat that was the talk of the city, its owner crumpled inside it.

"Don't go near, don't touch her." A man was holding back the onlookers.

"I know her," she hissed. "Let me pass." As Grazyna knelt down she could feel the deep cold in the hand, but somehow there was life inside it.

Ania was lying on her side, knees drawn up almost to her waist. Her left eye opened.

"Ania, it's me—Grazyna. It's all right. I'm here, I'm beside you."

The breathing was labored. Someone shone a pool of light near the face, and she could make out the blood on the ground, the awful stillness of the body.

"My flat . . ." The voice was barely audible, and for a moment Grazyna wondered if she'd imagined it. Ania tried to cough, but her body shook in pain. "Stay with me." The mouth barely moved. "I want a friend . . . stay with me."

Grazyna doubted whether the girl ever heard her reply. For the eye closed again and didn't reopen and she got to her feet, feeling the terrible stabbing cold for the first time. Down on the road it didn't seem as though there had ever been a human being, and yet she couldn't help noticing that the body was lying almost in the fetal position, as if to link the events of birth and death, to square the circle.

39 _____

As he set out across the city Tristram reflected on what the years had taught him—not to stay waiting for action but to provoke it, invite it, make it work for you. It was like judo, he recalled. You can turn your opponent's strength against him, make him fear, make him slip and fall.

He had telephoned Reuters news agency from a pay phone. "I'm a British reporter. Can you help out with a phone number?" The man had gotten the diplomatic list and found the name of the consul. Soviet. Klimov. Wilna 3. And now he was on his way.

Of course it needn't have been the consul. But Tristram had learned the protocol, practiced the etiquette. If the consul is not the resident intelligence officer, then he will know how to find him. There are patterns and there is custom and all sides observe them.

An ancient Mercedes picked him up by the roadside. A slim man in his thirties at the wheel, distant somehow, almost aristocratic. They drove in silence, but there was no hostility. The man was a Pole and these were tense times. You asked no questions, shared no information, forgot the faces that emerged from the night.

Tristram walked the last mile, where the snow was thicker and the houses modern and expensive. There were front gardens deluged with snow. Like icing, it perched on gates and fences. Smoke came from the chimneys.

How well you live, Comrades, he thought. All the little luxuries. He looked up at the chalet-style house, with its long sloping roof, bright lights in the front windows, and heard the sound of laughter and raised voices. Klimov was entertaining. The Klimovs at home. Dinner for six, or eight, or nine. Tristram laughed inwardly, remembering all the ghastly diplomatic dinners he had ever attended, reflecting how much more fun this one was going to be. Quietly, unhurriedly, he moved to the back of the house and searched for a path.

Klimov couldn't remember when he'd enjoyed such an evening. He had invited no one from the embassy, no one to report to the ambassador, no one to spy on him in his own home. There'd been enough of those evenings.

Instead he had thrown open his house to a Yugoslav couple, two loud Italians, and a Canadian businessman and his girlfriend. Fun people, with a lively sense of humor. And if they wrote reports on him, who cared? He would write about them too. Tonight even his wife had cracked her face. And in the intervals between her incessant diatribes, they had told all

the dirty jokes they had ever known and were down
to the last bottle of Georgian wine.

I need to relax, he told himself. Too much pressure.
Especially when there's an operation in progress.
Time for laughter was essential. It restored perspec-
tive, calmed the nerves.

Later, as the maid cleared dinner, Klimov moved
over to the cassette player and pulled an old tape recording from a drawer. He had placed it there in advance—a special tape played only for special friends.
It was the balladeer Vysotsky—famous throughout
the Soviet Union. But these were songs he had never
played in public. Protest ballads, available only on
underground recordings. And one of them had gone
to Klimov.

He turned it on and the deep, rasping voice filled
the room. The tape, he recalled, hadn't just come to
him. He had seized it years earlier from a Jewish dissident, a student leaving the country. Klimov had
wrested it from the suitcase at Moscow airport, along
with all the other valuables and mementos the Jew
had planned to take with him.

Now as he listened to the music it brought out the
tears just as it always did. Tears for the motherland,
for the greatness of Russia, for the grandeur that the
ballads evoked. And no thought at all of the Jew.

His wife brought coffee and then hurried back to
the kitchen, discomfited by the music. She would
bitch to him later about making a display in front of
foreigners. She didn't realize that it was safer to do it
in front of them than his own people.

Such a simple creature, he reflected, one dimensional and stupid. Loyal, not from conviction, but because she had never thought to question.

He shook his head sadly. She still believed that Communists were supposed to act as if they'd just come from one funeral and were on their way to another. No fun, no laughing. Life stripped of entertainment and joy.

Not anymore.

Klimov yawned and settled himself farther back in the chair. Two of the guests seemed to have dozed off. Maybe, after all, the music was a little heavy for them.

He glanced up to see his wife walk stiffly back into the room. She looked like a wrinkled old prune, he decided, and just about as tasty. She had probably come to berate him. And then he noticed she was gesturing wildly with her eyes and eyebrows. The two Yugoslavs laughed. Klimov sat up. What the hell was she doing?

He rubbed his eyes and it was as if he was suddenly seeing everything in slow motion—the gun pointing toward him, a plump figure in a beige raincoat emerging from behind his wife. And they all gasped simultaneously from deep down in their throats as the tape played on.

I'm too old for all this, Tristram had thought, his heart thudding away in his temples.

But the garden wall had been easy and then he had tried the door—the living room first—no luck there. It was locked and barred. From where he stood, crouching on the snow-covered terrace, he could see the Russian woman in the kitchen. As she carried out the coffee tray he had clasped at the sliding window, releasing it, pushing it aside, stepping into the cramped, narrow room.

Breathless, he looked about him. There was filth everywhere. Dirty plates had been piled high on top of each other. Open packages and cans littered the stove. He stepped backward onto a saucer of milk and cursed. He kicked it aside, took out the gun, and waited.

She had taken only a few seconds. As the door had opened he had thought to himself—*What do I do if she screams?* But she hadn't. Tough old bird! She had simply stood there in shock, staring at the barrel of the revolver, frozen by fear.

"Don't make a sound." Tristram spoke in Russian, but in that moment he realized words were unnecessary. The woman was transfixed by the gun. Perhaps she'd even seen it used. Her respect for it was automatic and total.

"Let's go back to the others," he whispered, and they moved silently over the thick carpeting to the living-room door.

To Tristram it was an extraordinary sight—the little group cowering in their dark suits and dresses, sipping coffee, listening to some harsh whining singer. Instantly he had picked out Klimov. You could put him in a hundred suits but you couldn't alter the anatomy of a thug. The jaw gave it away and the dirty white shirt, frayed at the neck. Aggression seemed to ooze out of every pore. Watch him. Watch that one, he thought.

As Klimov rose from the chair Tristram fired a foot to the left of him, watching the bullet tear into the

plaster beside the mantelpiece—and Klimov wasn't
going anywhere. One of the women screamed. And
all of a sudden, as if someone had switched it off, the
music died away.

He spoke quickly and in Russian. Really, it didn't
take more than a few sentences. Klimov was in the
business, he didn't need a bloody preamble. Everyone
on the same wavelength, except of course the poor
blighters who'd come around for some free caviar
and hadn't expected a gun waved in their faces, not in
this place, not here in Communist Poland.

He told Klimov about the little girl called June,
told him in the kind of clear uncomplicated language
that all professionals use, that if they harmed her
Klimov would not survive to return home to Russia,
neither he, nor his wife, nor anything that he cared
about, if there was anything beyond himself. There
would be a further message and a rendezvous. And
Klimov sat there as he left the room and let himself
out of the front door. He would have assumed Tristram had backup, wouldn't just walk down the street
and disappear into the suburbs, because that wasn't
the way a professional would operate.

He smiled to himself, and as he reached the gate he
looked down and saw the reason for the milk saucer
in the kitchen—a large tabby cat, fat and old, and
none too friendly. Tristram reached down, and in a
move he never fully understood, put his right hand
under the cat's jaw, jerked it back, and broke the animal's neck. He flung the tiny bundle onto the porch
and made his way hurriedly down the street.

Of course, he decided, it needed to be done. A little
reminder of his serious intent, the kind of calling

card Klimov would understand. But it horrified him
to have killed with so little thought, to have acquired
such a violent reflex. He shuddered and put his hands
in his pockets. Perhaps the quiet, sheltered life of
Wimbledon had gone forever.

He had to survive. Out there in the winter jungle,
where you died, if you couldn't kill first.

Long after embassy security had left and the
hatchet men in the black Volgas had cruised the area,
and the guests, scared and disoriented, had gone
home, Klimov sat alone in his living room and examined the bullet hole in the wall.

They had beckoned, he reflected, and Tristram had
come running. He would have seen June's televised
"confession." Klimov recalled the anger and determination in his eyes. But there was more, something
they hadn't planned for. The kind of strength and
agility normally found in much younger men.

Klimov had met the British before and hadn't enjoyed them. One summer he had been on temporary
assignment to the embassy in London and had had
his every footstep dogged by MI5. He had done nothing and they had let him do nothing. A total waste of
time. And he hadn't gone back to London since, because the British never forgot you. Those bumbling,
lazy, decadent people. But they had a hard edge that
you couldn't ignore.

He heard a light knocking at the front door. Hadn't
security finished yet? Was he to get no peace that
night? Angrily he flung open the door and immediately took a step back.

The Russian strode past him without greeting and

made his way into the living room. His eyes took in the damaged wall, the plaster on the carpet. He turned to face Klimov.

"I thought you might want to know about your Polish friend. The man from the Interior Ministry. Passent."

"Know what?"

"His body was found an hour ago."

Klimov sat down. Later, when he thought about it, he could trace his sense of foreboding back to that moment, when he had sat there watching the Russian, seeing for the first time the extent of the danger they now faced.

It wasn't till the Russian had left the house and was on his way to the airport that he realized his error. Klimov's intruder had gone. So, too, had the embassy security men. But it wouldn't end there. That wasn't the way it was done. Out of sight, at least one unit would have been watching the house, checking for any unusual visitors. They wouldn't have told Klimov. They'd just sit there in case something happened. And now they would have locked on to him. Damn the bastards.

He looked into his rearview mirror. Four cars behind him. Get the colors. Two white, one red, one light blue. Check every minute.

He turned off the main road. Go around the houses, try a shortcut, see who follows. The two white cars were still with him.

If only he'd known about Klimov's visitor. But they should have expected it, should have planned for it. Tristram wasn't going to sit around and do nothing.

The Russian rejoined the highway. **And it** goes only one way now, direct to Okecie airport **and** back again, so there's no choice anymore. You're committed. He joined the flow of trucks and cars and glanced again in the mirror. One of the white cars had stayed the course. Maybe genuine, maybe not. But you don't live long on maybes.

You have to make a decision now. Once inside the airport, they can bottle you up like an insect. You're stuck in the departure lounge, armed guards and soldiers all around. You can't put yourself in that position if there are any maybes.

Never mind that the rendezvous in Switzerland was definite. They had set that rule just to keep track of each other. You had to make it. Unless you were dead or dying, a no-show would be taken as a critical change of plan. And yet he had to risk it. While he was free there was still a chance to make something of it. If they caught him . . .

But he didn't finish the thought, just drove to the departure complex and out again, cruising slowly, attracting no attention, like a taxi driver looking for business.

Only when he was close to the city did he spot the white car again, half hidden behind a bus. They were being casual, he thought. Three or four of them by the look of it, joyriding. They wouldn't be difficult to lose. This time.

40

Every January there comes a day when the weather tricks you, when the cold wind softens and a warm sun sparkles down over the city and you imagine winter has gone. But it doesn't last, and when the sun goes down the melted snow freezes over and the roads and pavements become more treacherous than ever.

Grazyna knew it wasn't over. Nothing in Poland ever ended. Things only began again, harder and more intense than before. Each vaunted economic reform brought a different shortage, each battle brought new casualties and another battle, somewhere else, some other time. No one forgot, she decided, and yet no one ever remembered—where they were, who kept the keys to the tanks, and what always happened when they hit the streets.

So unreal it was to live in Poland, where half the country pretended they were somewhere else, half free or half repressed. Enough for some, but never the majority.

She left the apartment and wandered into the

square. The ambulance and police cars had left hours ago, and Ania had gone away in a black plastic bag. And she wouldn't be the last. Grazyna was certain of that. You don't declare a war footing and go off to pick mushrooms. You go and fight and bring back flowers for the gravestones, and maybe they'll light a candle for you on a street corner in the time-honored fashion. And maybe they won't.

She wondered what little Maya Angelica was doing, out in the wood near the Soviet border, safe with her cousin. And if it all went wrong, what would it mean to her?

It's come so quickly, she thought. Two weeks ago we were a bunch of stragglers, crusaders without a cause. We printed leaflets, held meetings, hid and protected the ones who were on the run. But it wasn't going anywhere. It never becomes a war because we knew we could never win. Now, suddenly, it's a war, and we could lose it all.

Jozef had done all that, taken the sleeper from Berlin, carrying the orders of battle, just the way he had in the seventies. Only then they had been building the movement out of nothing. Behind them were the grim years of Stalin, when you hardly dared let your mind dream a dream, when a disloyal word could slip from your mouth and hang you. They had lived through that. And then came the spring—hesitant, weak, and oh so unpredictable. Of course that was almost worse than the blanket repressions. For the informers had penetrated every meeting, noted every encounter, wormed their way into everything.

Grazyna looked up and saw blue sky and felt the sun warming her hair.

The seventies had been a good time. The government was weak and wanted to buy goodwill. Many Poles had traveled to the West, peeked over the wall, breathed the capitalist air. They had seen something worth fighting for, so they'd come back and cranked up the unrest. In 1980 they were ready for the Solidarity union, better organized than they'd ever been before. And a year later the authorities had used tanks to break it all up. And that, as her mother had always said, was that. End of story. Lock away your memories and don't let anyone steal them, because in Poland that's all we've got.

Grazyna had made good progress toward Constitution Square, and the private market traders were out on Polna Street, selling white cheese and chickens, some cucumbers and radishes. All of it expensive. But people would pay what it took.

She recalled the early months of her marriage to Garten, how poor they'd been, how Zbig had taken them in. And as the days went by she had grown to admire him and care for him. A giant among men, she had thought. Brave and resourceful—a man who ran an underground network that surpassed even that of the Catholic Church. As a carpenter he had traveled right across Poland, working in factories and shipyards, fulfilling his commissions and moving on. And while he worked he had sucked in the information. Who was up, who was down, where the Party was weak, who was bribable, who had a secret they didn't want told. Always he would return to Warsaw and share his stories. Grazyna recalled the countless evenings she had listened enraptured by his knowledge and recall.

Zbig had known the real Poland, with all its scabs and wounds. And still he had loved it, even as it beat him to the ground.

Almost without thinking Grazyna had crossed Warsaw to find herself outside Dyadek's apartment. Along the street coal was being delivered from a horse-drawn cart. Two elderly figures in blackened coats were shoveling the blocks onto the pavement, where the customers would collect them. All around her, she reflected, were reminders of the past—Poland still struggling into this century when other countries were preparing for the next.

She stopped across the street from the main door, trying to collect her thoughts. But there wasn't time. From around the corner a gray Fiat sedan was flashing toward her. Even as it pulled up she could see three figures emerge from the building, hurriedly and ungracefully pouring themselves onto the backseat. Instinctively Grazyna turned away, and yet, even as she did so, she could see his face—Dyadek's face, transfixed by fear, staring straight ahead, the white hair, the long arrogant nose.

A few feet away some boys began chasing each other, and an old woman walked past the car but refused to turn her head. *You've got to stop this*, Grazyna told herself, but the car was moving off. Dyadek was being abducted in broad daylight and no one was lifting a finger. The car was accelerating rapidly. She ran out into the road, shouting, waving her arms—and then stopped, realizing no one could hear her. Suddenly the car had gone. She turned to see one of the coal men leaning on his shovel as if it were a walking stick.

"Give it up," he called across to her. "Give it up. This is Poland, remember? It's not worth the tears and the pain." And he looked at her almost pityingly, as if she were destined to suffer both.

In the distance, over the mountains, the sky was a deep, dark blue and the Englishman could see the colored lights around the lake as the plane dipped down over Geneva.

It was the last time he would make the journey—he would tell the Russian. Too risky for a man in his position. Too many eyes at the airport, too many remote cameras. You can't go on putting your head in a noose and playing with it.

He should have ended the Polish operation long before it had gotten to this stage. But each action carried a risk. And he had thought the Russian more capable, more ruthless, more efficient in his own backyard. If he couldn't hunt down James Tristram, he couldn't hunt at all.

A taxi took him to the hotel, its radio pinging and sputtering as they crossed the half-empty city. It was, he decided, a monumentally boring place. Sterile, closed. An air-raid shelter under every house, where they could all sit and fiddle with their watches while the rest of the world fought it out.

As he stepped from the taxi he could feel the stillness. Lights burned in a few of the hotel rooms, but the Englishman took no comfort from that. You were on your own here, the country neutral, the people deaf and unseeing. Years ago the Swiss had made clear they would tolerate no intelligence violations in their country, no little wars or killings. At the first sign all sides would be out. Since then the rules had been kept. But they all knew it was only a question of time.

The proprietor, Herr Leck, was installed at the reception desk.

"Good evening, Herr . . . ah?"

"Thomas. Good evening."

"Of course, Herr Thomas." There was a quick smile, quicklittle movements that produced the room key and the registration card, summoned the boy for the luggage. Herr Leck at his most clinical.

At eight-thirty the Englishman descended to the ground floor and walked to the back of the hotel, as he had the last time. He didn't knock, but pulled smartly on the handle, and, with a grunt of surprise, stepped back. Twice he tried it and then returned to the reception desk.

"I take it my colleague has been delayed."

Herr Leck did not look up from the register. "I know of no colleague, Herr Thomas. My guests meet with many people, and I take the trouble to forget them all. Nobody, and I say this with some pride, takes any account of who comes and goes. Complete discretion, you understand, Herr Thomas. Complete discretion." The bald head rose and nodded pedantically.

"I quite understand."

The Englishman returned to his room and opened the door to the balcony. The room seemed hot and close. For a second he lost his balance, reaching out to the chest of drawers to steady himself.

There are no innocent changes of plan, he reflected. If two agents set a rendezvous, there is no stomachache or back pain that will prevent them from keeping it. Only danger, real danger.

He wasted no time gathering up his coat and the unopened suitcase, reaching for the telephone.

"A taxi, please, Herr Leck."

"At once, Herr Thomas."

And he was back out into the night, back across the sleeping, ignorant city.

Too late for planes, but there was a night train to Paris and from there a hundred different connections to London.

As they drove he could see there were fewer lights burning. Some of the passersby wore thick ski boots and woolen hats. It would be a cold night, cold and uneasy.

Of course the danger might not be to the Russian. You have always to consider betrayal. You have always to consider that a double agent may revert to his handler, that a traitor may reform, that the Russian could have sold him to save his own life. You can't be charitable, he knew that. You can't be soft or sentimental. If there was going to be treachery, it would be as well to commit it first.

Long before he reached the station the Englishman had drafted an urgent message to the British Embassy in Moscow. He would send it as soon as he got to London.

41 _____

The General Secretary leaned back in his chair and gazed out at Moscow. There were times when he thought it beautiful, but now was not one of them. Years earlier, as a rising star in the Party, he had been allowed a visit to France and Italy. There he had seen beauty. He recalled the way he had examined the cities, with their history and culture, stared at the people in bars and cafés, noted the freedom and ease with which they walked the streets. The absence of authority. Often a voice would come to him from the classrooms of his old school in the Transcaucasus and remind him of Western crime and unemployment, of drugs and exploitations. And yet each time he had looked about him his eyes had told a different story.

Something inside him, he recalled, had longed to stay. Maybe he could have lost the car, lost his passport, gone to the Americans or the French. But that would not have been his way. He would return to Russia, he had decided, and take what he had learned with him. He could do nothing about the past. But the future was not inevitable. There could be a dynamic in Russia, an energy, a force for invention and creativity. Ultimately, he knew, it could occur only in a freer society.

The cabinet officer buzzed from the outer office. The General Secretary flicked on the green light above the door and the man entered carrying a leather file.

"Leave it by the door."

The officer gave a hint of a bow and turned on his heel.

Freedom. He looked down to the river. Dotted along the frozen surface were a handful of fishermen sitting on stools, dangling their lines through holes they had cut in the ice. What use did they have for freedom?

Of course things would have to change. But he had no illusions about the task. He got up, picked up the leather file, and reset the blinds, letting the sun stream through the triple windows.

There were terrible dangers in tampering with the system, for it was built on human insecurity. Power came only from the top. Therefore it had no security or legitimacy other than what it gave itself. The entire edifice was founded on fear. And if you altered the balance, upset the equilibrium, you could easily meet a terminal accident.

He knew it had happened before. He had arranged it himself.

From the file the General Secretary removed a sheaf of papers and settled back in the chair. The final details of his visit to Warsaw had been compiled and awaited approval. He ran a finger down the list and groaned inwardly. Trips to factories, trips to war me-

morials, and dinner after dinner. At the end of it
would come the inevitable stomach upset. Maybe it
was he, maybe it was the disgusting food, covered
with rich sauces, the tables groaning under overloaded trays and bowls. In the West, he recalled, they
never gave you half as much. But then they had nothing to prove.

He reached the final sheet and raised an eyebrow in
surprise. The British were requesting a meeting and
that was well out of the ordinary. Ambassadors were
supposed to go through channels, first the Foreign
Ministry, never directly to the Kremlin.

He read the note again and buzzed the outer office.

"Comrade General Secretary?" The cabinet officer
had entered immediately.

"What is this thing with the British ambassador?"

"I have no idea, Comrade General Secretary. The
man is highly agitated and said he had information
from his government that must be communicated directly to you."

"The Minister of Foreign Affairs is still in Iraq?"

"He returns next week."

"And what is your recommendation?" The General Secretary looked the man straight in the eye.

"We would suggest that you decline the request.
The British should not think they can have access to
you whenever they wish. It would, I believe, set a—
how shall I put it?—an unfortunate precedent."

The General Secretary looked down at the paper
on his desk. "Your suggestion is noted. Make an appointment for the ambassador at four o'clock this afternoon." He glanced up contemptuously. "I might
remind you that this is a government, not a prison

camp. Sometimes we should talk to the outside world —not slam the door in their faces. Too many games, Comrade, too many silly games."

Britain's ambassador to Moscow sat in the diplomatic reception area and marveled at the simplicity of it—the absence of glitter and pomp, so beloved by previous Soviet leaders.

Everywhere he looked there was understatement. Dimmed lights, plain woodblock floors, white walls unencumbered by frantic tapestries of the revolution. A Picasso, a Degas. After centuries, it seemed, the Kremlin had ushered in the outside world.

Of course the biggest surprise had been the summons. Sir Harold Stebbings put his elderly gray head in his hands and recalled the message London had sent him: "Seek urgent audience with the General Secretary, matter of national security, exceptional circumstances. Do it and forget it. No answer back. No acknowledgment." It had sounded like the ravings of a madman.

His first reaction had been to dismiss the whole thing. But he'd been a diplomat long enough to know when London was playing games. And what they were suggesting struck him as so damnably silly that he knew with complete certainty they were serious.

For a moment the thin black-suited diplomat, with the brogues and the gold watch chain, seemed lost in thought. From across the corridor he could hear the faint clatter of teleprinters and high-speed transcription machines. No tension, no bustle. He could have been in the headquarters of a major industrial corporation.

And it seemed quite natural for the General Secretary to open the door himself and usher the ambassador inside. A hand fell on his shoulder and he was shown to a simple antique chair across from the desk. But there was no warmth in the greeting.

"We have, as always, limits on our time, Ambassador. You wished to see me on an urgent and exceptional matter. I have made an exception and agreed to see you. Please state your business."

Sharp, thought Stebbings, sharp and hard with it. The private face of the new Soviet star, so much feted around the world. If only people could see him now.

He cleared his throat. "I'll come straight to the point, General Secretary. . . ." And then he stopped, uncertain of how to continue, aware that once he had relayed the message, there would be no going back. Nothing would be quite the same again. He sat up, straightening his back.

"I have to tell you, sir, that my government believes you to be in considerable danger."

The Soviet leader rose and walked over to the window. The ambassador fell silent. Should he proceed? Was this a signal of some kind? The man was staring out over the city. Then he turned abruptly.

"Sir Harold," he said quietly, "why don't we take a walk?"

The General Secretary led him through a side door that he hadn't seen before, cut in the wood paneling. The corridor was stone. At the end of it, a tiny two-man elevator.

The Soviet leader held open the door. It sprang smartly shut and they began to descend. Cold air wafted upward and Stebbings shivered. The light in

the elevator was dim. He could see only the General
Secretary's profile, not his expression.

Abruptly the elevator halted. Uniformed hands
pulled open the wrought-iron gates, boots snapped to
attention on either side. They stepped out and stood
still for a moment. Suddenly Stebbings was aware of
powerful hands helping him into a coat. It was dark
and heavy, and there appeared to be a fur collar. The
General Secretary was receiving similar attentions.
He could see the man pulling a scarf across his face,
wrenching the hat down low over his forehead.

"Let us go this way, Sir Harold." The ambassador
counted five steps, and then without warning a door
was opened and the daylight and the wind streamed
in. And suddenly they were out between the Kremlin
wall and the Council of Ministers. In the gray distance Stebbings could see a chain of dark figures,
maybe tourists. Thin, flat snowflakes swirled about
them.

He suddenly realized that they were heading toward the people, the General Secretary striding out
ahead of him. The ambassador shivered, and for a
moment he felt unaccountably afraid. And yet the
man was unrecognizable, just another wintry shape,
nothing to distinguish him from the crowds.

As they walked the Soviet leader turned to him and
spoke through the scarf.

"Ambassador, you were talking, if I remember, of
some danger to me. Perhaps you would explain."

Stebbings struggled to catch his breath. He drew
level with the younger man. Only his eyes were visible, the same blue eyes in the wide, open face.

"It concerns your visit to Poland."

The General Secretary stopped. The ambassador pulled down his own scarf and felt the wind sting his nose and chin. Better to have everything in the open. He took a deep breath. "We strongly suggest you cancel the trip."

They had cleared the walls of the Kremlin and were enveloped in the swelling crowd along Revolution Square. The streets had been glazed by ice; the people looked numb. And Stebbings was struck by the silent trudging all around him, like an army in retreat.

What the hell was going on? He looked in disbelief at the Soviet leader. The fellow was behaving like an invisible man among his own people. What sort of madness was this? A game? If so, why was he playing? In all his years of diplomacy he could find no precedent for it, no explanation.

At times the two of them were buffeted by the oncoming crowd—homegoers, old women, men in uniform. There were the dark, swarthy figures from Georgia or Central Asia; Mongols, too, with their flat noses and high cheekbones—part of the Soviet patchwork spread out over a sixth of the globe.

The General Secretary's scarf still covered his mouth and nose. But in the eyes Stebbings could see he had relaxed. And then he understood it. The man felt safer out on the streets than at the center of his own empire, safer among strangers who could never vote him in or out of power, safer without the colleagues and advisers who would scheme and plot and one day force him from office.

Stebbings had no doubt that there were bodyguards around them. The Soviet leader might be unconventional. He was not suicidal. Some would be on foot, others in cars. Perhaps a camera was following their progress from a high building. In Russia, he knew, they could track you across snow or desert, through cities or wasteland. Their power was unfettered and absolute. Nothing could stand in its way.

He had talked uninterrupted for more than twenty minutes and then he paused.

Stebbings felt the Soviet leader move closer to his side.

"You had better give me the names," he said. "All of them." And the steam blossomed from behind his scarf. "We don't appear," he added, "to have much time."

42

Garten felt the snow turn to rain and shivered.

In the early morning light mist hung in patches above the grass. And yet there was no mistaking the towers and walls of the monastery on the hilltop high above him. He shivered again. Not just any monastery—this one, the Church of the Black Madonna, Poland's most sacred shrine, a symbol of strength and defiance through the ages.

Wearily, Garten began the climb. His stomach was empty, and the morning wind seemed to drive straight through his clothes. He had spent a lousy night in the university hostel, where the central heating had rattled until dawn, where the air had been hot and humid, and the students clumped and shouted in the corridors well into the small hours. Garten had known the rector from years ago. A fat little man with a nerve in his nose that quivered constantly. Sometimes he had been in the movement, sometimes out. "Take the room and move on," he had told Garten. "I have a family. These are hard times. They watch us all."

Garten had felt the anger surge inside him, anger at the uncommitted, the afraid. It had been the same in the shipyards at Stettin. There he'd encountered the young firebrands of eighteen and nineteen, some with the first sproutings of hair on their cheeks and upper lips. Kids who imagined they could undermine the state with a clenched fist and a slogan. Naive, primitive, Garten had seen them all before. He hadn't been happy to see them again.

As he walked he counted the places he had visited, the hours by road and rail, by truck and bicycle. Through the dirty, bleak villages he had sought out the sympathizers, the men they had positioned and buried years before. They were to be the underground's last and only shot. Saved and nurtured for the time when the movement would rise up, play all its cards, and go for the big one. The time now fast approaching.

Garten stopped and caught his breath. Below him the town of Czestochowa slept along a wide shallow valley. Only in the monastery would they be awake, singing their morning prayers, dedicating to God's greater glory a day in Communist Poland. And yet here, he knew, there was a light that could make a difference.

From the trees he crossed to the monastery wall. A small wooden gate had been cut close to the corner. His father's gate, Zbig's gate, and only God, it seemed, had watched the men and women who entered and left by it.

Garten hadn't seen it for years. But he remembered the day. A blazing summer, just before sunset. They had climbed the hill, quickly, eagerly. "When you come here," Zbig had told him, "you come only to this gate. Day and night there is a monk who stands guard behind it." Zbig had told him of the people for whom it had been designed—Communist officials, men and women of the government, soldiers and policemen who would steal in with their faces covered, often with a child wrapped in blankets. They came for baptism or marriage, in a country where the revelation of their faith could lose them their jobs. Hesitant, frightened, they would gather in the tiny chapel near the door in the wall. There the service would be conducted with maximum speed. Later, under cover of night, they would leave the building and return to their own world.

There were no banns published, no public records kept. But Garten knew that deep in the archives of the monastery the clergy kept a list—detailed, up to date, and most certainly explosive. As he knocked on the door he knew he had to find a way to get it.

The monk led him to a small cell. A mattress lay on the floor. A small electric fire fizzled dangerously in the corner. It was cold, just as cold as on the outside. Garten could see moss along the bare stone wall.

"You are . . . ?" The monk removed his hood. Pale blue eyes watched Garten unflinchingly.

"Tell the abbot. I'm Zbig's son. Come to talk to him. It's urgent. Vital. He'll understand."

"The abbot is sick. He will see no one."

"He will see me. There is no other way."

For a moment the two of them looked at each other in silence. Then the monk moved to the doorway and, still without speaking, let himself out.

He had been gone for less than ten minutes when Garten heard footsteps in the corridor. The monk had not returned. Instead a young woman in a white nurse's uniform entered the cell. Her thin face held no greeting.

"Please follow me. You may see the abbot, but for only a short time."

They climbed stone staircases and headed along dark corridors. In a few of the rooms Garten glimpsed some of the monks at work. There were desks, and libraries, an office, and no names on any of the doors. They go to ground, thought Garten, that's how they survive. You could hide an army in this place and they'd never be found. And he knew some of the people they had hidden, didn't he? Some of the underground leaders on the run during martial law. The police had never found them here, never even looked for them. The clergy had their own friends in high places.

Abruptly the nurse turned right and pushed open a large oak door. For a moment Garten thought the room was empty, but as his eyes got used to the light, he could see the long, wide bed in the corner.

"Don't shout at him," the nurse whispered. "He hears everything. People always shout at him because he's ill, but it's not necessary."

Garten approached the bed. A jagged shaft of daylight shone through the poorly fitting curtains, striking the abbot on the right side of his face. The old man looked tired and immobile, and yet Garten had expected worse. The skin still had color and texture. There was strength around the mouth and jaw.

"Zbig's son, you say." The voice was steady.

"Yes, Abbot. You knew my father well."

The old eyes seemed to darken. "I have been mourning your father." He paused and his breathing came more heavily. "You should know that he was a man with many regrets." The abbot paused. Garten said nothing.

"Most of them seemed to revolve around you."

Garten turned away. "I didn't know that."

"Of course you didn't." The abbot shifted onto his side. "You were away in England. Perhaps you were resting, perhaps you needed time to think. Who among us knew what you were doing? Your father was bitterly hurt."

Garten got up from the bedside. Deep down he had known in advance what the abbot would say to him. Finally he would have to answer for his time away, for the sudden panic that had gripped him so many years before, for the feelings of guilt that had made him stay silent, out of touch, cut off from his family, from the movement.

"Maybe I did need time to think." Garten stood at the end of the bed.

"You could have come here. You could have lived among the fathers as long as you wanted. We would have given you peace and comfort. You would not have been the first."

"I know. I know that now. I was afraid. But you must see . . ." He wrung his hands. "What we were doing then had no point. Surely you knew that. We were knocking on brick walls, shouting at the wind. Nothing we did made any difference. Wherever we went they blocked us, arrested us, took our equipment. All over Poland they had traitors, right in the midst of us. Wherever we ran to, they got there first. I . . . I had to get away from that. It was terrible, simply terrible."

"And yet you came back." The abbot's voice was quiet. In the corner Garten heard the door open and watched as the old man ushered the nurse away.

"I came because I believed the time was right to do something." He returned to the bedside and sat down again.

"No, not right, Abbot, vital. We have to stand up and fight while there is still time. The underground is lazy, soft, lulled by the Communist aggression and the new man in Moscow. They're *blind*. They don't realize they're being duped with fancy phrases about reform and democracy. It's like a bulldog stepping forward to have a new collar put round its neck. This one feels looser, more comfortable, but it tightens much more quickly. One strain on the leash and it cuts your throat. The Communists are simply waiting for the government to fail."

"You are not describing anything that is new." The abbot's eyes began to look tired. "Each time they change it is for the worse. Each year they perfect and refine their evil. . . ."

"But this time we have a chance to end this love affair, this so-called coalition. Moscow's new man is coming. That will be our signal. Do you know what I have been doing? I've traveled this country north to south, waking up our people, instructing them. And now they wait for a radio message that will activate them in their tens of thousands."

Garten looked over at the abbot. The old man had

shut his eyes, but he wasn't asleep, lying there in the dim, dull daylight.

Garten lowered his voice. "But I need one more thing, Abbot. I need to know who supports us in the Party, who can we pressure, who can we count on. Only you know the whereabouts of the list."

Slowly, purposefully, the cleric opened his eyes and eased himself up onto his elbows. He shook his head sadly.

"In the forty years that I have been here, no one"—he wagged his index finger at Garten—"no one has ever asked for the list. No one, you hear me." He sank onto the pillows and coughed violently. "Your father would never have asked for such a thing."

"My father is dead."

"And he died with honor," the abbot cut in quickly. "He did not live with disgrace. What you ask of me is to violate the trust of hundreds of frightened people who turned to God because man would have persecuted them. . . ."

"Thousands of people may die if you refuse."

"We all die, my friend. We all die. What matters is how we get there. How many times we deceive along the way, how many people we betray. Not the lives. They will go anyway."

Garten's voice rose angrily. "You are wrong, old man. This is a final chance to show the world that the Poles can fight, that communism can be resisted, must be resisted."

The abbot had shut his eyes. Garten heard the door open again and the young nurse stood in the doorway.

"You must leave now. You have stayed too long." She began moving toward him as if to pull his arm.

"Abbot, you have to . . ." And then he realized the uselessness of it. As he turned to go he heard the voice, older suddenly, more frail it seemed, echoing from the edge of the room.

"It would have been better if you had not asked, my friend, and not come here. I cannot find it in my heart to wish you either happiness or success."

Looking back, Garten could see the old man, motionless on the bed, his face without expression, just as if they had never spoken.

43 _____

"I feel as though I know you."

Tristram had spoken quietly, comfortingly, and yet the words seemed to punch right through Grazyna and she slammed the door shut, standing there helpless in Ania's flat, with Ania no longer alive to claim it.

Strange how close she was to her picture, the one on file back in London, taken light-years before.

"My name is James Tristram. I'm a colleague of your husband's."

She looked at him in disbelief. "Don't assume then that you are a friend of mine."

Grazyna moved into the center of the room. Elegant, headstrong, he thought. She was a woman who could manage alone, just as she'd had to. She sat on the sofa and put her bag on the coffee table.

"You knew Ania?"

"I know Ania." Tristram frowned. "Where is she?"

"I'm sorry to tell you this. She's dead. Died in a traffic accident." Odd, she thought, the way it sounded so matter-of-fact. No tears even in the distance.

Tristram got up and went over to the kitchen and began opening cupboards, slowly first, then more quickly. "I thought I might find some coffee," he said, and then stopped. Ania was dead. Presumably she'd been identified. That meant a police check very soon. How soon? Maybe a day or two, maybe less. Who knew what still functioned in this country? Sorry, Ania, he thought. So very sorry.

"We'll need to leave shortly," he told Grazyna. "But I have to contact your husband."

"Who are you?"

"I told you. Name's Tristram. We worked together in London. You might as well know that we worked together before he came out here."

"Which means what?" She looked at him, knowing what it meant.

"I don't need to answer that, do I?" Tristram sat down again, pulling the sport jacket across his swelling stomach. He was too tired to persuade or cajole. And there wasn't the time for it.

"It doesn't matter anyway," she told him. "He's out of contact. Even I couldn't find him."

"Until when?"

She looked hard at him, making up her mind. "Till the day after tomorrow. Six A.M. Dawn. You know what happens then?"

"He gives the signal for the uprising."

"That's right. My brave, intrepid husband, Jozef. He gives the grand signal." Sarcasm seemed to drip off the words themselves.

"Where?"
She didn't hesitate. "Auschwitz."

Even as Tristram sat there they were moving. The
urgent, coded signals from Moscow, ambassador
only. Direct to Warsaw. No distribution. The Foreign Ministry bypassed. Direct from the Kremlin,
with a signature leaving nothing to the imagination
or chance. You simply obeyed because this was
power. This was your career and your family. This
was a home in Moscow or the tiniest, smelliest village
in central Asia. And the Soviet ambassador was not a
man to try his luck.

He had his own security detail. That was the rule,
because nobody was completely trustworthy. They
were there to watch him and watch over him. They
carried out his orders, the two of them. Ivan and
Sergei, good boys, who were outside the control of
the local KGB resident, unknown to him, except as
the secretaries they purported to be.

Specific orders. No room for error, except if you
fail to carry them out. Ivan and Sergei drew their
sidearms and stuck them in the waistbands of their
trousers. And now, they felt, they could do anything.
One of them made the phone calls, the other brought
around the car. And the ambassador personally ordered the aircraft and leaned on the immigration authorities. Amazing what you could do with a little
shouting and weight-throwing. Your own.

Into the car then, the one with the Polish plates.
Still early. Still dark. The roads cold and tricky and
the snow drifts high and thick along the pavements.
And now quietly to Klimov's house. What had he

done? wondered the ambassador. How does a lowly
KGB chief in Warsaw provoke the most powerful of
them all? What awful transgressions had he committed? The ambassador hadn't been told, he certainly
wouldn't ask. Don't interfere, don't get involved,
don't think about the little summer house or the
grandchildren's future. If only he'd been out of Warsaw on vacation. If only.

No lights in Klimov's house. Let me do this. You
stand by. The ambassador glanced at Sergei and Ivan.
They looked crestfallen. Could have been their
chance to get back at Klimov, rough him up a bit,
intimidate the family. A joyous occasion snatched
from them.

He knocked at the door, quietly at first, then impatiently. All the lights seemed to come on at once, and
he could hear Klimov's solid frame descending the
wooden staircase. There was a muffled cry in the
background and he knew who that was. Well, she'd
have a fright, too, wouldn't she?

He stood there in his dressing gown, a dark figure,
the light behind him, the jaw jutting outward into
the dawn.

"My God, Ambassador. What's happened? What's
going on?"

"Urgent matter, Klimov. Just come up. They want
you in Moscow at once. You'll have to get your things
and leave immediately. There's a plane standing by."

A moment of silence from Klimov. He was weigh-
ing it all up. He would know all about these early
morning encounters, thought the ambassador. No
need to feel sorry for him. He's been on this side of
the door plenty of times.

"And my wife?"

That was the clincher. Now Klimov would really know.

"She comes too. That's the instruction."

Klimov inclined his head in resignation, seeing it all for what it was. Because when they take your family as well, then it's real trouble, and a special plane, and a dawn flight and no good-byes, then you're not going home to a medal and a celebration.

This is the journey back that you hoped you would never make.

"Give me a couple of minutes. . . ."

"Klimov, don't . . ."

Klimov looked past the ambassador to where Sergei and Ivan were standing, kicking their heels in the snow beside the car, and that seemed to change his mind.

"It's all right, I understand," he told the ambassador. "That's the way it happens, isn't it?"

They drove slowly toward the airport. Klimov's wife sat whimpering in the backseat. He made no attempt to comfort her. Sergei and Ivan cracked jokes in front. Denied their quota of physical nastiness, they told tales of prison camps and executions and laughed uproariously until the ambassador ordered them to be silent.

Klimov ignored them. Only when they reached the airport perimeter did his mind begin to race. What had gone wrong? Who had talked? Where was the Russian?

They drove directly to the aircraft. A tiny Yak 40 jet, the Soviet version of executive transport.

"Get her on board." The ambassador gestured toward Klimov's wife, who appeared to have passed out. Sergei and Ivan bundled her out of the car and carried her up the steps.

"I haven't anything to tell you." The ambassador put his hand on Klimov's shoulder, steering him away from the plane. "I shouldn't even be talking to you. But it's serious. That's all I know. And it comes directly from the Kremlin, none of the usual channels. It's from the man himself. So it couldn't be worse."

"Why are you telling me this?" Klimov turned up his collar against the wind.

"I don't know. You're as much a shit as the rest of them. But it's a tough way to go. We should have moved on a little but we haven't. Not in things like this. Once that plane lands in Moscow, you're a dead man. It's your choice what you do between now and then. Oh and one thing. They'll want to know about the old man—all of it, right back to the war, chapter and verse. That's what they really want."

He watched Klimov get aboard. A final shove from Sergei and the pilot closed the door. Ivan was riding shotgun. He was the lazier of the two, the slower. If Klimov was to have a chance, Ivan was it.

The ambassador stood on the tarmac and watched the Yak scream down the runway, the takeoff, it seemed, near vertical. In a few seconds the plane had disappeared into the snow-filled clouds that hung low and thick over central Poland. For some reason he felt sure it would never reach its destination.

44

Tristram examined the street carefully in both directions. Another fifteen, twenty minutes and it would be light. And now you play postman, he thought, and felt in his inside pocket for the note, the ultimatum he had promised Klimov. The rendezvous.

Up the path and he pushed the envelope under the door. The simplest drop of all and the most reliable. And that's what they'd always told him. Keep it easy. Intelligence is like one, two, three. Don't try to be clever. Don't make two trips where one will do. Don't nail messages to trees when there's a mailbox. Be normal.

Normal! Tristram recalled laughing. But he didn't laugh now, scanning the street again, suspicious suddenly of the stillness around him. The house had looked deserted. Why should that be strange? Klimov would be asleep next to his pig of a wife, soon to wake and plot the machinations of the day. He'd get a jolt in a little while, though, finding the postman had called early with an invitation to go south. An invitation to Auschwitz.

* * *

The Russian watched him go. Slowly he released
the curtain and let it fall back into place. The room
across the street had been highly convenient, the
apartment of a diplomat from Libya, a man who had
owed him a favor from many years ago. And now was
the time to call in the payments. Wherever you could.

It would have been so easy to kill Tristram, to have
reached through the window and fired. Even at that
distance he could have done it. The pistol had a
shoulder brace and a laser sight. He'd managed
harder shots than that. And yet it would not have
been satisfying.

The Russian reached for a tissue and blew his nose.
The room was cold and drab. On the table in front of
him lay a half-eaten salami and some rolls.

Tristram was certainly the enemy, but he wasn't
the main one. Not for now. Someone else had blown
the operation, someone else had squealed in Moscow.
And he had watched Klimov taken out of his house
like a runaway dog and led away to the killing farm.
Only they wouldn't let him die till they were ready.

He felt no pity for the man. Klimov had gone in
with his eyes open. Why the hell should he be pitied?
But someone would have to pay for the betrayal.

The Russian sat back in his chair. Who had the
motive? Who had the information? And then he remembered the canceled visit to Switzerland. Regret-
table, of course, but there had been no choice. Would
the Englishman have panicked? After all these years
would he have smelled a trap? Worse, would he have
seen the chance to bury his guilt for good and erase
the tracks?

His mind computed the odds. They didn't add up. But then, what else was there?

He got up and went to the door. Better move fast. In an hour or so the embassy would send around the security detail and the house would be ransacked. They'd pull everything out, right down to the cockroaches.

Already a few people were on the street. Middle-class Warsaw on its way to work. A BMW roared to life in one of the driveways and the Russian nodded amiably to a passerby.

It took only a sharp shove and the door gave. And there it was on the mat, sitting so stark and simple. A gift, thought the Russian. And not a moment too soon.

Back in his room, he tore open the envelope and read the contents twice.

What a clever man Tristram was trying to be. He had nothing to bargain except himself, and here he was calling the shots, demanding freedom for the little woman in London—June, that was her name— and setting a rendezvous in Auschwitz.

The idea was ludicrous. The Russian snorted into his handkerchief. And yet, the more he thought about it, the more it appealed to him. As he sat in the little room he could think quite clearly about the future.

Finally he reasoned they had gotten him. That much was undeniable. In the end everyone lost. Whatever you learned in life, it was important to absorb that. You can win only for a while.

Still, it was vital to leave something behind . . . or take something with you. He recalled a few of the men he had executed. One or two had even managed to spit in his eye, so they had been dispatched with the glint of triumph in their expressions. They had enjoyed their moment. And now, the Russian promised himself, he would enjoy his.

He moved to open the door and then rapidly changed his mind. He hadn't missed the skid of rubber on ice. From the window he saw them getting out of the Volgas, all in their identikit coats and shapkas. A dozen men with a mission.

Something inside him enjoyed the spectacle, for it brought back so many memories, so many raids, a lifetime of terror and intimidation to which he had dedicated himself. And they all moved so well! Professionals. They didn't talk, didn't waste energy, but their shapes were lean and fit, and they walked with a swagger and took pride in wielding the state's sword.

The Russian sighed. He had commanded men like that, trained them, earned their respect. And now, like the professionals they were, he had no doubt they would find him and hunt him down. But not yet. Not till he was ready. His age and his experience would win him that.

45

The two men had wakened June early. At least she assumed it had been early. But there was no light in the room and she had lost all track of time.

"Get moving, come on. Get your things together. You're going on a journey."

June sat up on the bed and threw off the blanket. The nights were cold and she had asked for more clothes and they had gone out and bought her a woolen cardigan. Now she wore it both day and night, as if it could somehow ward off danger.

"Where are we going?"

"Long journey." It was the younger man. She could see him now in the light reflected from the corridor. "Going east, I shouldn't wonder."

"East?" She gasped suddenly and held her hand to her mouth.

The man lowered his voice. "Look, I don't know, do I? Anyway, it's bound to be somewhere cold."

Odd, she thought, how humans come to accept the awful and the extraordinary. And she recalled the hours of panic when they'd first put her in the room, the shouting, her own shouts, and the solid block of depression that had weighted her face down on the rough, hard mattress as the hours jumbled past.

Emotions came and went, but the resentment didn't go away. That sick, nervous hand, gripping the lower stomach—always there, whatever you thought about, whenever you ate or slept. And at times she had pounded the mattress with her fists and screamed her innocence. But who had spoken of guilt? I'm a physics teacher, a good one, and I met a man and danced with him a few times and liked him. And I shouldn't be here! For the sake of Jesus Christ Almighty, I shouldn't be here!

And then came the calm, just as now. You can hear every little sound, every scratch of a bird, and all the traffic you could ever want, in the distance so far away. Once, she remembered, she had wakened in the middle of the operation to remove her tonsils. And she could hear it all, the sound of gas and suction, instruments being put down and picked up, the chatter of the surgeon—and she, yes, she, powerless to open her eyes, powerless to sit up, powerless to scream. Then as now, she thought, and stood up, wrapping her coat around her.

The older man had led the way, down the corridor, down two flights of wooden stairs that bent and creaked under their weight. And, oh God, the rain and the wind, and as they stepped outside into darkness she turned her head upward to drink them in, aware suddenly that they were in a courtyard with tall buildings and chimney stacks on all sides. But at least it said London to her as they opened the back of a van and pushed her in.

June crouched on the hard metal floor, trying to stop herself keeling over. They were driving fast, far too fast, slamming in and out of the gears, the engine whining and jerking.

Then something seemed to go wrong. For they must have pulled over to the side of the road. The van had stopped. She pressed her ear to the front partition, hearing the static of a radio transceiver. One of the men was arguing, protesting. She couldn't make out the words. But the tone said abuse, invective, puzzlement.

They were turning the van. That much she could tell. A three-point turn in the middle of the road, careering around, heading back the way they had come. Or were they? How do I know? But she did know, hearing the sound of a railway station, the same sound she had registered a few minutes before, a distant signal, clatter on tracks.

There wasn't any doubt in her mind. So she settled back on the metal floor and waited till they opened the back of the van, led her out under the drizzle, back up the stairs. They slammed the door and she stood alone in the darkened room, wondering if she had imagined it all. But she could still feel the rain on her face, and her hair was damp and windswept. And for a brief instant she had felt free.

Through the scatter of South London, through Brixton and along the M23, Cornish drove, his mind on the traffic, refusing to think of anything else. It was only when he reached the outskirts of Brighton that his thoughts began to wander. Turn right under the railway bridge, up onto the downs past the old windmill and into the sprawl of Hove. And the gray of the sea met the gray of the sky.

The Director had disappeared. No, not disappeared, gone sick. That's what his wife had said. But she wouldn't say where he'd gone. And that was irregular enough. It really was most worrying.

The line of traffic had come to a halt and Cornish sat impatiently, playing with the dials on the radio.

Funnily enough, though, no one else in the office seemed to be worried by the man's departure. Apparently the Cabinet Office had been informed, the under secretary at the Foreign Office knew all about it, even the Prime Minister had received a memo. So what did *they* make of it all? A man who came and went at will, who seemed to carry on the business of the Service in the street instead of in his office. Did they think that was any way to behave?

And there were other reasons why it worried him. For the unusual can always be a sign or a symptom. An eccentric can be a wise man or a fool. A wild gesture can be a reflex or part of a pattern. And everything has two sides, and some things have more. Cornish knew that.

But he wasn't sure why he'd come to Brighton. It was only a sense that something was missing. What a worrier I've become, he told himself. Never used to be. And he thought back to his escapades during the war, and the way he had never worried or cared about anything. Just done what he thought he should.

The traffic moved on again, and his hand came away from the steering wheel hot and clammy.

Cornish pulled in and stopped about a hundred yards from the Director's block. He could see both entrances to the building, with the ocean lapping just a few feet from it across the causeway.

The couple lived on the first floor—an apartment that looked directly out to sea. Years ago they had sold their house in London, children had grown up, and they didn't want to live over the shop, as so many others had done. The Director was always on call, people were always dropping by late at night with documents to sign, permissions to obtain. Now, of course, there were fewer people to drop in. Brighton was far enough away. So all they had to cope with was the phone.

Outside the building Cornish could see the porter repainting the wooden gate. Not a man in a hurry. He'd met him a couple of times. Ex-Navy, a bit too comfortable, found a sinecure and wouldn't want to give it up—"Know what I mean?" Cornish had known all right. Wouldn't have minded one himself, when he thought about it.

On instinct he got out of the car and went over to the man. There was a nod of recognition.

"Morning, my friend. Is he in?"

"Morning, sir." The porter put down his paint-brush and pursed his lips to look important. "Seems to me there may, just may, mind you, have been a slight misunderstanding. Know what I mean?"

"No, I don't know what you mean."

"Well, sir, it's like this. He"—the porter leaned on the word—"he ain't here anymore. Left a few days ago. Just a wave and a fiver stuffed into me hand. And that was it. I'd come out to clean up—you know, the droppings. Well, it's like that here with the filthy gulls. And there he is with his missus and a few bags, and suddenly they're in the car and off. I mean I don't even have an address, although nobody's been round. 'Cept you."

"What about the keys?"

"They took them as well." The porter put his hands in his pockets and stood upright. He had the look of a man who wasn't going to say any more. Cornish took out his wallet and handed him a ten-pound note.

"And you don't have a spare set?"

"I wish I could help, sir."

"I'm sure you do." Cornish turned his back on the man and returned to his car. As he drove away the fellow was watching him, still smiling, still holding the money in his hand. But he couldn't drive for long. His fingers wouldn't hold the wheel and his knee began to tremble involuntarily.

Think. Think! What did it mean? The Director had disappeared and yet there were no alarm bells. Nothing out of the ordinary. The office was functioning as normal. Cornish didn't like it.

He drove on for a mile or two and then stopped again. He was missing something. Across the downs the sun was setting in great orange streaks, gold and orange with jagged edges. And he sat back in the car and thought how much it reminded him of the wartime skies—the contrast between natural beauty in the heavens and the devastation on the ground.

Suddenly he wanted to get back home, back to the family and the lawn mowing, and the wife with her endless tea parties. He put his key back in the ignition but couldn't turn it. He was scared to move.

* * *

"There's a point, Dyadek, when you get down to the wire, when you peel away all the talk and the playacting, the masks, the finery, the lies, and the horse-trading—and then there's just you and me in a room. And no one else to hear what we say."

"I know."

"But do you?"

"I think so."

The Soviet ambassador looked across his desk. In front of him an elderly, frightened priest, brought in by the new team. The new team sent from Moscow. Kremlin security ordered out to work with him, and if that didn't suit them, to work against him. A wonderful, flexible society we have, he told himself. Everything's negotiable.

"I think you should tell me what you know."

"Too late for that." Dyadek stared at the floor.

"Maybe not. Many people could be harmed. Many could be saved. You have faced choices like that in the past—and behaved responsibly."

"I have done, as they say, that which I should not have done."

"We could argue about it."

"Not about that. Anyway, I'm tired."

The ambassador sighed. "I have been most patient. You agree? But in turn you must see my position. I am being pressed for information. My people want to repair the damage. We want peace and understanding. What is past we can do nothing about. But the future is always there."

He went over to the sideboard and poured coffee, watching Dyadek from the corner of his eye. The tactics had been right, he was sure of that. Take it slow. You can't just keep bashing the Poles. People had been doing that for centuries and getting nowhere.

The priest set down his coffee. Maybe, he reflected, there was a point at which you couldn't go back. You've sold your soul to the devil so many times that he won't return it. And one more transaction hardly seems worth the effort.

So he sat back in the easy chair with the ornate wooden armrests, ate a pastry, and told of the things he had seen and heard, of a man called Garten, where he had gone, where he would go.

He was interrupted only for a moment by the phone call, barely noticed the jerk of the ambassador's eyebrows, and ignored completely the draining of color from the man's face.

When he'd finished he was shown out and driven to within two blocks of his apartment. It was, after all, important to maintain appearances.

And the ambassador remained sitting at his desk, going over in his mind the news that he had expected. A military telegram about a missing plane that had left Warsaw hours earlier bound for Moscow, carrying a man they had much wanted to interview. Disappeared, they said, off the radar screens. No sightings or wreckage reported.

He didn't know whether to feel happy or sad.

46

They were dying slowly. That was how it felt. The KGB major looked around the forest clearing at the soldiers, fatter, more idle, and lazier by the day. They'd become a rabble. Another few days and the smoldering hostility would turn to outright insurrection. He'd seen it before. The men were animals. They should have been kept badly fed and exhausted. It was the only way to handle them.

Yet the orders had been to wait and stay out of sight. And the promise had been that they would see the kind of action they liked best. Easy targets, outgunned, outmanned, and maneuvered into a dead end. Like shooting ducks at a fairground. A pleasant, fulfilling outing, then back to barracks.

From across the clearing he could see one of the lookout patrols returning to base, a six-man unit dressed in their winter battle capes. It was of no interest. And yet, as he looked again, he could see someone else with them. He picked up the field glasses and focused them. A civilian. At least he was dressed as one—a large, lean figure with short black hair. Confi-

dent. The major could see it from the walk. Long,
unhurried steps through the dirty, trampled snow.

He left the command post and approached the lieutenant leading the patrol.

"Who is this with you, Comrade?"

"He wishes to speak with you." The lieutenant
grinned insolently. "You are, we're told, in command."

"Come with me, please." The KGB officer led the
civilian over to the officers' tent. He wouldn't look at
the lieutenant. His anger wouldn't let him. Later, not
too much later, he would personally knock the man's
teeth out with the butt of his pistol. Things had dete-
riorated far enough.

"What can I do for you?"

They sat in semidarkness on folding canvas chairs,
the only light from a grimy plastic window in the
side of the tent.

The civilian leaned forward. Only then did the major notice the deep diagonal scar on his forehead.

"Major, I come from Group Headquarters, Ninth
Army Command. Here, see for yourself." He produced the military identity card and a letter in a
small plastic folder.

"You will see that I have full authorization for
what I am about to say. And this is for your ears
alone." He looked about him. "At 1830 hours tonight,
in two hours time, you will move out of here. Everything, everyone. You are to leave behind not a single
trace of your presence. Is that understood?"

"Go on."

"You are to rendezvous with additional units of
ours in Poznan. They're already in position. The Pol-

ish civilian authorities are expecting joint maneuvers. You may travel freely on open roads."

"But this can't be correct." The major got up suddenly, overturning his chair. "This is against everything we have tried to do. I . . . There was no intention of us traveling to Poznan. Our objective is Warsaw and always was. The moment the underground rises up we were to move against them."

"Then the orders have been changed."

The civilian stood up and the two men faced each other. "You have not bothered to read the letter I brought you."

Angrily the major flicked it onto the ground and put his boot on it.

"I do not deal in letters. I have orders and I obey them."

He strode rapidly to the door of the tent and began undoing the flap.

The voice behind him was cool and unperturbed, but quiet, very quiet. "I should stop that if I were you," it said. "If you go outside, I'll kill you."

By six-thirty it was dark, and the entire unit was ready to leave. The official estimate gave them eight hours to reach Poznan. It took them nearer ten.

The KGB major traveled in a specially provided staff car, but he traveled in handcuffs. And when he and his senior staff reached Poznan they were transferred to transport aircraft that took off directly into the sunrise.

Shortly afterward their soldiers followed them, still in Polish uniforms, their stomachs empty, a night without sleep behind them. They were going home.

The civilian watched their departure. He hadn't been a civilian long. Soon after his last assignment in Poland as a soldier he had returned to congratulations in Moscow and promotion. In the Kremlin it was considered that a man with his skills was a man whose hour had come. Polish language, a marksman, and a rare Soviet ability to obey orders until he could devise better ones of his own.

They noted that he had killed a man and a woman and rescued a woman and a child. They liked that. A killer wolf who could still carry an egg in his mouth without breaking it. A true Slav, someone decided. A man who could hate and love.

From a hotel in Poznan he called the Soviet Embassy in Warsaw and spoke directly to the ambassador. He had expected only one target, but then he wasn't going to argue about that. In any case, for once they had asked something more of him than merely to dispatch bodies. They needed one piece of information. He turned the ignition of a brand-new Mercedes and headed toward the monastery of the Black Madonna.

As he drove the sun came up and the icy roads glistened in the fresh morning light. And yet he knew how easily you could skid and how treacherous the roads really were.

The abbot awoke in the late afternoon, feeling the stillness of the monastery wash over him. All his life he had been used to rising well before dawn and go-

ing to sleep soon after dusk, and he knew now that he
had reached a turning point.

Of course the nurse had said nothing. But there
were fewer pills to consume, less observation of his
vital signs, and the doctor had not been summoned
for three days. He was either getting much better or
much worse, and he had no doubt which it was.

For a moment he thought about writing a letter.
There was a brother in Lublin, at the Catholic University. Perhaps he should confide his fears to him.
But he recalled that the two of them had not communicated in years and he wasn't sure if the man could
be trusted. Not with this. Not with something so vital.

The abbot leaned over and pulled the bell cord by
the side of the bed. It seemed to take a long time for
the nurse to arrive. But perhaps he had fallen asleep
again. He blinked and she smiled down at him.

"Please call Brother Andrew." The request came as
a whisper. "If he's not inside the monastery, send
word. But he must be found and brought here."

He turned his head away and waited. The room
seemed suddenly much colder. "Another blanket," he
mouthed, but he didn't know if the nurse had heard.
Pray God they would hurry. There wasn't much
time. Why had he not acted sooner? Sleep. That was
it, too busy sleeping. Always a weak point. He had
always been far too attached to his bed.

In the distance he could hear the bells of one of the
parish churches. The men would be leaving the factory soon, change of shift, the world rumbling on.
Good men, he thought, strong and true to their country. Good Catholics, so poor, so deprived, but they

never lost their principles. Not like the man who had visited. Not like Zbig's son.

The abbot closed his eyes. He saw in front of him the small, wiry figure, the brow permanently furrowed, the nose jutting upward like one of those anti-aircraft guns. Such a dangerous man, that one. In all the years at the monastery no one had ever mentioned "the list." No one would have dared. Even in Poland, even with all the evil and deceit, not even the Communists had come looking for it. That had been the unwritten rule. The only one. But now if they thought Garten had broken it, they would break it themselves, without a second thought, without a scruple. And he couldn't have that. He couldn't die with that on his conscience.

All at once the anxiety seemed to renew his strength. I have a goal and a purpose, he thought. My way is clear.

The monk had tiptoed into the room, nervous of what he would find. But the abbot had heard the door, recognized the footsteps, and his face brightened.

"It does me good to see your face, Brother." He looked up from the pillow as the man came into view. Such a big man, such a giant of the Pauline community. Andrew, his own novice, the pride of his life, the son he could never have, the joy he had never expected.

The abbot held out his hand, and the young man scooped it up into his own, large and rough. They were hands that worked.

"What is it, Father?"

"Help me to sit up."

"But is this . . ."

"Do as I ask, boy. Don't argue with me."

Gently the monk lifted the old man, straightened his pillows, and propped him against them.

"I . . ."

The monk leaned forward to catch the words.

"You remember when you were younger, the services that we gave, not the public ones—but the people who used to come in secret. You recall that of which I speak?"

"Yes, Father."

"There's a list. I showed it to you once. Each abbot bequeaths it to his successor. It is the list of those whose names can never be revealed, Communists who believe in God, men and women who came to us for help and sanctuary."

"I know, Father, I know."

The abbot seemed not to have heard. He stared straight in front of him. "I cannot leave this list behind. There is danger, great danger, my brother. Go to that chest over there. You see it? Pull out the top drawer, yes, yes. But if you pull it farther, you'll see that there is a hidden compartment right at the back. There's a small box. Bring it. Bring it to me."

The abbot removed a large key and two smaller ones. "Take them, go to the archives, open the safe behind the painting. Bring me the list. Go on, do it."

For a moment the abbot thought he was dreaming. The book lay on the bed beside him. A candle had been lit on the table close by and the light seemed to pick out the red and gold colors on the leather binding. It felt solid and secure. He knew it by touch alone. There was no need to turn the pages.

"I thank you, Brother." The old face smiled at the monk. "Now I think I will sleep for a while." And he turned away, realizing that for the first time since childhood he had willfully told a lie.

"One thing before you go," the abbot added. "Whatever may happen here, you are to make sure that there is news of it. Everything. Even about the book . . ."

"Father, I don't understand. . . ."

"Don't be impatient, Brother. In time you will understand everything. Didn't I always teach you that? Now listen to me again. Whatever happens to me, whatever happens to the list—all this is to be told to our friends, told to the town. There are to be no secrets anymore. D'you understand?"

The abbot gripped the young man's hand.

"I understand, Father. It shall be as you say."

"Good. You had better leave me now. I need my sleep."

The monk made for the door.

"May God be with you, Andrew."

"And with you, Father."

The abbot had never known there was a fire, they said. A candle beside his bed must have fallen over while he was sleeping. A beam had fallen across the door, preventing rescuers from gaining access. In all other details, though, the version was correct. Throughout the local schools and churches people were told of the events, told that the abbot had died a sick man, that his papers and personal effects had been destroyed, and that the monastery's list of all baptisms and marriages had been destroyed. All. There were plenty who knew what it meant.

As the town learned of the tragedy a special Mass was said. People shook their heads in sorrow and wondered how something so simple and yet so fatal could have occurred.

On arrival it didn't take the civilian long to work out what had happened. Everyone was talking about it, as much about the list as the abbot. For, as often happens in Poland, they all knew the rumors, knew the mythology.

He informed the Soviet ambassador by telephone that he had no reason to disbelieve the accounts, and therefore no reason to stay. But he would have a meal and spend the night and move on early the next morning.

He was told in no uncertain terms to forget the meal, and the night, and move south with all possible speed.

47

June sat in the room, half dozing, half thinking, playing word games in her mind. Something was wrong, something was different, but it hardly seemed to matter.

As the days went by she found her anger and depression giving way to lethargy. Her thoughts seemed unfocused, almost disconnected from daily living. In the beginning she had imagined she would surely be killed, a simple hostage in some distant and unfathomable drama. But now she couldn't even think it. She was tired, she wanted her peace, she no longer communicated with her captors, nor they with her. June had retreated inside herself and shut the door.

In the end she got up to go to the lavatory and banged on the wall. There was no reply.

For the sake of it, she tried the door handle.

"Look, you two, I'm coming out." Not a very brave voice, she thought, but she didn't want them rushing at her, slapping her, pushing her back into the darkness. Again there was no reply. She raised her eyebrows, shrugged, and went into the bathroom.

In that instant she knew they had gone. There were creaks from the stairs, a window rattled, a tap dripped—tiny echoes of loneliness from empty rooms and corridors. The house stood used and discarded.

She didn't hurry. She gathered up her coat from the little room she had lived in. She walked carefully downstairs.

Daylight now. And the first feelings of desperation began to hit her. Choices instead of orders. What should she do?

Must get to a phone. She started to run, pushing open the door, down stone steps into the courtyard. It was afternoon, after lunch. After all this time, she thought, I must call the police, find out what happened, get help.

At first she had no idea where she was. The courtyard gave into a side road, all sixties semidetached houses, with little front gardens and low wrought-iron gates and names like "Belleview" and "Rockley Sands" and "Whitehurst Cottage." The street sign was at the crossroads. "Harper Lane—London Borough of Acton." Oh God, no distance at all from home. About a mile. Oh for heaven's sake. What a terrible . . .

There was a row of small shops about a hundred yards away, a pay phone on the corner. She ran again. Don't let it be vandalized, or full up with coins, or one of those silly card phones that they'd brought in, because no one has a card and it's just too . . .

I'm back, she thought suddenly. What am I thinking of? I've been kidnapped for days, locked up in a strange house. This is an emergency.

She dialed 999.

The voice answered immediately. "Which service do you require?"

"Police." Slowly, deliberately, June put down the phone and leaned against the side of the booth as the sense of hopelessness hit her. Why tell the police? There was no evidence of anything, the men had gone, what use were the descriptions? And the people who might know something—the friends of James Tristram—how could she contact them?

Outside, a man rapped on the glass. "You finished yet?"

"No."

On instinct she picked up the telephone and dialed her school. The secretary answered.

"Is that you, June?"

"Yes, yes it is."

"Everything all right, dear? You feeling better?"

"What d'you mean?"

"I didn't want to pry, dear. But when your doctor called and said you wouldn't be in for a little while, well, we thought it might be something serious."

"No, no. I'm fine, really."

"Oh, good. Did you want the headmaster?"

"I tell you what. I'll call him back a bit later, all right?"

"All right, dear. Take care now."

She left the phone booth and walked past the row of shops, feeling the cold for the first time. So they had covered all her avenues. No amateurs these. They had wrenched her life from her, tied up all the ends, and tossed her back.

June went into a café, sat, and ordered coffee. The day was turning to dusk and a newly developed instinct kept telling her that it wasn't over.

The train was crowded. Everyone had bags or boxes or baskets. Tristram had realized quite suddenly that he stuck out from the rest of the travelers. They all owned things in a way they hadn't ten years before. Even here, he thought, even in this godforsaken land of nothing, they had moved on. Young people wore jeans and colored parkas, their hair was styled and waved. Some carried skis or skates, heading south for a winter holiday.

I can remember when each winter was a national disaster.

But the people he saw around him knew nothing of the deprivations of the fifties, of the misery and homelessness, the lack of heating, the sick and the wounded who had lived in tents in the ruins of their cities. Bad as it was now, they didn't starve.

Three rows in front of him, he could see Grazyna's blond hair. He had pushed her into the only vacant seat and she hadn't complained. She lolled limp and lifeless as the train rocked its way through the southern suburbs of the city.

He tried to see through the dirty windows, but gave it up. After a few minutes the lights spaced out and disappeared and he didn't want to stare at his own reflection. He thought of June. Professional thoughts, first. How they'd gotten her, where they'd taken her, was it Poland, had she even left the London area? But he couldn't work out the answers. Define, analyze, assess, he told himself, but it wouldn't come.

June wasn't a professional problem. She was personal. Had been all along. That was the trouble. You can't admit it, can you? You were touched by that woman, not because you fancied her (which you did), but because, somewhere in that miserable dancing class, your two stars crossed.

Tristram made a face. The woman opposite him looked down at her book.

Something about June had been different from the others. Not, he conceded, that there had been many others. He had not found it easy to show his emotions, and his friends had had difficulty in reading them. Tristram had gone to boarding school at the age of eight, a place where you learn to cry in the darkness of a dormitory, where you learn to blend in with the crowd, where the meek watch the strong inherit the earth. All the little laws of the little jungle.

Some of it had been a good lesson for the future. Cement, backbone, they had called it. But Tristram had been a hard boy to reach. By the time he went to public school he no longer cried tears at night. He no longer felt much of anything. For what they took out of him was replaced with ambition. He had known simply that he wanted to get on, to pass exams, to get to a good university. Girlfriends were for sissies and suckers. Some of the students used to talk about "doing it" and "having it." But he wasn't sure what "it" was and didn't miss it.

Not till university, at least. Oh they had gone out

in groups, and there were plenty who had paired off and gone home together. But somehow he often seemed to be in the wrong group, seldom invited in for coffee, his mind on his books. A constant comfort and no risk of rejection.

The train jarred suddenly to a halt, breaking his thoughts. For a moment there was silence. Then everyone began to talk at once. Tristram was listening for the slam of doors. And down the train, two maybe three carriages away, he heard the first of them.

Then the jeering began, like a football crowd, angry, insolent, and he knew what it was.

He peered down the gangway. Grazyna's head remained propped against the side of her seat. Probably still asleep. That wouldn't last long. He had no doubt they'd been stopped for a random security check. Perhaps, if he had been on his own, he would have jumped the train, made a dash for it. But with the woman in tow there was no chance. This time he'd have to risk it. After all, they couldn't check everyone. There'd be a riot.

It took longer than he had imagined, but it wasn't thorough. Three uniformed officers, three in plainclothes. By the time they reached Tristram's carriage they were looking nervous and awkward. There was plenty of abuse coming from the passengers. "Cleaning up for the Russians, are you?" an old woman called out. "Such good little boys. Now go home and wash your faces."

Everyone laughed. They didn't bother with Tristram, but he noticed one of them glancing at Grazyna. Hardly surprising. As they got off he could feel his muscles relax. Outside, the clouds blew away for a moment and the winter moon shone down over the countryside before the train moved forward.

In the rear compartment the civilian grunted and sat down among the parcels and packing cases. It was bitterly cold and he was tired and hungry. There had been no problem identifying the girl. She looked much the same as when they'd last met. But the man was older, fatter than his picture. He hadn't worn well at all.

The civilian pulled his coat tightly around him. A trying business, he reflected. Difficult for anyone to wear well.

48

The General Secretary looked hard at the faces around the table. They were the men charged with his security at home and abroad, the defense of the state against any threat, real or imagined. The same men, he reflected, who would have him visit Poland in the middle of an uprising.

"There is, of course, a notable absentee from this meeting." He looked down at his papers. "Our old comrade is, I hear, temporarily out of touch."

"Indeed." The chairman of the KGB shifted in his chair. "He is at this time in Poland, concerned with the . . . ah . . . intimate details of your forthcoming journey."

"How comforting."

"As you know, Comrade General Secretary, his experience has benefited us on many occasions in the past."

"I'm sure you know better than I."

The KGB chairman beamed with pleasure. It was not every day that a public compliment came in his

direction. It had taken two years even to become a
full member of the Politburo.

"Am I to assume from all these files and submis-
sions that you are satisfied with the arrangements in
Poland?"

Around the table heads nodded.

"And can I also assume that there are no last-min-
ute details to which you wish to draw my attention?"

The heads nodded again.

The Soviet leader got to his feet and looked down
the length of the green baize table. "Amazing. Such
unanimity. Such complete identity of views and opin-
ions. It is almost, Comrades, if you will forgive me, as
if we have gone back to the old days." He laughed.
"You know what I have in mind—that practice of
fobbing off the General Secretary with any old nonsense because it was what he wanted to hear." He
laughed again. "But that is of course a joke."

None of the faces even approached a smile.

He turned away from them. It was nothing less
than a gesture of supreme confidence. And they read
it for what it was. Not many Soviet leaders had felt
powerful enough to turn their backs on the security
apparatus.

The General Secretary looked out of the window.
Across the Moscow River he could see the Union
Jack flying in the courtyard of the British Embassy.

"My friends"—he turned back to them—"just to
make sure that we have not slipped back into the old
ways, and of course this is easily done, I myself have
decided to make use of some old methods."

The KGB chairman got to his feet.

"You will kindly stay seated." The General Secretary's voice was not to be challenged. "It may interest you all to know that our old comrade is not in Poland looking after our interests. Instead he is being urgently sought in connection with some pointed questions that we"—the voice rose—"that we wish to put to him."

All eyes were fixed on the Soviet leader. No one saw the main door open.

"Comrade Klimov, from our embassy in Warsaw, was to be brought here, but we have reason to believe his aircraft crashed. There are therefore plenty of questions still to be asked, plenty of people still to answer them." He pursed his lips. "Of that I have no doubt."

The six men in the dark green uniforms of the Kremlin guard took up position in the doorway.

"Regrettably, I do not have the time to pose such questions myself. But fortunately we have a number of trained and highly sympathetic personnel on our own staff who can carry out such matters on our behalf. Some of them would like to talk to you now, should your arrangements permit that."

The Soviet leader picked up his papers and moved jauntily toward the door. "One or two of you," he added, "may not, for administrative reasons, be coming back. The rest . . . I shall look forward to welcoming. Good day, Comrades."

The guards moved aside to let him pass, and he strode quickly along the corridor. He looked at his watch. It was just after ten, and the morning flight from Poznan, bringing a new batch of detainees, would just be arriving.

* * *

In Moscow the British Embassy employs upward of thirty Soviet nationals—telephonists, drivers, messengers, mechanics—and of course the cooks and maids. Without exception they answer to another and more secret employer as well.

At times, therefore, it can be a difficult relationship, and Sir Harold Stebbings counted himself lucky not to have experienced major problems. As a widower he relied heavily on his maid, a former Aeroflot stewardess called Zina, to order his domestic arrangements.

True, she broke a lot of plates and glasses, but he put that down to her limited experience in working on firm ground. Anyway, despite all the warnings and provisos, he liked her. She was different from all the other dumplings that the Russians supplied to the foreign community. She was slim, even graceful, and although not wildly attractive, she had at least a pleasant manner. She brought back memories of a school mistress who had taught him years before.

It would be wrong to say they shared confidences. The ambassador talked to her frequently, perhaps more than is usual, but then he enjoyed practicing his Russian. And Zina would sometimes correct a case ending, or a verb tense, gently, almost hesitantly, as if anxious not to hurt his feelings.

Sir Harold saw no harm in their conversations, always about the weather, or the sights of London, or the markets. He was pleased that she never tried to flirt. The relationship was mutually respectful—and that was the way he intended to keep it.

But he couldn't ignore her that morning when she

arrived in tears, couldn't help but put his arm around
her and lead her to the sofa and provide an ear for the
troubles that she poured out to him.

It was difficult to make sense of them. Zina said she
had been called to the Soviet Foreign Ministry and
asked for her weekly report. "You know that, don't
you? We all have to report. They give us no choice."
Sir Harold smiled indulgently. Zina sobbed into a
dirty checked handkerchief.

"They said you would not be here much longer.
You did things that were against the interest of the
Soviet state. And I was to leave your employment
immediately. A new maid would be found." She un-
wound the handkerchief from her fingers and blew
her nose.

"What nonsense." Sir Harold patted her shoulder.
But he could feel his thoughts begin to race. What
kind of hook was this and why was she alerting him?
If she was a plant, it was exceptionally clumsy. And if
she was genuine, she was risking a lot. All the embassy rooms were swept regularly for electronic bug-
ging. But there were always microphones that
slipped through the net. It wasn't the time to tell her.

He got up and took her arm, leading her to the
door of the private apartment. "You had better go,
my dear. We shall not meet again. I'm afraid this is
often the way it happens. But I shan't forget the
friendly conversations we've had." He smiled. "And
you've done wonders for my Russian."

He looked at her. The tears were still rolling fast.
So much grief over a departure, albeit an unpleasant
one. And yet nothing had ever passed between them.

There was something she hadn't told him. He was certain of it. There had to be more to it than this.

Clumsily, she took his hand and tried to kiss it, then hurried away down the stairs without turning back.

Sir Harold shut the door and returned to the sofa. His heart was beating fast. Maybe he was more worried than he thought. The Russians always had a go at the ambassadors. That was nothing new. But why now? Why straight after delivering the message to the General Secretary? Did they really shoot the messenger who brought bad news?

There had been times when he had thought back to the meeting with the Soviet leader and imagined he'd dreamed it. Such an extraordinary thing, he whispered to himself. What a way to run a government!

But his heart wouldn't keep still and he went into the bedroom to look for his pills. Six years earlier he'd suffered a mild coronary, and the doctors had looked carefully at his body and his mind and diagnosed a nervous man. The pills were an insurance policy.

Sir Harold got a glass from the kitchen and poured water. Then he took the pills into the sitting room.

That was odd. There seemed fewer than he had expected. It was time to order some more.

He stretched out his feet on the sofa and pressed the remote button for the tape player. It was Chopin's First Piano Concerto, a longtime favorite that had often helped him to think things through. After ten minutes, though, he kicked off his shoes and decided to take a nap. It didn't seem to matter that there was work to be done in the office, the Foreign

Ministry to see, a lunch to go to at the American Embassy, coffee with the Australians, a dinner, lecture, files to read.

But Sir Harold died where he lay, long before the music ended.

Zina moved quickly along the crowded embankment. I don't know what will happen, she told herself. I just took the pills because they told me to, gave him some others, probably just the same.

And then the tears started again, and she began to run, knocking into the passersby, feeling arms and coats and baskets all around her, knowing, really knowing, what it was she had done. She didn't stop till she reached the bridge, pulling the pills from her pocket, scrunching them in her fist, flinging them far out over the gray frozen river, solid and immovable, like the Russia she had always lived in.

They had told her to keep the pills, hand them over. Now she had disobeyed. It wasn't much, but it was better than nothing.

49

Krakow in the early morning. To Grazyna the city seemed like a sleeping beauty, with its narrow cobbled streets and churches, the market square deserted, the snow pure and unmarked.

So peaceful standing here, she thought. So innocent. None of us is guilty until the day begins, till we leave our houses, till we turn intention into fact.

She led the way. Tristram followed. Who was he, anyway, this so-called colleague of Jozef's, a man from London? Such an ordinary man, going to fat in his fifties, more tired and slower than he wanted to be. And yet he was determined. She could see that. He didn't sleep much, didn't let up. Driven, that was it. Like so many of the men she had known. Driven to fight or to lie, to leave a mark in the quicksand before it covered them over.

Which would he do? She guessed he would lie when the time came for it. Maybe with that thin, nervous smile. But the eyes would hold steady. That came only with practice. In any case, they would soon know.

Grazyna led him to the north side of the square, away from the covered arcade, to the left of the Mariacki church. They stopped in front of a fifteenth-century mansion. Number 8. She pointed to the sign—"House of the Salamanders"—and pushed at the green front door. It opened immediately.

The warmth and the darkness hit her and a firm hand guided her down a corridor and then they were in a basement kitchen, high ceilings, no windows, a table and three wooden chairs. This is where we'll do it, she thought. This is perfect.

Under a flickering neon strip they made their introductions. Three men, all in their sixties or early seventies, and she could see Tristram sizing them up. She'd told him they would stay in the house until heading for Auschwitz the next morning. It was a safe house, she'd said. The best. But she hadn't told him why they used it.

One of the men made coffee. He couldn't straighten his back properly, and only his right hand appeared to function. "I'm a survivor," he said.

Tristram looked up at Grazyna.

"He means a survivor from the camps," she told him. "They all are. Now they work with us. There isn't anything they're afraid of."

Tristram nodded. "I understand," he said quietly. "I was once a prisoner for a while. Nothing like the camps, though."

"Where was that?" The man beside him moved in closer.

Tristram looked around at all the faces. "I don't think this is the place to discuss it."

"Oh, but we'd like to hear it." An old voice spoke

right into his ear. He spun around, and at that moment his arms were pinned to his sides and someone took hold of his feet, and he was falling backward fast, his head banging on the linoleum floor. "What the bloody . . . ?"

And as they brought the chair right side up, Grazyna moved in front of him and his eyes began to focus.

"I'm sorry that we have to do this. . . ."

Tristram coughed painfully. "You shit . . . what the hell d'you think you're doing?"

She pulled up a chair and sat just a foot away from him. "No, Mr. Tristram, what d'you think *you* are doing? You appear like some magic trick from nowhere. You say you're my husband's colleague—and we all know what that means. I don't know what it means." She got up and paced over to the other side of the kitchen. "Difficult times here, my friend. And we're careful. We don't wear uniforms but we're good. We're better than the other side. But sometimes, you know, they manage to get in among us and play games." She came back and sat in front of him. "You wouldn't play games with us, would you?"

The man behind him slapped Tristram's head with the back of his hand.

"Answer!"

Tristram winced. "No games. I'm too tired for games."

"You said you had information for Jozef. What is it?" Grazyna ran a hand through her long hair. "You say you were once a prisoner. . . . Where? You say this and you say that. Tell us about yourself, James

Tristram. We have plenty of time, a whole day in fact, and we like to be entertained."

She could see his anger. But he wasn't desperate, wasn't afraid. You've been this road before, she thought, you will know how to treat us, how to maneuver it your way. Long ago someone sat down and taught you. Only which side was it? Where are you from?

If you've never been there, you think it's easy to sing—just open it up, tell all the secrets, hold nothing in reserve. But it's the hardest thing in the world, and Tristram knew it. Because when they train you they make you lock it all away, and no one can ever get at it. Not your controller, not your colleagues, not your agents. No one. And it doesn't just stop with their secrets, does it? You begin to build a whole world and fill it with other secrets. Little things that you don't tell your wife, or your friends, or anyone else—not because they're important, but because it becomes the way you live. You don't tell.

You don't say when you're leaving the office, don't say what time you're catching the flight, don't say who you met on the street or who you spoke to. And pretty soon you *can't* say it.

Tristram had forgotten where it started or how it developed, but he knew it was time to draw a line. You know the turning points in your life, the major decisions, the doors you close and can't reopen. And you've got to stop pretending that everything lasts forever, that next Christmas will be like the last one, and that there's more coming into your life than leaving it.

So he talked to them, slowly, hesitantly, of the dangers they faced. He told them of the Polish underground in 1944, of his arrest in Prague, of the death of a friend in London, and a traitor, so finely cloaked and masked that he could lie his way up the ladder of the Secret Service for four decades.

"It stops here," he told them. "It has to. You're caught up in something you don't understand. One day we'll do it. Not this time."

He didn't know whether they believed him. Not until Grazyna reached forward and held his head in her hands, and the five of them sat silent in the high-walled kitchen below the ancient city of Krakow.

Like ducks in a row. Some there, others still to come. The civilian counted them off. He had been told about the House of the Salamanders, told that it often played host to a different kind of wildlife altogether. And he had smiled, and part of the smile was for the woman, the blonde that he'd carried to safety a lifetime ago across the Tatras.

She had style, that one. Maybe it was the hair or the way she walked. But he could see she had depth. In Moscow the girls always handed it out up front—the whole lot, body and mind, take it or leave it. Anyway, no time to piss about on a cold night. Or maybe it was just the way he'd seen it. But this one was really different.

He knew they'd stay in the house. This was the jumping-off point. Had to be. From there they'd head for Auschwitz. All of them with their different motives. It wouldn't be a hard job, not if they played it by the book, and they were all professionals.

As he watched a few people began to move about on the streets. Krakow was set in motion. He would go to a café, get some breakfast, maybe even find a hotel and sleep. Although that would be hard. Always hard to sleep before a kill.

The Russian saw the dawn from the inside of his stolen car. He had taken it just south of Warsaw and had assumed it would be days before the number was circulated. Wrongly. For even in the most chaotic and confused societies, the strangest of little tasks are sometimes faultlessly performed. And the Warsaw police, who were, according to their own commander, incapable of catching even a gnat, noted down and circulated the number of the stolen vehicle. So effectively in fact that when the car shunted past a patrol unit just south of Radom, it was instantly recognized.

There was, however, a special reason for the vigilance of these particular officers. Alone among their colleagues, they had failed to apprehend a single motorist in the course of their previous shift. That meant there had been no bonuses. That meant they were desperate.

Not, of course, that the police department paid extra for arrests. Not at all. The bonuses came rather from the motorists who were stopped. The game was simple. You invited them into the patrol car, read them a few paragraphs from the state criminal code, and then proposed a Breathalyzer test. Since most of the drivers were drunks, this was the point at which their jaws would fall open. From then on it was easy. "Perhaps there might be a way around this, after all," one officer would whisper audibly to the other. "Perhaps you're right," his colleague would say. And by this time the driver would be delving into his wallet with the kind of enthusiasm he hadn't previously experienced. Bonuses.

The Russian knew all about the system, and so he wasn't surprised to be pulled in. But something offended him about the two officers. Maybe it was their swagger, or the silly grins they carried, or the fact that he had so little time left and knew it. But when they moved to clinch the shabby deal, it required very little effort to grab the hair of the officer driving and smash his head through the glass of the side window. Instantly his colleague reached for his pistol, but it wasn't easy to get at, stuck hard in a leather holster, with a buckle that hadn't been oiled for well over a year. And he never saw the punch that broke his nose, sending him unconscious onto the plastic dashboard.

Satisfied, even entertained, the Russian got out of the car and returned to the one he had stolen. He rubbed his knuckles. God it was good to use your hands. Years since he'd done that. So many times he'd ordered others to do it for him. But he could still hold his own, still teach discipline to the pigs around him.

For a final journey, he felt calm, even elated, humming a song as he drove south.

Like all Soviet ambassadors to Warsaw, he had known how quickly his star could fall. He leaned back in his chair and looked unkindly at the photograph of the General Secretary on the wall of his office. He had known it the moment they'd an-

nounced his appointment, known it the moment he
had set foot in Poland. There was simply no way you
could win.

Either you offended the Polish government by mis-
take, tripping into one of those gaping emotional
wounds they all carried around with them, or else
you were ordered to do it on purpose by Moscow.
Cables would arrive instructing you to take the government to task over an article in the official press, or
a program the Kremlin hadn't liked, or a chance in-
discretion from a Polish diplomat at a cocktail party.
Whatever it was, he would have to go to the Poles and
wave his stick.

That was all very well, but they always got back at
you. Your mail would be held up, shipments would
be delayed in customs. Once the telephone exchange
had altered the embassy numbers without even telling them. The tricks were endless.

The fact was that, with few exceptions, the two
countries loathed and despised each other, but neither had the guts to admit it in public. The ambassador picked up his internal phone. It would have made
everything so much easier.

"Show them in."

He was on his feet by the time the door opened, the
smile already in place.

"Geniek, my dear fellow, and you, too, Bogdan,
how good of you both to come."

The two of them stumbled in nervously—the Minister of Foreign Affairs and the head of Polish radio
and television. Both were new to the post. In Poland,
the ambassador reflected, they never kept them for
long.

"Well, gentlemen"—he gestured toward the sofa—
"and what about the plans for tonight and tomorrow?
Mmm? An important visit!" He smiled effusively.

The Polish television man opened a briefcase. "I
have brought the schedules. You will see it includes a
list of references to the General Secretary's trip. I
believe"—he sat back in the sofa—"that we have ex-
celled ourselves this time. An hour-long documentary
about ties with the Soviet Union at 9 P.M. tonight, a
selection of one or two speeches—scripts are, of
course, included—yes, yes there at the back—and
then a final mention on the look-ahead, with arrival
times, motorcade details. That'll be at midnight. I
trust that all meets with your satisfaction."

The ambassador put his hands to his mouth. "You
don't think all this is a little overdone, Geniek? After
all, you and I know that the audience for your documentary will probably amount to six people, when
we've taken out your family and mine. Wouldn't it be
cheaper to bring them round in taxis instead of transmitting the thing?" The ambassador looked amused.

"Old methods, gentlemen, old thinking. The time
has surely come to manage things a little better,
mmm? I have to tell you that the General Secretary
does not wish for this elaborate and overblown fan-
fare. He wants to arrive quietly and in a businesslike
manner. Contrary to accepted practice, he does not
wish to be seen either as Santa Claus or Jesus Christ.
In fact, there is some doubt about whether he will
even be coming tomorrow."

The Foreign Minister looked as though he had
been slapped across the face. "I don't understand. Are
you mad? This has all been arranged weeks ago. Ev-

erything is organized—the visits, the busloads of children and workers, the meetings. Have you any idea . . . ?"

"I have every idea," the ambassador cut in sharply. "Evidently you do not even keep abreast of your own internal security, let alone that which is provided for us. Suffice it to say that it will not be clear until morning whether it is even safe for the General Secretary to be here. I myself have the gravest of doubts. In the meantime I suggest you confine your propaganda to the barest and most innocuous of reporting. Do I make myself clear?"

He watched the two men shamble out of the office. From his window he could see the stooped gray backs disappear into the government limousine. Give them twenty minutes, he thought, and they'd be back in their offices screaming like stuck pigs. And it wouldn't be long before the telephone was ringing, and the screaming would be going on all the way up the line.

He turned away. It didn't matter, of course. They could say what they liked. Whatever happened would be decided a long way from either Warsaw or Moscow, down south, where the Sola and the Vistula rivers converge, where the Nazis had exterminated the people in their millions, and where, in the morning, a few more would have to follow.

50 _____

She couldn't go to the school.

"June," the headmaster had declared into the telephone, "come back when you're better." But he had said it not knowing what was wrong with her.

Often she would sit in the back room, gazing out at the concrete wall and the two hydrangeas given her by her mother. She thought of Tristram and wondered whether he would return. And she wasn't even sure she wanted him to. He was no longer relevant to her life or her feelings. She wouldn't dance again, she told herself, wouldn't go looking for company, because you never knew if you might find a man who said he did "not much" for a living "in an office in the city." And to her that was lying enough for a lifetime.

Anyway, I made too much out of too little, she reasoned. We never did anything, never really got to know each other.

She stood up and decided to go to the shops. Food was running low, and her mother would call in the evening and expect to be fed. I can't stay, she would always declare. And then she'd stay and eat everything there was.

It was nearly four when she arrived at the supermarket. Too early for the crowds, and yet there were plenty of pensioners milling about, some chatting, out only for the company.

As she passed through the checkout an elderly figure in a tweed overcoat smiled at her. "Here, let me give you a hand." And he had taken her shopping bag, with the canned soup and the whole-wheat loaf, even before she had realized it, guiding her gently to the entrance.

Outside, he turned to face her. And for the first time in such a long time she looked into cold, steady eyes that made no attempt to avoid her.

"I'm glad you got out all right." The Director handed her the bag and in that instant she thought she'd be nervous, but she wasn't.

"I've been waiting for you," she said gently.

"Me?"

"Someone like you. I didn't think it was over. Not after all that, you see."

"Have you time for a cup of tea?"

"No, I've had enough tea, thank you," she sighed. "Oh, we could talk about all sorts of things, but what difference would it make? You wouldn't tell me anything."

The Director nodded.

"I suppose," she went on, "that I'm sorry to see you, but really it's only for one reason. If you're here, it means Tristram isn't. So there isn't any good news, is there?"

She walked slowly toward the bus stop and the Director fell in beside her. "As things go I don't get much in the way of good news across my desk. I expect you can understand that. It's been hard for all of us these last few days. Not that that's your problem, but . . . just occasionally we try things, out of what we think are the best motives, and they go badly wrong. And we all have to take the blame."

She looked at him more carefully. He wasn't what she'd expected. The hardness in the eyes and the face seemed to have been dented. Whatever he'd been in the past, he was no longer the same man.

"Why did you come to see me?"

They had reached the bus stop. The line of waiting shoppers seemed endless.

"You're something unusual in this business."

"What's that?"

"Innocent. We don't see many of them. Most people on both sides get involved because that's what they've chosen to do. You didn't. I'm sorry about that. If it's any consolation, I'm out of favor, myself, at the moment."

Suddenly, June wished he'd go. She didn't want his problems, she didn't want his pity. For some reason, she realized, she didn't even want any explanations. It could be over, really over, that would be enough. And yet she would ask just one question, even though she didn't want the answer.

"Is Tristram all right?"

For a moment the Director turned away. It didn't really matter to him that he had no good news to impart. Just occasionally, though, it would have made a pleasant change.

"I'm not sure," he said quietly, "but we'll know soon."

51 _____

Garten didn't notice the wind that swept down from the mountains. In the ice cold he stood motionless by the roadside, where the truck had dropped him, with his heart pounding double time inside the flimsy coat. Still dark, and yet close to dawn, and he knew that far away in a hundred distant towns they would be crawling from their beds, from blankets on the floor, from chairs and mattresses, adjusting their radios, awaiting the signal.

Hurriedly he moved through the snow toward the camp. Across the frozen countryside not a light shone, not even a flicker. But the two of them would be there beside the gate, the two who had brought the radio to Warsaw so many days before. They would not let him down.

It was hard going. The frozen snowdrifts obscured ridges and ditches. Once he fell headlong, fearing the shadow of a tree. A bird called out and an animal rustled in the undergrowth and then there was silence. And if I stopped now, he thought, we could end it all here, where the evil began. But he couldn't turn back.

You go so far, he thought, and you follow your star. You see no light but your own, heed no voice but your own, take no account of the world as it is but only as it should be. You're lost in your own visions and dreams and no one can take you home.

Garten could see it all clearly as he headed for the gate.

They greeted him in silence. Little more than boys, with their smiles, and hugs, and the nervous set of the jaw. They were cold beyond all their expectations, but they wouldn't have admitted it.

Under the wrought-iron gate they moved, over the railway lines where the cattle cars had disgorged their prisoners, past the wall of death. So many ghosts to watch us, thought Garten. We do this for you, for all who have lived under tyranny and oppression, we offer this, our gesture. In the darkness he could see only the barbed-wire fence and the outline of the camp buildings. But the boys knew their way.

They led him to Block Ten. And that was the place least visited by the tourists. Even with the passage of forty years it was hard to stomach what had gone on there—medical experiments of a kind so willfully cruel and senseless that, still, people would avert their eyes from the building in shock.

On the first floor they entered a storeroom with no windows. A kerosene stove stood on the bare floorboards.

"We've kept it here," said one of the boys. "It's all

set up." He gestured to a khaki field bag. "We can take it in this and it won't be heavy."

"I'm taking the transmitter." Garten picked up the bag and weighed it in both hands. "You two had better get out of here. They'll have the detection vans out, and they'll also be flying around in those special listening planes. It'll be safer."

"But there's been no sign of any trouble at all," the elder boy protested. "You got here without even a document check. We've been here for days. Nothing has moved."

"You're right." Garten peered out of the window. "And maybe that's the problem."

They had left Krakow behind, its towers and spires enveloped in darkness. Grazyna's mind was on the narrow, slippery road that carried them westward. But there was no traffic to be seen, no passersby, no travelers. Tristram watched in silence. A land of nothing and nobody, he reflected. A sad, bleak little plot of Central Europe, sitting uncomfortably where the Russians had put it all those years ago.

All the moves had been made, and now they would come to him. Sure, they were curious—they were the chess masters, they would want to know his game and his strategy. But beyond that and ahead of it, they wanted his blood.

The Russians always used force as a first, not a last, resort. If you had power, you employed it. You crushed and you demolished, you rooted out, and you did it with passion and belief—the faith of the moment, no matter what it was.

He watched Grazyna drive. It was a noisy old van,

full of rattles and jarring noises, and yet the engine was tireless and strong, built, it seemed, to drive to eternity. And maybe they would if the plans came tumbling down around them. For however good you are, you can only guess at the man who faces you. Is he cleverer or quicker—or are you? Is it your day or his? All of us lose once, they had said. Gets it out of your system. You can't afford to lose again.

Later, he thought, I'll look back. I'll trace back to the man who betrayed Senya and me. But for now I have to stop the movement, stop the signal, turn them back.

The drive was painfully slow. Tristram looked at his watch. It had taken almost an hour to drive thirty miles.

He leaned over to Grazyna. "You all right? Want me to take over?"

"Don't panic." The hard edge was in her voice. She didn't look at him. "Helps me concentrate. Lot to think about."

They passed a house with lighted windows—the first for miles.

"When we get there," he said, "you stay out of sight, find some cover. You've got a gun, haven't you? I don't know how the Russians will play this, but there won't be many of them. Maybe even just one. This was a renegade operation for them. They won't want to advertise it."

He peered out of the van. They had reached the edge of the village. Grazyna pulled up under some trees.

"Look." She was whispering. "If the uprising went

ahead, if Jozef gave the signal, how can you be sure it would end so badly?"

Tristram shivered. The heating in the van was totally inadequate. "I just know that they never use half measures. You'd have your uprising, but you'd have it only for a day. Then they'd move in, smash it, smash you, anything they could get their hands on. That'd just be the start. D'you want to die? D'you want to throw yourself under a tank driven by a Mongolian who doesn't even know where he is? Is that the ending you always dreamed about?"

Grazyna's mouth fell open and she stared hard into his eyes.

"I don't exaggerate," he told her. "I know what they can do."

The civilian waited in Block Eight. He had arrived first and would leave last. That was the pattern. Do your homework, walk all the routes, draw the map in your mind.

Some were there already. He could feel it. Didn't need to look. You got to know the way of these things as the years went by.

For now he'd let them get on with it. Their business wasn't important. All he needed to do was stay by the gate, the final guard. He alone would decide who left and who stayed. And he reveled in the thought of such power.

When he'd entered the block he'd paid no attention to the ground floor. In rows and rows of glass cases there were the supplies of camp garments, hair, spectacles, and photo after photo of the inmates. But none of it had moved him. Death was something you delivered face-to-face. Numbers weren't important. In Russia they never had been. How many hundreds of thousands had died at Stalingrad, defending just a few meters of ground? The struggle was important, the cause. And you took it wherever you had to.

But he wondered about the girl. Polish. Of course she was Polish. And yet the blond hair reminded him of the Baltic Republics, of summer holidays in Estonia, where the Finnish tourists had come, where he'd grown up.

Suddenly his muscles tensed and he heard the sound a split second later. Boots on snow. He crouched beside the window. Three shadows moved along the wide path between the camp buildings. Idiots! They were quick but they were noisy. Dark clothing against the snow. Not a thought for camouflage. He could pick them off in pitch darkness. Later, though, when they'd done what they'd come for, when their confidence would be high and their guard down.

He watched them slither out of sight, two in one direction, the other letting them go, a bag on his shoulder. He knew all about that one.

Of course he'd chosen his vantage point well. It was the tallest of the old dormitory blocks, windows on three sides. There was a view, even the chance of escape. A large, bare-floored attic, with packing cases strewn haphazardly across it. The dust and cobwebs told him you could hide there a month and not be found.

He sat down again on the floor and spread out the arctic combat gear. Used properly, it would take you to the North Pole and back. And he'd been plenty of places in it where Russians weren't supposed to go. He fingered it carefully, the padded down jacket with the Thinsulate lining, the face mask, the beaver hat and the sheepskin boots, waterproof and molded by hand. In his sack he carried a favorite possession—mittens made from the fur on a polar bear's face—a gift from Eskimos, who thought they were giving to someone completely different. But he wouldn't wear them until it was over.

For a moment he shut his eyes and raised his head. As he did so his forehead connected with a block of smooth, cold steel that flashed downward and he could feel himself falling, such a long way down, tumbling, twisting, his hands reaching out and finding nothing to hold, the darkness blotting out the light.

The Russian looked down at him and smiled with genuine pleasure. The boy was good, but, like all boys, far less good than he thought he was. His senses were acute, his planning excellent, but there were things that only age could give you—practice, intuition, and a knowledge of all the tricks that have ever been played.

And yet the Kremlin must have had faith in this man to send him on such a mission. Or was he the only one they could trust? In Moscow they doubted everyone. Always that clinical obsession with treachery.

He bent down and felt for a pulse at the temple. It was still there. The creature was as strong as a horse and breathing heavily.

Hurriedly the Russian searched the gear laid out on the floor. Twice he went through it, patting each garment, squeezing and prodding. He found two guns—a 9mm Browning with silencer and an especially adapted pistol that carried no markings at all. He picked it up and cradled it in both hands. He knew where it came from. Deep under the Lubyanka they crafted weapons as good as any in the world. This one, with its mat-gray sights and shoulder stock, was a precision instrument, made in the U.S.S.R.

He put it down and knelt beside the inert figure. The car keys were in an inside pocket. There was Polish money together with dollars. But not a scrap of identification and, more important, no communications equipment. It was a standard one-man operation. The Russian had seen dozens like it. There was no backup.

He checked the chamber on the Browning and brought it around in a practiced arc to the back of the man's head. The move was almost automatic. You disarmed and disabled your victim, and then you got rid of him.

He felt for the base of the neck and tightened his grip on the pistol, although he knew the kick would be minimal. And then for some reason his arm relaxed and he laid the gun on the floor. A cloud must have moved, for he could suddenly see the man's face lit up in the moonlight. Not a young face, for killers can never look young. But the skin was unlined and unmarked.

The Russian stood up. His head hurt, his breathing was labored, but he knew it was time to draw a line. So strange, though, not to finish the job. And yet if he killed this agent, another would come looking for him, just the way they had gone out in the thirties and forties. Not this day, maybe, but not many days after. Besides, he had something else to accomplish. He took a last look at the boy and walked away.

Outside, the Russian was struck by the haze that had come in with the night. It was hard to make out the more distant buildings. And yet toward the east the sky had lightened perceptibly and he knew he'd have to hurry.

"What time will he move?" Tristram yawned. Inside the freezing van he could see his breath swirling before him.

"He has to set up about ten to six. The transmitter will not need much preparation. But he must be quick. In this cold the batteries don't last long." Grazyna rubbed her eyes.

"How much does he have to send?"

"About two minutes. It is a recording of one of the Pope's speeches when he was here in '79. But it's been edited to make him say something he didn't. Once they get to that portion, then they'll have it all."

"Why so complicated? Wouldn't a piece of music have done just as well?"

"You surprise me, Mr. Tristram." She sat up suddenly in her huge red parka and stared at him in disbelief. "Music can come from anywhere, and so can the voice of the Pope. But these words come only from us. Besides . . . the monitors will think it's just a foreign radio station transmitting on the wrong wavelength. I doubt they'll listen to what it's saying."

"And what does it say?"

"Take your struggle forward, open your heart, listen to what it tells you. From the Baltic coast to Silesia, from the sea to the mountains, come out and carry your people to victory."

In that instant he could see tears in her eyes.

"It's beautiful," he told her.

She didn't answer at once, just turned and looked at him, as the first of the tears traveled down her face. "It would have been beautiful," she whispered, "but they'll never hear it."

Tristram got out of the van and headed for the main gate.

Garten felt afraid. He was on his own now, the key in his hand, and once he turned it, Poland would get out of bed and march. No better springboard, he thought, looking around as the sky came up gray and blue through the barbed-wire fences on which so many had died.

Quiet footsteps through the snow. To his right stood the low bunker where the Nazis had incinerated the bodies; behind it the showers where the inmates had been gassed.

For an instant he stood still, listening. But there was no sound of birds, no morning chorus. What was it the two men had said?—"We've been here for days and nothing has moved." And now, when he looked back on it, everything had been so safe and easy. The train journey from London, the rendezvous in Warsaw, the travels across Poland. Of course he'd been careful. But there should have been more trouble than this. Much more.

Ahead of him was the gate, the guard post to the right of it. Only a little way now. Up the ladder and he'd send it from the lookout platform. Quickly, because the wind had come up, gusting at the frozen snowdrifts. He couldn't stay out for long.

It should have told him something, that the door opened unprotestingly, wasn't frozen to its wooden frame, and yet he didn't notice it. He didn't even notice the footprints beside the lookout tower. He didn't see the rickety old van parked two hundred yards away beside some bushes. He didn't see and he didn't hear, and when he reached the wooden platform he had no idea that James Tristram stood behind him.

In the village northeast of Warsaw the farmer had been awake for well over an hour. Now he sat in the darkness of the kitchen, with the old radio receiver whispering and hissing at him, the curtains pulled, the rest of the house silent.

For the twentieth time he reached for the book of recipes, turning to the page where he had scrawled the frequency. For now there was only static, but he knew it would come.

He got up and pulled the curtain back an inch. Along the road to the village the houses stood gaunt and ramshackle. Inside, he knew they'd be awake, coffee on the table—and their heart in their mouth.

Despite all his misgivings, he was glad the day had arrived, because there'd been so much thinking and talking—and in the end it was better to act. Poles had always been like that. They could moan and groan and regret, but when it came down to the wire they would stand and fight.

He hadn't heard his wife come in, but as he looked

up she was standing there in her dressing gown, her eyes puffy, hair thin and straggly.

"Go back to bed, woman." He spoke gently, quietly. "I'll tell you when it comes."

She smiled nervously. "I'll make some tea." She moved to the sink. "How long before they send?"

The farmer looked at his watch. "About five minutes."

She came around behind him and put an arm on his shoulder. "You didn't really think I'd miss it, did you?"

The General Secretary awoke suddenly and for a long time lay staring at the ceiling before he remembered. In the distance he could hear the noise of a truck droning along Kutuzovsky Prospekt. Moscow was never quiet, never at peace—and yet, he reflected, nothing ever seemed to get done.

Ten miles away, through the southern suburbs, his plane stood ready at Vnukovo airport. The entourage would be arriving shortly, the massive array of advisers, hangers-on, stenographers, and communications experts—all prepared for a trip to Poland that might never take place.

Before going to bed he had summoned the head of Kremlin security and asked for the interrogation records of the KGB men returned from Poland. They had not been instructive.

No doubt the methods had changed. Torture was no longer applied with the gay abandon of previous years. But the questioning had yielded precious little.

The man who possessed all the answers had yet to be found. And what if he were? The General Secretary got up quietly from the bed and tiptoed into the study, anxious not to wake his wife. Surely this was just the first attempt to crush him. Among all those loyal and dedicated faces that welcomed him each day, how many belonged to the treacherous or disaffected? Was he hurrying toward a bullet in the back?

The Soviet leader sat in an armchair and looked out over the rooftops of his city. Whichever way it went this time, he could fend them off. He had been lucky and they had been clumsy. But who knew what would happen the next time? Where would the knife be aimed, and who would be holding it?

He yawned and thought of going back to bed. But he knew he wouldn't sleep. He'd wait now for the signal, either way.

Tristram clamped his hand over Garten's mouth, but he hadn't expected the speed with which the younger man moved, swiveling under his grip, turning inward, battering with his head and fists. He had forgotten the creature was twenty years fitter.

"For Christsake . . ." And suddenly he felt himself winded and falling, the wooden platform rushing up to meet him as he sank, dazed, to his knees. Only then did Garten catch sight of his face.

"My God. You! What in the name of God . . ."

Tristram felt the vomit rising in his throat. There was no holding it. The nausea gripped his stomach and he was violently sick.

Garten leaned against the side of the platform and watched. There was no sympathy in his expression.

"You of all people. You come here. I . . . I'm amazed, I really am. What is it—did you think Jozef

couldn't manage on his own? You think Jozef's some
sort of useless bum. Uh? Not bad to have come all
this way, uh?"

Tristram rose unsteadily to his feet. He wiped his
mouth on the sleeve of his coat. "Look, we don't have
long—"

"You telling *me*? I have to send the signal in three
minutes. You can't teach me about time. This is business, this is what we prepared for."

Tristram reached for the man's arm. "Listen to me
quickly. The whole thing is blown. It's no good anymore. There's a faction in the Kremlin that wants
you to succeed. They've been holding your hand all
the way along. You were betrayed even before you
reached Poland, but you weren't picked up, don't you
see? Don't you realize why it's been so easy?"

Garten said nothing, but his dark eyes took it all in.

"Look, the moment you start the uprising they'll
use it as an excuse to crush everything. They'll bring
the tanks in. There'll be terrible bloodshed. You have
to stop."

He could see Garten's breath coming in short jerks,
his cheeks raw from the cold. The bag had fallen
from his shoulder during the struggle. Now he knelt
down and opened it on the floor.

"Garten, this ends here—now, do you understand
what I say?"

But he didn't look up. "I hear you, but it makes no
difference. The people have built themselves up to it,
don't you see that?" He brought the transmitter out
and unwrapped the blanket that surrounded it, rais-
ing his eyes to Tristram. "Look at it. They're waiting
for just a few words and then it begins, all over Po-

land. Understand me, they want to fight. After forty years they have to fight. If it doesn't happen now, it may never happen again. I cannot take account of the risk."

"I order you to stop."

"It's my country, Tristram, not yours. My rules, my operation, and you are getting in my way."

Deftly he removed his gloves and attached the battery wires to the back of the radio. Beside it he laid a small cassette recorder, but as he did so Tristram was on him, launching himself the three feet across the platform, landing heavily on Garten's side, punching him against the wooden wall. It was a clumsy movement and Garten was instantly on his feet. And in that moment Tristram saw him remove the steel spanner from his pocket, and he knew it was coming for his head. He put up a hand to defend himself, a pathetic gesture, he thought. He must have shut his eyes, for suddenly there was a woman's voice that seemed to come from another life.

"Jozef—stop there. Stop it now. It's over."

He was struggling to hear her, fighting another burst of nausea that tried to settle over him.

"What . . . you too?" Garten seemed to chuckle. He returned the spanner to his pocket. "You and him. This is quite ridiculous, my dear. Put that gun down and come and help me. Just one more minute."

Tristram looked up. He couldn't see Grazyna. She had to be standing at the bottom of the steps. But he couldn't move. As the wind whistled through the cracks in the wooden floor, he couldn't move.

"I said stop, Jozef. Stop now. This cannot be."

He wasn't taking any notice. Tristram could see him snapping in the cassette.

"This is going to be quite impressive, my dear. I think even you will be pleased." Garten's voice so controlled, preoccupied, clinical, quite unlike the scream that followed it.

"Stop, Jozef. I won't say it again. I'll shoot."

Tristram tried to move, tried to shout. His hands clawed at the wooden wall beside him.

"Just one more wire to fix." Garten's voice higher now, more excited, teeth chattering in the cold. "There, now we are ready." And the terrible silence as Tristram seemed to hang on the edge of the world, willing it to stand still. And he turned away, as if he knew there was nothing to be done, just before the shot rang out over the camp and the desolate countryside into the bitter gray cold, where all the millions of lost souls had found freedom in death.

52

The civilian put his head in his hands. Only anger had forced him to sit up, for the pain was all but unbearable.

He had no doubt about his assailant. Such an old man, yet still so quick and so agile, a man who could walk on air, his feet soundless, his hands lethal.

He looked about the attic and slowly stood up. His arctic gear was intact, the gun there too. He checked the magazine. Trust nothing, he told himself. Check again. Forget about the wound in your head. Separate yourself from the pain. Think around it, through it. And all the old lessons came back to him.

As he got ready he felt the question nagging at him, worrying him like a dog, but he couldn't identify it. Only when he got out into the snow and the cold air hit him like a brick wall did he realize the problem. He was alive, when by all the patterns and precedents that the KGB had ever created, he should have been dead.

* * *

Tristram was being dragged, pulled to his feet.
God, she was strong! Maybe he'd blacked out, he
wasn't sure. Half of him didn't want to look down at
the floor, but he couldn't prevent himself. And there,
huddled in the corner, as if bracing itself against the
cold and the agony, was Garten's body, belonging
somehow to a different time.

"Wait!"

But she was still dragging him downward on the
steps, until he fell half on top of her. She was shaking
from the cold and the tears.

Slowly his strength returned. "We should go back.
We can't just—"

"No."

Half running now, they passed through the main
gate. Left now. All that way to the parking lot. And it
looked so much farther this time across the snow.
Nothing to be done about Garten. Look at the sky,
coming up gray and mottled, and more snow on the
way, to freeze the dead.

Tristram could see the van, and maybe he was
thirty or forty yards away, when the figure stepped
out from behind it. But he went on walking because
this was the Russian, and whatever the cost, you have
to meet him and deal. Not for your sake but for
June's, even if it all ends here and she goes home—
and you don't.

Twenty yards, fifteen. Not Klimov, but a much
older man. Military parka, boots, and a face oblivious
of the temperature, flat, with a red and battered nose.
No emotion there. Instead a single expression of dis-

dain and contempt. A figure that could neither laugh nor cry, frozen like the head on a coin.

Tristram stopped just in front of him. "Get in the van," he told Grazyna. "Go on now."

She did as she was told, skirting the stranger, her resistance and her strength sapped.

"She has nothing to do with our business." Tristram spoke in Russian, but the man waved his hand dismissively.

"English will do fine, Mr. Tristram. Your day has already been difficult enough."

"Where's June, the girl you took from England? Where is she?"

"Mr. Tristram, she was never taken out of England. She was photographed in a house not far from her own. It was made to appear that she was in Poland in order for us to try to locate you."

Tristram shivered. "Then you've done that. You have no further need of the girl. Let her go."

"If my guess is right, she has already been freed." The Russian turned away from the wind and blew his nose. The sun was rising above the horizon, sending long shadows over the snow.

"I don't understand. . . ."

"It is not my concern whether you understand or not. In any case, I shall not waste time. You will have concluded by now that there is a man working in your organization who is not entirely loyal, uh?"

Tristram remained perfectly still.

"This man's identity is known to me and I wish you to know it as well." He took a sheet of paper from his pocket. "In three days time I should have had a meeting with this . . . ah, gentleman. . . ."

There was scorn in his voice, and he let the word hang there out of place in the wind. "Yes, a meeting at this hotel, here in Switzerland." He pointed to a name on the page. "Perhaps you would find it interesting to go in my place. I should tell you, however, that he has recently proved himself rather . . . unreliable. . . ."

Suddenly the Russian looked back over his shoulder. What was it? Tristram had heard nothing. The Russian stared for a moment and turned to face him.

"It's time for you to leave. Say nothing and go. Now!" He pushed Tristram toward the van. "Get in —go. Cross the border as soon as you can."

Grazyna had already started the engine. She flung open the side door and he caught hold of the cheap plastic seat, pulling himself in, bracing as the van shuddered violently over the ice and the potholes.

As he looked around the Russian was standing stock-still, back slightly stooped, his arms hanging loose by his sides in a gesture of finality.

Even when the van had coughed its way out of sight, he didn't move, didn't turn around. The first telltale sound he had caught was followed by more— his ears picked them out of the wasteland where others would have heard nothing.

He could almost compute the distance and direction, and he looked toward the sun, judging the best angle to fall, feeling the gun against his belt, working out the equation.

But suddenly he felt tired. The cold had wormed its way into his boots and gloves. And he realized with a jab of regret that this time his feet would not obey him—this time his finger would not find the trigger when it had to.

In any case, he had done what was right, betrayed the Englishman, in all his pin-striped arrogance, just as the man had betrayed him. The law of every jungle in the world. Never die alone. Always take someone with you.

And then he knew there was little time left, because he heard the run, and knew what the boy would do. The soft, light jog weaving across the snow, giving yourself speed and flexibility if the target should ever turn and fight back. The Russian smiled, put his head back, and stared at the winter sky.

As he did so the civilian shot him on the move at a distance of twenty paces—a difficult shot, but something of a specialty, practiced and perfected over many years.

In the farmhouse northeast of Warsaw they looked at each other in silence. The radio squawked and hissed at them and after a while the farmer turned it off.

The tea had gone cold and he pushed the cup away from him, standing up, drawing back the curtains. Daylight streamed into the little kitchen, not the day he had expected or wished for. Not the day that would raise them up off their knees and give them hope.

This was the lousiest, most disappointing day that had ever broken over such a godforsaken country.

The cold draft blew in through the cracks in the

window frames and he pulled the cardigan more
tightly around him.

All right for him, but what about the boy upstairs?
He would have had something to believe in, a light to
guide and direct him when he was older, a faith that
could withstand all the lying and the propaganda
around him.

Now there was nothing.

He looked toward the kitchen table. His wife had
slumped forward and was crying soundlessly into the
sleeve of her dressing gown.

The General Secretary reached his aircraft and
glanced back. Beside the terminal stood the row of
black-coated, black-hatted officials, like mourners
rented for a funeral. As if by a single command, they
began a slow wave with the right hand.

He could bear it no longer and climbed the steps,
vowing to put an end to the ritual airport farewells.
Apart from being a waste of time, he reflected, a single terrorist could dispatch the entire Soviet leadership at one go.

He sat in an armchair and waved the stewardess
away. Out of the window he could see the gaggle of
officials was still there. And yet, however much he
loathed them, and he did, it was them that he had to
satisfy. They were his constituency. Not the 280 mil-
lion people who until recently had never been asked
for their opinion on anything, but the fifteen or so
"colleagues" who alone could vote him into power or
throw him out.

He recalled Andropov's words of advice: "When
you go abroad, take as many as you can with you.

That way, they won't be around to misbehave while you're gone."

A military pilot was leaning over him. "Comrade General Secretary, will you give permission to depart?"

"Yes, yes of course. Why else are we here?"

For a moment he closed his eyes. It had been an early start to the day. All the worrying and waiting, and then at breakfast time they had brought him the signal from Poland. It was safe to travel. Safe.

The word was, of course, relative and applied only to today. In the months to come, he realized, it might not apply at all.

Tristram took the wheel and steered them northwest to Poznan. Nine hours on the road and they made it by midafternoon.

Tristram knew Poznan, knew it the way the Service always taught them cities—street names, stations, depots, learned by rote, and you didn't set foot in the place until you had them all off pat. It had been back in the sixties and he'd gone in for the June trade fair. An annual outing for the Service, like a trip to Brighton. Go in and see what happens. Will you get lucky? Will you make a contact? Will a nod or a smile turn into something else?

Still, all these years later, he knew Poznan.

"I leave by train," he told Grazyna. "It's too long by road through East Germany and we don't have papers for the van."

She hadn't replied, and Tristram could see the signs of a mind in shock, a vacant expression, acute tiredness. She had shut out the events of Auschwitz and wouldn't return to them for hours, maybe days.

They crawled through the rush-hour traffic and he pulled up in a side road beside the river. It had started to rain, and through the droplets on the windshield they watched the crowds hurrying home.

Suddenly she sat up. "D'you have any idea how many people we'd have had on the streets today if it had gone ahead?"

Tristram shook his head.

"Tens, maybe hundreds of thousands. Our last bullet, the one we were keeping until we could bear it no longer. Could've been any of these people. How d'you tell? They don't wear badges."

Tristram put a hand on her arm.

"I wish I could say something that would make a difference."

He turned away. You can't make promises in Poland. You can't improve the past—you can't offer hope for the future. The whole of Central Europe had been clogged up with thirty years of worthless assurances. Why add to them?

"Where will you go?"

She didn't answer.

Suddenly he leaned over and kissed the wavy blond hair, but she wouldn't look at him, wouldn't say good-bye.

Slowly, stiffly, he got down from the van and walked away.

She waited until she was sure he was out of sight, then moved over into the driver's seat and turned the engine. It took her more than an hour to clear the dreary suburbs and then the road was hers, dark and straight through the snow all the way to the south.

She hadn't thought about it, but she knew she had to go. Back in Auschwitz she would find and bury the man she had once loved, because that was what was expected. And then on a street corner in Warsaw or Krakow she would drop a few flowers and light a tiny, thin candle to put beside all the others.

Later, much later, she would return to Maya Angelica. Later—because she would have to think it through in her own mind, find answers to the questions that the little girl would ask. That would take time, and in the years to come, how much would she remember?

Grazyna gripped the wheel tightly and stared straight ahead into the gathering night.

53 _____

Across Lake Geneva the morning light struck the peaks of the mountains, leaving the foothills in shadow. And for a long time the Englishman was struck by the contrast—darkness and brilliance, side by side, touching one another.

As the train climbed steadily he committed the sight to memory, aware that he wouldn't be seeing it again. This was the last of the journeys. Almost sentimental, he reckoned. For he was sure the Russian would not be joining him. And yet you had to check, had to be certain.

He put down the newspaper and sighed with contentment. The General Secretary's visit to Poland had received only minor coverage. And yet that in itself said a lot. The visit had been the usual gushing success. Crowds of precocious children and sweaty-handed bureaucrats—all in an orgy of self-congratulation.

No mention of threat or betrayal, of an operation aborted, or arrests or interrogations. Like the best of the stories—never revealed, never told.

At the hotel reception desk stood the manager, Herr Leck, and there wasn't a sign of recognition. Only when the Englishman greeted him did he return the compliment. "Herr Thomas. How nice to see you again. Number eight is, of course, at your disposal."

That was the way it had always worked. No questions about length of stay or purpose. He would come and he would go and there would be nothing to record his passing. Herr Leck, who knew everything, would pretend to know nothing. It was more than professional discretion. He would know that his own position depended on it.

Now, safely ensconced in the little room with the twin beds and the balcony and the Swiss duvets in their blue-and-white covers, it was just a matter of waiting.

Most likely nothing would happen, but if it did, he would take his chances. Unhurriedly he snapped open the black leather suitcase, removed the automatic with the single clip, and put it in his jacket pocket.

Tristram called the number from West Berlin. Getting off the train at the Bahnhof am Zoo, he had been struck instantly by the noise, the bustle and affluence. Hard to hear even the phone ringing so far away in another country.

He looked around, feeling out of place. The East had been like Europe in the fifties—drab, making do, frayed at the edges. It was like returning to another planet. He held the receiver tight against his ear, but there was no answer.

Tristram left the station, found a travel agent, and checked connections to Geneva. An hour later he tried the number again.

He felt his cheeks redden and his throat was dry, hearing the voice on a crystal-clear line seven hundred miles long—Geneva to London.

"June?"

He could feel the shock, the anguish—all built into that moment of hesitation.

"Are you all right?" So quiet, she sounded. Almost a whisper.

"Fine. I'm fine. June, what happened?"

"I don't want to talk about it. Later. You know."

"Yes, okay."

And then neither of them could speak. He wanted to say he'd call her when he got home. But it didn't seem right, trying to invest in the future when he'd taken so much from her past.

The receiver trembled in his hand and he had to press it tightly against his cheek. "Anyway, I'm glad things are all right."

"Yes."

"Well, take care." And he cut the line, without thinking, without meaning to. It was too late to get it back. On the other side of the wall he could see the clock and knew that his flight left in an hour. It was going to be tight. And yet he couldn't hurry, couldn't find a reason or a motive. Not now that he'd lost his chance, without ever really having it

They always tell you that the most dangerous time is when you make it back across the Wall. Because you think the battle's over, you think you got away with it.

But they can follow you so easily. They slip through the Western checkpoints any hour of the day or night, and nobody even asks for a passport. Walk through, do as you please. Welcome to Freedom.

And they do come across in their thousands. So why should Tristram have seen the man?

Besides, they know how glad the Westerners are to get home. They know how relieved they are to have left the big, bad East without any fuss or trouble.

They knew Tristram would be a soft target, with his guard not only down but somewhere around his ankles. And they weren't wrong.

Herr Leck watched him arrive and went through the well-practiced act. He could tell an Englishman all right. Americans wore their trousers too short; Englishmen let them dangle in the mud. There was nothing pressed or crisp about the English, and this fellow, with his red face and runaway belly, fitted the pattern.

He showed him to the first-floor room, waited while he fumbled for a tip. He went back to the reception desk, wondering what it was that worried him. The name in the register said James Tristram, but that was hardly going to be genuine.

This time he would watch carefully, study. He was anxious about the future. Perhaps it was time to keep some records. A little insurance against rough times.

He looked out of the window. The sky was overcast, clouds low over the mountains. Maybe it was nothing at all—just the gloomy weather.

* * *

The General Secretary lay on his bed in the ambassador's residence nursing his stomach. The banquet marking the end of his visit had been quite horrendous. Six courses would have been excessive in a land of plenty. In Poland they were totally absurd.

He wasn't pleased when the door opened and his private secretary appeared carrying a leather file.

"This just in from Moscow, Comrade General Secretary."

"It's two o'clock in the morning there. Can they not sleep?"

He put on his glasses and opened the folder. Only half a page. Couldn't be that bad. If it were serious, they'd have written a book, as they always did, blaming everyone in sight for some act of incompetence or rank stupidity.

And this time? No, this time it was good news, and, more unusual, from the head of Kremlin security. It seemed the KGB major who'd been arrested in Poland had finally and unexpectedly decided to talk. Fired by new feelings of candor and openness, he had identified a contact at the peak of British intelligence.

As he read with mounting pleasure the Soviet leader realized that this was, after all, the final mile, the last of the locked doors. No one else would be hiding on the other side.

He scribbled a note on the margin of the message and handed it back to his assistant.

"It would seem that this information should be passed to Switzerland," he said. "Our little friend might find it useful."

The man bowed and left the room and the General

Secretary found himself wondering what induce-
ments had been offered to the KGB major to persuade him to talk. It seemed odd that the man had
confessed everything without a fight. Perhaps it was
better not to inquire.

The civilian was cold. For he hadn't had time to
acquire the proper clothing. They had ordered him to
leave behind his arctic gear in Poland and there had
been no opportunity to replace it. He'd been outside
for almost two hours, in a thin raincoat and jeans, as
the sun disappeared behind the mountains. There'd
be no thanks for that. No extra bonus, unless he took
it himself.

All they had done for him in Geneva was give him
a name and a photo. Another elderly man by the look
of it, but he wouldn't underestimate him. Not after
the last time.

He circled the hotel for the second time. The trees
hid him, about three hundred yards from the building. Now he'd go in closer, search the downstairs
rooms. If that was no good, he'd check in and take it
from there. It was a small hotel. If the target was
inside, he'd find him.

The first-floor balconies had been raised a few feet
from the ground. He swung himself up from the frozen terrace, his feet landing lightly on the icy boards,
his balance perfect.

The first window had its shutters closed, but he
passed it without waiting. Inside, an elderly German
woman was complaining that her husband never took
a bath. Next to that there was pop music. Only at the
third window did he stop and listen. Not a sound

could be heard from the room. The civilian picked up a piece of ice and made a mark on the wooden frame beside the window. He'd come back to it. Two other windows were similarly shuttered, and he was beginning to think the task more difficult than he'd imagined when the curtains at the far end of the building were thrown open and a bright light splashed onto the terrace.

He could see a shadow gazing out, yawning. He crept forward on his knees. At the outer edge of the light he stopped and peered into the room. Even from the low angle there was no mistaking the face, solid and gaunt, the stiff military deportment beneath the wine-red cardigan.

What a find, thought the civilian. And for the first time he wondered what it was that the man had done.

Not that any of them would ever tell you. Not that you would ever give them the time.

At seven-thirty Tristram left the room, his shoes squeaking on the dark wooden floors. The corridor was clean and bare. A family hotel, they called it. No frills, just the basics. Solid and dependable. It would be there forever.

As he reached the ground floor he heard muted conversation from the dining room. Take it slowly, he thought. They won't hear you, won't see you. He reached the door to number eight and stopped for a moment, realizing that after all the treachery, the dying and the deceit, it would be easy to kill. And yet, even in that instant, he recalled the warning from the Service instructors: "If you have to pull the trigger, no need to worry about living with yourself afterward—just make sure you don't enjoy it. Because if that happens, you're finished."

He opened the door and stepped into the semidarkness.

The man had his back to the door. He was sitting on the farthest bed, looking out beyond the balcony. And even with the cardigan around his shoulders Tristram recognized him instantly.

He stood just inside the doorway and waited for the figure to turn.

"Don't tell me you're surprised, my friend." Clumsily and with evident weariness, Cornish swung his feet around to the other side of the bed. "You probably had an idea, didn't you?" He sighed. "Just one request—don't ask me why or how long. That would be just a little pathetic, don't you think?"

"I wasn't going to. I'm not interested in your motives."

"Good. Besides, I've pretty well forgotten what my motives were. It was such a long time ago." The arrogance was still there, but he didn't look at ease. "I'm glad we can be adult about this," he added.

Tristram hadn't moved, and yet something had distracted him. Something outside.

"What about your family?"

"My business, I think. Don't you?"

"Whatever you say." For a moment Tristram let his eyes wander past the man. There *was* something on the terrace.

"Anyway, what would you know about family?" The question was a sneer. "You never did go in for that sort of thing, did you? Mmm? Bit of ballroom

dancing more your style, wasn't it? A quick grope
and a feel during the fox-trot, and maybe a peck on
the lips at the end of it all. Nice and safe, eh? No
commitment there. Let's leave my family out of it."

Tristram moved over to the chest of drawers and
leaned against it. The room was overheated. And yet
suddenly he felt elated. For what he had seen was the
light from the room reflected on steel. And he *knew*
who was outside, knew what would happen.

"You don't even answer me, do you?" The sweat
began to appear on Cornish's forehead. "You really
are rather spineless, if you don't mind my saying so.
Aren't you going to take charge, order me home? Do
something, man, for God's sake, let's get on with it."

It was then that Tristram felt the surge of anger.
"You're not worth taking home, Cornish. Can you
understand that? Why would we want you back in
England?"

"Don't try to mess me about. I've handled a few of
these things myself, remember? At the very least,
they'd want a debriefing."

"Don't you believe it. They'll know everything
they need. Besides, what's the point of talking to you?
You wouldn't even know where one lie ended and
another began. No, I don't think you'll find much of a
desire on our part to get anything from you. As far as
I'm concerned, you can go over to your friends in
Moscow." And he caught the flash of fear in
Cornish's eyes. He's starting to see it, he thought. He
doesn't have anywhere to go.

Cornish stood up and frowned. "Well, if you have
no further need of me, perhaps we can say good
night. I'm very tired."

Tristram moved away from the chest. "I'd like nothing better," he said quietly. "I'm pleased to say I shan't be seeing you again."

"Oh, you're pleased to say . . . are you?" Cornish mimicked the words. "I don't give a damn whether you're pleased or not. Go back to your pathetic files and your boring little friend. I met her, you know. Stupid little—"

And he didn't even see the punch coming, and Tristram hadn't even planned it, but almost involuntarily his right hand came up, striking Cornish's cheekbone, knocking him backward. He should have done it again, he wanted to. But in that moment he was afraid he'd enjoy it.

So he turned his back without a word, shutting the door behind him. He didn't need to imagine the hand outside, smashing the glass, the silenced pistol swinging in that smooth, calculated arc, didn't need to see what the bullet would do to Cornish when it finally reached him.

Quite enough to know it was on its way.

54 _____

He wasn't used to the rain. Not daily. Not for hours on end. In Moscow it could be cold and overcast, but the sky never spat down at you ceaselessly, the way it did in London.

The civilian was glad when he could move into the underground, pressed tight against the afternoon shoppers and the tourists. They all carried bags and baskets, just as they did back home. But here, he reflected, the baskets were full—and in Moscow they were empty, carted around from place to place on the off chance there'd be something to buy.

The doors opened and he watched carefully. Don't be distracted, keep your eyes open, mark and follow, because that's what Moscow wanted. He knew the signs. They were assessing the fallout, the potential. Was there still a danger? Would they have to act again?

He looked once more at the faces. The British really were a people without passion. Nobody was laughing. Not many even spoke. In what bag, he wondered, did they carry their emotions?

Then he put the question out of his mind and concentrated on the job—working, the way he would in any city, with the same single-mindedness and detachment, building the general picture, assessing the subject, waiting for the final order. One way or the other.

As the doors opened again he felt the mass of bodies contract and expand around him. He edged closer to the subject, anxious not to lose sight, even for a moment.

And yet, even after all this time and distance, it wasn't much of a subject. A man who appeared to have little occupation. A man who stayed long hours in, what even the civilian could see, was a pretty miserable house. No friends came to call, and he paid no visits himself. Occasionally a trip to the public library or the shops. Once he'd gone into the West End to buy a pair of trousers. And that had been the high point of the week.

It seemed to the civilian as if James Tristram had simply gone somewhere else and left his body behind to represent him. Three feet away he sat hunched on a seat, a group of women glaring down on him as if they expected him to relinquish his place. But his eyes were half closed and maybe he hadn't seen them.

It would be odd, thought the civilian, for an assassin to pity a potential victim. And yet, as he focused on the plump, red-faced figure, alone among so many people, he experienced an unusual sensation. Of course, in his position, Tristram might look on the prospect as a blessed release, a timely end to an otherwise wholly unsatisfactory affair. The civilian felt a little better and his features brightened.

He would definitely look at it that way if the time came.